under a
new york
skyline

FOUR ROMANCE NOVELLAS BY

KATHI ORAM PETERSON ✦ NIKKI TRIONFO
MAUREEN L. MILLS ✦ TERESA RICHARDS

under a
new york
skyline

Teenacity
BOOKS

Title: Under a New York Skyline

Summary: Romance in New York has never been so loud with hip-hop, so frenzied with Comic Con fans, or so alluring with teen pop sensations. Authors Kathi Oram Peterson, Nikki Trionfo, Maureen L. Mills and Teresa Richards whisk you away to four of the Big Apple's sweetest, hippest teen romances ever.

Published by Teenacity Books, an imprint of Caguas Publishing.
Riverton, Utah

www.NikkiTrionfo.com/TeenacityBooks

contents

 foreword

Welcome to Teenacity Books, dedicated to providing readers the sweetest, hippest romances evah!

As an emerging writer who is also a massive fan of young adult romance, I've had the chance to meet dozens of YA authors. We often edit for each other. For years, we batted around the idea of writing together despite having different publishers. We knew it would be a lot of work, since we're not exactly "halfway" kinds of authors. Finally, we decided to bite the bullet and created Teenacity Books. It's our chance to romance-out in novella and full-length novel form.

A huge round of applause to everyone at Wasatch Mountain Fiction Writers—Charlene Raddon, Ann Chamberlin, Linda Aagard, Roseann Woodward, Dorothy Canada and most especially Brenda Bensch for copyedits. Kathleen Dougherty, no content editor holds a candle to you. Best friends, professionals, fellow actors in mannequin scenes. I can't love you more.

Please enjoy our debut release, *Under a New York Skyline*, as it brings you heart, spunk, and more than a handful of kisses.

In love with love,

Nikki Trionfo

Editor, Teenacity Books

KATHI ORAM PETERSON

new
york
holiday

 chapter one

Dressed in his Madison Square Garden security guard uniform, Logan O'Brian smoothed the crease in the *New York Times*, which lay on the dinette table before him. He glanced at the digital clock on the stove. He had an hour before he had to check in for tonight's concert. He stuffed the last of his microwaved burrito into his mouth, gobbling it down as he returned his attention to the paper.

"Don't tell me you're still reading about the Facebook stalker?" His sister, Sara, rushed in wearing Mercy Hospital scrubs, ready for her four to midnight shift in the ER. "You had your nose stuck to that article an hour ago, before I took my shower."

Mr. Whiskers, her tabby cat that was ornerier than a longshoreman, lazily followed her into the room, plopped his fat behind down on the black speckled floor tiles and proceeded to bathe himself.

Ignoring the feline he barely tolerated, Logan leaned back in his chair. "Seriously, you think there's something more important than finding a pervert who preys on unsuspecting women?" He couldn't believe his sister's cavalier attitude, especially after being raised by their police-officer father. "You know the cops believe he's the one who murdered the two women they found in Central Park, don't you?"

"Yes, and I feel bad for them and their families. I just don't like dwelling on bad things. I'd rather read about the rich and famous." She grabbed the paper and turned it over. "Like this." She pointed to the headline. "*Prime Minister Patrick Templeton Speaks at U.N.* Oh, and he has his teenage daughter with him. She looks about eighteen." She gazed at their picture. "Pretty thing."

"Dad would be all over this." Logan snatched the paper from her hands and flipped back to the article he'd been reading, sitting down as he studied it. "Some guy lures innocent women to bogus Facebook pages he sets up under different names. He arranges to meet them in public places. The police traced one who went to the Garden, which makes my antenna go up. Anyway, they go, thinking they're safe, until they turn up dead several days later."

"How does he get them to leave a public place and go with him alone?" Standing behind him, Sara rested her hands upon Logan's shoulders, trying to read the article in front of him.

"The authorities don't exactly know. That's why this is so puzzling. Dad would be working up scenarios and looking into case studies. It's the kind of mystery he loved to solve." For over thirty years their father had been a detective on the NYPD until he had been shot and killed during a drug bust. Though his father died when Logan was only fourteen, he still remembered the dismal, rainy day of his funeral. Logan had pledged to devote his life to the cause of continuing his dad's legacy of keeping law and order.

With no mother to lean on, Logan and Sara only had each other. Though at the time of their father's death, Sara had just started her career as an RN, she willingly took on the responsibility of raising her younger brother. Now the job was done, though he still lived with her. But he hoped that was only temporary.

"Dad would." She squeezed his shoulder before turning to the fridge. "He loved solving tough cases. But you're not Dad *and* you're not a police officer."

4

"Yet." If he let her, Sara would climb on top of her big-sister-knows-better, high-horse. "I'm twenty-two now. You don't have to worry."

"I'm not." She scowled for a second. "At least, I don't mean to. It's just you'll always be my little brother. You're still the boy Gorilla Gonzales gave a black eye."

"I caught the guy stealing from the school's vending machine. I couldn't let him get away with it. Dad wouldn't have."

"Gonzales was four years older than you and weighed at least a hundred more pounds. Honestly." She stared at him. "I just realized something. You suffer from David and Goliath syndrome."

"What?"

"You know, David in the Bible went after Goliath, the giant. You're always picking fights with people bigger than you are."

"What kind of hemp shampoo did you use in the shower? You're hallucinating."

"I wasn't hallucinating when I had to save you from Trish the Dish."

Logan burst out laughing.

Sara opened the freezer and pulled out a Lean Cuisine. "You weren't laughing when she cornered you in the city library to make out. If I hadn't come along, you would have died stumbling over your big feet and blushing from embarrassment."

Trying to ignore that embarrassing moment, he said, "I don't have David and Goliath syndrome."

"David turned to butter in Bathsheba's hands." His sister winked at him.

"Will you always hold that over my head?" He folded the newspaper. Mr. Whiskers jumped up on the table where the paper had been, purring, and trying to cozy up to Logan. He half-heartedly stroked the critter's head, then set the heavy feline on the floor. "Anyway, that happened six years ago, and I've gone out with plenty of girls since. *And*

5

I'll have you know I haven't blushed once, nor stumbled." Truth be told, he liked to date, but kept girls at arms-length. He didn't have time for them. Logan had a plan. A plan that would put him on the path to becoming a police chief. Since graduating high school, he'd attended NYU majoring in Criminal Justice while working part-time as a security guard at the Garden.

"Don't I know it?" Sara gave a sigh, looking at him. "Liam Hemsworth's got nothing on you, little brother." She tried to pinch his cheek like she used to, but he dodged her and stood.

"*Little*. Really?" Logan looked down at his five-foot-four sister. Way down.

"Height isn't everything." She elbowed him in the side.

He playfully acted as though she'd delivered a power punch.

She chuckled as she packed her frozen meal in a thermal lunch bag. Sealing the top, her face sobered. "But about following in Dad's footsteps. You can still do that and not become a cop. Before sending in your application to the New York Police Academy, you might want to look into some law graduate schools. Lawyers fight for justice too. Dad wouldn't want you to become a cop, just because he had been one."

"Give me some credit." He understood his sister only had his best interests at heart, but she needed to give him space and let him make his own decisions.

"I do . . . well, I'll try. Just promise me that you'll meet with Max before submitting your papers to the academy?" She blinked her wise-sister eyes at him.

Max worked at the midtown NYPD precinct and had been Dad's junior partner. After Dad died, Max visited them occasionally, and then frequently. Before they knew it, Sara and Max had fallen in love despite her swearing she'd never, ever get involved with a cop. Not long after that realization, they'd become engaged.

"I already have and he's one-hundred percent behind my decision." Logan hoped that would stop her going on about it.

"Hmm." Sara bit her lips together, the way she always did when she pondered something of importance. "Well, we'll talk about this later." She grabbed her light coat, sliding her arms into the sleeves. "I should be home a little after midnight; that is, if the ER isn't too busy. You know how crazy it gets come spring. May has been the worst month this year."

"I'll probably beat you home, though it's Austen Zeiss's concert tonight. He tends to attract an unruly bunch of pop rock fans." He tugged on his hat and zipped up his black blazer, with "Security" sprawled in bold white letters on the back, intending to follow her out.

"Remember, you promised to buy me an autographed tee shirt." His older sister had a soft spot for the teeny-bopper rock star.

"Yes, I remember. You've only reminded me every day for a month." He shook his head as he followed her from their apartment. Locking the door behind them, he turned to find Mrs. Shapiro, their nosey neighbor, returning home with grocery bags under each of her short arms. Sara skirted past her, but Logan wasn't so lucky.

"Goin' to work, are you?" She set her groceries on the floor and mined her keys from her coat pocket. "Make sure you're quiet when you come home tonight, will you, hon? When Mr. Shapiro hears someone in the hallway, he thinks burglars are breaking in, don't you know?"

Opening the door, she gazed up at Logan. "Glad you're in security work. Makes a woman feel safe in these troubling times." She patted Logan's cheek. "And if you've a mind to, you could buy me a Zeiss tee shirt, if it's not a bother."

"It's not a bother at all." Logan picked up her grocery bags, handing them to her.

"Such a good boy." She took the bags and went inside, using her foot to close the door.

What was it about Austen Zeiss that made young women nearly crawl over people just to get a glimpse of him and older women want his memorabilia? Logan had no idea, but knew his night would be filled with checking purses and keeping his security-guard eye on as many fan-crazed women as possible.

It was going to be a very long night.

Glorianna Templeton stared at the Facebook message once again. Austen Zeiss had personally messaged her. She placed her finger on his image of long platinum blonde hair caught up in a man-bun, his black brows sheltering his soulful brown eyes, and though she was a hip seventeen-year-old going on eighteen, she swooned just a little, like she could actually touch his face.

She read his message aloud, "When I sing, *Only You*, and tug on my ear, that will be your signal to meet me backstage. Can't wait to see you in person."

She couldn't believe her good fortune. She had joined Zeiss's online fan club several months ago, and shortly afterward he'd sent her a brief message. She'd never forget it. He'd written: "Hey, you seem like a nice girl. I've dreamed of having a normal life and meeting someone like you." His feelings mirrored her own, but she couldn't tell him that. If he knew who her father was, he might not want to meet her. And she desperately wanted to meet him. When he proposed they get together after his concert in New York, she'd jumped at the chance.

The stars had all aligned. Either that or the earth had tilted completely off its axis and plummeted toward deep space. But it really didn't matter what the cause had been. Glorianna Templeton, the Prime Minister of England's sheltered daughter—who wasn't allowed to even listen to that "ungodly" music—was going to meet her true love, her soul mate. Ever since Zeiss had given a TV interview with that gobby, elderly woman who always made her interviewees cry, Glorianna hadn't been able to shake him from her mind.

She stared at his picture. "Oh, sure, you became weepy-eyed when she asked about your mother's fatal car accident. We've both lost our mothers to fatal crashes. That's why I've had the collywobbles for you. No, that's not what they say here in the states. They say, I've got a thing for you. Yes, I like that."

After Zeiss had brought up the idea of meeting in person, Gloriana had begged her father to let her come with him to New York. He always caved when she brought up what a handsome babe magnet he was, how terribly alone she felt when he was gone to his top-secret meetings, and how she didn't mind the sacrifice for her country because she loved him. So, he let her come, but her plan had always been to meet her idol. Her father didn't suspect a thing. And all had been going as she'd expected . . . until she came down with the flu.

Tosh!

She even had a temperature of a hundred and two. Every muscle in her body ached, but not as much as her heart did. Her heart would shatter if she didn't meet Zeiss. Fate had turned against her.

At that very moment, her governess, Miss Rae, was escorting the doctor to the door. He had passed on Glorianna a sentence of staying in bed and getting some sleep. He had also prescribed medication guaranteed to lower her temperature and help her rest. She'd swallowed two tablets. They might be helping her body heal, but her heart was a different matter, especially if she missed her chance to meet the man of her dreams.

Footfalls neared her bedroom door. Against common sense, she quickly typed in her reply. "Can't wait to meet you too." As she hit send, the door to her room opened. She logged out of Facebook and cleared the screen.

"Okay, young lady. It's lights out. And who said you could use my laptop?" Rae had watched over Glorianna since she was six and had taught her everything from how to tie her shoes to what clothes the daughter of a PM should wear. She took the computer from her, closed it, and set it on the nightstand. Tall and slender as a willow, the older woman had a few gray hairs mixed in her nicely trimmed bob. Rae's finely-tweezed brows bunched together as her worried eyes studied Glorianna.

"I was online, looking at some places we can go while we're in New York." That she was on the web rang partly true. Well, maybe more like barely true. She hated lying to Rae, but if she hadn't, Rae would put the brakes on meeting Zeiss and Glorianna would miss this once in a lifetime opportunity. After this trip, all Glorianna saw ahead was study, study, and yes, more study. Oxford University loomed ominously in her future this fall and she had to be ready.

Glorianna needed to move away from the topic of what she'd been doing on the lappy. "I've always wanted to see the Statue of Liberty, Saint Patrick's Cathedral, Times Square, and the Empire State Building." She lay back on her pillow like she planned to be an obedient patient and do what the doctor had said.

"Your father has laid out your schedule and it doesn't allow time for sightseeing. However, unless your fever comes down, you won't be able to meet those obligations either." Rae pressed her hand to Glorianna's forehead. "You're still hot. And your eyes are dilated. Do you feel dizzy?"

"No. Just tired. Do you remember that movie where two lovers planned to meet at the top of the Empire State Building?" Glorianna couldn't think of the title. "You know, it had that handsome guy, somebody Grant."

"Cary Grant." Rae settled on the side of the bed. "I see my fondness of classic American films has rubbed off on you. Guess that's what happens when you're stuck with a stodgy governess as your best friend."

"You're not stodgy. Besides, I like being with you." And Glorianna meant it. Over the years, Rae had become her surrogate mother. "Who else would tutor me on my university courses?"

"Which reminds me, young lady." Rae smoothed the blankets on the bed. "I brought my remedial calculus textbook. You can start on it when you're feeling better."

Glorianna closed her tired eyes. Anything that had to do with equations made her want to chunder.

"However, I suppose it can wait a fortnight. After all, you are on holiday." Rae smoothed Glorianna's hair away from her face. "Your pretty brown eyes are bloodshot. Get some sleep." She picked up her laptop, reached toward the light, and stopped. "*An Affair to Remember.* That's the name of the movie with Cary Grant."

"Yes. That's it." Glorianna feigned a yawn as Rae clicked off the lamp.

"By the way, I like being with you, too." Rae slipped out of the room.

Glorianna lay perfectly still for a moment, the old classic movie playing in her mind. *Yes, my meeting Austen Zeiss will be an affair to remember in more ways than one. Fever or not, I'm off to have an adventure.*

As the Waldorf Astoria tower suite fell quiet, Glorianna slipped out of bed. The room swirled a little, but soon righted itself. Despite her achy body, Glorianna grabbed her mobile phone off her night stand and tapped on the flashlight icon. She couldn't risk turning on the overhead light, just in case Carlton, the secret intelligence officer assigned to her family, should notice and investigate.

She hurried to her closet and pushed past the many proper dresses, suits, and boring slacks Rae had helped her purchase. She grabbed the small bag she'd hidden in back. Before leaving home, she'd packed a few clothes she'd managed to buy with the help of housekeepers: jeans with thready tears, a form-fitting black tee with Zeiss's silver guitar logo on the front—won't he be impressed?—and makeup. She even had a pair of black combat boots, but the *pièce de résistance* was the black, long-haired wig with streaks of bright purple. No one would recognize her without her honey-colored hair. And if she painted her face, she'd fit right in with screaming fans. She quickly set to work on her disguise.

Finished and feeling a little wobbly, Glorianna crept back to her nightstand, setting her mobile down. Because her father was the Prime Minister and for her security, the device had limited access to the net. However, her father's men could ping the GPS and find her if she took it with her. She couldn't have that. She had to leave the phone behind. In case of an emergency, she would have to find an internet café. She knew of a website that would mark a call as unknown and mask the incoming IP address, so she could let her father know she was okay without getting surrounded by security.

A twinge of doubt over doing this raised its head. *But I want to have fun. It'll be fine. I'll be in a public place. Nothing will go wrong.*

Spying the medication the good doctor had left for her, she stuffed one of the bottles in her hoodie's pocket and turned her back on her paranoid fear. Resolutely, she walked to her door, opening it just a touch.

The spotless traditional living room basked in the soft glow of a table lamp. Sitting in an overstuffed chair beside it reading a newspaper was Carlton, Mr. Kill-A-Good-Time. He made it his life mission to sabotage her. However, his soft spot was his love of watching Red Dwarf reruns, which came on in the States at nine.

As the clock down the hall struck the hour, he neatly folded the paper and cast his gaze around the room, which forced Glorianna to close her door. She counted to ten, allowing him time to exit, before opening it again.

The coast was clear. She tiptoed the best she could—feeling woozy and wearing combat boots—and hurried out of the suite's entrance door. She madly dashed down the marble corridor to the lift and pushed the button.

When the lift doors slid open, she found Lady Chesterfield, the hotel's stuffy busybody. Glorianna held her breath, hoping not to draw the woman's attention. Dressed in an evening gown, the lady stuck her nose in the air, stepped out, and headed toward her flat without saying a word.

Brilliant! Glorianna's disguise worked! The old crone hadn't given her a second glance.

Glorianna got on the lift and pushed the down button. For a second, she wondered if she was doing the right thing. She didn't like being deceitful or doing something she knew her father would disapprove of. But she wouldn't be gone long. And she'd gladly keep to the schedule her father had given Rae if she could just have this one night out.

One night to herself.

One night of being someone else other than the proper Prime Minister's daughter who had to smile and grin and do what she was told. She deserved a night away.

chapter two

Glorianna paid the cab driver with cash she'd squirreled away. She escaped the yellow taxi and stepped out in front of Madison Square Garden. Despite her hoodie, a cool spring breeze blew strands of her black and purple wig into her eyes. Smoothing it aside, she gazed up.

Despite her dizziness from medication, she could clearly see the marquee overhead had a picture of Zeiss. No man-bun this time. Instead, his wild platinum hair hung down his bare back and dangled to his gold lamé pants as he played his magical keyboard. His name blazed in audacious white letters across the top, and underneath in red, hard-to-miss lettering were the words "sold out."

She wasn't worried. She'd already purchased a cheap-seat ticket in the West Balcony behind the stage. And she really didn't care that the concert was more than half over. All she needed to do was find her seat and wait for his signal, which she knew would come near the end. And then, somehow, she would make her way backstage.

As she walked into the foyer, she stood amazed by the high ceilings where two huge screens showed events that would soon come to the arena. The wooziness she'd experienced earlier returned, but she shook it off and pulled her ticket from her black messenger bag. She showed it to the stout, busty ticket lady scanning bar codes. A green light appeared on the hand-held device. She motioned Glorianna through to a security guard, who took her bag. While he looked through it, he had her step through a metal detector. No flashing lights went off. He met her on the other side. "Here you go. Follow the concourse around to the escalator tower." He waved her in the direction she needed to go.

"Isn't there a lift?"

"Lift? You mean elevator? Those are only for people with disabilities, media, or employees." He again motioned for her to be on her way.

At first, she was surprised by his brusque manner toward her. But tonight, she wasn't the pampered Prime Minister's daughter. Nope. She was merely Glory Smith, a normal, everyday person. Her skin tingled with the excitement of being incognito.

She noticed a few other stragglers in the hallway: people buying snacks, others rushing to the loo, and caretakers attending overflowing garbage bins. Her heart pounded; her hands grew clammy. Flu symptoms. Oh, tosh! Taking a deep breath, she made her way to the escalators.

Beside them was a kiosk with a map of the building and seating of the arena. Her seat was on the top floor, the backstage dressing area on the third. That's where Zeiss said he'd meet her. But first, she had to take her seat and wait for his signal.

Turning toward the escalator, the moving steps made her dizzy. *Look forward.* As she stepped to get on, a couple of giggling girls sped past. Their bright shiny bling made her wonder if they'd set off the metal detector as they'd come in. One had a pink mohawk and diamond earrings, the other's wild hair appeared hardly contained beneath the baseball cap she wore sideways on her head. They climbed the electric stairs, prattling and laughing. And then they heard the thrumming of Zeiss's signature song, *Forgive Me.* The girls squealed and raced each other to the top.

16

Even though Glorianna couldn't hear the exact words, the music spoke to her. A warmth filled her core and trickled to her arms and legs. *I'm really here. I'm hearing his music live.* She even felt a little lightheaded, which had nothing to do with the flu or the medicine. No! It had everything to do with getting to her seat to see him in action.

She rode escalators that seemed to take forever before reaching the top floor. Glancing at her ticket for her seat number, she followed the signs directing her to her assigned section.

Dizziness clouded her vision as she walked through the small dark passage that broke out into the arena. She covered her nose to block the overpowering smell of pyrotechnics, which nearly gagged her. Staring down, she saw flashing lights and flames around the stage.

And there he was.

Zeiss!

Though he stood far away, the spotlight found him. He seemed drenched in golden magnificence. On the Jumbotron's curving screen, she caught a close-up of her star. His eyes caressed her, melting her heart. His throaty voice filled the arena accompanied by screams of adoring fans. A tingling sheeted over her skin.

"I'm walkin' here." A loud nasal voice boomed from behind her.

Glorianna turned to find an older, fuzzy-haired woman, who looked like she'd eaten a few too many American hotdogs. She burped as she huffed by.

"Sorry." Glorianna walked down several rows and finally spied row J. Then she had to squeeze by perturbed fans until she sat in her assigned seat. As soon as she settled, her eyes once again went to the jumbotron, to Zeiss in all his splendor. He sang another song and then another and finally the music softened as he began "her" song, *Only You.* He peered over the crowd and tugged his ear. His signal to her and her only. She had wondered if she'd see it and now she had. Smashing! It was time!

Time to make her way backstage. She had to hurry. If she remembered correctly from the kiosk, the dressing rooms were on the second or third floor. But which one? Oh, tosh!

Stepping on a number of toes as she exited the row, she quickly retraced her steps to the escalator and fled down to level three. *I simply can't mess this up. This is my chance, my only chance.*

She raced down the concourse, passing a few stragglers at the concessions. Finally, she saw where she needed to go. A sign over a door read Employees Only. That had to lead to the star's dressing room.

Glorianna glanced about. A security guard spoke to some women, mothers probably looking for their teenage daughters. But no one else. A couple of caretakers pushing garbage pails went through the door.

She dodged through behind them.

Stationed backstage, Logan surveyed the area. All seemed normal. A few of Zeiss's people walked around, along with some press who'd been allowed in because of the lanyards dangling from their necks. As soon as Zeiss exited the arena the mood would quickly change. Pictures would be taken as the media begged for a quote and to be noticed. Things could get dicey, so Logan must stay prepared for anything to happen.

Regardless of his dislike for Zeiss, Logan had to admit he enjoyed the beat of the boom-baba, boom-baba music. He could never figure out why stars like Zeiss were always grabbing their crotches while singing, like that was normal. Any guy who did that out on the street would be arrested or, at the very least, issued a ticket for lewd behavior—especially around underage girls. But Zeiss, and his type, got away with it on stage in front of thousands of screaming fans. Logan just didn't understand.

The radio attached to his belt vibrated. He grabbed it and placed it to his ear. "What's up, Cazara?"

Cazara was one of the guards stationed in the concourse on the third floor. "Just glimpsed a girl with black and purple hair slip through the Employees Only door with some janitors. I was stuck helping a couple of women. See if you can catch her. Over."

At that moment, the maintenance workers pushing their carts walked by and trailing a safe distance behind was a slender girl with black/purple hair. "Got eyes on her. No problem."

Logan secured the radio on his belt, all the while watching the girl—walking as though she were a little tipsy—cautiously make her way down the hall. Just as he was about to greet her, the press sprinted toward the arena exit.

Zeiss must be coming. Though the star had his own bodyguards, Logan's job was to make sure nothing happened while Zeiss moved around backstage.

But first he had to get the girl!

He turned around, looking for her.

She'd been swallowed up with the crowd and appeared in the middle of the media flocking toward the arena exit. Dang, he had to fish her out before she reached Zeiss. As he hustled, he tried to radio the star's bodyguards, but they either couldn't hear him or just ignored him. Logan would have to do this the hard way. He shoved through the wad of teeming reporters and photographers, all the while keeping an eye on her black and purple hair.

She'd pushed her way to the forefront. By her hopeful expression, she was ready to meet Zeiss face-to-face. Just as Logan thought he could reach her, she moved to the left, displaced from her prime spot by a journalist. He dodged for her as Zeiss made his entrance.

Lights flashed, questions were shouted, arms and legs were thrust everywhere. Still he remained focused on the girl who had positioned herself once again directly in Zeiss's path. Oblivious to what lay ahead, the star ambled forward.

Logan lunged and grabbed her arm, jerking her away from the limelight. She glared at him, as if he had some nerve and elbowed him in the side, kicking his shin. Still, he didn't let go of her thin arm as he hauled her away from the fray. "You're coming with me!"

The media mobbed around the star like hungry wolves, following him to his dressing room around the corner. The hall grew quiet.

"Who do you think you are?" She seethed and jerked away from him. He thought he detected a British accent, a Queen's English accent to be exact.

"I'm security. The real question is, who do you think *you* are?" Logan stared down on the slender girl dressed in black from her hoodie and torn jeans to her combat boots.

"I have a date." She smoothed her hair away from her face and staggered a little. "Thank you very much for your concern, but I'm expected."

He noted that her pretty brown eyes reminded him of Hershey's rich dark chocolate as she stared at him like she'd never been treated so harshly in her life. "A date?"

"Yes! With Zeiss." She straightened her jacket and righted her bag to her side as she shivered as though she had the chills.

"Can I see your pass?"

"Pass?" She squinted.

"How about ID of any kind?" He should escort her to the door, but there was something about this girl, something he couldn't quite put his finger on. Could be the way she'd sneaked in with the janitors looking all innocent and yet purposeful, or could be the how-dare-you-touch-me air about her, but mostly, he just wanted to hear her speak. He loved hearing her accent.

"ID? You mean papers of some sort?" She nervously twisted a strand of hair around her index finger.

20

"Yes."

She opened the flap of her bag and mined inside it. "My name's Glory Smith. Why don't you ask Zeiss? He's expecting me."

"Well, your royal highness, he's expecting a lot of people, but I have a feeling you're not one of them."

"I'm not *royalty*. Like I told you before, my name is Glory Smith. He messaged me on Facebook to meet him backstage." She stopped looking in her bag, and gave Logan a glare that dared him to question her further.

"If only I had a dime for every girl who used that line to get closer to a star." He folded his arms. "Do you honestly think Austen Zeiss would take the time to message a girl he's never met before on Facebook?"

"Yes. In fact, he told me when he sang *Only You* and tugged on his ear that was a signal for me to come backstage." She folded her arms and attempted to stand still, but swayed a little.

"Zeiss always sings *Only You* for his last song." He hated bursting her bubble, but someone had to. "And that tug on his ear is a message to his little daughter that he loves her. He does it at every concert. I would think, being a big fan and all, you'd know that."

Undeterred, she glared at him. "Do you have a lappy? I can prove it." She waited for him to do her bidding.

"Lappy?"

"Yes, a laptop. I can show you my account."

"Okay, that's it. Come on. Move along." Queen's English accent or not, he'd wasted too much time with her. He gently nudged her to take a step. "If you go out the same door you came in, I won't take you to the office."

As though heartbroken, her shoulders slumped. "He really did message me."

"I've no doubt someone messaged you, but it was probably a catfish."

"Catfish?" Her cheeks flushed a bright red, making her look even more innocent and naïve.

"Yeah. Someone posed as Zeiss. Happens all the time. Don't you watch MTV or read the news? There was a big article in the paper about a catfish on Facebook." Where'd this girl been living? Didn't she know how risky it was to agree to meet anyone from online?

"I just arrived today and haven't seen the news. And I can't waste time watching MTV." She appeared worried for a second but then found her resolve once again. "Won't you please check with his people?"

Even though he'd explained things, she still seemed to have no idea what a catfish was and didn't realize that people can be impersonated online. "Look princess, I don't have to. I'm positive you're not on their list of noteworthies."

She swayed and leaned against the wall.

"Are you all right? Had a few too many?" He was downright worried about her. She needed to learn what a catfish was and how dangerous they could be. But there was no time to explain it now. She looked like she might hurl at any moment.

"I'm not legless, if that's what you mean. Do you have a loo?"

"A loo?" Oh, yes. Even he knew that loo was British for bathroom. "Yes. Go back through the Employees Only door and there's a restroom next to the concessions booth."

She nodded and took off, holding her mouth, exiting where he'd told her to.

"You're welcome." He called after her.

Before coming to work, he'd read that article about the Facebook stalker luring girls, and here's a girl being lured. Wait. People met online all the time. But the article said the authorities believed one of the girls had met the catfish here at the Garden. He decided to follow, just in case he was right and a catfish had set her up. As he opened the door,

22

he caught a glimpse of her disappearing into the crowded restroom. She'd be okay in there.

At that moment, his radio vibrated again. Grabbing the device, he clicked it on.

"O'Brian, where the heck are you? I got a call from Zeiss's manager. They need help." That was his boss.

"I'm on it, Chief." He'd wanted to see her one more time, maybe even follow her out to make sure she was okay, but duty called. With that he spun around and headed for the dressing room area. Once he made sure all was well with Zeiss, he'd swing around here to double check on her.

chapter three

Glorianna had never been so sick. She'd lost the contents of her stomach and made such wretched noises, she didn't dare come out of her stall until the loo grew quiet and seemed empty. Venturing out, she looked about the disheveled room. Garbage bins overflowed with damp paper towels; water spotted the brilliantly lit vanity and sinks. Her gaze went to the mirror. Even with all the makeup she'd slathered on before leaving the hotel, she looked knackered. She stuck out her tongue.

Slimy green. And beneath her eyes, dark circles had appeared. No wonder that guard thought she'd been drinking. Still, he could have at least checked with Zeiss's people. That would have been the courteous thing to do.

She should have insisted. She should have stood her ground. If she'd felt better she would have given him the ear-bashing he deserved for not making an effort to see if she had a date with Zeiss. It would have taken him all of a few minutes to verify.

She patted a pocket for her mobile. She needed to message Zeiss and apologize for not meeting him. But her phone wasn't there. That's right. She'd been paranoid that her father's security would follow her

GPS, so she'd left it at the Waldorf. Common sense told her it was too soon to venture out of the restroom. She needed to wait.

Besides, her knees felt spongy. If only she could sit down for a bit, maybe the room would quit swirling. She remembered the medicine bottle in her jacket pocket and pulled it out. Grabbing a paper cup, she filled it with water and downed a couple of tablets. That should help clear her head, or did the medicine make her dizzy? She tried to read the label, but long medical terms boggled her mind. Too late anyway. She'd already taken them.

Gazing around the room, she saw no chairs. Wooziness overwhelmed her so much that she could hardly stand. The only place she could rest would be . . . her eyes drew back to the stall she'd recently vacated. That might be best anyway. At least she wouldn't have to talk to anyone should concert stragglers come in. Besides, she would only wait fifteen or twenty minutes and then venture out.

Not long.

Not long at all.

The night finally died down. Logan had watched as Austen Zeiss and his entourage safely left the building. The press dutifully followed. Now, all Logan had to do was make a final sweep through the hallways and he could leave. Fortunately, he'd remembered to buy his sister and Mrs. Shapiro the Zeiss tee shirts they'd requested and had stored them in his jacket pockets. That would score him some major points with his sis, might even make her let up on the don't-become-a-cop lectures for a while. And he liked making Mrs. Shapiro happy. With her elderly husband to care for, she deserved some pleasure. Plus, it would keep him in her good graces.

When he passed through the Employees Only door, he thought of the British girl and wondered if she'd left the building. He'd made a sweep past this spot forty-five minutes ago, and there'd been no sign of her. Surely, she had left. He paused at the restroom door. Maybe he should check.

No. Don't be stupid. He started away.

But then stopped.

As a security guard, he needed to make certain the building was empty except for employees. He turned back and pushed open the door. Walking farther in, he scanned the messy room. The place appeared vacant. All stall doors hung open.

All except one.

He glanced beneath. Black combat boots.

The little Brit.

What was she doing? Was she ill? He listened closely and could swear he heard a petite snore. Had she passed out sitting on the toilet? Well, sick or drunk, it didn't matter. He banged on the stall. "Anybody in there?"

A startled gasp came from within, followed by a raspy voice. "What are you doing in the ladies' loo?"

"The Garden is closing. All concert attendees have to leave. Come out."

"I must have fallen asleep." A moment passed, and then, she gave a little cry. "My legs are numb. I can't stand up."

"Do you need help?" He didn't want to open the stall, afraid of what he'd find, but she sounded in dire straits.

"Yes, please."

He pushed on the door. It didn't budge. "You have to unlock it."

"I don't know if I can."

"You have to."

"Oh, tosh." She groaned and after what seemed a good full minute the door swung open. Mascara smudged her cheeks, black/purple hair hung in disarray. "This feels so strange. Even though I'm standing, I can't feel my feet."

"Take it easy." He knew she could seriously hurt herself if she stepped wrong. "Let your circulation start flowing."

"My legs and feet tingle like thousands of needles are pricking me." She slowly edged her way out of the stall.

"You don't look so good." He hovered close.

"I bet you say that to all the girls you haul out of the bog." Her face grimaced with each slow step.

"Just the ones I'm concerned about. Is there someone I could call to come get you?" Logan followed as she slowly left the restroom, staying near in case she should fall.

"Has Zeiss gone?" She glanced up and down the empty corridor and rubbed her eyes, smearing more mascara over her eyelids.

"You have a one-track mind. He left a while ago."

"Because of you, I missed him." She stamped her foot and flinched before glaring at him like he crushed all her hopes and dreams.

"Look, I've been pretty patient. I should have escorted your pretty butt to the security office after you came backstage, but I didn't. However, I still can, if you'd like."

Her chocolate-colored eyes grew wide. "No need. I'll be on my way." She slowly ambled down the hall, appearing a little tipsy on her wobbly feet.

He thought of the Facebook stalker and how she'd been lured here. It might be a good idea to stay with her until she was safely in a taxi, heading home. He caught up with her. "Why don't you let me hail you a cab?"

"That would be ever so smashing." She leaned against him.

The nearest exit would be the back way. Placing her arm in the crook of his, he guided her through the Employees Only door, down the corridor, coming to the freight elevator the rock stars, basketball and hockey players used. He pressed the button, opening the gate to get on.

"Hold up." She looked around at empty hallways. "Why did you bring me backstage again? Where are you really taking me?" Concern creased her pretty mascara-smudged face.

"This is the quickest way out." He showed her his security ID, hoping that eased her mind. "I'm glad you're on your guard about going somewhere private with a stranger. The 'cage' doesn't look like much, but Zeiss took it not more than an hour ago before he got into his limousine and sped away." He hoped hearing her heartthrob had come this way would alleviate her worry.

She seemed to mull over that, then relaxed a little as she cautiously stepped on. Logan should have guessed this night would end with him babysitting some strung-out, though very pretty, teenager. Could be worse, he supposed. He could have been stuck going to the airport with Zeiss. He closed the gate and pressed the ground floor button.

As the elevator descended, she clutched his arm, keeping her balance. "You know, he really did send me a message on Facebook." Her eyes pleaded with him to believe her.

"I'm sure someone did." He couldn't help it, but he felt sorry for the kid. When they reached the ground floor, he opened the gate, and let her step out first. Then he guided her past the giant garbage bins being filled by the janitorial night crew.

"Hey, O'Brian. Find a pretty chica?" Hector Garcia teased, as they walked by him and his fellow maintenance workers, wearing the standard grey jumpsuits. One was short and squat though muscular, another tall and wiry thin, and another medium height. The tall, thin guy's eyes lingered on Glory as though admiring her good looks. They all snickered. Hector had been one of Logan's down-on-his-luck friends he'd helped get a job at the Garden. Hector wanted to be a guard, but there had been no openings, so he'd taken the janitorial job until a security position became available. Logan hoped Hector could take his place once he was accepted at the academy.

"Just helping this young lady hail a cab." Ordinarily Logan would crack a joke, but he didn't want his friend to make more of this than there was.

Hector finished dumping the bin from his cleaning cart. "Too bad for you, *muchacha linda*. O'Brian shows the ladies a good time. Hey?" His round face creased with a grin. The other workers chortled.

Logan glanced at Glory, wondering if she understood that they weren't threatening her, but simply thought she was pretty. Red blushed her cheeks. Yes, she knew.

He pointed behind his friend. "You missed a spot."

Hector spun around, then laughed, waving him off as he pushed his cart toward the hallway. "Take care with that *hombre*, girl. That one, he's cunning." He bowed and left with his buddies following.

Logan guided her to the back door and down the alley, which led to the main street. A man sat in the doorway of a building across the road, taking a swig from a bottle in a brown paper bag and a stocky man wearing a pea coat hustled by, but no one else was around.

Her steps grew slower and slower. No cabs were in sight. Usually the streets were wall to wall with taxis, but that would have been earlier, after the concert had let out. Now, nothing.

She swayed into him. As he helped her stay upright, his hand brushed her forehead. "You're burning up. I'm taking you to the hospital."

"No. I've already seen a doctor." She dug in her jacket pocket and pulled out a prescription. "He gave me these. I'll be fine."

He took the bottle from her and by the street light saw they were tranquilizers. No wonder she had trouble staying awake. Poor sick kid had dragged herself to this concert all in the hopes of meeting Zeiss. "Look. There are no cabs right now, and I can't in all good conscience leave you on the street." Logan tried to think what would be the best thing to do. "Let me drive you home. I get that you hardly know me, but I work security, so you know I'll keep you safe."

"That would be smashing." She yawned. "What did you say your name was?"

"Logan. Logan O'Brian." He steered her along as they retraced their steps into the building and the cage, so they could descend to underground parking. As they reached the garage, she seemed to grow steadier and stood on her own. He opened the gate and stepped off the elevator. "Fortunately, I scored a prime parking spot. It's not far."

She nodded, like she understood.

He started for his father's rundown Toyota Tundra, thinking she'd followed. Halfway to the vehicle, he turned and found she'd ventured off in another direction.

Doubling back, he took her arm, leading her once again. "This way."

"Logan." She smiled up at him; her eyes glazed. "My father will be very grateful to you. He's a very, very busy man."

"Is that so?" He kept her walking, not really listening, intent on getting her into the truck.

"Yes, *very* busy." She choked. "He's going to be so upset."

"I'll talk to him. It will be all right. You'll see."

"You don't understand." She shook her head. "I've cocked up the situation something awful. I sneaked out. I've never done that before." They'd reached his vehicle. He steadied her against the truck as he unlocked the passenger door. He quickly helped her get in, shielding her head with his hand so she wouldn't bump into the door frame.

"I always do what Papa expects. But Zeiss wanted to meet me." She gave a deep sigh. Her stale-medicine breath fanned Logan's face as he buckled her in. He coughed and looked at her.

Pink full lips curled to a grateful smile. Cheeks flushed; eyes filled with appreciation and something more. Something she wouldn't be feeling if she had her wits about her. Something that made his gut sizzle. Being this close to her—kissably close to her—felt awkward and wrong.

He quickly pulled back and banged his head on the truck's frame. Muttering a curse under his breath, he slammed the door. He had to get this young lady, this teenager—even though she only looked a few years younger than he was—home as soon as possible. He raced around to the driver's side, got in, and started the engine. "Okay, where to?"

She didn't answer.

He glanced over to find she'd fallen asleep.

Could this night get any worse?

chapter four

Now what? Logan noticed the bag beside her. Her ID might give him some idea of who to call. He grabbed it and opened the flap. Inside he found a makeup kit, a couple of twenty dollar bills, tissues, and breath mints. She could certainly use those. But no ID of any kind. Who leaves home without proper ID on them in case of an accident? Or at least a cell phone? He hated to do it, but he had to get her to come around. "Hey, wake up." Logan nudged her.

She opened her heavy-lidded eyes and smiled. "Logan! Are you taking me to Zeiss?"

"Sure, as soon as you tell me where you live."

"I can't go home. I live in London. Papa will go bonkers." She swiped at a stray hair that had fallen into her eyes.

"Look, I either take you home or to the hospital. You pick." He started the car and backed out of his parking space.

As he pulled from the plaza onto the street, he realized she hadn't answered. Glancing at her, he found she'd drifted off again. "Hey, you." What did she say her name was? Oh, yeah. "Glory."

She moved a little.

"Glory Smith!" he yelled.

She blinked awake, and then, as if remembering what they'd been talking about, she became teary-eyed. "Please don't take me to hospital. I just need to sleep a little while."

What had he gotten himself into? Sure, do a good deed, he'd told himself. Hail her a cab. Make sure she gets help. Keep her safe in case she was being stalked by the Facebook catfish. That one hit home. If he were to drop her off at a busy hospital, the stalker could nab her. He'd seen plenty of movies where that happened. And after hearing from Sara what went on in the ER, he believed it possible. But was he being too suspicious? Then he remembered that she'd said her home was in London. Could her family afford to pay for an ER visit in a foreign country? Oh crud! He glanced at the clock on the dashboard. Nearly 12:30.

Sara would be home. She could help Glory. Together, they might find out who Glory's father was and get in touch with him. Against his better judgment, he headed to his sister's apartment.

Once Logan parked under the apartment building, getting Glory out of the truck was no small task. He managed to turn her so he could pull her out of the vehicle and onto her feet. But after he got her standing so he could reach inside to snag her bag, she slumped over like a sack of rags. He grabbed her and boosted her over his shoulder. If his luck held, he should run into Mrs. Shapiro, waiting for his return. Even though it was the middle of the night, he wouldn't put it past the woman to want to collect her Zeiss tee shirt, or at the very least tell him he was making too much noise. And what would he tell her about the girl over his shoulder?

To avoid running into anyone, he opted to take the stairs to his sister's third-floor apartment. Even though he considered himself in prime shape and Glory was fairly light to carry, he grew winded by the time he exited the stairwell. Fortunately, the hall appeared clear. No one about.

He tugged keys from his pants pocket while balancing Glory on his shoulder and slipped inside his sister's apartment without incident. He turned on the light, laid Glory on the leather couch, set her bag on the floor beside her, and hustled down the hall to his sister's room.

Peeking in, he saw her bed still made. She wasn't home yet.

Now what?

Walking back to the living room, he found Mr. Whiskers had jumped on the back of the couch and was staring down on the intruder to his domain.

That dang furball! Logan couldn't leave Glory where the cat could bother her. For all he knew, she might be allergic. He had to put her in a room where the cat would leave her alone. Sara's? That would probably be best.

He shooed the cat off the couch, lugged Glory over his shoulder, and took her to his sister's room. Walking in, he quickly flipped on the light and closed the door behind him, banishing Mr. Whiskers. He set her on the bed. She groaned and curled on her side. As she did, he noticed something strange.

Was that blonde hair near her ear?

Fascinated, he leaned over, studying her hair more closely. Was she wearing a wig? He tugged on the black/purple hair and it slipped off her head. Long luscious honey-colored locks spilled over her shoulders.

Whoa! Why cover up such beautiful hair with this thing? He dropped the wig in the armchair by the bed. Kids today. Who knew how they thought or why they did things? Was it only three years ago that he'd been a teen? Seemed a lifetime. Whatever her reasoning, at least she was safe here with him and Sara. He grabbed a throw and covered her. Feeling her forehead, he found she was still feverish. He thought of that moment when he'd fastened her seatbelt and the sizzle that had stirred in his gut as he'd gazed into her bewitching eyes. He shook his head as though to erase such notions from his mind. Yet, still he stood there gazing at her.

Fascinated.

Intrigued.

And . . . attracted?

What? No! He hit himself in the forehead. What was he thinking? He couldn't be attracted to her. He must think of himself as her guardian angel, her port in the storm, her safe harbor. That's it. That's all. He had to think like a cop, think like Max, think like his father would have.

Before leaving the room, he turned on the soft light of the lamp which sat on the nightstand. Should Glory wake up, she might be frightened in the dark. He quietly closed the door behind him as he left.

Mr. Whiskers rubbed against his legs. Of course, the furball had been waiting for him. He glared down on the cat. "Don't you dare rattle that door."

Mr. Whiskers had been known to reach his paw beneath and shake the door for attention. "Come on. I'll get you some treats." Logan went to the kitchen with the cat chasing him.

First, he dropped cat treats in the feline's bowl, then opened the fridge and grabbed a yogurt for himself. Yogurt had been his and his sister's go-to food when they were worried about something. He headed to the couch and sat down. He set his yogurt on the coffee table and took off his jacket. In doing so, his foot kicked against Glory's bag.

She sure seemed convinced Zeiss had sent her a message. Curious, he grabbed his laptop, turning it on. Logging onto Facebook, he entered Glory Smith in the search line and hit enter.

Several faces appeared. None of them Glory. So, he entered London. Her image with black and purple hair—not blonde—appeared. He clicked on her picture and her page opened.

He pressed his finger on the "Message" tab. A window opened so he could write Glory a message, but it didn't show posts she'd received. He'd have to get her to log on. Following a hunch, he entered Austen Zeiss's name.

The rock star's page popped up with pictures of him. Five million followers. Popular guy.

Logan heard a key in the front door. Sara! Finally. He shut his laptop as she walked in.

"It's nearly 1:30." She tugged off her jacket, hanging it in the coat closet. "I thought you'd be sound asleep."

"Ran into a bit of a problem." He went to the kitchen. "Let me grab you a yogurt as I tell you about my night." He fetched her favorite black-cherry, collected a spoon from the utensil drawer, and handed them to her.

"This must be bad." She climbed up on the bar stool, peeled back the foil, and took a spoonful in her mouth before looking expectantly at him.

"There's a girl asleep in your bed." Logan recounted how he'd met Glory and why she ended up in Sara's room.

Without saying a word, Sara set her yogurt down, slid off the stool, and hurried to her room, not even knocking as she entered. Logan followed.

Leaning over Glory, Sara felt her forehead. "You're right. She's feverish. Let me get my bag."

Sara kept a medical bag handy in the apartment. Every once in a while, a neighbor would fall, or become ill and rather than call the doctor, they called Sara. She returned, bag in hand. Pulling out a forehead thermometer, she swiped it across Glory. The reading came back 100.5. "That's not too bad. You said she took some pills."

He nodded and at the same time tried to think where Glory had put them. In her pocket? Her bag? He couldn't remember. "Check her jacket."

37

Sara found them right away. Bringing the bottle to the lamplight, she said, "You're right again. This is a tranquilizer. You said you couldn't find any ID on her?"

"Well, I didn't dare pat her down like you just did." No way would he have done that. Not after realizing he was attracted to her. "You check."

Sara searched her jacket pockets, and her jeans.

Glory stirred, but went on sleeping.

Sara motioned Logan out of the room with her. Once the door closed, she said, "She's resting very well right now. There's a chance the fever will break when it's run its course. I'll bunk on the couch and check on her every few hours. When she wakes up in the morning, we'll take her to her father."

"Why don't you sleep on my bed and I'll take the couch?" Logan wanted his sister to get her rest.

She nodded. "You owe me. Big time. And what about the Zeiss tee shirt?"

"In my jacket." He picked it up, pulled out the shirt, throwing it to her.

"This helps." Sara smiled as she checked it. "And, don't worry. Things will look better in the morning."

Glorianna blinked open her eyes. This was not her room at the Waldorf. Where was she? Bits and pieces of the night came back: Zeiss's music, the smell of smoke, and . . . the security guard—Logan O'Brian.

Was this his place? Though her flu-body aches were gone, panic bubbled through her as she glanced around the room. Paintings of beautiful landscapes graced the walls. The room was neat and orderly, nothing out of place. A vanity had pictures on it. On the other side of the bed rested an armchair and on the seat waited her black and purple wig.

She stood up. Felt a little dizzy for a second, but soon her head cleared. Her father would be worried out of his mind. He'd been hyper-protective of her since her mother had died. She could picture him pacing, dressed in his Manu Melwani tailored suit, anxiety creasing his noble brow, and a cig in his hand.

He always smoked when stressed. She'd begged him to quit. And he would for a day or two and then some international crisis would arise, and he'd cave. Her disappearance would cause an *international* crisis for him. She had to get word to Rae.

She sank down on the bed, remembering she'd left her mobile in the suite. Drawn to the dresser, hopeful to find a phone there, she recognized Logan in one of the pictures. He sat at what looked like a restaurant table with an older man and a twenty-something woman with long brown hair. A kind smile lightened her solemn dark eyes. She resembled Logan. In another picture, the older man wore a policeman's uniform. Their father, perhaps? Knowing Logan's father was a police officer made her feel a little better. A notepad with what looked like a grocery list lay next to the pictures along with several pens.

A light tap came at the door. The woman in the picture entered. "How are you feeling this morning?"

"You mean other than embarrassed and a bit peckish?"

"Yes." She smiled and held out her hand. "My name's Sara O'Brian. And yours is?"

Already she was fishing for information Glorianna couldn't tell her because it might leak to the press, and that was the last thing she needed, the last thing her father needed. "Glory Smith."

"Glory, you gave my brother quite a fright last night." She felt Glorianna's forehead. "Your fever is gone. You're probably hungry. While you wash your face, I'll fix you some scrambled eggs and toast. The bathroom's down the hall and to your left."

"Thanks. Skip the eggs though." Glorianna held her upset tummy. The mere mention of gooey eggs stirred her queasy stomach. "But the toast sounds wonderful. Do you have tea?"

"Sure. I'll have it waiting for you." Sara disappeared into the kitchen. Glorianna hustled to the bathroom. After refreshing herself, she gazed into the mirror. Mascara smudged her cheeks and eyelids. She quickly washed her face and ran her fingers through her hair. And that's when it hit her. They'd seen her without the wig. Surely, they'd ask why she'd worn one. The key would be not to make a big deal about it.

She made her way down the hallway to find Logan seated on the couch in the living room, laptop in front of him.

He smiled. "Hey. Are you feeling better this morning?"

"Yes. Thank you for taking care of me. I apologize for being such a burden." A huge picture window took up much of one wall and looked out on New York City. An array of towering buildings stood before her. And with them, possibilities. There was so much she wanted to see and explore. "Is one of these the Empire State Building?"

"No. That's farther south. And don't worry about being a burden." He smiled and a dimple flashed in his cheek, a sparkle kindled in his eyes.

All at once, she remembered him buckling her seatbelt in his truck, and how close he had been to her face, *and* how she'd been sooo attracted to him—even wanted him to kiss her. Embarrassed, her cheeks grew hot. Blushing always gave away her thoughts. She had to think of something else. Her father's stern image came to mind. "Could I use your computer to call my father? I need to let him know I'm all right." She was glad she'd had the forethought to set up voice call on the Internet that would mark her call as unknown and not show the IP address.

Logan handed her his laptop.

She couldn't call here. Logan would hear her entire conversation. "Do you think Sara would mind if I used her room?"

"Not at all." He waved her to go ahead.

Glory hurried down the hall and quietly close the door behind her. She moved the wig from the armchair and sat down, then dialed.

"Rae Fleming speaking."

"This is Glori—"

"Glorianna! Where are you? Your father is sick with worry."

"I'm fine." She had to choose her words wisely. "I'm so sorry. I went to a concert and met a friend."

"You what?! What concert? What friend?" Behind Rae's voice she heard her father's booming tone.

As soon as she returned to her Prime-Minister-daughter's life, she'd be pressed to go to luncheons and keep to the schedule her father had made for her. And before she knew what hit her, she'd be back home tromping around Oxford up to her eyeballs in studies. She thought of Logan. If she left now, she'd never see him again. They would say they'd keep in touch, but that never worked. Spending time with him now was far better.

Maybe, just maybe, she could use this opportunity to breathe a little and see the sights with a guy she was attracted to and who she was pretty certain was attracted to her. "Tell Papa I'll be back this evening, and not to worry, I'm fine." She abruptly ended the call.

Today was her chance to see how normal people lived, and she was going to take it.

"Was your dad upset?" Logan took his laptop from her when she returned.

"Yeah, but at least he knows I'm all right. I'll give him the day to calm down and then go home." She sat beside him on the couch as Sara brought in her tea and toast. "You're an angel. Thank you." Glory took a bite and sipped the steaming brew.

"I looked up Zeiss's Facebook page." Logan showed it to her. "Does this look familiar?"

She stared at the screen. "Kind of."

Logan moved his laptop in front of her. "Why don't you pull up your page, and let's take a look at the message he sent you?"

She took a big bite of toast, then laid it on the plate next to the tea cup, brushing crumbs from her hands. "Sure. Then you can see I wasn't lying." She tapped in her passcode and her page appeared, with a picture of her with black and purple hair.

"I have to ask. Why do you wear that wig? Your hair is pretty enough."

A smile came to her lips. And he realized he may have showed a little too much of his liking for her.

"I mean, the blonde hair looks more natural." Had he mended the damage?

"It's fun to be someone else every once in a while." She smoothed a stray hair off her shoulder.

He could understand. Many times, while growing up without a mother and father, he'd wished he could pretend to be someone else. He glanced at Sara. She watched him a little too closely. Did she suspect he was attracted to Glory? That would not be good. Straightening in his seat and putting a little distance between himself and their guest, he waited for her to open the message folder.

"There. See." She turned the screen. "He's even left a new message. 'Where were you last night?'"

The photo with the message was indeed Zeiss, but someone with hacker skills could have accessed Zeiss's page. "Glory, I'd bet a million dollars this isn't your rock star."

"Who could it be?" She took another sip of tea, her pretty mocha-colored eyes staring at him.

42

"I don't want to worry you, but there have been some women abducted in the city who have been linked to a catfish on the net. This could be that guy." Logan showed her the article in the paper that he'd read yesterday morning.

"Are the women all right?"

He glanced at his sister. Sara didn't move, just stared at him like he'd better know what he was doing.

"No. Their bodies were found in Central Park."

"Oh no!" Glory's hand covered her mouth. "Do you think this catfish person pretending to be Zeiss could be the one who killed those women?"

Logan set the paper on the coffee table. He had to be truthful. "There's one way to find out."

"How?"

"Have him meet you this afternoon at Rockefeller Center, near the statue of Prometheus."

She hesitated a moment as if this was too cops-and-robbers for her, yet she typed in a reply, stating she was sorry to have missed him, but could he meet her at 3:00 by the statue. She hit send. "You know, he might not be on his computer right now. It may take him a while to answer."

Sara walked over, standing in front of them, arms folded. "You guys are playing with fire. This could be a murderer."

Logan shrugged. "The guy probably won't reply anyway."

"But if he does, promise me you'll call Max." Sara gave him her big-sister-knows-best look.

"Sure. If he answers the message, I'll call Max. Happy?" Logan gave her an I'll-do-it-your-way smirk.

"You know, you really should rethink your career choices. You're pulling good grades at NYU and I'm sure your professors would give you a good recommendation to a law school. Harvard. Princeton. Yale. Lawyers make more money than cops, and they still help bring justice to the world, like Dad did." She gave a shrug like she knew his mind was made up, but she still had to voice her opinion.

"Let's not talk about this in front of our guest." He hoped Sara could take a hint and let the subject rest. In case she wanted to go another round, he turned to Glory. "So, you're here on holiday. What are the sights you want to see?"

"All of them really."

"That could take several weeks. How long are you in town?"

"Just a few days. Papa is here on business and that doesn't give us a lot of time to become tourists. However, I have today."

"I'll take you around. Want to see the Statue of Liberty?" Logan hated fighting the crowds, but to spend more time with Glory, he'd tolerate them.

"That would be smashing. Oh, and could we go to the Empire State Building? Ever since I saw the classic film *An Affair to Remember* I've wanted to go there." Glory clamped her hands together like she was uber excited at the thought.

Sara shook her head. "Before Logan takes you anywhere, I think you should go see your father. I know if Logan had been gone all night when he was your age, I'd want to see him as soon as I could."

All the joy in Glory's eyes vanished. And as much as Logan wanted to make her happy, he knew Sara was right. "What would it hurt? We could stop, see your father so he knows you're all right, and then head out."

Glory looked as though she'd been trapped. But then something flickered in her eyes, like she saw the wisdom in what they were saying. "Okay. Let me gather my stuff together. I'll only be a minute." She jumped up, grabbed her bag off the floor, and dashed to Logan's room, maybe going after the wig.

His sister sank down on the couch beside him. "She sure is a pretty thing. Beats Trish the Dish in the looks department."

44

"Are we back to that?" Logan couldn't believe it. "Please don't bring that up in front of Glory. I'm begging you."

"So, you like her, don't you?" Sara nudged him with her elbow.

"What's not to like?" He had no intention of telling his sister he was attracted to Glory. Mostly because she probably already knew. His sister had eyes and could see for herself.

Sara stared towards her bedroom door. "There's something about Glory that's very familiar. It's like I've seen her before. It nagged at me all night, but I couldn't place her." She picked up the saucer and cup Glory had used. She also grabbed yesterday's newspaper and stopped, staring at the front-page.

"What's wrong?" Logan stood beside her.

"Look who it is." Sara pointed to the picture of the Prime Minister and his daughter.

Logan didn't understand. "So, it's England's Prime Minister."

"Look closer at his daughter."

Staring at the photo, he suddenly realized who Glory really was. "Oh, crud!"

He tore off down the hallway to Sara's room. Throwing open the door, he found the window to the fire escape opened and Glory long gone.

# chapter five

ogan looked to the armchair where he'd put the wig last night. It was gone. Glancing around the room for a clue, he saw a note with his name on it. Grabbing it, he read, "Forgive me."

Sara had followed Logan and stared at him with deep concern clouding her face. "She's gone?"

He showed her the note. "Looks like it."

"Oh, this is not good. We've had the Prime Minister of England's daughter in our home and now she's gone. What are we going to do?"

"I don't know." Logan paced the room. "We need to think."

"*We?* Don't you mean *you?*" Sara pointed at him.

"She can't have gotten too far on foot." Logan dashed back to the living room and grabbed his jacket. "She called her father, so it's not as bad as you might think. I just need to find her and take her safely to him."

"But—"

Logan didn't have time to argue. With every second, Glory got farther away. He charged out of the apartment and ran smackdab into Mrs. Shapiro.

"In a hurry, are you?" Pink sponge rollers covered her head and her terrycloth bath robe was cinched tightly around her thick middle.

"Mrs. Shapiro, did you see a girl with long blonde hair leave our apartment through the fire escape?"

"Heavenly days! That fire escape has more rust than an anchor chain. Don't tell me she used that?" Her wrinkly-lidded eyes peered up at him.

He couldn't listen to her inevitable rant about the lazy maintenance manager and what dismal state of disrepair the building was in. To distract the woman with something new to think about, he remembered the tee shirt. He pulled it from his pocket and thrust it in her hands. "Here's the shirt you wanted."

"Aren't you a good boy? Your father would have been so proud. It's for my ungrateful niece, who never comes to visit unless she needs money." She patted his cheek and held out the tee shirt inspecting it.

Mrs. Shapiro took a deep breath, preparing for another barrage of conversation.

He couldn't afford to waste time. "Can't stay and chat. If you have any questions, talk with Sara." He glanced back at the doorway.

His sister had stepped in the threshold and heard him. She shot him blazing stink-eye, but quickly flipped her expression to a smile when the elderly woman turned to her.

"How are you, Mrs. Shapiro?" she said through clenched teeth.

This was Logan's chance to make a clean get away. As he dashed to the staircase, thinking it would be faster than the elevator, he heard Mrs. Shapiro. "Oh hon, I'm glad you asked. My lower back is killing me and the mister, wouldn't you know, he's constipated again. I've told him once, if I've told him a hundred times, you've got to eat the greens and prunes I give you every day."

Logan thundered down the three flights of stairs and burst out onto the sidewalk. He scanned up and down the street. No sign of Glory. The newspaper article had her real name. Thinking as he ran, her name finally came to him. Glorianna Templeton. He'd just keep

48

thinking of her as Glory. That was easier and didn't make him feel like an idiot for not recognizing her.

Where could she have disappeared so fast on foot? And where was she going? Obviously, she wasn't in a hurry to see her father. When Logan had asked her what sights she wanted to see, she'd mentioned the Empire State Building. Said it had been in one of her favorite movies. That she'd gone there was a long shot, but the only one he had.

Sitting in the taxi's back seat, Glorianna nearly had her face smashed against the passenger window as she peered out at the bustling city. Sidewalks teemed with lively crowds, but in the back of her mind she wondered—would Logan remember what she'd said about the Empire State Building and go there hoping to find her? How romantic would that turn out? And so much better than the movie because she wouldn't have an accident and become paralyzed like the main character.

And then she worried. What if she did have an accident on the way? Or worse, what if *he* did? She'd never forgive herself. *Nice one, Glory.*

She was into the scheme now. She might as well see it through and hope Logan turned up. But what would it have saved her? He could still insist on taking her to her father. But with any luck his sister wouldn't be with him, and Glory might be able to talk him into waiting.

Logan should have driven his truck, but finding a parking place downtown was a nightmare, so he'd hopped on a bus at 14th Street. As it lumbered near 23rd traffic came to a standstill. He heard the radio dispatcher telling the driver that an accident on 5th Avenue had stopped traffic. Logan opted to go the rest of the way on foot.

Dodging between people, his mind went to Glory. He had to watch for blonde hair and black/purple hair just in case she wore the wig. Why would the Prime Minister's daughter take such a risk and go out in the city alone? Why hadn't her father's people taken her to the concert? Maybe the prime minister didn't like Zeiss. Or maybe he didn't even know of her crush on the rock star.

Logan reached 33rd Street. Sprinting to the entrance of the ESB building, he hurried inside, vigilantly watching for Glory. Chances were she'd still be in the tourist line for the elevator. Apologizing and saying he wasn't cutting in as he passed surly-looking faces of many nationalities, he found no trace of her.

Had she already gone to the top? If so, it would take him forever to stand in line to ride up and check. Spying a security guard, an idea came to him. With firm resolve, he made his way to the man who looked like he worked for the mob: thick neck, massive shoulders and a scowl on his face that would scare a pit bull. "Hey, I need a favor."

The guy stared at him.

"I work security at the Garden." Luckily, he still had his MSG ID in his jacket pocket. He showed it to him. The unimpressed guard looked at the ID then back to him as if to say, "Big deal."

"Here's the thing. I need to get to the observation deck in a hurry. I'm looking for a girl and it's vitally important I find her."

Still, he said nothing.

"If you could please help me, I'd score you some Ranger hockey tickets, rink-side seats."

He appeared a little impressed. "Throw in Knicks playoff tickets, too?"

"Sure." Logan didn't know if he could swing it, but what the heck.

The guard started to lead him to a service elevator away from the public.

"Logan. Is that you?" Glory decked out in her black/purple wig, walked toward him. Relief seemed to wash her face.

He couldn't believe his good fortune and rushed to her. "Why did you take off like that?" He looped his arm with hers. She wasn't getting away again.

"Still need to go to the observation deck?" The brusque guard glared at him, as if he could see his Ranger and Knicks tickets evaporating by the second.

"Nope. Found her. Thanks, though." As Logan guided Glory toward the exit, he felt the guard's glowering stare in the middle of his back.

"You remembered what I said about the movie and you came." She smiled warmly with a beaming expression and glowing cheeks.

"Yes. I came, *Glorianna*." Logan scowled.

All the brightness left her face. "You know who I really am."

"Yup." Logan stopped and glanced out the glass door and then back down the hallway, checking to see if they had drawn attention or if some of the Prime Minister's protection unit had found them. People hustled by, not paying the slightest attention. Even the gruff guard had disappeared. "You should have leveled with me."

"But if I had, you would have insisted that I go to my father, like your sister wanted."

"You better believe it." He tugged on her arm.

"Please, Logan. Don't make me go. This is my chance to be a normal person, and see the places I've heard about, but could never visit because it would be a hassle for security. I've always wanted to have one great adventure. My schedule never allows it and sightseeing certainly isn't as important to Papa as making the right connections to further Great Britain's influence. I know I have a good life. And I'm grateful. It's just . . . sometimes . . . as I look at my future and what Papa has planned for me, I can hardly breathe."

"At least your dad is alive. Be grateful for that."

"Oh, I am. I love Papa. But . . ."

"But what?"

"I need air every once in a while. When Mama died ten years ago, Papa became obsessed with keeping me safe. She died a year after he was elected, and he has always suspected her car accident to be foul play. I've hardly had a moment to myself. I think that's why I joined Zeiss's fan club and set up that Facebook page, so I could be Glory Smith, an ordinary girl who could go where she wanted, when she wanted. I became like everybody else. Don't get me wrong. I like having a governess to talk to, servants who clean and cook, but every once in a while, I wonder."

"Take it from me, ordinary isn't for the faint of heart." He thought of how hard it had been for him and Sara. "My sister gave up a lot to take care of me after Dad died. We only had each other, no maids or cooks, no special service guys to watch over us."

"Your sister is smashing. I wish I had a sister. Or even a brother for that matter." She paused for a moment. "I watched you and your sister this morning. There's a strong bond there."

"You have your dad."

"Along with the entire country."

He and Sara did have a strong bond, but that's because of everything they'd been through. His greatest desire was not to become a burden to her. And getting accepted at the academy would help him become more independent and show her that she could get on with her life and marry Max. Logan would be fine.

He studied Glory, standing before him, trying so hard to be independent even though she shouldn't, and even though her father would probably come down pretty hard on her. Could Logan take away the few hours she desperately wanted and return her to her father?

"Your safety comes before your longing to sight see." He'd said it to her, but he also said it to himself to reaffirm that he was turning her in for her own good.

"But, Logan . . ." She bit at her pink bottom lip and her bright brown eyes begged him to listen. "You're a security guard. If you came with me, I wouldn't be in danger. You'd keep me safe."

"Don't do that."

"Don't do what?" Again, she blinked those innocent, British eyes that he could easily get lost in. Eyes that had tantalized him last night, even made him want to kiss her.

He glanced up at the ceiling. "Don't go dragging me further into your scheme. I've only had a few hours sleep *because of you*." He focused on her again. "Besides, what makes you think I'd want to babysit you all day?"

"Because you might hear from the catfish. If he replies it will be on my Facebook account. You need me to set the trap." Her gaze no longer pleaded with him. Instead she appeared rather smug.

"That is not even on the table right now. You are the—" Some people were walking toward them. Logan could not risk anyone overhearing so he leaned close to her ear and whispered, "—Prime Minister's daughter. And I refuse to put you at risk."

"Okay, so we don't try and catch the guy. I can sightsee alone."

"Seriously?" He couldn't tell if she really would or not. Part of Logan wanted to grab her and shake some sense into her, the other part couldn't help but admire her tenacity and determination. He knew he could keep her safe. He never doubted that. The question was, was it the right thing to do?

"And, if Carlton or the other members of Papa's security team catches us, I'll tell them that you'd been trying to take me to Papa and I wouldn't go. I'll make everything right, and you'll turn out to be a hero." She rubbed her hands together as though wringing every ounce of hope from them.

"I don't know." Even though she made it sound like everything would be fine, a gut feeling to take her by the arm and haul her to the British Embassy nagged at him.

"Come on. You know me. It will be all right."

"I don't know you at all. I only know that you're the Prime Minister of England's missing daughter and the odds are if his people find me with you, my butt will land in jail!"

"I promise I won't let that happen. You'll be a hero."

If she really could deliver on her promise, he would gain high marks with the police academy. In fact, it might even clinch his acceptance.

"Okay." She didn't wait for him to agree, but took his arm and guided him toward the door. "Let's go see your city and get to know each other better."

He took one step and then another. Had Logan lost his mind? If they got caught and she didn't defend him, he could kiss his dream career good bye. But on the other hand . . . she seemed earnest and believable. Why not take a chance and spend the day with a beautiful young woman? He'd keep her safe. "You have to promise me when the time comes to return to your father you won't argue."

She smiled up at him, not saying a word as she led him out of the door.

 chapter six

Glorianna walked beside Logan as they made their way west on 34th Street's busy sidewalk. She couldn't believe Logan had agreed to go with her.

He texted his sister. Glorianna supposed he did it to let her know everything was all right. "When we get to Herald Square, we can either take a bus down to Battery Park, where we can catch a ferry to Liberty Island. That will cost twenty-two dollars. Or take the subway which will cost twenty-three." He studied her "For each of us, I might add." He waited for her answer.

She only had one twenty-dollar bill left. She'd given the other twenty to the cab driver. "I'm a little low on funds at the moment. But I'm sure Papa will reimburse any of your expenses, whichever way we go."

Logan grimaced like he'd expected as much, then stopped and glanced at his mobile. "Here's the deal. It's close to noon now. It's a good hour and fifteen minutes to the Statue of Liberty whether we take a ferry, bus, subway, or cab. That's not allowing for time there. Or we could head north, hit Times Square and Broadway, then on to Central Park, but we'd have to double back to see St. Patrick's Cathedral."

She knew he wanted to head north so he could deliver her to her father and meet the catfish at Rockefeller Center, just in case he made contact. But Logan still had two problems: he didn't know where her father was staying, and there was no way she was letting him meet the Facebook catfish without her. Deep down she wanted it to be Zeiss. Since Logan didn't know the answers to either of his problems, she said, "Let's go north."

"All righty then." Logan stopped at a metro pavilion. "We can use my MetroCard to hop a bus north. Now, where did you say you and your father were staying while in the city?"

"Good try, but until we've seen all the sights, I'm not telling you." Glorianna wasn't about to give away key information. Not yet.

"Can't blame a guy for trying," he muttered, as they stepped up in the newly-arrived bus.

Glorianna made sure she sat in a window seat. Logan settled beside her. "You must be planning to attend a university soon. What college are you going to?"

"Oxford. That's the only college, isn't it?" She dreaded the structured boring life of academia. The thought of being stuck in a drafty classroom pouring over books made her shudder.

"There's Cambridge and Eton." He'd said it like he knew hundreds more.

"To Papa there's only Oxford. All the Templeton family throughout history attended college there. It's tradition." She'd seen her stern-face ancestors' pictures dressed in black graduation robes. "Of course, women were only admitted after 1979, but still."

"Sounds like you need to stick up for yourself. I know how it is though. Sara is constantly trying to convince me to become a lawyer. But that's not what I want to do. It's my life and I need to make my own choice." Logan's brows raised and his face gentled into a thoughtful smile.

"That's what I think. I should be able to make my own choice, but I would never dare say so."

"Why not?" His noble forehead furrowed, like she'd said the most absurd thing he'd ever heard.

"Being Prime Minister of Great Britain is a high stress job, and Papa doesn't need grief from his daughter on top of everything else he has to manage day in and day out." She was nearing a dangerous topic and had to switch him to something different. "Are we getting close to Times Square? I've heard there are naked women with paintings on their bodies who frequent the place."

He rolled his eyes. "Yeah, but I know their hangouts. And we're not going there." Logan leaned closer to her, gazing out the window, his eyes scanning the buildings. "We have several more blocks yet." He moved away from her, as if worried he had invaded her personal space, much like he had last night, when he'd buckled her seatbelt and she'd wanted him to kiss her.

Why did she have to remember that? Except, golly, he was movie-star handsome. Besides the dimple in his cheek, he had a little one at the bottom of his whisker-stubbled chin. She caught his faint scent of musk she remembered from last night and all she could think about were his strong muscular arms, and that she wanted them around her. Why were these romantic thoughts swirling in her head?

As if reading her mind and fighting the attraction he must feel as well, Logan sat up. "Telling your father that you'd like to attend a different college shouldn't give him grief."

He was back to the subject which haunted her in so many ways. Why not tell him a little more? Glorianna couldn't betray her father by telling Logan how grief-stricken he'd been after her mother had passed, that there'd been days he hadn't come out of his room and only allowed his top aides to come and go to keep the government on course. "I haven't wanted to do anything to make him upset."

"Oh, and sneaking out to attend a concert so you can meet some strange man, that wouldn't cause him stress at all." Logan playfully nudged her.

"Austen Zeiss is not some strange man. And I intended to return before my father knew I was gone. That I got sick and ended up at your place was not intentional on my part. But now that I'm out and about, I might as well make the most of it. I mean, when will I ever have another opportunity?" As she spoke, she saw the smirk on Logan's face grow and the dimple in his chin became more pronounced.

"Nothing like giving it your best shot, huh princess?" Shaking his head, he added, "Just remember to tell him, I'm the one who found you and brought you safely home."

"Deal."

As Logan herded Glory off the bus and started walking up Times Square, he scanned the area looking for anyone who could cause her harm or anyone who could be with her father's security. Only the normal tourists and New York locals bustled about. Still, he vigilantly kept watch as they made their way.

He wondered about her home life and how trapped she'd said she felt. But even despite that, she seemed protective of her father, even called him papa, like an endearment. Many Brits referred to their fathers as papa. He liked it. But from what Glory had said, it sounded like her dad pretty much ignored her. Logan couldn't blame her for wanting these few hours of freedom. He felt sort of honored that he was her guide and protector. Determined to keep her safe and also show her a good time, his entire mood changed.

With more gusto than he ordinarily felt about his city, he said, "Times Square has a rich history, but something you might find interesting is on New Year's Eve atop the Times Tower." He pointed to it. "See that ball?"

She nodded.

"It lights up at 6:00 and descends as the clock nears midnight amid dazzling lights and pyrotechnic effects."

"I've seen it on the telly. That's brilliant." She appeared impressed.

He glanced around making certain they weren't being followed and were safe, before guiding her over to Broadway. He gave a brief history of the theater district and the few plays he'd attended. "I'm not a fan of *Cats* which had the longest run, but as a kid I enjoyed *Les Miserables* and *The Phantom of the Opera*."

"What about *Hamilton*? I hear it's spectacular."

"You surprise me. I wouldn't think a Brit would think so."

She shrugged. "Well, I haven't seen it, but we've made our peace with your country's Founding Fathers long ago. And I've heard the music. It's brilliant."

The word brilliant must be the equivalent to American's awesome. They came across a hotdog vendor, so Logan bought their lunch.

"I've never eaten an American hotdog." She giggled and slathered a small package of spicy mustard on it before taking a big bite. A smudge of yellow dotted the tip of her nose.

Curious, he asked, "Do you like it?"

"It's absolutely scrummy." She took another bite.

Without thinking, he leaned over and wiped the mustard off her nose. Her beautiful chocolate eyes warmed as she smiled up at him. Once again, the urge to kiss her claimed him and all he could focus on were her full lips and what they might taste like. He awkwardly fought off the notion by remembering his duty to keep her safe.

As he ate his lunch, he scanned the area once again. All seemed well.

"Let's hop on the next bus heading to Central Park." He dropped his napkin and empty paper cup in the trash.

"Isn't that where the women's bodies were found?" She took another bite of her hotdog, trepidation flickered in her eyes.

"Yeah, but it's a big park and we'll stay away from the area where they were." Though he thought she looked a little frightened, at the same time she seemed disappointed.

"Don't you want to check out that spot most? It might give you something you can use in case Zeiss doesn't meet us at Rockefeller Center and my Facebook friend turns out to be this catfish person." She finished off her lunch and balled up her napkin and hotdog wrappings.

"First, there is not going to be an 'us' at Rockefeller Center. And second, I doubt we'd find anything the police missed. They're pretty thorough."

She shrugged as she dropped her garbage in the trash.

Once on the bus, he found only one seat vacant, and offered it to her. But an elderly man had boarded behind them. Glory gave the seat to him, and stood next to Logan. At each stop, they became more and more crowded, making her lean up against him. He yearned to hold her.

What was wrong with him? His job was to keep her safe from danger. But the longer he was with her, he knew another real danger was falling in love with the Prime Minister's daughter. How stupid was that? He'd only known her for a night and a day. Yet, he couldn't stop these unwanted emotions, despite the warning bells ringing in his head.

When they finally got off the bus, he did reconnaissance once again. All seemed normal, so he took her to the pond, Gapstow Bridge, and even strolled under the leafy canopy of The Mall. Time stood still as he listened to her talk with her Queen's English accent, watched her eyes sparkle with delight as she took in the sights, and he noticed she had a quirky habit of tilting her head as she listened to him. He wanted this moment to last forever, but reason soon found him. He needed Glory to check her Facebook account. After tapping the Facebook icon on his cell phone, he handed it to her. "Why don't you log on and see if you have a message?"

"I thought you'd never ask." She entered her password and opened her messages. "He says he can't meet us until 5:00." Nervous excitement flashed in her eyes.

Logan leaned to see the message. This was his chance. Either Zeiss would show up, or the killer.

"Tell him you'll be there." Of course, Logan had no intention of taking her.

Within a few seconds, she handed the phone back to him. "Okay, we're set. Now what?"

"I need to call Max, let him know my plan." Logan dialed his soon-to-be brother-in-law and told him about the stalker and the meeting at Rockefeller Center. He told Logan he'd check it out. That done, he turned to Glorianna. "It's time to take you to your father."

"But we still have time and we haven't seen St. Patrick's Cathedral. I believe it's close to the place where Papa and I are staying."

"Which is?" He waited, expecting her to tell him.

"The Waldorf Astoria." She hung her head, finally surrendering the answer.

He took hold of her hand, guiding her to the curb. "If we take a cab we might have enough time to see the cathedral before I drop you off."

"But Logan. If you take me to Papa, you'll miss meeting the catfish."

He caught the attention of a taxi driver heading their way. "No, I won't. I'll have . . ." In mid-sentence, he realized she was right. Her father's security would detain him with questions that would take at least an hour because he'd have to explain about last night, why he hadn't taken her right home, and a million other questions he knew would come his way. That would take until well past 5:00.

As the cab pulled up, she added. "You know I'm right. I'd love to see the statue Prometheus."

He got her meaning. She wanted to see who showed up and still hoped it would be Austen Zeiss. Avoiding the subject, he opened the vehicle's door ushering her in. As he climbed inside, he intended to tell the driver to take them to the Waldorf, but instead he went against all sane reasoning and made a snap decision. "Take us to Rockefeller Center."

chapter seven

Glorianna could hardly dare believe what she'd heard Logan say. She stared at him. He didn't look at her, just sat there, apprehensive. Speaking softly so the driver couldn't overhear, she said, "You're doing the right thing. I'll be fine. I promise."

He took a deep breath as though centering his thoughts. "You don't understand how quickly things can go horribly wrong. Imagine how your father would feel if the worst possible thing happened to his daughter."

She hadn't really thought about how her father's life would be without her. Her father would blame himself for letting her talk him into bringing her to New York. Even though he'd worked more than ever after her mother had died, she knew he did it for all the right reasons, and when he came home he was genuinely happy to see her. She felt it by how tightly he hugged her and saw it in his tired eyes. Everything he did was to help others. And that was why she wanted to see this through, to save others from becoming victims in the future. "It would be horrendous, but I'll be fine. Once Papa learned the facts he'd understand why we took the risk." She searched Logan's face. "If you're so against this, why are you taking me with you?"

"Because there isn't time to take you home, and I can't let a chance to stop a murderer go by. My father wouldn't have."

"Seems we both have honorable fathers. I saw your father's picture on Sara's dresser. He looked very noble in his uniform."

"He was. He died trying to make this world a better place. When I buried him, I vowed to continue his legacy." His gaze trailed back to her. "You mentioned that you wanted to have an adventure. Well, this is it, princess. If we play our cards right, we could both come off as heroes. Or . . ."

She knew what followed. Things could go badly. But they couldn't think about that. They needed to lighten up. "Or Austen Zeiss will meet us there."

As he realized she was joking, a broad smile came to his face.

She smiled as well. "I know you're right, and he probably won't. I just hate to think how terribly naïve I have been."

He took her hand, threaded his fingers with hers. "I'm glad you were, otherwise we never would have met. And, despite everything, I'm glad we did."

An electric tingling flashed up her arm as his fingers rubbed over her knuckles. Was this really happening? Was she truly on her way to a "stakeout" with a handsome security guard who believed in truth and justice and that he could right the wrongs of the world with her by his side? Well, maybe that was a stretch, but they were in this together. She'd landed right in the middle of the most thrilling and dangerous adventure she could ever have imagined. She was blindingly happy.

She stared into Logan's hazel eyes and saw a sureness, a confidence, and even determination. Was it because he had growing feelings for her like she did for him or because of the surprising path they were now on?

Her gaze went to his mouth. She couldn't help but lick her lips as she leaned toward him and he toward her. Just then his mobile jingled, alerting him to another text.

The magic spell was broken, so Glorianna straightened in her seat.

Logan pulled his phone from his pocket and frowned. "It's Sara. I guess . . . Max called her and she's worried." He tapped in, "We'll be fine." He got an answer immediately, but instead of replying, he glanced at Glorianna.

"What is it?" she asked.

He shook his head and put his phone on vibrate. "A matter for another time."

"Here we are," the cab driver said, pulling up to the curb.

Logan swiped his palm over his face before digging into his jacket. He handed some bills to the man, then got out, waiting for Glorianna to join him.

Slinging her bag over her shoulder as she stood, her mind stayed on that wonderful moment when the world halted with Logan holding her hand and leaning towards her as though he intended to kiss her.

"Come on." A new seriousness edged Logan's words. He glanced at his cell. "It's a quarter to five." He scanned the area: Channel Gardens, the grey buildings of the Promenade, and down to the ice rink in the center where the gold statue of Prometheus stood. Behind the statue loomed the Comcast Building—30 Rock. Glorianna had read up on the center, hoping to take a tour. Logan hustled her down the sidewalk. "Watch for anyone you might have seen last night. That drunk we saw in the ally, or the guy in the pea coat. *Anyone*."

Fear sliced through her, which surprised her. Before this it had been a great adventure, now it had morphed into something that could turn treacherous. She quickened her pace to keep up with Logan, all the while assessing those they passed. Had she seen that person before? Could he or she be the catfish? And could her father's security team pop up and ruin everything? She clung to the fading dream that Zeiss would appear.

Logan didn't take the stairs going down to the ice skating rink now filled with shade umbrellas and tables and chairs for outside eating at the restaurant. Instead he went around, descended some concrete steps and dashed past a row of flags, heading to a vantage point looking down and at the side of the golden statue. She sprinted to keep up.

All at once, he stopped and turned his back on the statue. "Did you notice anything?"

"Other than you're very fast and hard to keep up with? No." She caught her breath as she followed his lead and scanned the crowd around them.

"We need to blend in with others, like we're merely sight-seeing." He smiled at her and did recon on the crowd. "Look at people, but don't be conspicuous."

"Okay." She tried, but her mind went to the romantic moment they'd shared. "What happened back there in the cab?"

"Huh?" He glanced at her for a second.

"Just before we got here. I felt something. Did you?"

He kept his eyes on the people. "What do you mean?"

"There was a moment, when you held my hand."

Again, he glanced at her. "This is not the time to talk about that. We need to stay focused."

"Things could go . . . not as planned and we might not have another chance to say some things." Her words grabbed his attention.

For a moment, his eyes caressed her. "Yes, I felt something." And once again he shifted his focus to those walking by. "Happy?"

"Extremely." She tried to sound casual. This adventure had everything she'd ever dreamed of: intrigue, mystery, and a handsome hero. The only down side was someone could kill them.

Major drawback.

The fear she'd felt a moment ago returned.

"Are you all right?"

"Yes," she muttered.

And then he froze as his gaze shot past her shoulder. "Oh, no."

"What?" She swung around and found the janitor from the Garden, the one who had heckled Logan as he'd taken her out the back way. He seemed to be hiding as he stood near the Comcast Building.

"I can't believe the catfish is Hector." Logan appeared crestfallen.

"Maybe it's a coincidence he's here." She doubted it, but wanted to give Logan hope about his friend.

Logan guided her behind a bush where Hector couldn't see them. "I don't believe in coincidences. Why else would he be here at this time, hiding, and acting all weird?"

She turned as inconspicuously as possible to see Hector again.

"Don't look at him. He hasn't seen us yet." He pulled out his mobile and tapped a number. When no one answered, he said, "Where the heck is Max?"

"Why don't I go closer to the statue and see if he comes out to talk to me? I mean, if he's the catfish, he's here to meet me."

"No way. I'm not putting you in danger."

"But you have no solid proof. He's just here. Let's see what he has to say. If I get in trouble, I'll . . ." She couldn't think for a moment. "I'll tug on my ear."

"No. That's what he told you Zeiss would do. He'll know he's been setup. I know we need more solid proof, but that's why I called Max. All we can do is keep an eye on him."

"Okay, but in the meantime, why don't I see if he comes over to me. I'll ask him why he's here, get him talking and see if I can get him to say that he posed as Zeiss in order to meet me. If he tries something I'll scream, or tell him that you're here and wave for you to come over." Glorianna stepped to the side to keep an eye on Hector.

Another person, a tall, thin man, blocked her clear line of sight for a moment. When she spied Hector again he was looking straight at her.

"He's seen me. I have to go." With that, Glorianna screwed courage to her backbone and left before Logan could stop her.

67

# chapter eight

All at once someone grabbed Glorianna from behind. "Miss Templeton. I think it's time you came with me."

She'd recognized that voice anywhere. Dread rippled over her as she spun around to find grim-faced Carlton, her father's security intelligence officer. He'd found her. And at the worst time. His stern don't-give-me-trouble expression told her he was very upset and greatly disappointed.

Another plain-clothes security officer was with him.

"Look, you don't understand." Logan tried to plead with them.

The other security officer took hold of Logan's arm, trying to guide him away. "The Prime Minister wants to talk with you."

"There's been a big mistake." Glorianna had to make him understand before Hector got away.

No sooner had she said it than Hector bolted.

Logan jerked free from the guy holding him and took off after Hector. The security officer sprinted after Logan, but he wasn't nearly as fast.

"Carlton, listen to me." If Glorianna could explain what had happened, he'd understand. She pointed to Logan as he sprinted in front of the Comcast Building. "He's chasing a man who stalked me on Facebook."

Carlton's busy brows that made him look like a major general slammed together in disbelief.

"Please, trust me. You might be letting a killer get away."

Logan's feet pounded the sidewalk as he dodged people, trying to catch up with Hector and stay ahead of the security guy chasing him. He fought for breath, forcing air in and out of his lungs. Hector was twenty feet ahead. He had to be the catfish, why else would he have taken off like that when he saw the security guys talking with Logan and Glory? Running always condemned a person. He thought of himself, running this very moment.

Logan stole a look behind. The plain-clothes security man wearing a suit was nearly to him. Oh, crud! This looked bad. Real bad. He had to catch Hector before Suit caught him. A shot of adrenaline coursed through Logan's legs driving him on. His lungs burned with each breath.

Hector cut across 50th, bringing a car to a screeching halt. He skirted around the Lincoln, never looking back. Logan slid over the vehicle's hood, rapidly gaining on his friend. He didn't dare check behind him. Precious seconds would be lost, and Suit was on his tail.

Hector came to 5th Avenue and stopped, looking up and down the street. Logan lurched forward and grabbed him from behind, pulling him around.

"Logan!" He seemed surprised. "What the—"

"Don't even try denying it."

"Denying what?" Hector again looked up the street, as if Logan was a minor distraction.

Suit caught up to them, seizing hold of Logan as he gasped for breath.

"Who's this?" Hector glared at Suit, confused.

"Admit you're the Facebook stalker." Logan had to get him to say it.

"Are you crazy?" Hector started away.

Logan yanked free from Suit and lunged forward, barely grasping Hector's jacket, jolting him back. Hector swung around and hit him with a right cross in the jaw.

Suit must have realized something more was going on. He grabbed Hector, wrenching his arm behind him. But Hector managed to pivot around and break free. Logan kicked Hector's legs out from under him, and he fell to the ground.

The British security man Glory had called Carlton arrived, gun drawn, with her a few steps behind him. "Miss Templeton explained who you were chasing."

Sirens wailed in the background.

"What the freak, man?" Hector glared at Logan. "What's got into you?"

"As if you didn't know." Logan rubbed his aching jaw.

Hector spat out, "I don't."

"You're the one who catfished Glory into meeting you at the Garden during Zeiss's concert." There. Logan had said it. Let him counter with some lame excuse.

"Have you totally lost your mind?" Hector blanched as if confused.

"I caught you before you could hurt her."

"Is Glory the *chica* with you backstage?"

"Yes. And she told me how you 'friended' her, posing as Austen Zeiss, and asked her to meet you after the concert. Is that how you grabbed the other two women whose bodies turned up in Central Park?"

"You been smoking some bad weed, man." Though he spoke to Logan, he glanced at Carlton and Suit, like it finally sank in that he was in deep trouble. Sirens grew closer.

"Then why were you at the Center, why did you run, and why did you haul off and hit me?"

"Okay. I've been training that new crew the Garden hired. They were with me last night, when you and your girlfriend left the back way. The tall, lanky one, Nils Merrell, he's been acting pretty strange. I thought I saw him pick-pocket some concert goers last night, but I wasn't sure. And on top of that, he has messed up ideas about women. Said he was going to make some bi—" he looked at the people around him, "*witch* pay for standing him up. The way he said it gave me the creeps, so I followed him."

"I only saw you." Logan was not letting him off.

"Doesn't mean he wasn't there. He took off like a bolt of lightning, like something was wrong, so I chased after him. And yeah, I hit you. You practically tackled me."

"Where's this Nils Merrell fellow now?" Carlton injected himself into the conversation.

Hector looked up and down the busy one-way street. The sidewalks were crowded with pedestrians. "Because of you, I've lost him."

"Your employer must have his home address. When your police officers arrive, you can have them check into him. In the meantime, Mr. O'Brian." Carlton focused on Logan.

Glorianna must have told Carlton his last name. "Yes."

"You and Miss Templeton have some questions to answer as well."

Logan looked to the place where she had been standing. But she wasn't there. In all the fracas with Hector, Glorianna had vanished.

Glorianna had tried to scream when he took her, but his large hand had clamped over her mouth, making it impossible. "One peep and you're dead," he said next to her ear, like he was whispering sweet nothings to her. He shoved the barrel of his gun hidden in his coat pocket into her ribs. Shocked, she didn't know what to do.

So many people walked by, and yet no one seemed to notice. His long-limbed arms held her close, like they were lovers. He smelled of cleaning fluid and body odor. He towered a good foot taller than she was, and his arms were like steel bars. She only managed to see his profile. A long thin pointy nose, shallow cheeks, greasy hair. He forced her across the street and up 5th Avenue. With every step, they grew farther and farther away from help.

How could this be happening?

A numbness blanketed her. She couldn't feel her feet. Her mind spun. Think! She had to somehow get away. If she didn't and he got her alone there was no telling what he'd do to her before he killed her like those other two women Logan had told her about.

Saint Patrick's Cathedral's two gothic spires came into view.

The church! She'd be safe there. Somehow, she had to get away and hide inside. A couple of business men deep in conversation walked toward them. This was her chance.

As the men were about to pass, Glorianna shoved her attacker into them.

Startled, he let go of her for a second, but it was long enough for her to bolt away, race up the steps of the church, and push open the huge bronze door that, surprisingly, moved with ease, then slipped inside.

An usher met her with a smile.

Catching her breath, she spat out, "There's a crazy man—" Before she could finish, the two men she'd shoved her attacker into hauled him into the church, following her.

"Lady, did this guy pinch something from you?" one of the good Samaritans asked.

All at once her attacker pulled out a gun, raised it in the air and fired.

"Everybody out!" he yelled.

As Logan tried to explain to Carlton what had happened, he glanced down 5th Avenue and saw people fleeing St. Patrick's. "Glory!" He suspected whatever was going on in the cathedral had something to do with her.

As Carlton, Suit, Hector and Logan dashed across the street, they were soon joined by Max and his partner. Sara's fiancée was in excellent shape and barely out of breath. "What's going on kid? I came as soon as I could."

"A girl's been kidnapped," Logan told him as they approached the church. They became surrounded by people running away. Old women crying. Shock-faced men glancing around as if afraid of being attacked.

"Officer." A woman with a black scarf tight around her head ran up to Max. "He's got a girl in there. You've got to help her." She sobbed. A couple of harried ushers and a Catholic priest came up to him as well.

"Stay here." Max told Logan as he turned to them, getting their statements.

Logan looked at Carlton, who had his cell phone stuck to his ear, probably calling Glory's father and getting more help. Solemn-faced Hector stood next to Suit. They were all in shock and trying to get their bearings.

Logan knew every second mattered if they were going to reach Glory in time. His growing attraction for her had made him let down his

74

guard. And he had even let himself be swayed when she said she'd put in a good word for him at the academy.

Now, look where his selfishness had landed them. Glory could die. And it was all Logan's fault. He had to do something now.

As soon as her attacker fired the shots, he grabbed Glorianna and pressed the gun's barrel to her head, making everyone leave the building. Blinding fear swallowed her. She hardly dared blink.

Once everyone was gone, he eased the gun away from her head as he dragged her over to each of the two front doors and locked them. Done, he shoved her away. Keeping the gun on her, he tried to peer out the stained-glass windows. "Can't see what they're doing."

"I could look out the door, if you'd like." Maybe she could get away.

"Not hardly. You're the one who got me in this fix." His eyes were drawn to the cathedral's pillars and high vaulted ceiling, then down the center aisle where at the end stood the sanctuary, holding the main alter.

"Why couldn't you just come with me, quiet like?" His index finger rested on the trigger.

Was he going to shoot her right here, right now? Too scared to answer, Glorianna said nothing.

"You were more than eager to go where I wanted you to when you thought I was Austen Zeiss." A craziness glinted in his eyes as his right eyebrow quirked up. "I watched you sneak backstage. Planned to grab you but that guard caught you first. Thought I'd lost my opportunity. So, I messaged you again. Imagine my surprise when you answered and wanted to meet me at Rockefeller Center. I should have listened to my gut. Too public. Too risky. But when the girl's cute and she's primed with the excitement of meeting a rock star . . ." He looked at Glorianna with a heat in his eyes that made her skin crawl.

Gobsmacked that he'd watched her all that time and could have grabbed her if it hadn't been for Logan, her stomach roiled. Bile rose in her throat. She couldn't lose her cool now. Had to keep it together. Oh, how she wished she'd done what Logan had wanted and gone to her father this afternoon.

A phone in the back of the rectory rang and rang. The police must be trying to reach her attacker, but he ignored it.

The man tilted his greasy head from one side to the other as he studied her. "You're not like the others. Oh, you've the black hair and as naïve as they come, but I sense something more."

Maybe Glorianna needed to level with him. Let him know this was worse than he thought. "You're right. I'm not like the others." Taking a big gamble, she said, "I'm the daughter of Prime Minister Patrick Templeton of Great Britain."

To prove it, she pulled off her wig. Her blonde hair fell passed her shoulders.

His mouth dropped open. He stood still as though dumbfounded. Then, a wildness flashed through his eyes, and he threw his head back, cackling. All too quickly, the psycho's mood flipped, and he became angry. "You're a bigger liar than I thought. All women lie!" He glanced at the confessional booths on the north side of the building. "You need to confess your sins."

He shoved her toward them.

She tripped and fell to the floor, biting her tongue and banging her knees hard on the marble. A hymnal lay under a pew, not far from her. When everyone rushed out, someone must have dropped it.

"Get up!"

Though rattled, Glorianna knew once he had her in the booth, she wasn't coming out. He'd become her judge and would carry out a death sentence. She had to stall and see if there was some way she could get her hands on the hymnal. She might find a way to defend herself with it. Blinking away tears, she uttered, "I'm hurt."

He stood over her, staring with dead eyes. "Get up!"

"Please." She had to get him to talk. "Please have mercy on me, umm, I don't know your name."

"Nils," he said warily.

"Nils, I didn't lie. I wanted to meet you so badly, that I had to sneak away." She moved off her smarting knees, sitting on the floor, all the while watching him.

"Who you fooling? You thought you were meeting Zeiss."

"Still, I deceived Papa so I could meet you." The word papa made him glower even more. Maybe she was onto something. "Did you ever sneak away from your father?"

"Men are the victims in this world. Never forget that. Women are the deceivers and liars."

Out of the corner of her eye, past the first pillar, she saw movement. It was Logan! He must have sneaked in through a side entrance.

She had to keep Nils talking. "Surely, not your mum."

"She was the worst." He seemed caught up in a distant memory.

As Logan rushed Nils, the phone in the rectory started ringing once again, drawing Nils attention. Seeing Logan, he swung the gun towards him.

At the same time, Glorianna reached under the pew and grabbed the hymnal.

As Nils's index finger squeezed the trigger, she threw the book, hitting him in the face.

The gun went off and miraculously missed Logan.

He tackled Nils, pinning him to the floor. Glorianna sprang to her feet and kicked the revolver away.

"Good girl," said Logan. "Now, open the doors and let the police in."

77

She sprinted to the bronze doors and unlocked them. The cathedral flooded with officers, Carlton among them. He took hold of Glorianna and gave her an awkward hug. "I thought we'd lost you."

"No. Logan kept me safe, just like he said he would." She glanced over at him. The police had taken over dealing with Nils. Others were questioning Logan. His eyes met hers and he winked like it had been no big deal what he'd done. She wanted to go to him, tell him how grateful she was, but now was not the time.

Carlton seemed to notice their nonverbal exchange. "Do not worry. I'm sure your father will want to meet this young man. I promise you will have your chance to tell him thank you and say good bye."

Another officer stepped in front of her, asking her questions. She took comfort in what Carlton had said and planned to hold him to his word.

The next morning, Logan and Sara arrived at the Waldorf Astoria. Logan had hardly slept the night before, especially after receiving the call that Prime Minister Patrick Templeton wanted to meet him and his sister in his suite.

Last night after answering endless questions, Logan had arrived home. He and Sara ate several containers of yogurt while he apologized for not replying to her text messages. She told him how she'd had to endure the PM's security intelligence officers grilling after they'd traced Glorianna's computer usage to Sara's apartment. She'd told them over and over again she knew where neither Glorianna nor Logan had gone, and all the while Logan didn't answer her text because he didn't want to interrupt the stakeout. All was forgiven because her little brother was alive and well and had become an international hero saving the prime minister's daughter.

And if that wasn't enough, Max stopped by later that evening and asked Logan to go to the precinct tomorrow. Seemed Nils was rambling incoherently and they needed to ask Logan more questions. If Nils kept up the crazy act there was a chance he might get a light sentence, especially if they couldn't connect him to the two women who had been murdered in Central Park.

Logan couldn't believe after all he and Glorianna had been through, that the guy wouldn't be punished to the fullest extent of the law. He'd heard Nils taunting Glory as he'd crept between the pews. The guy sounded sane to him. Plus, he'd threatened to kill her. That should bring a hefty sentence. What good was law enforcement if the courts let criminals go free?

After Max left, things seemed to settle down. The prime minister's secretary had called with the invitation. So, that was why Logan could hardly sleep, going over what had happened and what he'd say to the leader of Great Britain. Was it any wonder that, as the maid guided him and Sara into the posh suite, Logan became even more nervous?

They were met by Carlton. "Ordinarily, I check visitors for weapons, but after what happened yesterday I think you two can be trusted. Prime Minister Templeton is finishing breakfast with his daughter right now. Please have a seat. They'll be with you shortly." He disappeared down the hallway.

They walked farther into the immaculately clean living room. The mahogany side-tables trimmed with gold scattered throughout the area seemed to shine in the morning light. Logan was tempted to sit in one of the traditional blue and gold armchairs, but Sara guided him to the cream-colored couch. She must want him to stay close. On the coffee table in front of the couch rested a very British-looking tea service along with mouth-watering finger pastries.

As Sara sat, she straightened the black skirt she'd worn. He hadn't seen her in it since their father's funeral. In fact, she rarely wore dresses of any kind.

Logan heard a door close down the hallway. Soon Glorianna and her father walked in. Logan and Sara stood to greet them. He gave Glorianna's dad a quick glance. He was tall, blonde, and very British. But Logan's full attention went to Glorianna. Her beautiful blonde hair cascaded over her shoulders. Her face had just a hint of makeup, that enhanced her chocolate-brown eyes. "Papa, this is Logan and Sara O'Brian."

"Nice to meet the hero who saved my daughter's life." They shook hands. He turned to Sara, shaking her hand as well. "And the woman who tended to her when she was sick. You both have my deepest gratitude."

"But I shouldn't have put her at risk in the first place. I should have brought her home to you." Logan didn't feel like a hero.

"Mr. O'Brian, I know how stubborn and persuasive my daughter can be. She told me how you took care of her even when you didn't know she was my daughter and how you risked your own life to save her from that Facebook catfish man."

Mr. Templeton glanced at his daughter then back to Logan. "My men have looked into it. Seems the Austen Zeiss's Fan Club site had been hacked. That was probably how this Nils person found her. Now that I know she has a presence on Facebook, I'll take precautions to keep her safe.

"After everything that has happened, Papa, I'll take my own precautions as well. Safety is not to be trifled with." Glorianna sat in one of the armchairs and gave her father a respectful nod.

The prime minister turned to Sara. "My daughter told me that your father passed away many years ago, leaving you and Logan alone."

"Yes, he did, your excellency."

He smiled at her and motioned to the couch for her and Logan to sit. "Glorianna and I understand how difficult it is to lose a loved one. It's just been the two of us for many years. Though it is rather early, shall we have tea?"

Logan watched as a very mature Glorianna poured them each a cup and let them pick what they'd like to eat. Where was the teen who had disguised herself to meet Zeiss? She didn't look or act at all like Glory Smith, more like a young woman who had the poise of her father and the confidence of someone who'd faced a killer. Maybe almost dying made her see things in a different light. It certainly had for Logan.

"Mr. O'Brian. Glorianna said you want to become a police officer. If you'd like, I could put a good word in for you." Mr. Templeton looked straight at him, waiting for an answer.

"That's very gracious of you, but I'm rethinking my career path."

"You are?" Sara cut into their conversation.

"Yes. I'm thinking that becoming a lawyer, like you've always wanted, might be safer and I could keep Dad's legacy alive that way."

Sara set her cup and saucer on the coffee table and despite their present company, threw her arms around her brother. "I'm so happy."

"Let me congratulate you for deciding on such a noble profession." The prime minister placed his cup and saucer on a side table. "Let me help you with the expense. And, of course, you'll go to Oxford. I know people who can make things happen."

"Oh, Papa, that is brilliant!" Glorianna's eyes sparkled much like they had yesterday gazing at some of New York's sights, before all the craziness at Rockefeller Center.

"That's settled then. If you'll excuse me, I have a meeting at the U.N. so I really must leave. But please stay and finish your tea." Prime Minister Templeton met Carlton at the threshold of the room and together they left.

Logan didn't know what to say. The prime minister's offer was too good to pass up, but it was too much. He was about to say so, when a tall, slender woman entered the room.

Glorianna got up. "This is Rae, my governess. Rae, this is Logan O'Brian and his sister, Sara."

"I'm pleased to make your acquaintance." She had a nice smile which put Logan at ease with her. The woman turned to Glorianna. "I wanted to remind you that we need to leave in a few minutes. You have that luncheon with the royal family from Norway."

"Oh, yes. I'll be right with you." She turned to Logan and Sara.

"Don't let us keep you." Logan rose to his feet.

"Yes, please. Your father has been so thoughtful and gracious. We really should be going." Sara got up.

Glorianna looked genuinely sorry as she walked with them to the door and opened it. "I had so hoped to spend more time with you."

"Think nothing of it," Sara said as she walked out. "We understand busy schedules." As Logan was about to follow Sara to the elevator, Glorianna motioned for him to wait.

"Be with you in a sec, sis."

Sara continued without him.

Logan stepped back inside the suite. "What is it?"

Glorianna pulled him down as though to whisper something to him and then kissed him ever so tenderly on the lips. Surprised, Logan didn't know what to do at first, but then he melted into it, savoring the moment and never wanting it to end.

When she finally pulled away, she said, "That's a proper thank you for saving my life. Do you think you'll take Papa's offer and attend Oxford?"

Gazing into her eyes, he said, "That's the only college there is, isn't it?"

She smiled and kissed him again.

 about the
author

KATHI ORAM PETERSON worked on her craft of writing while raising her family, finishing her bachelor's degree at the University of Utah, and working. She has had nine children's-concept and biography books published through a curriculum publisher and has sold two children's activity books. Her passion has always been novel-length fiction. Her ninth full-length novel *Breach of Trust* was released in February and her tenth novel will be published in 2018. Reach out to her on Facebook at Kathi Oram Peterson or visit www.kathiorampeterson.com.

About *Breach of Trust*

After being rescued from Afghanistan by Navy SEAL Axe Talbot, Cooper Lane thought her troubles were behind, however, upon returning home she is plunged into a dangerous nightmare that only Axe can help her unravel.

NIKKI TRIONFO

CrossTrain
my heart
and hope
to die

Teenacity
BOOKS

chapter one

With a bounding step, I jump into a headstand stall and balance upside down. I bend my arms. Muscles trembling, I press my cheek and a shoulder into the hardwood flooring while keeping my feet high in the air. The stench of my own sweat nearly overpowers the smell of varnish inside Dance On's east studio. I hold, *hold*. A still body is a perfect one. Excellent. Without flaw.

Exactly on the 16th down-beat of Nicki Minaj's breathy R&B ballad, I let my legs fall and stand.

Whistles and claps come from Mom's advanced hip-hop class, middle-school-division.

I point at the girls standing in two lines, awaiting my instructions. "That's what you're going to do." I've been their instructor since I turned sixteen a few months ago.

"Um, excuse me and yeah right, Lina," Cora says with a grin. She's my sister. Her nearly black hair is in a heavy bun above her head. She wears too much eyeliner for a fourteen-year-old if you ask me, not that she ever does.

"See these trophies?" I answer. "That's why we're doing a headstand stall."

Walking to the floor-to-ceiling display case in the corner, I double-tap the control panel on the back. Overhead lights switch on, illuminating championship trophies, some of them three feet tall. Sunlight and the glare of cars waiting in the traffic of Queens, New York shows through the window next to it. No comparison on which shines brighter.

"You're going to do something the competition can't do," I say. "To prove you're good. To prove you're the best. There might be more to life than being the best, but there's nothing more to dance."

I take a deep breath, absorbing the shiny gold and silver. But mostly the gold.

Finally turning back to the girls, I notice them wiping sweat from their brow. I mimic them, secretly wishing we could turn on the air conditioning. Mom owes seventy-four dollars and ten cents to the electric company. The first payment she's been unable to make since before I was born, she told me yesterday. It was that or be late with our apartment's rent.

I turn off the lights to the championship case. No wasted electricity.

We used to leave those lights on all the time.

I shake off nostalgia, overtaken by the drive to dance. To be excellent.

"We're doing a headstand stall. Ready!" In front of the room, I announce the actions to the class as I do them. "Knee down! Lean! Do a headstand! Drop your cheek and one shoulder to the floor. Hold!" My voice is muffled as I demonstrate. I hear bodies dropping. My mouth is pressed into smooth wood. I drool.

I keep yelling. "Hold!" Lots of drool. "*Hold* . . . release!"

I stand, wiping my mouth. Ugh.

Girls are all over the floor.

If wishes were dimes, I could pay for a truck of ballet pointe shoes. I stand, picturing the glory of placing another regional trophy into the case. Cora's division came in second last year. Her friend KJ got a first place in the singles division. I want a first place for the entire team so bad. That would solve Dance On's membership trouble. Everyone would want to take dance lessons from us. We need to prove we're still a championship kind of studio, not a late-bill kind.

"Look at you!" I call, pacing. "Bunch of slugs. Get up!"

During our third try, Cora holds the headstand stall for five seconds before tumbling. KJ—my blond power-house of a cousin—is still upside down, counting the beat. I don't know where she gets the blond from. All of us cousins are second-generation Romanian. The class counts with her.

Rather than count, Cora wipes her brow. "I held it for almost as long as KJ."

". . . nine . . . ten . . . ," the class is saying on KJ's behalf. Meanwhile, Cora sets her jaw and tries another headstand stall.

At fourteen, KJ falls and everyone cheers.

Cora is upside down, redder than a tomato. ". . . four, five," she says. Most of the class ignores her, practicing on their own.

When my sister gets to sixteen, her voice gets urgent. "Look, look." She tests her stability, playing with it, stretching it. She does a free-standing pushup from the ground to come out of the headstand directly onto her feet, nailing the landing. Holy freak. Whooping and cheers erupt.

KJ's wide-necked tee-shirt slips over one shoulder, exposing her black leotard. "Dude, Cora!" She tightens her ponytail—the dancer equivalent to rolling up her sleeves—and gets into another headstand.

Cora and KJ aren't just cousins. They're best friends. And ever since KJ beat out Cora for first in regionals, they've been in stiff competition.

A glance at the clock tells me I've gone three minutes over time. I wish we had ten minutes more. If we had ten more, I'd wish for twenty more.

"Homework is twenty pushups a day." I shoo the girls toward their cubbies and dance bags. "You hear me? Twenty. Push-ups. A Day. I'll know, too."

I glance out the window. Two stories below me, a police officer tickets a van double parked under branches kissing each other from either side of Queen's narrow roads. The leaves have a touch of fall color. The van has speakers and a satellite dish on top. A brightly-colored ad-wrap features a picture of a blond woman and says, "Karenina Crowton, INS Cable *Inspirational Reality Showbiz*." That'd be the life. No money trouble. No one thinking anyone is better than you.

With a flick of my finger, the driving beat of hip-hop silences, leaving soft Tchaikovsky floating in from Mom's ballet class in the west studio. The sound of voices approaches from the lobby. *Male* voices.

All of us dancers turn to the door, our confusion reflected hundreds of times in the mirrors.

"*Sainted One*," Cora whispers in Romanian, brow high. She switches to English. "Marky's gonna pick up on Lina again!" She loses all body structure—and brain power—and falls into KJ, each of them giggling.

"Hush." I smooth my leotard, and take quick strides to the lobby.

My body is prepped for amazing news like maybe I've won the lottery or maybe my hangnails have decided *all at the same time* to stop attacking my fingers. I'm acting like the girls who get la-la. The girls who make me want to vomit. Anyway, I was pissed last time I talked to Marky and maybe I still am pissed. It's hard to tell when the thought of him gets me walking on air. I change my expression to bored and force my steps to slow.

Inside the lobby, Marky is not alone. He's got his younger brother with him.

Great.

Tito pokes a pair of sunglasses on the counter, like he's never seen such a thing. Sweat glistens at his abs, running in rivulets down the center of his brown chest. Marky has offered the world the courtesy of wearing a tank top—a tight teal one that hugs the curve of his pecks. He has thick brown hair styled back, forming a gelled wavy pattern like shadowed ripples in a fast-moving stream. The left leg of his shorts is caught on his thigh, revealing a green mesh under the black fabric. He's probably half a foot taller than me. He has rich sideburns, a straight nose, and the dark-brown skin of a Dominican.

My bangs stick to my forehead, partially blocking my view of the boys. I wipe my brow and address Marky. "What up?"

His lashes flutter as he nods at a roll of paper towels in the crook of his biceps. "Trade you this for a few rolls of toilet paper? I'll restock you next week." He pronounces the final *r* in paper, all proper. He sounds like a tourist, trying to look smart.

No smile on his delicious lips.

Girls from the studio slip past us and out the exit. Not even the boldest of the fourteen-year-olds dares to address him. Mom's class of young elementary-aged kids won't end for half an hour, so they're staying put, too.

Marky isn't smiling. He's talking formal. No way he's here to pick up on me. No way. What I thought I saw of his interest in me before, I didn't see. Or he lost interest. I feel like I just bit into a triple cheeseburger with pickles and got cardboard instead. All saliva and desire and nothing of substance to go with it. Just hunger.

Swallowing to keep from breathing funny, I head to the supply closet. "Of course I'll lend you toilet paper. I'm your neighbor, duh. The gym as busy as ever?"

Marky doesn't answer for a moment. I stiffen at the pause, uncomfortable with how aware I am of him. Maybe he's shrugging. "We can't maintain customers. Everyday Fitness took two more members yesterday."

Nodding, I grab three rolls of toilet paper to prove I'm not stingy—not very stingy. Everyday Fitness is a nation-wide chain of gyms that moved in two blocks away. It offers kid classes—tumbling, jump-rope, and jazz-dance. Two of the same classes we offer. Mom didn't graduate high school in Romania. We will own this dance studio and be super poor, or own this dance studio and be not so poor. There's no other option.

"We've tried doing stuff to get more members," he says. "The only thing that worked was a fundraiser. One of our members had thyroid cancer. He's in remission."

I pause from gathering supplies and send him a look. "You asked people for money and they joined your gym?"

He smiles. "We hosted a community workout. You didn't see our posters? Fifteen dollar admission fee. That went to the fundraiser, but some people enjoyed the exercise. They signed up to be regulars."

"Oh." I stop fantasizing about a fundraiser. I figure zero fabulous dancers are likely to notice a poster taped above food vendors and bus stops.

"Dad's talking right now to some cable show about advertising," Marky says.

"Let me guess. *Inspirational Reality Showbiz?*"

He whistles.

I shrug. "I saw their van."

He nods but doesn't answer. I become anxious about the silence.

"Here you go." I motion to the toilet paper I'm holding. We're alone in the lobby except for Tito, rocking out to something on his earbuds.

Marky and I approach each other to switch supplies, me hugging the toilet paper rolls in one arm. Marky deposits his paper towel roll into the crook of my other arm. He brushes my skin with the back of his fingers. I hitch my shoulder to indicate the toilet paper is available. Leaning into me, he slides a warm arm under mine, relieving me of all three rolls in one shot. A whiff of sweat hits my nostrils. I forgive him. No big. What's a little sweat? I catch it again. *I'm* sweating. Mortified, I hug my arms to my sides.

"The closet's right there." I turn. I don't want him to see my face is red. "You should've taken the toilet paper straight from the shelf. I'm an idiot."

Tito calls to us, snickering. "Marky likes to get close to the ladies. It's a family trait." He is now sitting on the counter, ear buds around his neck. Mom hates it when people sit on the counter.

Marky rolls his eyes.

I look between them. Did Marky tell his brother we grabbed a soda together last week?

Rubbing the back of my neck, I step away from Marky completely. I've got to say something. I've always got to say something when I'm anxious. I've got to act like nothing's up.

I notice the beads of sweat on Tito's naked abs. "How was your workout?

Marky shakes his head and answers for him. "Haven't started."

"'Less you count twenty push-ups as a start." Tito hops off the counter and heads for the exit.

Marky takes an audible breath, trailing Tito. "That's not a workout."

"Nothing's a workout but a full CrossTraining routine," Tito agrees.

The anger-fire smoldering in me for the past week kicks into flames.

I tsk as Marky walks to the exit. "Good thing you guys cleared that up. Someone might think *ballet* was a workout."

Marky stops. Turning back, he levels his dark gaze at me. "Tito's an idiot. Dancers get a good workout."

I put my hands on my hips. "Just not as good as yours."

Tito comes up to us, dropping his gaze to my navel and back up. Gross. He's two years younger than me. "Work out with us and see. That's what Marky wants to say, in his dreams where he ain't no wimp."

As Tito gets nearer, the stench of sweat and spoiled milk makes me step back and put my wrist over my nose. I fake a cough. I drop my arm, embarrassed by my behavior. But seriously. Cologne. A bath. Breath mints. There are solutions to his problem.

"Tito, you reek," Marky says. "We installed a shower for you." His Adam's apple bobs.

"Try one workout," Tito challenges me.

"Why would I want to grunt for an hour pushing around heavy objects to lame metal music?" I ask Tito innocently.

"Ho, ho, ho!" Tito says. "She's harshing on you, bro. Throwing shade! Girl, what's your damage?"

Marky licks his lips. They stay wet, full and perfectly proportioned—like some kind of gummy candy that has yet to be invented, but needs to be. "I like my music."

"I like your Dominican music," I answer.

Word on the street is that Marky's been in the states ten years, all of them with his father who owns the gym next door to ours. I didn't connect his last name Alvarez to the Jose Alvarez next door until freshman year. Marky was in my art class in seventh grade at Daniel Carter Junior, back when I was dating my first boyfriend. I've had three boyfriends since. My last guy figured it was time for me to lose my virginity. I figured it was time for him to kiss my butt. Just not literally.

For the past year I've rocked the single life. Maybe I'm waiting for Romeo. Maybe I'm sick of guys. I'm not really sure.

"Your salsa and bachata music," I say. "Why don't you play that during workouts? Something with rhythm? Latin music is *it.*"

Tito steps in front of me. "Rhythm don't help you throw heavy objects."

I wince. "Get out of my face."

Marky nudges his brother to get him away from me. Tito backs off, laughing.

94

"I never said dance wasn't a workout." Marky folds his arms, which highlight how well-proportioned they are. Good thing he's tall or he might be big and bulky instead of broad-shouldered and cut. "I said dance wasn't a *sport*."

I sniff, getting a trace of Windex from used rags in the closet's laundry pile. "We get scores. We beat people when our scores are higher. Have you ever thought ballet might be *harder* than flipping tires? You've got to hit the poses at exactly the right time. There's no time to scratch yourself and burp."

I flush, but *1)* the shoe fits and I know it because I've done my share of spying, and *2)* he started it.

A few weeks ago, our tradition of sharing casual smiles and five-minute conversations slipped into something new. Marky started coming to Dance On for no reason. Five minutes stretched to fifteen. His smiles at me flashed on with anticipation and off with tension. The girls in my dance classes spied on us, inventing reasons to lounge in the lobby after class ended.

On Monday when I mentioned after ballet that I was thirsty, he said I should try a cherry pomegranate soda from the newspaper stand on the corner.

We went together.

Together together.

Or that's what I thought. It was like I'd won a lotto jackpot. We were sipping our drinks under street lights, and I mentioned how sore I was. He asked if I was sore because I *didn't just dance but worked out or did a sport or something.* Um, excuse me? He got pissed that I was pissed. We walked back home all silent. We haven't spoken since.

I lift my chin. "Dance is a sport and the dancers at Dance On are elite."

He shakes his head, eyes flashing. "*Bendito, chica.* I agree. You're elite." With a final lean into me, he turns for the door.

"Dancers're stuck up," Tito whines.

He and his brother exit. Only five feet of sidewalk separates the front doors of our building from the buzzing traffic of 45th Avenue. I spot a plastic bottle on our lobby counter and roll my eyes.

I pull open the glass door.

"You forgot your protein puke," I call over wind flapping the stiff fabric eves of the building.

"Muscle Milk," Marky answer me, glaring over his shoulder.

I shrug. "That's what I said."

He changes direction over a sidewalk vent. It's twilight. The days are getting short. The long shadow of the single-pole corner street light darkens his face as he walks back.

He grabs the milk and I let the door shut, hearing Tito start talking about me. Something about how I'm too skinny and how can Marky think something? Maybe he wants to know how Marky can think I'm good enough to catch his eye. I think I want that. I think I want that very much.

But maybe that's not what Tito said.

I tell myself I don't care. I don't care that I don't know everything about how to get on with guys. Marky can take his monster truck tires and shove them up his nostrils for all I care. For years he's never paid attention to me at school, and that's okay because I'm a year younger than him and kind of shy. But I'm a great dancer.

I can't respect anyone who can't respect dance.

Three hours later, I stride through the lobby of CrossTrain Gym, trying not to cringe from the smell of body odor. Telling off Marky would have been cooler if Mom hadn't needed to borrow his dad's floor buffer.

Their space is bigger than ours. This late, all classes are done. The lobby has a TV, an empty couch, and a bin of toys.

I head into the main gym area, which is stuffy even with fans blowing. CrossTrain Gym has never used air conditioning that I know of. Maybe they're too tough for it. Or maybe they couldn't afford it even before the recent financial hit.

Tito and Marky talk to an older lady in heels and a tight skirt. She looks like a reporter. She has a row of gold bracelets on each wrist. No one else is here.

"Oh, we'll come in with an entire film crew," she's saying.

Tito doesn't notice me. He overturns a five gallon bucket and sits. It now reads, "3-2-1-PUKE!" upside down. Gross.

Marky glances at me. His expression shifts, and he turns away.

Ignoring them, I duck under a rack of pull-up bars. The buffer I need is leaned against weights stacked along the opposite wall. I look over my shoulder at Marky to see if he's looking at me. He is, from under the rim of a Mets cap. He has this dark handsome thing going on which his sideways-look enhances. I jerk my head forward, taking a breath I hope isn't obvious. Is it obvious?

"We highlight how inspirational your gym is," the lady is saying in the practiced, rapid speech of a newscaster. She has a slight accent. Maybe Brooklyn. "We do this by challenging the best members of a boutique gym to take on the members of a powerhouse gym. I'm talking with Everyday Fitness now. Did you know they train an entire indoor football league? You pick half the workout and they pick the other half. Can you beat *their* athletes on *your* own turf? It's a hometown fitness challenge in hometown America. We call it *David Versus the Grand Goliath*. I talked to your dad about it before he had to run off to his other job."

I frown as I lift the buffer by its handle. I recognize the lady now. She's the face plastered on the van outside. Marky and Tito get to be on TV?

Marky's voice is animated. "We'll set up a workout. Those big-box gym members won't know what hit 'em. We've had over a dozen men and women compete in regionals—that's a CrossTrain thing. It's like the NFL or the NHL. CrossTraining's a real sport."

I accidentally bump the buffer against the wall at the words "real sport." Marky notices. His lips part and then press together.

The lady claps, gushing. "We film Thursday. No delays. Think of the free advertising you'll get. Once we air, you'll have dozens of new members wanting to try out your gym. Or more. Everyone loves rooting for the little guy."

"We're not the little guy, Everyday Fitness is," Marky answers solemnly. "CrossTraining is the best workout there is."

I stop in my tracks and hold the buffer at my side. The *best?* Forget that.

I call to the lady. "If you're looking for the best, you should highlight Dance On."

The lady barely glances at me. "We're looking for exercise venues."

"Dance *is* exercise!" Setting the buffer down in a huff, I approach the lady. "Dancers are *strong*. Way strong. Our studio would be the best challenger you'll ever get."

"Yeah, right," Tito cries, standing. Marky steps to head him off.

The lady puts a hand on the hip of her pencil skirt and faces off with me. "Who are you?"

"Lina Constantin. My mom owns Dance On. We do ballet, tumbling, jazz, hip-hop—all of it at the highest level of cardio and all of it beautiful and . . . well, film-ready. If you want the indoor football pros at Everyday Fitness to . . ." I wrack my brain to remember what she said she was looking for. *Dozens* of new members? ". . . to get a challenge, test them on something they *haven't* done."

"Aw, ha, *ha*, ha, ha. Look at you rattle off your qualifications. Delightful!" She shakes my hand. "Karenina Crowton."

"Nice to meet you," I say, soothed by her new enthusiasm.

Tito ignores Marky and heads toward us, fists clenched. "Nah, nah, wait a minute. This lady's looking for gyms."

I keep my voice calm. "She's looking for unique fitness venues to challenge the big guys. What do you do here that they don't? Pull-ups? That's the only thing you call exercise." I wave at his weight rack.

Marky's jaw tightens. "She's looking for a competition people can root for. One all about fitness, not performance."

"She's looking for an *exercise* venue, such as for example a *dance* venue," I snap. "You know, a real sport?"

The anger around Marky's lips travels to his eyes.

I smile sweetly at Karenina. "My mom was a top dancer in Europe before injury ended her career. She was professional for only eight months, but she's coached twenty years. She'll come up with a new, um . . . innovative routine to teach your challengers. Our dancers will win."

Karenina rubs her hands together, rings clicking. "No, no. *You* have to come up with the routine and teach it."

"*Me?*"

"My dear, you are passionate." She runs her hand down the length of my ponytail, making it sway. "And photogenic, too. Granted, they don't do too badly." She throws a glance at Marky.

Marky put his hands on his hips, hitching up the side of his tee shirt. "Ma'am, you'd better talk to *Papi*, my father. I don't think this is fair. He's the one who contacted you and volunteered. We lend out our floor buffer to be kind . . ." His quick glare pins me in place. ". . . but we can't let our neighbor talk you out of filming with us . . . not right here inside our own space. That's not cool." His eyes become pleading and he speaks more fluidly. "You're an inspirational show, you say. We need inspiration. We need this. If we don't get more members, we've got to shut our doors."

Tenderness buzzes in my arms, like I want to reach for him, like I'm harboring some tightly hidden need to hug him ferociously. Marky has never said anything like that before. His gym needs members, and he's been open about that—more open than me. But to say it out loud how he needs inspiration?

He's as far from Mom as she is from Romania. Last week, we lost five customers. Five. She said nothing. Every feature on her face moved from heightened, enlivened positions to worn, settled places carved into her skin. She needs steady places like that to help her shoulder a new country, a dead husband, two daughters, rent payments, and the lost hope of going big in the European dance circuit.

I cut my sympathy for Marky into long skinny pieces. They wrap around my heart and twist like a tourniquet. Who's Marky to Mom?

"Use us. We're better." My voice is brittle. "Think how entertaining it'll be to watch muscle-bound dudes try to master dance. And dancers trying to out-macho weight-lifters. The visuals would be priceless."

Karenina drums her fingers together. "Think you're that good, huh?"

"I know I'm as good as CrossTrain Gym," I say.

Karenina claps. "Ah ha! That's it!"

The three of us teens stare. Karenina absorbs our attention like a sponge soaking up water.

"Don't you get it?" she asks. "Why should Everyday Fitness get all the challengers? They'll take a challenger in Episode Two." She points at Marky. "For Episode One CrossTrain Gym will be our goliath." She points at me. "Dance On is the challenger."

Marky droops with relief.

Tito rears back, yelping, "We have to learn to *dance?*"

"And teach dancers how to CrossTrain," Marky says, tilting his head with the idea.

Picturing the glory of winning, I jump up and down, but Karenina isn't finished.

"But," she says. "Only *one* of you will be highlighted in the advertisements."

Tito stops cheering. "What?"

"*Our* gym gets the advertising," Marky steps forward. "Or else that's not fair."

Karenina stares him down. "The leader. The team with the most points going into the final competition gets the advertising. Period."

Whoa. If Dance On beats CrossTrain Gym, we steal their advertising spot.

An advertising spot we need, need, need.

She turns to me, handing me a business card. "My dear, on Thursday bring five dancer-contestants to The CrossTraining Gym to compete against Marky's team. Afterward, the gym will send five contestants to dance for points at Dance On. We repeat that the following Monday. The main competition will be next Saturday—*live*. It will count for twice the number of points as the first two shows. Lina, dear, I want you to choreograph the dance, no one else. I want teen dancers. It's an angle. Teen coaches, all teens. Have your mom call me."

Her heels click on the floor as she leaves.

When she's gone, Marky glances at me from under the rim of his flat-brimmed hat.

"I can't believe you!" Tito says with a blast of sour breath. "We're supposed to get that advertising!"

I don't even blink at Tito. I stare at Marky. The taste of cherry pomegranate materializes on my tongue.

"My mom needs this. She hasn't got a second job like your dad." I think I'm asking for forgiveness. I never meant for CrossTrain Gym to lose its advertising.

Marky hitches a shoulder. "Looks like you'll try out CrossTraining after all."

Long lashes frame his brown eyes. Their shape is rounded, not narrow, giving his expression an open, confident look. A smile tugs up one side of his lips. "Could be kinda fun."

Flutters make my shoulder blades tighten.

Then I get a vision of Karenina lifting Marky's hand above her head and declaring his gym the champion. What, does he think that's the only outcome possible? He's not even worried.

Eyes glittering, Marky sticks out his hand. "May the best gym win."

All sympathy for him flies. I squeeze his knuckles as hard as I can. "Count on it."

 chapter two

"Ten dance moves," I say the next day. "We mix and match 'em for a total of thirty-five steps. Boom. Good luck memorizing *that*, Marky."

Cora and I stand in front of a whiteboard in Dance On's lobby. We grin at the list of moves we've created for an ultra-fast hip-hop performance. For scoring, the judges give a thumbs-up or a thumbs-down for each move. All we've got to do is print a list of all the moves and that's the score sheet. Each dancer gets one point per thumbs-up move.

Cora takes her marker. She crosses out the words *8-count* under the words *headstand stall* and writes 16-count. "One dancer—me—will hold the headstand stall for sixteen total counts and everyone else can come up into the splits. The CrossTrainers can't provide a contestant who does that."

I yank the marker out of her hand. "No."

"Why?"

"KJ's not good enough yet."

She yanks back the marker. "So? I can do it. KJ doesn't have to do everything."

"We'd need two of you for symmetry. Only you and it'll look awful."

"We'll get points and the CrossTrainers won't! Come on."

I fold my arms. "You don't have to be better than KJ to be good, you know."

Cora opens her mouth to protest, then winces. She looks like she got caught trying to steal my last French fry, which she always tries. Her heavy black ponytail brushes her neck as her head drops. "I know KJ's better than me."

I scoff. "Well, I don't know that."

Her delicate features register shock. "Of course she is."

"You're about even in my opinion. Cora, you're like . . . *really* good. You're going into the David and Goliath competition for a reason, you know. Besides, she's your teammate. She roots for you. Root for her."

"She roots for me because she thinks she's so good. It doesn't bother her that I'm getting good, too."

I get out my phone to take a picture of the whiteboard's brainstorming. "That's my point. Root for her because *you're* so good. You don't gotta be better; you gotta be amazing. Together. And be amazing soon, okay? The first filming is tomorrow."

Thursday dawns overcast and brisk, with fall leaves swirling under cars and buses that idle in 45th Avenue traffic. By afternoon, I stand alongside four girls—Cora, KJ, Jasmine and Meilin. An immense rack of chin-up bars separates us from five CrossTrain contestants. Marky is the trainer, with contestants Tito, three buff college-age dudes and a girl my age who's wearing stretch pants and a pink sports bra.

In the corner, a camera crew fills the gym with cords, metal boxes and billowing canvases to reflect the lighting they brought.

This is it. The start of filming. One set of contenders will burn out and the other will blaze with glory.

I intend to blaze.

When the cameras start filming, Karenina strides under the weight rack, motioning to the band of CrossTrainers. "Acknowledge the camera. Wave. Don't move too much."

Tito stretches his arm across his chest, pecs squeezed together. He winks. The teen girl spits into her hands. Marky gives a tight smile.

Next to me, Cora wiggles in excitement. She and KJ are only fourteen, but their training is impeccable. Sixteen-year-old Jasmine is our best ballet dancer. At nineteen, Meilin, our lyrical jazz teacher, technically still counts as a teen and . . . well, we're using her. We need all the experience we can get.

Mom is also with us. She's nervous. She said she doesn't want to get too hopeful about our chances of winning. I pat her on the back. Her leotard shifts against her skin, looser than it should be. She doesn't get new clothes for herself, saving that for Cora and me. I'm the only girl I know who gets begged to let go of my hand-me-downs because my mom is itching to wear them. She doesn't worry about her clothes. She worries about losing the studio, which means losing our income, which means losing our apartment and . . . I don't even know. Living with drug dealers. I don't even know. I only know Mom doesn't need one more thing to worry about. Our chances at winning rest squarely on me.

Setting my jaw, I accidently make eye contact with Marky's dad. He's watching from the doorway of the gym. He's shorter than both of his sons and darker—pretty much black. He grins, seeming to have no hard feelings against me as his gym's challenger.

I feel weird about that, like he's happy to do me a favor I didn't even ask for.

Clipboard under her arm, Karenina claps. "Girls, your turn to be filmed. Camera ready. 3, 2, and . . . acknowledge the camera."

I'm actually going to be on TV. This is epic.

I wipe the smile from my face and wave. I want to look intimidating.

After the introductory shoots, Marky takes a place in front of the contenders. He's like a Greek God. Well, a Dominican God. The hollows of his cheeks, his Adam's apple stretching his neck's smooth dark skin, the way he smooths down his hair with a flat palm—all self-conscious like. I wish I could . . . bottle him up. For preservation. You know, on behalf of posterity. In case the world's supply of hot guys dries up, then he'd be there, showing us the hotness that used to be.

"Hi, I'm Marky, the CrossTrainer who will coach you dancers. Today's competition will be fifteen minutes."

Focus, Lina. Focus.

He says more stuff. I know this because I'm staring at his lips.

". . . Lina will teach CrossTrainers to dance afterward," he continues.

I duck my head and bring it back up to wave.

Freak. Pay attention. So what if he's hot?

"Warm up is a half mile run," Marky continues. "The workout is three rounds each of twenty pushups, thirty sit-ups, and forty squats. After that, do as many handstand pushups as you can. Your time is the number of individual exercises you get through in fifteen minutes. Okay, let's line up."

I gather with the other nine contestants. A start line has been marked on the floor in scrawled spray paint, like gym members are too tough for rulers or stencils.

Marky nears, to show everyone where to go. As quickly as our eyes meet, he glances away. He's nervous, I can tell. He lines up next to me, like he feels natural there. My left arm is warmed by his body heat.

Blowing air out of my mouth, I drop my focus to regain my cool. Near my hipbones, two tiny triangular shadows separate my abs from the hem of my brief-style workout shorts, which hit way below the belly button.

I smooth the hem, conscious of my hip bones, like maybe they stick out too much or not enough. I wonder how they look from Marky's angle. What if he's right and dancers can't be good at CrossTraining? What if *I'm* not good? Pushups, sit-ups and squats sound like a cakewalk, but I can sense more than see the curve of Marky's brown skin. His shoulders are big. He has guns for biceps—the kind that guys can make jump when they want to show off. I saw Marky do that only once, for his friend at school. He stopped when he noticed me. He glanced back at me twice afterward. That was two weeks ago. A lifetime ago.

I swallow, jiggling my foot.

"Ten laps makes a half a mile." Marky's deep voice startles me, coming from so close. "Don't forget to count. And, go!"

The stampede of close quarters with other runners cramps my style. I pass Cora and KJ, following the cones to circle the gym. Marky doesn't run with us, heading to the center of the gym to coach. I pass Tito, who snickers. This is a warm-up. Am I burning my energy too quickly? I slow my steps.

Warm-up finished, Marky lines us up on a long mat. "Before we begin, I'm going to show you pushup form. Start in plank position, with the body straight."

He demonstrates as he speaks. The loose legs of his shorts dangle toward the floor. His back is stiff. His butt is tight. He wears a black shirt that's sheer in the back, revealing a hint of his pinched shoulder blades.

"Keeping the elbows in, lower your chest to the floor. Push straight up to complete." He does the exercise with no catch in his breath. I imagine him as a mini electronic toy, doing pushups effortlessly for hours.

He has the dancers and CrossTrainers take a few practice pushups.

"Elbows in!" he calls.

I move my arms so they brush my ribs as I push up from the floor. The movement is harder that way, but not impossible.

Marky walks us through proper form on the sit-ups and squats. Dancers call squats pliés, but of course we make them pretty by keeping our backs and necks straight. We're in plié position for minutes at a time. Marky must have had no idea what he was doing when he chose squats. If a group of dancers with ballet training don't beat gym members at squats, I'll eat Tito's sweatband. Which would be gross.

Marky fiddles with a remote control and a timer on the wall sets to 15:00.

He calls us to attention. "We start in ten seconds."

He hits a button. The timer switches to 00:10 and counts down. I get into plank position on the mat. At 00:04, sweat breaks out over all my body. My breathing is heavy like I've already started.

The countdown beeps the final three seconds and then buzzes.

I drop my frame to the floor and start my pushups. The mat smells sweat-stained.

Grunts of breathing from the CrossTrainers. They're going way faster than me.

I double my speed, muscles screaming. Cora's next to me, pumping out pushups at a record pace.

"Faster girls," Marky says. "Faster. Elbows in. Come on!"

His voice is incredibly encouraging.

"Lina, what number you on?" Marky calls. "Don't forget to count."

Suck, I've got no idea what my count is. There's a slap on the mat and an "oof!" It sounds like one of the CrossTrainers is rolling to a sit-up position. Karenina's wedge heels tap the flooring near Marky, like a rapid knock on the door.

"Is there a punishment for losing count?" she asks.

Next to me, Cora's mutterings become audible. "Sixteen, seventeen." Her cadence matches mine.

"Eighteen, nineteen," I say with her.

Sweat drips from my forehead to the mat. I don't know what else to do. Marky never answered Karenina.

"Twenty!" Cora and I cry in unison. It feels like cheating not to know my number.

"I didn't count. Do I gotta start over?" I shout to Marky as Cora flips to her back. I'm still in plank position, way out of breath and flushed with shame. Did it look like I was cheating?

"Of course not. Go!" Marky yells.

Karenina humphs. "Well, in the real competition, judges will verify the numbers."

Comforted at the idea of judges, I flip and start sit-ups. Three of the CrossTrainers have beaten us. Cora and I are the first two dancers done. Marky plants himself near the dancers' end of the mat. He coaches KJ, Jasmine, and Meilin on going faster. They are to keep their core and butt tight. They and the remaining CrossTrainers finish at the same time. He claps and yells, "Good job!"

He's training us for real. Helping us.

Fine, I decide. I'll train him in dance, too. We'll still beat him.

"Ten, eleven," Cora says.

"Twelve, thirteen." I say with her, reminded to count my sit-ups. Counting takes more mental effort than I bargained for.

On my twenty-first rep, Marky calls, "All the way down, Lina. Your fingers need to touch the mat when you're on your back and again when you come up to touch your toes."

Immediately I break rhythm and drop my back to the mat. My knuckles brush it and my hair. Curling up without my momentum is hard. My abs burn and cramp at the halfway mark, but I don't stop until I've completed all thirty. Feeling a rush of accomplishment, I scramble up. Cora's already up from the mat, along with three CrossTrainers.

I squat until my butt is parallel with my knees. I bounce up. Down, up. Down, up. I'm gaining on the CrossTrainers. All of the dancers are squatting now. We're faster than our competition.

Marky's eyebrows go up. Tito is huffing. His cheeks are red.

"How're you *doing* that?" he calls to Cora and me, upping his game. He matches our speed, exhilaration in his eyes.

Marky's dad claps from the doorway. "Not bad!"

Mom snaps at us dancers, yelling, "All the way down! Backs straight! Necks straight!" For a dancer to be picky about form is professional pride.

"No straight-backs," I yell, winded. "Go fast. Do it their way."

A loud clap rings through the gym, followed by Karenina's shrill voice. "Marky, don't let Lina take over as trainer."

I drop my gaze, chastised.

Marky only shrugs. "Well, she's right."

None of the dancers catch up to the leading CrossTrainers during squats. By the time I finish the second round of sit-ups, I'm dying of fatigue, but grinning. Learning something new, rising to a challenge—as long as I forget about Karenina frowning in the corner, it's fun. As I start my squats, I remember I'm doing CrossTraining, which I'm supposed to think is boring. I laugh at myself.

Marky catches my eye and laughs with me.

I let my face reflect my happiness even though I feel stupid at how much I like his smiles.

He pushes his tongue into his cheek and nods, gesturing at me with a twinkle in his eyes. He thinks my squats are legit.

Instantly red, I laugh and exchange glances with Cora.

"You know it!" she calls. "Dancers in the house!"

"Aw, talking smack? You're going down," Tito calls. I can't tell if he's excited or furious or a little of each.

At the end of all three sets, I'm in second place. The CrossTrainer ahead of me is one of the college-guys. I race on jelly-legs to the wall to start the handstand pushups. 00:59 shows on the clock, counting down the final minute.

I get into handstand position and lower my head almost to the floor. I push up. My arms tremble. Tito is on the wall now. He's got a rep in already. I straighten my arms.

"One." My voice box gives out.

I picture myself in ten minutes, how I'm supposed to be teaching the CrossTrainers dance. I can't have my muscles be so slammed I can't move. But I can't let myself lose.

I push harder. On my ninth handstand, my core collapses. I topple to the floor.

Punching the ground in anger, I hear girls counting.

"Eleven, twelve!"

Every muscle protests as I push up from the floor. Cora is against the wall, upside down and doing pushups. Jasmine, KJ and Meilin are all still squatting, yelling short, breathless encouragements to her. The college-dude and Tito have fallen and so has the sports-bra girl. Cora is on fire. Thirteen, fourteen. I crawl—scrambling to set up into another handstand.

The timer buzzes.

"Stop!" Marky shouts just as Cora yells, "Eighteen!"

"Individual first place goes to the dancers!" Karenina yells.

Cora collapses in a heap. Her face is fire-truck red.

The girls and I erupt in cheers and dogpile her. Only KJ stands apart, digging one sneakered foot into the mat. She's not used to being out-shown.

"Get over here!" I pull KJ to Cora.

They look at each other, about to say something. Maybe to admit they're trying to best each other. Instead, they explode into giggles.

Fourteen-year-olds. Gotta love them.

Marky gets us off the floor and to the whiteboard, where we list our numbers. Twenty pushups plus thirty sit-ups plus forty squats all times three sets is 270 points—plus however many handstand pushups we did. All girls get their scores increased by fifteen percent to account for their lower body weight, even the CrossTrain girl. That's CrossTrain rules.

Total average score for the dancers is 272.8.

Total average score for the CrossTrainers?

Marky pauses, green pen hovering as he consults a calculator.

280.

We groan, and they cheer. My muscles are so spent, it's hard to care about anything. I force mental concentration. In order for us to catch up to them, we need to beat them in today's dance portion by at least an eight-point average. None of us can post a word of the results on social media—not until the first show airs. We can post about the show all day long and in our sleep and during our showers. Karenina would love that. But no results, not even on Snapchat.

I try not to stress as we move with the camera crew over to Dance On. We set up in the east studio because it's the largest space we have. Even then, Karenina makes unhappy faces. She keeps talking about angles and making the operators try different positions.

At Karenina's signal, I have the CrossTrainers form a line in front of the girls. Their feet shuffle on the floor. I don't turn on music. I want them to hear me. We have thirty minutes exactly, not a second over. Karenina said it's not fair to let one competitor take more time than the other.

"A dougie is a step right, step left, step right, right." I demonstrate as I go, lifting my knees to highlight the movement. "Okay, do it with me."

The CrossTrainers mimic the movement. Their nervous laughs and sidelong glances show their insecurity. Meanwhile, every dancer is on step. We repeat the movement and by the fourth time through, the newbies have all picked up the rhythm.

I continue. "Now, to earn a point for the dougie, you've got to add one aspect of personality to it. You can punch left, right, left, left as you go. Or you can roll your arms. Or you can pop out both of your knees on each beat."

The CrossTrainers look like junior high kids afraid of their own skin—like they wish they could disappear. Behind them, the dancers look like, well, a dance team. In front, I pop my knees in double time for show and get a "Siiiicccck, girl," from one of the college guys. He laughs and tries it, falling off beat. He looked good, though.

"That's great," I cry automatically. "Try that again, but slower. One knee pop per beat."

He shakes his head and won't copy me, sticking to the much easier punches. I wave a hand at him. I'd stick to easy points, too, I guess. He did look good, though.

Karenina rolls her eyes and tells us to get to the good parts.

For serious, she is nuts. These *are* the good parts. Every part of dancing is a good part.

After teaching three more moves, I motion everyone to line up against the wall. I tap on the music. Usher and Pitbull rap to a gospel chant that gets faster and faster until a synthesizer takes over. I keep the volume low for now, foot tapping.

"Okay, right in the middle of the dance, we're going to move across the stage one at a time," I call over the music. "We're going to pause to give our best move. You've seen a dance circle where you go inside and show off? Only here you got the whole stage."

Cora goes first, shaking the little booty God gave her. She pauses in the center of the floor and does the worm. A crowd favorite. The dancers are all smiles.

Marky is up first for the CrossTrainers. Brow creased with concentration, he takes four steps and then leans back in an awkward hand-crossed-over-chest move.

"No, stop." I wave him back to the front of the line. "You need to step in time with the music. Watch."

I ready myself. With a diva-roar, Beyoncé's velvety, tart voice signals my favorite song is coming on. Feeling delicious, I get funky. I pop and rock all the way across the room. My lower back stretches with the movements, getting limber. Feeling free and strong.

Putting my hands on my hips, I turn to catch Marky's eyes and say, "Your turn."

He grins like he can't help it.

Everyone is watching him.

He hesitates. He takes a breath and—stomp, stomp—cuts loose completely.

He cocks his head and makes a bad-boy face. He shakes his hips. He leans to the right, folds his arms, and yells, "What?" as he goes. He may not shake his hips as well as me, but he keeps in time with music and gives just as much attitude as I did.

The girls clap and shriek with excitement. I belly laugh.

His teammates cheer him on. "You *know* it! Yeah! Bring it, sexy!"

Marky crosses the whole room, flushed with pride. He wipes his mouth like the smirk of pleasure will be erased, but no such luck. Hip-hop dance is way too fun to pretend to be bored by it.

The smiles on everyone's faces chase the stuffiness right out of the ballet room. I want to cut loose and do a body roll or something. A backflip even. Could anything rock more than teaching willing hot teen guys who have rhythm? I could die.

Marky comes up to me and shoves the brim of my hat over my face. "Take that."

He stays close. Everyone is watching. He puts a hand on my waist, guiding me back to the front of the line of CrossTrainers. "Get to your teaching, girl. I mean, I know I was good but . . ." His brown eyes are crinkled with pleasure at the corners.

I don't look away.

"It's gettin' hot in here," someone raps.

It's the college boy with the dreads. He gives me a friendly wave, like I'm a person he'll take note of from now on. I'm Marky's friend. Or I'm Marky's *something*.

Like that, Marky and I move apart from each other. Karenina and the top camera guy whisper next to a lighting canvas.

I smooth my ponytail, trying to calm the thrill of pleasure inside me. I send the dancers and CrossTrainers through their solo moves.

After the final solo practice, I glance at the clock and gasp. We only have eight minutes of filming left.

Thrill and pleasure, deleted.

"Line up!" I shout.

I teach half the dance and run out of time. I've got to start the competition now or it won't be filmed. But I'm not ready.

"Get on your marks," I call. This is going to be a disaster. A *disaster*. "One point for every correct move."

The competitors breathe and focus. Crew members tinker with their cameras. Mom lines up with two fellow dance teachers who will act as today's judges.

I ready the music, turning up the volume in prep.

"And . . . *go!*" I hit play. Drake's falsetto busts through a chorus of female voices, followed by a driving beat. The music vibrates the smooth wooden floor.

The dance starts well. Everyone stays in sync for the first sixteen-count. The CrossTrainers fall apart in the second count, coming in late on every move. Even the dancers hesitate in the third, unsure of what moves come next. Meilin freestyles the entire second minute. She looks amazing, but the judge can't give her any points.

When the one-and-a-half-minutes are up, the competitors don't even know they're done.

"Time!" I call, wincing. No one calls time at the end of a dance.

The performers stop and lean forward, breathing heavily. Judges tally the scores and display them on sheets they lay on the floor.

Cora and KJ each get 52 points. They're the highest. Marky gets a 38. None of the other Cross Trainers get more than 30.

Marky's dad punches numbers into a calculator. "Average Dance On score: 299. Average CrossTrain Gym score: 298.2. Good job, everyone."

"Now, *that's* competition," Karenina says, sounding more satisfied than she's been all day. She holds a microphone and faces the camera crew in the corner. "With one more day of training before the final live competition, anything can happen. It's an everyday fitness challenge in everyday America."

Finished, she simpers at the cameras for a full ten seconds.

I avoid standing behind her in view of the camera. My body isn't being filmed, but that doesn't mean my shame and triumph aren't caught on camera, the way they take up every bit of space in this studio. No one else is freaking out like me. I can't believe how terribly I coached the dance. I should never put in so many different moves. The dancers whoot and the CrossTrainers clap—a classier move than I expected.

As the CrossTrainers leave, I try to get one last look at Marky, but he doesn't notice my effort. The camera crew clears out in ten minutes. Once they're gone, dancers nudge me.

"Marky sure is motivated to learn," Meilin says. "I wonder if he wants private lessons."

"Shut up," I answer. Today's filming was a success, right? I mean, we won. I can relax.

The problem is that I encountered more issues than I'd expected, like me mishandling my time and the CrossTrainers' ability to do exercises so fast. The other problem is the fun and smiles and friendly prodding we give each other, especially Marky. We're enemies. No, that's too dramatic. We're . . . two people who sort of went on a date and sort of fought and sort of still like each other—assuming he still likes me or ever did.

Yes, that's more accurate.

But I still don't know if he feels a burning need to beat me, the way I feel the need to beat him.

I head to the lobby for a water bottle. Marky is there, drawing a pattern with his finger on the counter. His headband is gone, replaced by a Mets cap. He's alone.

Noticing me, he walks over. "Good job today."

I shrug, fantasizing that he was waiting for me—but he was, though, right? Ninety thousand muscles scream in agony when I move. Moaning, I wince and rub my shoulder.

His chuckle is husky, sexy, deadly. "Make sure to do some light cardio tomorrow. Takes the edge off."

I lift my palms, torturing yet another set of muscles. "Why are you helping me? Don't pretend you're not trying to win."

"Wait." His eyes light up like I'm flirting with him. "Are you trying to win?"

"Okay, you can shut it, sir."

He tilts his head. The base of his gelled hair is wet with sweat. His cheeks have color, showing off that he's been physically active. "Homegirl, Karenina's a straight-up drama queen. Being on TV will help with sales no matter who wins."

"Yeah, we'll see," I say, folding my arms. "We both want our name in the advertisements. You think you got nothing to worry about. Today proves you *better* worry."

He folds his arms, too. Smiling, he leans over me. His arms are a large presence. He has to come forward pretty far to make his face close. "Maybe I'm not thinking of the competition every time I'm with you."

I focus majorly on trying not to smile. "Maybe I'm not either." I've got no idea what I'm saying.

He unfolds his arms and turns his hat backward. With a glance at the hallway leading to the west studio, he lifts my chin with his finger.

I jerk back. He copies me, moving a million miles away. A rash of hot prickles spreads from under my bra to my neck and armpits. His finger on my chin was amazing. The vision of what it promised even more so. I want the moment back. Bad. We stare at each other something intense.

He presses his lips together. Coming close, he touches his fingers to my cheeks and hovers.

Lightly, I lean into him.

He kisses me.

Mom's voice floats in from the studio. She's speaking in Romanian. *"Lina, where are you?"*

We step apart. The huge grin on his face confuses me, like I wonder if he's happy at my expense. But I'm grinning, too. Well, not on the outside. The grin is more like racing down my arms and across my middle. My legs wobble with one part glee and two parts exhaustion. Best. Kiss. Ever. Makes me want to break up with my two previous boyfriends all over again.

Before leaving, Marky whispers, "See ya tomorrow."

As the door closes behind him, brisk air and the smell of Chinese food rushes inside.

Am I missing something? Is there some way for both of our teams to win? No, only one of us will get the advertising. That means bringing my A game, not losing my breath over the way Marky's skin lights my body on fire. I can still feel where his fingertips traced my jaw. Without permission my mind relives the scene, this time with no interruption. This time Marky's arms encircle me. His palm caresses my neck under my hair. He whispers that I don't need to worry about the David and Goliath competition when it comes to him.

Competition.

With a frown, I become aware of my surroundings. *Dance On* is stenciled backward on the glass front door. An encased poster of Mom as a twenty-two-year-old on stage in Paris is hung between the door and the window. The crisp smell of autumn promises that soon pennies saved on air conditioning will be spent on heating.

Winning the competition is supposed to save us.

Is that the point here? Is Marky distracting me so I won't focus on winning?

 chapter three

The weekend passes in a haze. My muscles are a chorus of sobbing cry-babies. If I don't move, I'm stiff. If I do move, I'm moaning loudly and rolling my shoulders and neck and thighs. Anything to ease away the pain.

I teach four dance classes Saturday morning, three on Sunday morning, and crash on the lobby couch in the afternoons until Mom finishes all eleven of her weekend load. We taught three extra because of the classes we have to cancel to make time for the David and Goliath show. The first competition hasn't aired yet. It won't air until a few days before the live finale.

Monday after school I head to CrossTraining Gym with Mom and my four teammates. I'm still sore, but I'm no longer focused on that. Each of my body systems is ready to physically react to Marky. My heartrate is prepped, my cheeks are already hot.

If he comes up to me all nervous, I'll smile and keep an arm's length. If he's smug and acts like we're already an item, though, I'll know he's using me. In that case, I'll ignore *him* and beat his butt at dancing *and* CrossTraining. I wipe my brow. Beating his butt is supposed to be what I'm doing no matter how he feels.

He and his teammates are with his dad, stretching out sore muscles with rollers. Industrial fans swirl the fresh scent of apple spice which comes from unlit candles. It's cute to see the gym trying a little harder in the smell department. In the corner, camera crews set up lighting equipment. Karenina's pencil skirt stands out as the only bright purple thing in the room. I let my gaze seek Marky. He doesn't look over, as if avoiding me.

I wasn't expecting to be ignored. I've got no plan. I fidget with the bottom of my shirt.

With folded arms, Karenina looks back and forth between Marky and me like she's at a tennis match.

She waves me over. "We're going to need a lot more drama if this production is going to make it on air."

"*If?*" I glance quickly at her. "Of course the competition will air. You're the producer."

"Nothing airs if it's boring. The viewing numbers came in for one of my previous shows, and they're awful." Tap, tap goes her foot. Tap, tap, tap, tap, tap, tap, tap, tap.

I glance at the weight rack and the people milling around. At Marky's shoulders bouncing as he jumps in place to warm up. At Mom smiling, smoothing her hair into her bun. All her hopes are wrapped up in the camera crew finally settling into place. Only one establishment will get advertising, but that's better than no one getting it. The David and Goliath competition *has* to air.

"The score last time was within one point," I say. "How can you have more drama than that?"

She raises her too-thin, too-high eyebrows. "Why don't you go over there and give Marky a more personal hello?"

"No way!"

I fold my arms. I mean, Marky can play to *me* but I can't do that to *him*. Wait, did Karenina already pitch this idea to him? Did he hate the idea? Maybe he doesn't want his feelings for me broadcast over all of

Queens, especially if he's only pretending anyway. Is that why he's avoiding me?

Karenina doesn't answer. Her interest is caught by Tito jumping from a stack of weights.

Marky hurries to his brother. "Don't jump from the weights. You could push the stack over and injure someone's foot."

Tito grabs a set of rings dangling overhead from the weight rack and hangs. He sways back and forth. "I didn't push over no weights."

Angry, Marky hooks a thumb onto his shorts, revealing skin that's much lighter than his arms. "Follow the rules."

Tito blows him off. His body gets momentum swinging on the rings. He jumps, landing too close to Marky for comfort. They exchange a glance that's none-too-friendly.

I could go to Marky. I could smile to tease his mind away from his anger. But not knowing if he wants me for real is like going up the stairs in the dark. Will the steps end? Will my strides fall on nothing but air once the cameras are off?

Karenina motions frantically to the camera guy. He gives her a thumbs up, keeping his face squarely behind the video camera, which he swivels to follow Tito's movement away from Marky.

Karenina's posture relaxes. "Time to start!" She actually smiles.

That woman makes me trust the world less. She wanted romance. Now she wants arguments?

Marky comes up to me. "Ready?"

His expression is careful and adorable. I mean, I'm sure he thinks he looks casual, but his breath is caught and he's watching me hopefully, ready to smile at anything I say. I can't help but notice his lips. They're full and wide and slightly chapped in the center.

I thought he had been ignoring me. Or did he simply not notice me earlier? I'm not sure. In fact, there are two sides to my brain. The side that has a crush on him and wants to die and possibly giggle—if I allowed myself to do that sort of thing. And the side that suspects him of playing me. Maybe he wasn't offended at all at Karenina's hints. Maybe he's teamed up with her and thinks I'm easy to fool. Plus, I'm reliving his kiss, how his mouth smiled but his eyes were serious. Maybe he's one of those psychopath people who charm you into doing what he wants without even realizing it. I watched a movie about that once.

Everyone is looking at us, and I'm sure the cameras are zoomed in.

I frown and step back from him.

I sense more than see Karenina scowling at me.

Marky's expression falls.

Leaving me, he positions himself in front of the contestants. "Today's section is only ten minutes. We will do muscle-ups and toes-to-bar."

Marky grabs a bar and does three pull-ups, facing away from us. The entire weight rack creaks with each effort. The gymnastics rings to his right swing in time with the rippling of his back muscles, displayed through a skintight shirt.

With a grunt that out-grunts even his previous best, he kicks as he does a pull-up. A spasm of contractions between his shoulder blades launches his shoulders over the bar. He pushes down on the bar and lifts his entire body until his waist is level with the bar.

He drops and faces us. Sweat lines his brow. He is so hot. Like, *so* hot. He looks like a Hollywood superstar playing the part of a plain-clothed superhero just in from saving the world.

"That's a muscle-up," he says, winded. "Try one."

Today is going to be freaking hard. I've only done a handful of muscle-ups ever.

I grasp the bar and try a pull-up. No trouble there. I try it again. This time, I lift my shoulders over the bar and push up . . . push up . . . flail my legs . . . *push up*. My body rises in slow motion. I lock my elbows, waist touching the bar.

I hop down and pump my fist. "Yes!" My voice shakes from the exertion I gave. No half-effort will produce a muscle-up.

Someone claps for me. It's Marky. I feel a brightening in my chest and even my toes. But I don't acknowledge him. I just can't perform for Karenina that way.

Marky shows us the exercise called toes-to-bar.

"Hang from the bar." He demonstrates, shoulders ridiculously large on either side of his head. He looks like an action-figure with those bulging arms that never change proportion, no matter how you swing them around their sockets. The only difference is that his skin isn't ill-colored and plastic, but smooth and inviting. Will I ever run my fingers along that surface?

I bite my lip and try to concentrate.

"Kick up both legs. If you're not flexible enough, you can bend your knees." He kicks his feet up to the bar. His body folds in half. His knees are comically bent, like a monkey's.

At his signal, we practice. The dancers—no offense or anything—kick *butt*. Our legs are straight, our backs rounded. The CrossTrainers all have to bend their knees. Once we get in a practice, Marky sets the clock.

A beep sounds at 3, 2, 1 and then a buzzer.

Pulsed with adrenaline, I hang from the bar and take a breath. A muscle-up. I can do it.

I kick my feet and do a pullup. I get my chin level with the bar, but I'm not high enough to get above the bar. I drop. I try again. I'm not high enough still. I hang, resting.

KJ gets in the dancer's first muscle-up. She quickly does a toes-to-bar and resets for a second muscle-up.

We need to win. Our dance studio needs that advertising.

With a grunt, I do a pull-up and get my shoulders above the bar. I'm crooked. My entire weight on my right wrist. It buckles and I fall.

I try over and over again.

After one failed attempt, I sag to the ground. I'm a complete failure. Above me, CrossTrainers move with measured effort. Long, deep breaths as they hang from the bar. Herculean kicks to get enough momentum to do a muscle-up. A jump to the floor. Rest. Back on the bar for a toes-to-bar. The dancers are less fluid, but KJ is killing it. She used to be in gymnastics. Meilin and Jasmine are pretty good also. It's Cora and me who are struggling. Marky's been working with Cora practically the whole time. Every time she squares off with the bar her face screws up like she's going to cry.

The next thing I know, Marky is at my side. His expression tells me he knows how upset I am. "Let me see you," he says.

Ashamed, I ignore my screaming muscles and drag myself to the bar, hanging with way too much sway.

I glance at the clock. Thirty seconds left.

Marky steadies my rocking with a hand at my hip. "You're going to bring your legs back before you kick forward. Now, tighten your core. Tight. Lina, tight!" He barks at me the way Mom does. "Now, bring your legs back! Kick! Push, push, push!"

I do a pull-up. I get my shoulders above the bar. My wrist trembles but holds. I've managed to balance myself, finally. I just need to press up my entire weight.

"Go, Lina, you can do it!" Marky's voice is joined by others rooting for me, Mom among them. She sounds desperate.

Mom's hopes and my weight drag me lower. I clench my teeth and press down on the bar. My body rises in slow motion and then more fluidly. I'm up. Marky cheers for me.

I drop, gasping for air. Only seven seconds left.

Fueled by pure determination, I grasp the bar and do a toes-to-bar just as the buzzer sounds.

"Look at you. That's the way to do," Marky yells for me. He pumps his arm.

Too exhausted to scowl, I drop to the floor, no strength for standing. My lungs burn. I want Marky to go away. He's happy I lost, that's all.

Coming over to me, he tries to get in my face. I roll onto my back to avoid him. I'm too weak to crawl. He leaves, taking with him the heat and tense energy his presence gives me.

Eventually my breath calms. My core obeys commands like, *sit up*. I test out walking, catching myself on stiff legs after each small step.

The scores are already up. CrossTrainers 29, dancers 10. They killed us. KJ is the only dancer with a good showing, at 32 individual points. I earn the lowest individual score at 2. We have to make up almost twice the points we had to cover yesterday.

The camera crews take down equipment in preparation for heading toward the dance studio.

An arm wraps around me. It's Marky's. "Great job—"

"Stop it!" I shrug him off me, muscles in agony at the effort. I sound like a savage.

Marky stands apart from me. His flash of anger crosses the space between us and punches me right in the face. "Fine, guess I shouldn't have helped you."

In the corner, Karenina shouts at her crew. "Why didn't you get that on film?" She points her fake nails at Marky stalking away from me. She's way more pissed than he is. Or maybe she just lets her emotions show more. The cameraman shrinks away from her.

The thought of Marky being as pissed as Karenina almost makes me sympathize with him—like, oh no, I'm sorry if I'm not ready to go all cuddly after pulling the lowest score for my team. He's got what he wants. He's got the advertising in the palm of his hands.

If there's any advertising at all, that is. Karenina isn't getting what she wants out of the show. So much for romance.

My mood darkens.

Over in the dance studio, I don't smile. I don't get funky. I teach one new move—the headstand stall. The CrossTrainers pick it up with ease. I focus the rest of my time on teaching the moves in order.

Karenina is bored stiff. Every time I glance at her, I tell myself she can take her ball and go home for all I care. I'm here to win, not entertain. But I'm not here to win, really. I'm here to get on TV and get new members. And that means advertising.

I frown harder and bark orders. Intrigued, Karenina snaps at her cameraman, eying me.

Fine, she wants drama?

I eye KJ holding a headstand stall. She loses her balance after six seconds and has to come down early. Cora is still upside down, balanced on one shoulder, ready to go all eight seconds.

Rushing to KJ, I clap so hard my hands smart. "Great job. Great! You're killing it today, KJ. You did the most muscle-ups, and now you're holding the headstand stall longer than ever. Here, stand where the camera can see you better."

I pull KJ forward. Cora drops down from her stall. She moves so KJ can have her place in front. Jealousy repaints Cora's face, dulling her skin and making her eye bright and malicious. Mastering her emotion, she lowers her gaze in submission. She even applauds for KJ.

"Cora, will you *please* pay attention?" I snap as I head to the front. "It's not like you're rolling in points like KJ."

Cora's gaze flies to me but I'm purposefully looking away, eying her only in the mirrors. KJ beams and high-fives Meilin. Cora folds her arms and hunches her back.

I feel bad, but tell myself to get a grip. It's not like I'm killing her.

"I want to end with a bang," I announce to everyone. "We're going to do a formation. A big human pyramid of dancers and CrossTrainers, basically. The bottom row goes on their hands and knees. The middle people kneel on the backs of one member of the bottom row, like this."

I get down on one knee, with one foot on the floor. "The last tier of people will go on top of the bent leg of the people under them—but they'll be *upside down.*"

Standing, I grin at the impressed faces. Think dance is easy now?

"Points will be awarded for form and balance," I continue. "I've talked with Karenina. The only way for her cameras to get a view of the whole formation is for us to be over here, in front of the trophy case."

With pride, I lead the group to the floor-to-ceiling glass enclosure. Inside, gold spires are attached to marble bases. 1st Places. Grand Prizes. Living proof of Dance On's excellence. Usually we wouldn't line up so close to an obstacle in case someone falls. But just this once for the cameras is fine. I want to make sure the viewers at home are impressed with Dance On.

"Marky, Tito and Lance, bottom row," I instruct. "You leap into a crouch and hold this position."

I leap and fall to my hands and knees. They mimic me.

Marky lands so his knee is almost touching my foot. He scoots away from me. Does he think that trying to avoid me is going to make me cry or something? We're in the middle of a competition here.

I stand. "Ignacio, you and Meilin are going to do a fan kick. KJ, show Ignacio."

KJ lies down so that her back is on top of Lance's back, with her feet on the ground supporting her lower body. She kicks each leg in a round-house motion. She goes to one knee on top of Lance's back, with her other foot planted on Tito's.

"KJ, that's wonderful." I clap loudly.

Expression pleading, Cora tries to make eye contact with me. I refuse to see her.

"KJ, show him again," I say. "Look to KJ, everyone."

Blond hair shaking, Karenina motions to one of her camera people. The metal supports for the lighting behind her make her look like a black widow spider plotting wickedness inside an evil web. A balding, thin cameraman moves so he can get a better angle of not just KJ, but Cora as she finally gets my attention. I send her a look so she'll know to back me up on being rude to each other. Instead of trusting me, she throws me a killer glare and spins away.

Anger primes my muscles like adrenaline. Oh, she thinks she's having a bad day?

Ignacio tries a fan kick. He can't do splits to save his life. No way he gets a point. No joy for me, though. I got nothing but fury. Cora thinks she's the only one with problems. She's got no idea how far into check I can put her.

I get everyone in place on the formation except our top tier.

"Time for KJ and Cora to do a forward hand spring onto the formation. While in the air, they'll do an extension split and land, leaning against the middle people." I smirk. KJ is well-known for her greater-than-180-degree extension. "We'll see who can do their extension the *best*."

Readying herself, KJ smiles at her reflection in the mirrors. Cora hitches her wide-necked shirt onto her shoulder like she's a bull stamping the ground. She plants a foot, ready to start. I exchange a glance with Karenina and get a slow, appreciative nod. The spider in the corner is wickedly happy.

"Cora, not *yet!*" I yell, super-rude.

My sister spins to face me, cheeks red. "I wasn't even going!"

"Girls," Mom steps forward from her position against the wall. Creases line her forehead.

"What?" I mutter to no one in particular. "The cameras have to hear me."

Karenina is animated with delight. "You're doing great, Lina. It's *so* stressful to be in charge, isn't it?"

Looking up from his position kneeling on the ground, Marky catches my attention—all concerned and how-can-I-help. Just playing his role like a stuffed monkey. Both of us, stuffed monkeys. Karenina the Spider and her two stuffed monkeys. Only a women as evil as Karenina could eat something ten times her size. I'm no one's monkey. Yet part of me stretches into my role easily.

130

I lift my chin. "It *is* stressful to be in charge. Especially when what you're teaching actually matters." I level my gaze at Marky.

His eyes narrow, pressed down by thick scowling eyebrows. Suddenly I feel awful. I don't understand why I feel so bad. I'm pretending to be a punk. That's the point.

Meilin sways as Tito shifts position under her. She hops off him. "Take a break."

"No breaks!" Karenina roars from her lair. "Ten minutes left."

Ten minutes. The boys on the bottom row will start fidgeting soon. I've been on the bottom row hundreds of times. I know how it works. Stay kneeling too long, and the hardwood floor starts to kill your knees. No matter how tough you are, you start fidgeting. It's practically a reflex. If I don't get the boys a rest soon, they won't be a solid foundation for the girls landing on top of them.

"Marky, you're center," I say, breaking out in sweat. "Call *go* when everything above you is steady. Everyone, get in place. Hurry."

The competitors regroup. Cora turns from them. She's mad, but I need her to be ready.

I move toward her so I can say her name quietly. "Cora, listen—."

She turns farther away from the formation, arms folded. "Shut up!"

"Go," Marky calls.

Behind us, KJ's footsteps drum as she runs into her forward hand-spring.

Cora's face screws into a rage at missing her timing. She pushes me aside and accelerates into her lead-in. KJ lands against Meilin. The formation wobbles. On the opposite side, Tito looks up to see why no one has landed on him yet. Meilin sways, moving more than a foot.

I race forward. "Cora, stop!"

I toss her my panic with my tone of voice, but she doesn't catch it. She doesn't want to catch anything I'm throwing. She goes forward full-bore.

The bottom row of CrossTrainers aren't well-trained. They don't know to hold position in times of trouble. They crane their necks to see what's going on just as Cora plants her palms on the female CrossTrainer's knee, flipping into an off-kilter handstand. Her body flies through the air. To her right, Meilin falls. Without Meilin, KJ careens left. She's upside down, about three feet above the ground.

With a yell, Jasmine moves to catch KJ. She ends up pushing KJ's knee into Cora. They collide with an audible thud. KJ ricochets backward. She crashes into the case of championship trophies. Glass shatters, raining from the ceiling to the floor like hail in an ice storm. Girls scream, falling in fetal positions.

Bodies land tangled. Vicious triangles of glass shoot across the floor. The case's entire front panel is broken. Crew members creep like insects closer to the destruction, holding their cameras steady. Karenina's long fingers tap each other in glee.

No. No, no, this can't be happening.

I scan for injuries, cringing like someone's about to yell at me. Please, no injuries.

"Girls, don't move." Mom holds out both hands. Her cheeks are red. She doesn't look at Karenina. She ignores what she doesn't respect. "Are you all right? Do. Not. Move." I expect her to send me a wild glance before making a decision. She doesn't.

She doesn't look at me at all.

KJ is on the ground, whimpering. No blood visible, fortunately. She rocks back and forth, holding her knee. A temporary thing? Like a bruise? No, she's got tears spilling down the fingers over her face. Pain. Real pain. Cora has stopped trying to crawl to her, frozen in place. She's saying sorry over and over.

My eyes feel dry and huge. "A broom?" I say to Mom.

Mom doesn't acknowledge me, instead directing Meilin to bring in garbage cans. Trembling with emotion, I get two brooms anyway. Guilt? Is that guilt I feel?

Marky also refuses to look at me. Everyone throws away the biggest pieces of glass. Leaning heavily on Mom, KJ stands and hops feebly on one leg, bending the other at her side. While people sweep, Marky goes to the lobby for another trash bag.

"Shocking results in today's competition," Karenina announces reporter-style for the cameras. She holds a microphone close, like it's a fly she wants to devour with her huge, red lips. "The dancer's second portion of the competition earns *zero* points. The dancers are cat-fighting and their competitors are on a roll. Will the dancers pull together? Will they overcome their 21 point deficit against the Goliath? Only one chance left, right here on Saturday's *live* airing of . . . *David Versus the Grand Goliath!*"

After smiling for a nauseatingly long time, Karenina makes a hasty exit toward the lobby. She rambles about important executives she now has to call.

I stand on flat feet and look at all the destruction. The trophy case is bare in front, with three trophies toppled.

"I'm sorry," Cora sobs to KJ. "You're just so good and I . . . I want to be as good as you,"

Still holding Mom, KJ looks up with tears running down her face. "*I* always want to be as good as *you*."

I step toward them, glass popping under my foot, emotions popping inside my vocal chords. "Guys, I . . . *I'm* the one making you feel that way. I'm sorry. I really am."

Like a flock of bluebirds in silent communication with each other, Mom, Cora and KJ turn their faces farther away from me.

"Guys," I say.

No response.

All that sorrow, that guilt, that fear of rejection—all of it melts together and boils, hot, hot, hot. I stamp my foot. I actually do. I said I was sorry. What do they want? I didn't have any choice. *I* was the one making sure Dance On didn't fail, and now *they're* pissed? Cora and KJ have been in a death match for a year to prove who's best. That's their problem. They're trained. Hello, you have to *think* before you launch into a formation. And everyone blames me? Forget that. Forget it. Forget *them*.

With a flip of my ponytail, I turn on my heels.

The lobby is like another dimension the way it's so silent. Silent like a silent scream. Not calm. Not peaceful.

Karenina speaks quietly into her phone near the couch. Marky is a shadow against the wall, arms folded. His glare at me is steady.

I recoil from his attention. Its rush of warmth is how I imagine a drug hit to be. A punch of pleasure and pain. Why didn't I dig my fingers into his hair and make out with him when I had the chance? Taste the cherry pomegranate soda on his lips? The thought of touching him now was all wrong, like rain falling up, right back to the clouds.

Cell phone at her ear, Karenina is breathless with excitement. "In SoHo? I can film it, sure. What time Saturday?"

"Saturday?" I exchange a look with Marky that goes beyond the gulf between us. She can't film someone in SoHo.

"You're filming *us* Saturday," I tell her.

Karenina waves for me to be quiet.

"Schedule it," she tells the person on the other end of the phone line. "We'll have time. I'll film only the dance portion of the competition Saturday. We'll spin the advertisements and drop CrossTrain Gym completely from airtime. It'll work; you'll see."

"What?" I cry.

With a small noise of air rushing between his teeth, Marky steps away from the wall, headed for us.

Still on the phone, Karenina levels her gaze at me. Her fake eyelashes are black and heavy, making slits of her eyes. "I've got a girl here who understands pushing people down so she'll rise to the top."

A barbell drops onto my throat, crushing my self-respect for good. Me. She means me.

I force croaking words out of my mouth. "You can't delete CrossTrain Gym's part of the show."

She hits end and tucks her phone into her purse. The picture of innocence, she puts a hand to her chest. "*Mi amor*, this is great news for you. After today, if I film the CrossTrainers, they'll win. They'll get the advertising. This way, you're the star. *Your* studio has the drama—the fire—that viewers want. Do you think they want to see nice people say nice things and get a nice workout? How is that dramatic?"

My head shakes and shakes and shakes. "INS is supposed to be inspirational."

She looks me dead in the eye. "INS is supposed get businesses to pay two hundred thousand dollars a minute for advertising. I will see you Saturday."

Her heels click as she leaves for the parking lot.

Me—I shake and shake and shake my head.

Marky races to me. He opens his mouth like he's about to tell me off.

I beat him to the punch. "Don't you *dare* make me the bad guy for figuring out how to really win. *You* wanted to win, too. Going for the romance angle?"

He stares like a Jack in the Box just popped out of the front of my leotard. "*Romance* angle?"

"Flirting with me . . ." My voice trails off. He wasn't playing anyone.

I'm the only one playing anyone.

He clamps his mouth shut and spins away from me. He winds up to punch the wall. At the last moment, he flattens his hand and slaps it instead. The thud reverberates through the lobby, proving how strong he really is. Strong enough to check himself before he put a hole in a wall no one can afford to fix.

He leaves without looking at me.

chapter four

Three days later, I drag a handheld broom over each shelf of the floor-to-ceiling case, scraping glass shards along the bases of the championship trophies. I sweep the shards into a dustpan. The trophies are dull and dusty.

Unlike the trophy case, the floors of the room are cleaned to perfection. We've danced in this studio. We've watched the cable network's advertisements on our phones as they named Dance On as the only contender in Saturday's live show. No mention was made of CrossTrain Gym. We watched the airing of the first show yesterday, which we won, and the second show today, which blew up on us. The disaster of the trophy case breaking looked insanely dramatic. Cora yelling, KJ crying, me stalking off when no one would talk to me. Lots of screams and shattering. They ran the video of the formation collapsing four separate times. Already, our studio has three more clients than before. The advertising is working and so is the extended guilt trip I'm on.

Tonight, classes are over. Mom is doing payroll in her office. I've got no more excuses to avoid the final chore left by the filming disaster.

While I clean, Cora paces in the center of the studio, a cell phone clenched in both palms. "KJ was supposed to call as soon as she got done at the knee doctor's," she tells me.

"KJ will be fine," I reassure her. Maybe that's the real reason I'm cleaning. I need a distraction. I'm as anxious to hear from KJ as Cora is and twice as guilty. We've been expecting news for hours. News that will be *1)* bad, or *2)* worse. It seems like those have been my two options for everything lately.

Kneeling, I finger the name etched onto a trophy I got in regionals. LINA CONSTANTINE, HIP-HOP DIVISION VI, INDIVIDUAL FIRST PLACE. That was three years ago, before I gave up competition and taught, like my mother before me.

Teaching makes better financial sense, I remind myself.

Well, it used to.

Cora's voice is urgent. She's still pacing. "If KJ needs knee surgery, it's my fault. But we're going to forgive each other. We've decided to stop competing and be amazing together no matter what."

Swallowing my nerves, I stay focused on the trophies. Seeing no more glass shards, I use the small broom to dust a golden figurine frozen in a pirouette. The dust smells slightly damp, one step up from moldy. Like a dreary basement.

"Good plan," I tell Cora. "Neither of you has to be better than the other to be amazing."

Better.

Amazing.

Two words that both scream *Marky* to me after trying so hard to beat him.

I haven't seen him since he stormed off three days ago. Here I am, telling Cora she doesn't have to win to be amazing, and I'd never tell myself that about anything to do with Marky. I sound how a dumb social media meme reads. For the David and Goliath competition, I *did* have to be better than he is to be amazing. Our studio needs more members or we won't be amazing—we'll be bankrupt.

I stand. Dusting the trophies is stupid. They're just going to get dirty again.

Going to the lobby, I notice a dark figure. He strides through the unlit space, holding something in his arms.

"Marky?" I ask in surprise.

Marky avoids my gaze, headed toward the supply closet. He's carrying three rolls of toilet paper under his arms. "I told you we'd restock you."

Keeping his back to me, he stacks the rolls so their edges line up perfectly. He traded us a roll of paper towels for the toilet paper. He's got no need to restock us, but here he is.

I imagine him taking a girl on a date and holding the door of the movie theater open long enough that it won't swing to hit her. I picture him leaning close to guide her through the dark aisles. That could have been me. Now it won't be, and it's my own fault. I'm exhausted holding up the dead weight my body turns into when I'm depressed.

Finished stacking, he faces me.

He's tall. The smell of him is coffee and cigar smoke. His dad's the smoker. He emits tension like invisible rays through the semi-dark. Stubble shadows his face. His handsome features seem to condemn me—the way he doesn't smile. The way he looks at me in silence.

Hope fills my voice. "You're going to have your portion of the competition ready in case Karenina changes her mind, right? For Saturday?" The final competition is day after tomorrow.

His profile comes into view as he turns. "She's not going to film us. She called Dad. You won."

Cue the swelling orchestral tragedy. My only redeemable action now is get down on my knees and beg forgiveness.

"You think I won?" I answer sharply instead. Do I ever stop defending myself—*ever*? "Karenina's going to make Dance On into a joke. She's making us into this drama-queen, cat-fighting place. *Everyone's* going to see we were led by a sucker who let herself get played."

Forcing my mouth to stop talking, I scuff the floor with the toe of my black jazz shoe.

"I guess there's no way to win." Marky says.

Heart hurting from the sorrow in his voice, I look up. We make eye contact. I've never seen him so sad. He looks like a child who buried his family dog.

"Mom, Mom!" From the west studio, Cora's desperate cries are followed by the thud of footsteps toward the office. "Mom, KJ and Uncle Vasile need to talk to you!"

Marky turns to the studio in concern, but I stop him, agitated like the sky is falling, which it may as well be. "KJ's telling Cora about the surgery she needs."

"From our fall?" he asks.

I drop my head into my hands, wishing a trophy case could drop out of the sky and bury me forever.

I uncover my face. My voice is monotone. "KJ dislocated her kneecap. She saw a specialist today so he could tell her if she needs the kind of surgery that takes six weeks to heal or the kind that takes almost a year. He said if it's the major one she needs, she has to get it within a week or she'll never be able to dance ballet again."

Cora may think the surgery is her fault, but I know it's mine. I'm the reason she's in pain and needs medical care. But that's not all. Oh, no. There's money to think about. KJ's family is well-off compared to ours, but not that well-off. Even with insurance, surgeries cost a lot.

How could I have done this? How? *How?*

"Lina?" Mom bursts into the room, anxious.

Cora runs in behind her. She notices Marky and covers her face, sobbing. She pulls her hair over her eyes like it's a sheet and she's a kid refusing to get out of bed for school.

My hand goes to my chest. "A whole year to recover?" I don't breathe.

Mom holds a cell phone at her ear. "Hello? Hello?" She looks at the phone and then drops it to her side. Her back is rounded, her eyes wide and frightened.

"KJ needs the major surgery?" I press.

Dazed, Mom looks at me. "A year to recover but the insurance won't pay. They're calling the big surgery optional, even though that's what the doctor recommends."

My head shakes, like someone else is controlling it. "If she doesn't get that surgery she'll never dance again."

"Never." Mom lifts her chin, displaying a firm yet delicate jawline. "I'm going to their house. Uncle Vasile needs to sue us."

"*What?*" I cry.

"We have liability insurance."

I step to stop her. "No, you can't. If we use it, our rates will skyrocket."

Running a hand over her eyes, she buries her pain deep, deep inside. I'm supposed to step back and pretend to see nothing. That's how to be polite in Romania. My older relatives have trained me silently on this since birth.

I am not supposed to get in her face like an American teenager. "Mom, I know we can't make payroll. I ran this month's numbers myself."

Flying at me, she drills her pointer finger into my chest. A hole burns straight through my attitude. "*Adelina Maria Constantine, you are not the head of this family.*"

She stares me down. Casting a shameful glance at Marky's huge eyes, she exits the studio. Cora runs into the bathroom. The lock clicks.

I tremble all over.

"Lina," Marky says gently. "Maybe you *can* afford it. That advertising . . ."

"Yeah, unless we don't get enough sign-ups. Or unless Karenina decides not to run the rest of the advertisements. Because, let me think, she's *evil?*"

My breaths come fast. I stare at the supply closet without seeing it. Uncle Vasile has to sue us. KJ can't dance for a year, if ever. Our gym has been highlighted to all of New York City as a laughing stock. Marky is being nice to me.

I want to kick his shins. Why couldn't *I* have been nice? For once, just be nice and not take an unfair advantage?

I cover my face, stumbling away from him.

He follows. "The advertising—"

I whirl at him like a cat attacking from an alley corner. "We don't need advertising! We need money for KJ. *Now.* How are Mom and Uncle Vasile going to come up with money for a surgery in a week? It's not like we have friends like that. Hey, give us hundreds of dollars. *Thousands* of dollars." One more word and I'll cry.

Marky scowls, but lowers his eyes. "My family could donate at little."

I breathe through my nose to hide the catches in my breath. A donation. His offer is too kind and won't solve anything, anyway. Still, my heart threatens to claw its way into my brain and *make* me say something nice to him.

"Maybe you could hold a fundraiser," he continues.

"Wait, like . . ." I take an enormous gasp of air. Memories of anything except my own meanness are fuzzy and difficult to piece together. ". . . like the fundraiser you held once? At your gym?"

"Yeah, for a member who had cancer. We earned two thousand dollars for him."

All the air leaks out of me, leaving me empty. "She needs more than that."

Nodding, he gives me a weak smile. "If only we could put the fundraiser on television instead of the competition."

I stare at Marky. My jaw drops.

"Lina?" he asks.

"The competition is live," I whisper.

142

He leans in. "The competition is what?"

"The competition is live! It's *live!*" I shout. I pace. I clap my hands to my forehead and laugh.

I face a totally confused Marky. "Karenina has no choice but to air whatever we give her. The show is *live!* She's already aired the advertisements. You know how freaked out she is, about how we have to show up. Well, we *will.* We'll show up *and* we'll invite a bunch of neighborhood people to show up. We'll have the fundraiser, *live.* People watching at home—well, maybe they'll feel sorry for KJ. Maybe we'll get more donations. A super rich person could watch!"

"But you might lose some advertising."

"I want Mom's gym to stay open, but getting money for KJ is more important. Plus, we might be able to avoid being sued."

"Karenina . . ." Marky grins in slow-motion. ". . . is going to be pissed."

"Won't she be?"

We lean into each other. Close. Sharing the deliciousness of Karenina's demise.

There's something about how his jaw is covered in a day's worth of perfect stubble and how his workout shirt is a little too tight and how his eyes are ridiculously handsome and his shoulders a hulking set of muscles. It reminds me how my body lit on fire when he kissed me. It reminds me of catching him looking away from me in the school halls and how cherry pomegranate soda tastes when I'm next to him and how much I want to never end this moment or any other moment with him.

A thought from far, far away flies into my head.

Gasping, I step away from him. He clears his throat.

"Suck, I don't know how to set up a fundraiser," I say. "The show airs in like thirty-six hours."

The brightness comes back into his eyes. "That's what you're worried about?" He laughs. "Easy. We gather our team."

He gets out his phone.

Eager, I get out mine.

"Mom doesn't hit me or beat her children or whatever you're thinking," I say out of nowhere. I didn't realize until now how worried I am about what Marky thinks of the way Mom yelled at me. Mom is a great parent. I can't bear to have her look bad.

He gives me a half-smile. "I know. You never flinched."

"I didn't?" For some reason, that news eases my sorrow.

He leans over me, entering my personal space. A flush runs the length of my body.

"Call everyone you know," he says in a husky voice that hits me in all the right places. "Tell them to meet us at Dance On tomorrow an hour after school lets out."

chapter five

After school ends the next day, Marky and I take an MTA bus from Flushing High to East Flushing. We hurry across a pedestrian foot bridge to a print shop on 156th Street.

"And 'ow may I help you?" The lady at the counter has a New York accent that's thicker than Tito's and a stunning array of gold earrings. She keeps her blank gaze on the cash register.

"Yeah, hey. We're looking for a donation in the form of free copies," Marky announces quickly. We want to get to the dance studio before everyone else arrives in an hour. The final *David Versus the Grand Goliath* airs tomorrow morning.

"We need two hundred fifty pages, cut into quarters. So, one thousand advertisements, total." Marky goes on to explain KJ's predicament and how local gyms are trying to help.

"Local gyms?" The lady wipes her nose. Her disinterested gaze floats in my direction.

Guess I've got to say something.

My chest and neck flush with heat. "Um, yes. A partnership of two . . . local businesses. A dance studio and CrossTrain Gym. Two good options for exercise." Yeah, I said that sentence out loud.

Saying something cheesy means I've got to catch Marky's eye to see if he noticed. He did. Apparently he's got to wink at me. So I've got to roll my eyes. So he has to laugh at me. I'd roll my eyes again but I can't. I'm too busy stressing about the cashier who has an intense issue with her nose. She sniffs nine times.

She stops sniffing. "Half."

I frown, but Marky steps forward. His sleeve brushes my arm. It's cool and silky, probably Dri-Fit material.

"Half price? Deal!"

"I get'a put my shop name at the top," she answers with zero excitement. "You got a design yet?"

My mouth drops open. Marky tells her we'll take any design. She types, asking us for color options and details like time and address. Meanwhile, Marky nudges my shoulder. I nudge back. For ten minutes, the two of us engage in shoulder-nudge war. We don't move more than three inches because we're in a public place and we're not ten.

The lady finishes, handing us our copies. They're about the size of a postcard. Blue lettering looks sharp on the orange paper.

"Dance with Dance On!" it reads. "For just $15 on Saturday at 11 AM, get a great dance workout which includes challenges from CrossTrain Gym. This event will be televised live on the cable network *Inspirational Reality Showbiz*. All proceeds go to fourteen-year-old championship dancer KJ, who needs career-saving knee surgery."

Marky pays the lady thirty-five dollars. He gives me a shy smile.

"My donation," he says.

How I think of anything other than Marky's eyes and Marky's lips and Marky's warm breath and Marky's, well, *everything* is beyond me. But as I lean closer and closer to him, a vision of our fundraiser sweeps over me. I get a hope that borders on despair. What would it be like to hand cash to KJ and keep Dance On from being sued? What would it be like to share my beloved dance studio with random strangers? They might look at dance the way Marky did, like it's a joke. Like we're not

146

excellent. What if they sign up to dance with us permanently and we really *aren't* excellent anymore?

Marky and I tear ourselves away from each other—after all, we're standing five feet from some lady at a business counter. We leave for Dance On.

More than thirty people greet us. Among them are girls from dance classes, Mom, Marky's brother Tito, Marky's dad, two of my uncles, and a carpenter who works out at CrossTrain Gym. I don't know if I want to tackle them in a bear hug or cry on them.

Instead, I yell, "Listen up! We're going to hand out fliers to every housing building that's within one mile. We'll go in pairs and map things out so we visit different places. We only have until tomorrow morning. Walk fast!"

Organizing everyone takes almost twenty minutes. I focus on hurrying. I can barely keep my thoughts straight I'm so hurried. At one point, Marky leans over my shoulder to see my map app. Our fingers entwine around my cell phone. The outside world—gone. We're alone. My skin tingles. My stomach tightens to a taut rope that reels me into him. I don't notice Mom and his dad watching until Marky steps away from me, dark red. My face gets hot.

A bunch of people nudge each other, including relatives. Mom gives me The Look. The Look is basically a cross between, *Marky is superhot; way to go, girl* and *Marky is superhot; you're never allowed out of my sight with him—did I mention I have access to nunneries in Romania?* She did not apologize this morning for yelling last night and did not ask for an apology from me. She simply made me a huge breakfast. Argument mended.

Marky goes to stand by his dad, who simply raises his eyebrows. Marky's had girlfriends before—school gossip supplies info like that.

And yet he still blushes around me.

I busy myself repeating a bunch of instructions I already said.

Half of our helpers leave to hand out fliers when Cora dashes into Dance On at a run.

"Sorry I'm late!" Her face is flushed.

Mom and I may have made up, but Cora is another story. I tried to talk to her, but all she did was ignore me and type on her phone and occasionally sob. I think she hates me, and with good reason.

She comes up, breathless. "Remember that guy DeAndre who likes me?"

"What?" I'm surprised she's speaking to me. "The one who shot you in fifth grade with the pink nerf gun?"

"No, not Luke. *DeAndre*. Whatever. His parents own Street Outfitters and they'll raffle off a $300 dollar gift certificate to anyone who pays some online fund thing for KJ. They already set it up."

"GoFundMe?" Marky asks, eager.

Cora nods. "I think so. It's up to like a hundred and fifty dollars already."

"Dude, what are you doing, Cora?" I cry. "Trying to be better at fundraising than *anyone*?" I hold my palm up for a high five.

Hands on her hip, Cora gets in my face. "No, I'm trying to be better than *no one*." Stepping back, she folds her arms, unable to hide a sly smile. "I just can't help that I'm amazing."

"Cora!"

I throw my arms around her, which I apparently don't do very often because she loses her balance and we knock into Tito. He steadies us with a touch at Cora's waist. Like, not a creepy touch. A touch like, *let me help you and move my hand away respectfully and look at you to see if there's any possible way I can do that again—can I?* You know, *that* way. Marky and I grin at Cora's blush. Tito goes back to his friends with a huge smile.

What is this, an alien takeover? Since when is Tito respectful?

I don't know what today is, but I know it involves wandering the brisk autumn streets of Queens, New York with Marky all afternoon.

And I like it.

148

Saturday. D-Day. The day of the final live *David Versus the Grand Goliath*. The day of the fundraiser. No re-do's.

"Get out!" Karenina screeches to the crowded dance studio. She is no longer a spider like yesterday. Here, in the middle of dozens of fundraiser attendees, she is a bat flying at breakneck speed into her cave. Her black wings spread from one mirror-lined wall to the other. Their bony edges scrape the wooden floors, tapping out the sound of high heels calling out terrible fury. "What are all you people doing here? Get out!"

"No, stay." I yell to the crowd.

About a dozen confused people shake their heads—judging me, judging Dance On, judging the world, the government, whatever. Each of them paid $15 to KJ's donation fund and now we're supposed to provide them with a workout featured on television. More and more people are arriving and paying at the entrance. It's amazing and epic and awful. The show is supposed to start in twenty minutes.

I'm drenched with sweat and nerves. The moment our first customers arrived, I lined them up and started going over hip-hop moves with them. I figured teaching them would help me feel prepared. Backfire. They didn't pick up on almost anything. I've never seen any of them before, these neighbors of mine. They are all sizes—kid-sized, overweight-sized, elderly-Asian-sized, strong-black-man-athlete-holy-intimidation-sized.

In the center of the studio, Karenina leans into the face of a middle aged, balding man with Jewish sideburns. "Get *out*."

I race to her. "Don't yell at him. We invited him. We're doing a fundraiser."

I stop as she spins to face me.

"A *fundraiser*?" The bat-wings swell. The black eyes widen, and then narrow to slits.

"A fundraiser." She leans over me. "How special. I'm. Not. Filming you." In a swish of fury, Karenina folds her arms. No more shadow-wings in the room. She is tall and skinny and closed. She is done with us.

She strides toward the exit of the west studio. The camera crew switches from setting up lighting in the corner to repacking supplies. Three college-age kids are with them, wearing lanyards that say "Official Judge." Men and women scurry out of Karenina's way. A dark lady with bright red hair holds up a cell phone to record her. Karenina crosses her hands in front of her own face to block her image from being captured.

"You've *got* to film us." I hurry after her.

Marky, Mom, Cora—everyone—is here, lined up against the wall, horrified. KJ leans into her crutches, resting her weight on them. Her injured leg is bent inside a thick black brace, full of straps and velcro. Aunt Tiny and Uncle Vasile pat her back.

What did I expect to happen? Did I really think Karenina would start the show without noticing that the filming was nothing like the set-up we agreed to? But she has nothing else to film.

As she cuts through the crowd, two more people get out a cell phone. They're upset, asking why an inspirational show won't support a fundraiser. They paid their money, they want to get on TV.

It occurs to me that *I* have a cell phone, too.

I get it out as Marky comes to my side.

I call after Karenina, "You going to let these people post the real you on Facebook?"

Karenina stops. She's suddenly right in front of me. The cell phone I wield like a weapon droops as I shrink from her.

"What happened to your competition? The dance you're teaching the CrossTrainers?" Karenina gets so close I smell her licorice breath mint. Her aggressively-styled blond hair shakes. "Our open *filming space?*" She gestures with a stabbing motion at the crowded room, which has gone silent. Five cell phones are out, recording. More coming out.

I glance at Marky. He nods to encourage me.

"You said INS was inspirational. If you don't film this, we'll show the world what you're really after."

"And what's that?" she cries, a Brooklyn accent sneaking out. "A story? That's what shows are. *Stories.* With no stories, we got no viewers, with no viewers, we got no money. How'm I supposed to help, to be inspirational, with no money? Huh? You wanna ruin this cable channel so you get help and not one more person does? You think I'm selfish? Huh? You think it? Airing an infomercial would be better than airing this. I can't *believe* this!" She assaults the air in front of her face with both hands.

She does not, however, walk out. She breathes through her mouth and glances at the cell phones recording her.

The camera crew watches her. Lighting equipment weighs down their arms. Stay? Go? They hesitate. One guy even holds a camera on his shoulder, filming.

I gather my courage.

"Please film us. Please," I plead with her. "This is a better show for fitness than a competition anyway. This is inspirational. You don't want to send the message that exercise is about being the best. It's about . . . being fit."

"You're *not* providing a competition. You're *not* fulfilling your end of the bargain. Anyway, your fundraiser is awful," she adds as an afterthought. "Your dance moves are too hard."

I frown. She could tell that in only thirty seconds? "They're good. I mean, we have to show a *little* bit that we're good."

Is that what I really value? Showing off again? I thought I was helping KJ. A feeling wells up inside me. I cover my mouth.

I'm still trying to be better than someone.

Karenina stares me down, icy finality in her voice. "If you won't do the original competition, I'm calling off the filming." She waits for my answer.

I swallow.

Competition. Proof of who's better. Always the drive to be better.

Mom looks at me. KJ glances at Uncle Vasile, biting her lip. Marky angles himself to see what I'll do.

The decision is mine. The show and its advertising, or KJ's fundraiser. There's no decision to make.

"No competition," I say evenly. Mom smiles.

"Good *bye*." Heels clicking, Karenina strides to the corner to bark orders to the camera crew. They burst into activity at her words. The guy filming swings the camera off his shoulder.

"Please," Marky calls, going after her.

"Let her go." I grab Marky's hand to stop him. He's sweating. Or I am. Or maybe the whole room is. "We have a bigger problem. We need to change the fundraiser. I've made the dance moves too hard. It's the same problem I've had the whole time."

I feel pressed by strangers watching us. They've backed up to form a semicircle around us so everyone can see. More and more people are showing up by the minute. Mom stops them at the door to the studio, keeping them in the lobby for now. I don't know what to do. I don't want to refund the money. Can we simply teach our attendees to dance without the cameras? I want to cry. I'm doing everything wrong again.

Marky glances at all the faces around us. He swallows. "I thought our trouble was that I'm cocky and you're determined to beat everyone."

Chuckles fill the room.

I give him a weak smile.

"What if the real problem is that we actually *like* having our main hobby be too cool for everyone else?" I redden, knowing my words aren't private. "What if you don't actually want people to join

CrossTraining unless they're going to feel about it the way you do—that it's life-changing and worth two hours a day? What if I treat people who think dancing is *just fun* like they're . . . well, stupid? I mean, I don't want dance to be seen as just fun. I want dance to be a real sport—a real, respected physical workout. Because it *is*."

He lifts his palms. "Dude, I'm on your side already."

"You better be." There's been this little fur ball of anger choking me for two weeks, ever since he said dance wasn't a real sport. It finally dislodges, letting me breathe easy.

He shakes his head like I'm crazy. "I. *Am*." He turns toward the camera, hitching his thumb in my direction. "Can you believe her? And she taught me how to do a headstand stall."

He stops talking. His jaw drops.

My gaze follows his, and *my* jaw drops. The cameras are pointed at us. Not just the one guy's, but *all* of the cameras. Karenina is directing the crew. She gestures frantically at them, using the silent—but deadly—gestures that mean the cameras are filming. She looks ready to break grandmas like small twigs if they stand in the way of a view of Marky and me.

Is the channel running the show? Early? What's going on?

Jumping in front of the center camera, Karenina speaks into her microphone. "Things are really heating up at *David Versus the Grand Goliath*. Lina and Marky, *joining forces*? What do they have in store for their competition—*or* their exercise venues? Make sure to join us . . . after this."

Without her usual smiles, Karenina yells at the crew. "Cut! Get that segment ready to patch in before the live section—and speed up the timing of the first set of commercials." She whirls to face me, pointing a stiff finger. "*If* we film this thing, because you *better* have a plan for what goes on air. Not the original plan, fine. But a plan with *competition*."

I jump up and down, hit by a vision that—not to brag—is pure, wholesome genius.

"I've got a plan! I do! A competition that's not about being better!"

I wildly motion for Mom, Marky, Cora and others to come closer, telling them we've got to change the entire fundraising choreography.

"What are you, crazy?" Cora asks.

"No, I'm brilliant." I turn to Marky. "We need to use every room in the studio and the big space in CrossTrain Gym, too. So there's space for filming. A group of contestants in each room, along with a few dancers and CrossTrainers as coaches. One camera per room."

I turn to Karenina. "Can we do that? Split up the cameras?"

She nods even though she's pissed.

I wave at the crowd. "Marky, take half of these people to your gym."

"No!" Karenina roars.

She's caught me. She knows I want CrossTrain Gym to get air time.

She whirls to point a long red fingernail at Marky's brother Tito. "You. And your dad. The two of you go next door." She touches her fingernail to Marky's chest. "*You* stay with Lina." She leans into him with a lowered chin and lifted eyebrows. "You get me?"

He nods like a bobble head.

"Fine." Karenina sweeps toward her cameras, her thumbs typing on her cell phone. "We'll get set up. I cannot *believe* this."

By now, more than fifty people must be crammed inside the studio or lobby, with more paying at the entrance. Marky's dad instructs men, women and families to follow him to his gym. The volunteers Mom asked to take money at the door confer with him. Half go to collect entry fees next door.

Half of the camera crew leaves for next door, too. Karenina shouts after them, calling instructions for how to know which camera will broadcast at which times. They leave. Still, she snaps to get her crew's attention. At one point, she has two cell phones at her ear while she, three camera people, and two judges confer next to their tripods. They're like physicians huddled over a dying patient. Around them, the vibe becomes carnival-like. Kids race under foot. People lace their shoes and wave at cameras.

"Thirty seconds to filming," Karenina barks. Apparently she plans to stay in the east studio with Marky and me. There's some other lady from the network with her, a director to direct the live-director on air. TV shows are so weird.

I take my place with Marky at the head of our fundraiser guests. I'm shot with nerves. With great and malignant presence, Karenina lines up next to me.

A man from the crew steps out from behind a camera. Flashing five fingers, he counts into a bullhorn. "Five, four, three."

He goes silent, counting *two, one* with only his fingers. He points forward.

"And we're *back*!" Karenina says, reminding me that she already aired that small segment of today's show. The part where Marky and I joke around, but admit that we've been held back by our pride. My emotions are all over the place. I'm satisfied with what I've learned and ashamed to have been so far off track before and scared at what happens now.

"This is Karenina Crowton, live. *David Versus the Grand Goliath* has a twist today you've got to see to believe. I've got Lina from Dance On to tell us all about it."

The mic appears under my face.

"Hi. Um . . ."

I'm on live TV. *Live freaking TV.*

Karenina's bat features are in full bat-mode. Maybe she's a vampire bat. Maybe she'll attack me and suck out all my blood if I don't say something good. I wouldn't be totally shocked.

"We . . . well, last week we here at Dance On were focused on winning a dance versus CrossTraining competition." I pause and lick my lips. "We were *so* focused, we had a . . ."

Karenina leans to gobble the microphone. "A *tragic* disaster."

"Yes." I nod. The mic appears under my mouth. "Our teammate KJ injured her knee. It was my fault. I wanted to be the best, so I pushed everyone too hard. You don't have to be the best to get good exercise. Exercise is for everyone. So today . . . instead of competing, we're here with our former competitor, CrossTrain Gym."

My gaze locks with Marky's. Our connection smooths a dozen points of anxiety inside me, like a hand running the right way across fur.

I take a breath. "We're here to hold a fundraiser for KJ. She needs surgery or she'll never dance again. Today, our neighbors and friends are competing for something good." I angle myself to face the crowd. I take a huge breath and try to mimic Karenina's uber-excited reporter voice. "Guys, each room has cameras. Just follow the instructors' dance moves or CrossTraining challenges. During open time, free style your own moves. And the competition? Get on television! The judges will decide which group of competitors gets air time. You don't got to be the best—you gotta be the most fun and entertaining."

Cheering interrupts me. I hear it even in the next room, where Cora is explaining without a microphone. In the crowd of contestants, a lady pushes her sleeves up to her elbows.

A zing of excitement races through me. The people here are really going to give it their best.

"And now . . . the competition!" Karenina tells the camera with a smile.

Marky and I race to the front, calling for the contestants to spread out. I hit on the the music. The melodic voice of Sam Harris with X Ambassadors plays, and I dance a basic dougie. I get some response, but most people are hesitant. A staccato drum beat joins the solo voice, and the song from the Suicide Squad soundtrack transitions to full-out rap.

"Aw, yeah! I gonna get on TV!" A mustached man in a sheer shirt comes to the front and shakes his hips. He does the stanky leg. He moon-walks.

When he fatigues, I take over. Marky follows my lead. Smiles infect the room. We whip and nae, nae. We groove to the cha-cha slide. We strike poses and dab and practically fall over giggling.

"Don't skip those 90's," some lady in a fanny pack calls. "Where's the Roger Rabbit?"

She thrusts her chest out and in, throwing her arms back and forward. She runs into the Jewish guy. He laughs and claps for her. I shuffle through songs until I find the 1990 hit Gonna Make You Sweat. It's obnoxious, but Mom claps in time. I drag her to the front.

"Free-style time!" I call.

While the room dances, I make Mom show off. Unaffected by the driving beat, her body transforms to soft poetry—still and graceful. A simple ballet pose. Her foot barely makes noise against the wooden floor as she lifts the opposite leg and lightly spins on the pad of her ballet shoe. She spots herself in the mirror. One, two—ten times. Ten pirouettes and her delicate posture is flawless. She drops into a relaxed position with a reserved smile, slightly out of breath.

A cheer rises from the room. Marky whistles.

Fifteen minutes into the fundraiser, Marky leads us through some CrossTraining exercises. I put on lame muscle music—LL Cool J. I figure "Mama Said Knock You Out" is trashy enough. We do pushups and burpees, too winded to laugh finally.

When it's dance time again, Marky wiggles his hips to copy my moves in front of the group. The dance should be Latin-swing, not Hawaiian-hula like Marky's doing. But still. He looks devilishly good. He's strong and tall and Hispanic. He'd be a knock-out doing a basic Salsa move.

I stop suddenly. "Marky, do you know any Latin dances?"

He looks over with a quick nod, ready to react. "The Dominican one. Bachata."

"Bachata. One, two, three, tap."

Breaking into a smile, he grabs my palm and presses his hand into the small of my back.

My frame both stiffens and melts at his touch. Iggy Azalea's soulful voice belts *Fancy* out of the speakers.

"This song is a march, not bachata!" I cry, scandalized. "It's practically a cheerleading beat."

"So?"

Stepping, he goes left, right, left, tap. Right, left, right, tap. I dance with him, keeping my elbow high so it doesn't rest on his shoulder. His body is strong and his face is close. He grins at me, pulling me closer. I resist, as I'm supposed to—our connection stronger than ever.

We maintain our close-but-not-close-enough position as we step the bachata back and forward. I match my hip movement to his, absorbing the feel of him having eyes only for me. It's like we're alone, except more intimate because we're not.

"Okay, now *that* is the hip swing we're going for," I say with a grin.

He leans to whisper and uses the movement to start me into a spin under his arm. "Come to a club with me Friday."

I'm so happy, I drop his hand. I stand there and nod like the drool-and-sigh kind of girls I hate.

"Oooh," says the fanny-pack lady.

She points at the camera. The camera guy is walking slowly toward me, hand up to indicate he's live. I blush.

After that, I don't know what the cameras do. *You're Mine* comes on. Romeo Santos's tenor voice croons the English version of a Dominican song. With a happy yell, Marky grabs my hand and the room disappears, replaced by Marky and dancing and our hands together and our breath mingled. Somewhere in the background Karenina narrates for the show again. I can only imagine the spin she's putting on the moment between Marky and me. She's probably announcing he asked me to fly on a magic carpet to watch the sunset.

The song ends. Marky flashes me a grin and releases me. My body hums with a drive to dive right back into his arms. Instead I watch him dance with a middle-aged woman dressed in wide-leg zig-zag-patterned pants.

Bursting with happiness, I find a partner. The elementary-age boy has a gap in his wide smile. I teach him the basic step. All around the room, dozens of partners step together.

Everyone dancing. Everyone learning and progressing.

"I ain't danced like this in years." Fanny-pack lady says to her partner, a girl barely older than me with a nose piercing. "This amazing. They make this an exercise class? Where we sign up?"

"They have a hip-hop one for adults, plus *Zumba*," the girl answers. "The owner, she signed me up for *Dance Step* on Tuesdays."

I glance at Mom near the door. She's showing a man and his daughter our class schedule. Her smile is soft and real.

And hopeful.

We're getting more customers. We can keep Dance On open.

I spin with the boy, around and around, laughing. I don't stop, even when Tito busts into our room to tell Marky he'd better watch out. A professional wrestler just decided to bring his entire team on at CrossTrain Gym. Tito predicts he and his brother will pump up and "maybe even get blood poisoning from shredding our muscles." Yes, that's a quote.

Based on the smile Marky gives me, I know he's not thinking about blood poisoning. He's thinking his gym is going to be okay.

The next thing I know, Karenina leads me and Marky in front of the cameras once more. Almost the entire thirty minutes have passed. We don't have a full hour because Karenina has to go to SoHo with the film crew. The traitor.

She stands shoulder to shoulder with us, the mic under her mouth. "This is Karenina with INS, the inspirational network."

She faces me. "Lina, it's been a wild ride. Your selfish drive to win brought disaster, but under your leadership, Dance On went on to partner with CrossTrain Gym. Together, you brought fitness to an entire neighborhood. *And* your friends tell me you've raised $1,545 dollars today for your injured champion. You've proven that *excellent* doesn't mean *exclusive*. Everyone watching is rooting for you. And the best part is, you don't even know the rest of the story."

I open my mouth to mutter something about gratitude for this opportunity, even though I'm still mad she never aired CrossTrain Gym's name in the show's advertising.

Instead I frown, my jaw continuing to hang open.

The rest of *what* story?

Karenina's eyes shine. Her face looks like an overfilled helium balloon ready to pop. She really does a great job of looking not-evil. "Our viewers have been prompted to call in donations to GoFundMe. INS has pledged to match every donation, dollar-for-dollar. KJ's online fund is at twenty-five thousand dollars and counting!"

Expressive as ever, she opens her arms, anticipating my freak-out. What am I supposed to do besides hug her, jumping up and down and screaming? We're joined by dancers, neighbors, Marky, KJ and Uncle Vasile. Twenty-five thousand dollars? That's starting to approach the kind of cash KJ needs and the show is *still* collecting money.

Karenina gets me in front of the camera. "So, Lina, what now?"

What now? Beats me. I'm still caught up thinking of what she said about excellent not meaning exclusive. I like that, even though it confuses me. It makes me wonder if Karenina is evil or not. I guess she helped us and got viewers at the same time. I guess the only way to keep helping people is by getting ratings.

Mm. I'm still thinking evil.

I decide not to say that, however.

"I just plan to teach everyone who walks through the door."

"That's it? That's your *only* plan?" Karenina makes a dramatic show of raising her eyebrows and looking from me to Marky. "I'd say by the look of you two, *someone's* got some *other* plans."

She puts the mic under Marky's mouth. "You? You going to tell us what the real plan is?"

His cheeks go red and he glances at me with that hesitation natural to him. Taking a breath, he pushes his hesitation aside, just like he did when he started hip-hop dancing.

He leans over me. His nervous eyes are adorable. The room whoops and whistles before he even touches his lips to mine.

I almost burst when I feel the warm touch. I want to stretch my arms and wrap them around him twice. I want to lean back and let him direct the kiss like he's leading me in a dance step with those killer hips and devilish grin. But I don't.

I save all that for Friday night.

about the author

NIKKI TRIONFO lives in Utah with five kids, a CrossFit-training husband who writes computer code, and lots of hip-hop background music. Her teen murder mystery *Shatter* won grand prize in LDStorymakers' First Chapter Contest and first place in the League of Utah Writers YA Manuscript Category. Alongside Heather Clark, she hosts the free *#50FirstChapters* writing webinars on YouTube. A committed party-girl, Nikki serves as the social coordinator of LDStorymakers Conference and chair of Storymakers Tribe. If you want to read more by Nikki, she sends out free short-story romances occasionally, because romance. No explanation needed. Reach out to her on Facebook or Instagram, or visit www.nikkitrionfo.com.

About *Shatter*

When sixteen-year-old Salem signs up to put a JFK conspiracy theory on mock trial at school, she doesn't expect to prove her sister died in a real-life conspiracy.

MAUREEN L. MILLS

if we
shadows

 chapter one

The despair I saw in the boy's piercing eyes stopped me cold.

I'd been hanging out at the back of my Summer Enrichment Program school tour group, silently reading the placards by the museum displays. The insane giggling, shoving, and excited voices of the other students around me was making me feel like I was going to explode. Stupid kids had no clue.

This boy, though. He got it. Life. Pain.

He'd already been in this gallery when Mrs. Wilkinson, one of the teachers who'd come along to ride herd, shooed us in here where it was relatively quiet. Most tourists wanted to see dinosaur skeletons, not History of New York dioramas. The boy had both hands against the glass of a display of old weapons from villages razed to make way for Central Park. Palm prints smeared out around his palms. He looked like he was about my age.

I moved forward, wondering what was so fascinating in that particular exhibit.

He turned his head and met my gaze. I froze in my tracks, feeling like I'd taken a fist to the gut. Breathing got that difficult.

He was beautiful, no question about it, with intense green eyes and black hair that fell over his forehead in a sexy wave. He had the kind of looks that would usually scare me off because I'd know a boy who looked like that couldn't possibly be interested in a mousy, pudgy bookworm like me. But that wasn't why I felt like I was going to throw up.

He held my gaze, and I knew what he was feeling. I could see all the tiny permutations and variations of emotion—the depth of loneliness, the utter conviction of powerlessness. And, seeing them, I could feel them, again.

I saw the exact moment he recognized the echo of his own emotions in me. His hand dropped from the glass case and he took a step sideways, as if he couldn't decide whether to move toward me, or run away.

"What are you looking at?" I asked, trying to make some sort of connection or something. But it came out all wrong. I'd meant to ask what he was looking at *in the display*. It sounded like I was angry at him for staring at me.

Pain flickered over his face, and he turned back to the exhibit.

I wanted to sink into the floor. Fantastic. Me and my big mouth.

Mrs. W moved to the center of the gallery, dragging the tour kids along with her. She fluttered her little green flag of authority over her head to catch our attention. Her loose arm skin fluttered, too. "You've got half an hour to check out the exhibits, then we'll meet in the planetarium for the star show." She pointed across the echoing white room with its coffered ceiling over rows of display cases, indicating the doorway leading, eventually, to the big glass box of the Hayden Planetarium. "Please don't be late."

The other students split into small groups and scattered like dropped marbles, only making more noise. Most headed downstairs to the Halls of Prehistoric Life. None of them stayed here, or waited for me.

Mrs. W gave me a hard stare. "That means you, too, Lila Deveroux."

She two-named me. Maybe I shouldn't have wandered off three times in the two days we'd been in New York. "My head hurts. Can I just find a quiet place to sit until it's time for Shakespeare in the Park?" I rubbed my head to add weight to the excuse.

Mrs. W sighed, admitting defeat. "Fine. We have to meet at the entrance to the museum in . . ." She checked her Fitbit. ". . . four hours. Don't be late, and don't leave the museum, you hear?" She shook her head disapprovingly. "I can't imagine why you even came on this tour, since you so obviously are not interested in being here. You could have saved your parents the money and stayed in Utah."

"Okay, thanks, Mrs. W," I muttered, unwilling to tell her I'd only agreed to the tour because my mom had pushed it so hard. Mom said I needed to "expand my horizons" and "get out of my own head" to help me get over her divorce.

Well, the divorce, and being abandoned by my big brother. He left the day he'd turned eighteen. He hadn't stuck around long enough to open the present I'd bought him, or eat the cake I'd made for him. None of us had heard a word from him since. And then Mom and Dad split up.

All because of me.

Mrs. W hurried off to separate a couple of the guys whose roughhousing was getting out of control. I hitched my backpack higher onto my shoulder and headed for a quiet corner to read for an hour or two. A couple of older ladies in matching "I Love NY" t-shirts finished taking pictures of every single display and left, leaving the boy and me alone in the gallery. I should've found someplace else to read. The boy looked like he wanted to be alone, same as me. But I couldn't force myself to abandon him. Not after that moment of shared misery. Not after I'd added to it.

I sat on a bench in the corner where I could keep an eye on him like some stupid guard dog, and rummaged through my pack for my tablet.

Two older guys, college-age, maybe, and football players by the look of it, entered the room and stalked past me like they had places to go and people to beat up. They didn't so much as glance at the displays of historical items around them. The boy leaning against the exhibit looked up in alarm as they approached. I don't know what I thought I was protecting him from, but it had been a stupid thought anyway. Not my problem.

The boy swore and tried to run. The two larger guys grabbed him and held him still, one on each side.

"What are you doing here, Kerry?" The large blond guy spat the words right into his face.

Kerry didn't flinch. "It's a public space."

The blond guy shook him. "You're not the public, freak, and you're not welcome here."

Kerry tried to shrug, but the bully on each arm made it difficult. "If you don't let go of me, security will throw you out."

Security would have to know about this altercation first. I slid back into the shadows of the corner and slowly stood up. I didn't want to attract the bullies' attention. They might come after me.

How long would it take me to find someone to help? They'd probably be gone by then, anyway. Maybe I'd be better off getting a snack instead. These guys could work out their problems without me.

"Come on." The blond guy tipped his chin at a dusty old door I hadn't previously noticed beside the glass display case. "Let's take the short cut out of here."

The bullies pulled Kerry to the door and wrestled him through into the dim hallway on the other side.

They were taking him to a more private place to beat him up.

I ought to walk away. After all, what could I do? Let's see. Two huge angry dudes. One dorky, slightly overweight girl. I didn't like the way this story ended. Besides, maybe he deserved to get beat up.

I couldn't forget that look he'd given me, though. I might not know him, but I knew how he felt. I'd lived with that feeling for too many weeks. Months. Years, it felt like. Since Dad and Mom quit yelling only at each other and started in on my brother, Abe, too. Because I couldn't keep my big mouth shut and ratted him out.

Had I turned into such a coward I'd do nothing to stop this bullying?

Or was it good sense not to get involved in something I'd probably just make worse?

I darted forward and caught the door as it swung closed. I wasn't trying to help, really. More like failing to help by not getting a security guard.

Stupid.

The door had no sign. Nothing that said, "Private" or "Employees Only" or, worse, "Men's."

I peered through the crack. Dim, greenish light coming from nowhere and everywhere barely illuminated a wide hallway very like the gallery behind me. Glass cases covered in thick coatings of dust lined the walls. Deep shadows veiled the tile floor at their bases, concealing who knew how many rodents, spiders, and roaches. It smelled funny, like the basement of your great-grandma's creaky old house. Or maybe an attic. Like old newspapers and rotting furs and mouse droppings.

The blond kid was taunting his victim at the far end of the hall, where it split in a T-shaped intersection. I slipped inside and the door shut behind me with a distinct click. I froze, hoping the boys hadn't heard.

The blond guy shoved his face into Kerry's. "It's not yours any more. It's ours. And we're keeping it." His harsh voice sent echoes bouncing off the hard floors and paneled walls. I tiptoed around a display of stuffed nutrias frolicking on a riverbank, looking like giant, yellow-toothed rats, and edged closer.

"It's not yours, either. You've never even touched it. It's been stuck in the museum's collection for a hundred years." Kerry smiled defiantly at the two bullies holding him.

The blond guy's face went red, and his hands clenched, squeezing Kerry's arm so tightly I was surprised he didn't cry out from the pain. Why didn't he shut up? Did he want to get punched in the mouth?

"It's ours because the museum is in our territory, Kerry. Not yours." The blond guy stepped back and raised his free hand—no, his free fist.

What could I do that wouldn't make things worse? I should have alerted a security guard, but no. I was too stupid.

And I was too chicken to yell at them to stop.

"Central Park is yours now? Does Seanan know you've claimed it?" Kerry lifted his chin defiantly.

"Shut up, Kerry," the blond guy said, fist still poised in obvious threat.

"No." Kerry didn't back down one bit. He stared at the blond guy as if daring the guy to hit him.

Hating myself, I stepped back behind the nutrias, not wanting to see the boy's beautiful face get split open.

My heel landed on something wobbly, and I went down painfully on one knee. My palm landed on a wedge-shaped block of wood—a doorstop, about as long as my hand, dark with age and grooved with multiple lines from the many doors it had propped open in its lifetime. I clutched it as I regained my feet, holding my breath in hopes my stumble hadn't attracted the bullies' attention.

The slap-thump of the bully's fist smacking into Kerry's jaw echoed in the silent halls. Kerry gave a grunting moan.

I was so sick of people hurting other people. If I could have wished that blond guy dead, I would have done it in an instant.

My hand tightened on the doorstop. I didn't think. I just acted. I stepped out from behind the nutria and chucked the doorstop at the blond guy's head.

The doorstop soared through the hall, missed the bully, and beaned Kerry on the cheek, right where it was red from the bully's fist. The hunk of wood clattered to the floor.

Wincing, I crouched behind the nutrias. Should have known I'd just make things worse.

All three guys stared down at the doorstop, then down the hallway in my direction. I tried not to breathe.

The red-haired bully spoke for the first time. "Dude, that was a shade. Let's get out of here, Jason."

A shade?

The blond guy nodded. "Yeah." He shoved Kerry, knocking him back two steps. "Stay gone this time, Kerry, or you'll get worse. Much worse."

The two bullies ran for the door—the one I was hiding next to. I pressed my face to my knees in order to hide its paleness in the shadows, I told myself, but mostly on the principle that if I couldn't see them, they couldn't see me. Stupid, but I did it anyway.

Whatever. It worked. I heard the door creak open, heard it slam shut. Heard the silence grow as the echoes faded.

Kerry sighed.

I unfolded myself from the floor and moved as quietly as I could to the door. I reached for the knob.

It wasn't there.

No doorknob. No door for the doorknob to open. Just a flat expanse of white-painted paneling stretching from one side of the corridor to the other, as if no door had ever been here.

"What the . . ." I gasped out loud.

Something moved in the hall behind me. I jumped a foot and whirled as soon as my Chuck Taylors hit tile.

Kerry stood not three feet from me, holding the doorstop in his hand. "Did you throw this?"

I clutched at my chest, trying to keep my heart from bursting through my ribs, it was beating so hard. "Oh, my gosh, you scared me so bad!"

"Sorry. And thanks. I was getting tired of Jason's company." He rubbed the side of his face. A dark red shadow spread from his jawline halfway up his cheek, punctuated by a darker splotch where I'd hit him with the doorstop.

I flushed. "I'm sorry, too. I meant to hit the other guy. Does it hurt?" I shook my head in disgust. "Of course, it hurts. I mean, how badly does it hurt?"

He shrugged. After all, he was a guy. "Stings a bit. I'll live. How did you get in here?"

I glanced over my shoulder at the blank wall that had, not two minutes ago, held a door. An exit back into the museum. "I followed you and those other two guys. I mean, I wasn't trying to butt into your business or anything. I was just exploring . . ." I trailed off, jerking a shoulder up in a half shrug, kind of like he'd done, trying to play it cool. Act like I dealt with disappearing doors all the time. "Yeah. So. How do we get back into the museum?"

He studied the wall where the door used to be. "Not this way. They locked it after they left."

"Did they take the doorknob with them, too? Plus the door? Because it's not here." My voice wavered despite my attempts to stay calm.

He didn't answer. His gaze stayed fixed on me as he waited to see what I'd do. I didn't see the pain this time; not from the bruise on his face, and not the emotional pain, but I knew they were there. His mask-face looked a lot like the one I saw in my mirror every day.

I patted the panels, searching. The door wasn't there, though. It was gone. Not locked. Not hidden.

It wasn't possible. Doors didn't just disappear. How was I supposed to get out of here? How was I going to get back to my school group? I dug out my phone to text Mrs. W.

No bars.

I wanted to grab the front of Kerry's shirt and shake him until he answered the questions I was unable to put into words. My breath quickened and I started to hyperventilate. How was I going to get out of here? Where the heck was *here*, anyway, that had disappearing doors?

"Don't worry." He set a steady hand on my shoulder. "I'll see you back to the museum. It might . . ." He paused, shifting uncomfortably. "It might take a little time, though."

Confidence and serenity radiated from where his hand pressed against my arm close to my collarbone. It felt strangely intimate, and yet not embarrassing or uncomfortable. No one, certainly no guy, had ever touched me quite like this before. Definitely no stranger had. Most especially not a strange guy who looked like this one.

I forced my breathing to slow. "How long? I've got to meet my school group in a few hours for Shakespeare in the Park."

He smiled his approval, and I felt my world steady further, which was weird because I didn't care what other people thought of me.

"We should make it by then." He took his hand away, and I missed the warmth and connection.

"I'm Lila," I said. "Lila Deveroux."

"Kerry Connor."

A soft scuffling came from deep in the shadows of the right-hand corridor. Mice, maybe? This was an old building.

Kerry turned and his eyes widened. "We need to go." He strode toward the T-intersection.

I hurried after, studying the dim, dust-covered displays as I passed. I didn't see anything, but the hair on my arms stood up. "What was that? Mice? A rat?"

He stopped at the entrance to the left-hand corridor and motioned me to go first. "No," he said curtly. "A ghost."

 chapter two

I stopped. "A ghost. Seriously?" New York was full of crazies. Stands to reason I'd run into one.

"Yes. Hurry." He pushed me in front of him, trying to move me along.

I whirled to face him. "I'm not an idiot. I may read fantasy, but I'm quite clear on what's real and what's—"

I broke off. Over Kerry's shoulder, a pale, washed-out silhouette—vaguely human-shaped, though short like a child—wavered at the end of the opposite hallway.

I sucked in a breath. "Is . . . is that an employee? Or . . . an employee's kid?" Because that's what it had to be. Right? I only had shivers running up and down my spine because Kerry was making a big deal of it. And I definitely could not see the vertical lines of the wall paneling through the shadowy young figure. No. No way. It was just a trick of the light.

Kerry looked over his shoulder and relaxed. "Oh, it's only Thomas. He's cool. Hey, would you mind waiting here for a second? I have to, um, talk to him really quick."

"Talk to him? Kerry, he's transparent!" My shivers intensified until I couldn't stop my hands from shaking. My breath came unevenly. The closer Thomas came, the more I wanted to run.

"Stay here," he repeated, and left me standing in the dim puddle of the light from some unseen light source that illuminated the intersection of the three hallways. He walked into the opposite hall, heading straight for the wavering figure. "Hello, Thomas. What are you up to?" His voice was gentle and quiet, as if afraid of spooking the small . . . ghost.

Thomas's outline swirled like fog in a breeze. His eyes darted around the hall until they settled on Kerry. He drifted closer. "Where's my mom? Have you seen her?"

Kerry crouched down to look Thomas in the eye. "I don't know, Thomas. Shall we go find her?"

"My name's not Thomas." He seemed to grow more solid as he spoke. The colors in his tight, striped t-shirt went from shades of gray to muddy oranges and reds.

Kerry nodded. "What is it, then? I have to call you something."

For a ghost, Thomas didn't seem all that frightening, beyond the fact that he shouldn't exist at all. I inched closer, taking in his red bellbottom jeans. He must have been dead for decades. Another shiver raised the hair on my arms.

The ghost, who wasn't actually named Thomas, shrugged and began to drift past Kerry. Toward me. "I don't like Evan," he said. His color began to fade.

"Who's Evan? Stay with me, Thomas." Kerry stood and reached out as if to touch the mostly transparent boy, but the kid dodged at the last minute, still heading vaguely in my direction.

"He called me a fag, and punched me in the stomach." The ghost came closer. I could touch him, if I wanted to.

"Is that what killed you?" I whispered. I sort of hoped he wouldn't hear. My weight shifted involuntarily to my back foot, ready to run away.

Not-Thomas focused on me. "I'm not a fag. I'm mean! I can fight!" His eyes went hard and squinty and his jaw dropped to his narrow chest, opening a gaping black hole in his face. He went from pale and sad to pale and terrifying in less than a heartbeat. Not that he had a heartbeat.

I scrambled back, but he rushed the last few feet between us and grabbed me with his cold, foggy arms. They sank into me, through my skin and flesh, and he clung like tar when I tried to scrape him off. I choked, trying to suck in breath and expel it in a scream at the same time, and everything went black as the inside of a tomb.

Everything.

I saw only faint, eerie outlines of the displays lining the walls—dim shadows in the Stygian darkness. I felt only blackness, inside my chest. Inside my heart. All the sorrow and guilt and frustration and helplessness and despair I'd been fighting for a year coated the inside of my head, of all of me, sticky like the tar of Thomas's hold, magnified by whatever he had done to me.

And then I wasn't in the back halls of the museum any more. I was in my own bedroom back home, still in the dark. It was night, and Mom and Dad were shouting at each other. Again.

"If you weren't so weak, you'd have been a better example for the kids," Mom snapped. "Now your son is gone, and your daughter has her head in the clouds as much as you do!"

Dad ducked his head, but tried to defend us. "He's your son, too, and Lila has a good heart. How can you be upset about that?"

"He's no son of mine! How can I ever hold up my head in church again after what he did?"

"You've still got Lila . . ."

"My son goes gay and all you can say is I've still got Lila? Do you know how hard I have to work to even make her get her homework done? No, you don't, because you don't care about practical things like grades!"

"Why can't you just shut up?" I moaned, jamming my hands over my ears. My knees ached as they hit cold tile. Odd. My bedroom was carpeted. "Shut up. Shut up. Shut up."

"Thomas, get away from her. Lila. Look at me. Lila!"

179

The cold arms at my waist vanished. Someone was shouting my name. It wasn't my dad or mom. The voice sounded younger, and not so angry. Extremely determined, though. I dragged my gaze from my hands pressed to the museum's tile floor. The swirls of marble showed faintly through the tips of my fingers, as if my body was becoming transparent. I shuddered.

Kerry knelt in front of me. He glowed in the heavy darkness, the one point of light in a sea of black. "Lila. Do you see me? Come back, now. I've got you."

He took my hands and pressed them together between his own, which felt like fire, only in a nice way. Warm and alive.

Darkness faded like the dawn, both inside me and in the museum. The outdated displays reappeared.

And so did the extremely cute guy kneeling in front of me, holding my hands, his knees touching mine. "Lila, are you all right?"

I flushed. "I'm fine. I'm good. Did I faint or something?" I felt like sinking into the floor and never coming back up, ever.

"No, you didn't faint." Kerry sounded grim, and faintly apologetic.

"What the heck happened, then?" I had started to fade like Thomas, that was what had happened, but I wasn't about to say it. I tried to retrieve my hands, but Kerry held on and pulled me to my feet. To be honest, I kind of needed the help. I was still a little wobbly.

Kerry let my hands go and stepped back. "Thomas got a little out of control. I'm sorry. He's never done anything like that to me."

Thomas! I spun, searching for the nasty little ghost. "Where is he, that slimy little monster? He tried to . . . What did he try to do to me? What *was* he?"

Kerry shoved his hands in his front pockets. "He's a . . . a ghost."

"Ghosts aren't real!" I shouted in his too-perfect face. He didn't even have a zit. Nothing but the beginning of a nasty bruise on his cheek. "This whole afternoon isn't real."

Kerry hunched his shoulders defensively. "Technically, he's a shade. The shadow of person who has lost himself."

"What does that even mean? And what did he do to me?" I thrust my fingers into the out-of-control hair at my temples, trying to throw off the miasma of truly awful emotions that had swamped me when Thomas tackled me.

"He showed you himself—what's inside him."

I shook my head, remembering too well from my own life the fight I'd overheard. "It wasn't Thomas I saw."

Kerry's eyes went sad, an echo of the loneliness and anguish I'd glimpsed in them before. He crossed his arms in front of his chest as if hugging himself. "No. They'll show you things in your past that resonate with their own misery."

I touched his hand. Didn't take it. Just—I had to touch him somewhere, to show him he wasn't alone. "He's caught you like that before."

"No, not Thomas." He drew a breath and let it out in a whoosh. "But others like him. Yes."

I frowned. "Why'd you go talk to him, then? What's the point?"

"I thought I could save him."

I stepped back. "You can't save him. You can't save anyone. Besides, he's dead."

"Not dead. Lost."

I took another step back. "You're crazy, you know that? Lost children aren't transparent." I laughed, a little too wildly. "Heck, maybe I'm crazy, too. Transparent children? Crazy."

"Calm down. You aren't crazy. At least, not more than most people."

"That's very comforting. Not. Can we go back to the museum now?"

"Fine!" Kerry stalked past me down the hall. I had to hurry to keep up. The damaged look had left Kerry's eyes, replaced by irritation.

"What happens if we run into another one of those shade things?" I asked, panting a little because Kerry was practically running down the hallway, which seemed to stretch too far to be inside any building smaller than a football stadium. Maybe not even that. "You're not going to talk to it again, are you?"

"I might."

I thought about that. "Have you ever 'saved' one of them?"

He slowed down enough for me to catch up. "Once."

I waited, getting my breath back at the slower pace, but he didn't continue. The floor grew rough, like the tiles had been laid unevenly. I stumbled, and Kerry grabbed my arm to keep me from falling. His hand lingered, and I wished, just for a second, that he'd leave it there. He was warm, and his hand felt good on my skin. Safe, and exciting at the same time.

He looked down at me from the six inches of height he had on me, his eyes sad. Haunted, I'd say, considering the ghost—shade—we'd just encountered. "Look, we *will* run into other shades. They live here. They don't usually bother people who walk through their territory." His fingers moved gently on my arm, right below the edge of my sleeve. I don't think he realized he was doing it.

I sure realized it. My breath caught, and I had to swallow before I could speak. "D-do regular people like us walk through here often?"

His shoulder twitched up in a self-deprecating little shrug. "It's a short cut."

And people liked short cuts.

A patch of gauzy gray wavered far down the hall, half-hidden by display cases and distance. I stiffened. Was Thomas coming back?

Kerry dropped his hand from my arm, darn it, and looked up, too. "We should go."

We passed a last display case, and the panels on the walls changed seamlessly to weather-grayed boards. The marble tiles petered out into bumpy cobbles. Piles of old trunks, burlap sacks, ragged clothes, faded photos, and cracked dishes leaned against the walls and teetered in unsteady towers directly in our path. We wove around them to continue down the hallway.

Gray, indistinct shapes lingered in the darkest alcoves. I shivered, and tried not to look at them as we passed. I couldn't help noticing, though, that they seemed to drift nearer, as if they'd been sucked into the little breeze we made as we moved. My heartrate picked up. "Um, Kerry? Is this supposed to happen?"

Kerry glanced over his shoulder and cursed. He grabbed my hand and began to run. The gray patches farther down the hall sped up, too, and joined the others until it looked like a low bank of fog creeping forward to engulf us.

"Kerry, where are we going?" My voice quavered. We had to get out of here soon. No way was I going through another Thomas experience.

He dragged me around another stack of old newspapers and a baby buggy full of unmatched socks. "Here." He tipped his chin toward the edge of a wooden access hatch mostly hidden behind an old wardrobe.

He got behind the massive piece of furniture and tried to shove it out of the way of the hatch. It barely budged.

"Let me help." I scooted past him into the narrow wedge of space between the wardrobe and the wall, braced my back against the solid boards behind me, and pushed. The wardrobe thumped over a couple of cobbles, sending a cascade of bent silverware clattering to the ground from a box stacked on top of it. I dodged a handful of forks, but the spoons got me, smacking into my arms.

"Is that far enough?" I asked, snatching up a fork. If the shades got too close, I'd see just how ghost-like they were. Let them dodge a fork to the face.

"We're good!" Kerry yanked open the hatch, grabbed my backpack, and tossed it through the small, square opening about two feet from the floor.

The first of the shades peeked around the edge of the wardrobe, her long, translucent hair trailing over puffy sleeves to her ankles. Her eyes fixed on me, and the hall dimmed . . .

"Go!" Kerry snapped. He shoved my head through the hatch and pushed.

# chapter three

The rough edge of the hatch door clawed at my t-shirt and snagged on the back pocket of my jeans as I squeezed through the constricted opening. I landed in a small room almost as dark as the hall I'd left. Thank goodness my butt compressed so well. If all of my size-whatever curves were as muscle-bound as the school cheerleaders' I wouldn't have made it.

Kerry dove after me, grabbed the little knob on the inside of the hatch door, and slammed it shut, blocking the pale fingers of mist that crept around the rim of the opening.

"Can they get out?" I backed across the small room, bumping into an enormous bundle of cables hanging down in the center. The metal mesh floor clanked as I moved. What kind of room was this?

"No. The lost can't leave the Halls." Kerry watched the hatch for a few seconds in spite of his words.

"The lost? I thought you said they were shades."

"They are. Shadows of people. Shades. The lost. Thomas lost himself to self-doubt." He shrugged. "Don't know about the others. There are lots of ways to lose yourself."

"You said people used this as a short cut. No one would voluntarily go through there with all those shades waiting to eat them!"

"They usually ignore living people." He turned away from the silent and motionless hatch and crouched, hooking his finger into a recessed ring on the floor and pulling open another square hatch leading down. White light flooded out. "Come on."

He dropped through, leaving me alone in the room that I suddenly realized wasn't a room at all. The ceiling was way, way, *way* too high. I was in an elevator shaft, standing on top of a really large elevator car.

I crouched and stuck my head through the hole created by the hatch Kerry had left open. Every inch of the white-painted elevator below was lined with lighted, narrow shelves displaying a bunch of weirdly ordinary stuff. A collection of toothbrushes. Some painted plastic backpacks. Different types of potato chip bags. A man's scuffed shoe in a glass box. It was like the world's smallest and least valuable museum.

Kerry stood in the open doorway of the elevator talking to someone I couldn't see. Maybe the person was around the corner, in the graffiti-decorated alley I spied through the wide doors. The smell of pee and car exhaust filtered up through the mesh floor, along with the sound of traffic.

"Hey, Kerry. You bring me anything this trip?" The voice was female, I thought, but so raspy it was hard to tell.

"Sorry. I didn't get the chance to find anything interesting." Kerry dug in his pocket for a couple of bills and slipped them into a plexiglass box mounted on the shelf nearest the open freight elevator doors.

I dropped my backpack through the opening in the roof, then stuck my legs through and tried to lower myself to the ground as gracefully as Kerry had done. My arms gave out, and I ended up dangling an unknown distance from the floor by my sweaty fingertips.

"I've got you." Kerry grasped me securely around the rib cage, just like we were a pair of ballet dancers doing a fancy lift. He seemed to know exactly where to hold on to avoid grabbing a boob or squishing the softer area around my waist.

He set my feet gently on the floor. "You okay?"

"Yeah." I sounded a bit breathless. Kerry was a strong guy.

And I was too dang easily impressed. I turned away from his expressive green eyes and his nicely muscled shoulders. Man, what was it about a guy's shoulders?

Maybe it wasn't the shoulders so much as the considerate actions of the guy who owned them. I scowled. Being helpful was a fool's game. Kerry was a sucker. "Where are we?"

"At the Mmuseumm," Kerry said, drawing out the m's extra long.

"Liar!" the raspy voice called.

I scooped up my backpack and stepped out of the elevator-turned-museum into an old, red brick alley. The arched windows on the wall in front of me had painted wooden shutters and black iron fire escapes. A battered porta-potty partially blocked the entrance to the larger street off to one side.

A young woman sat on a green folding chair to the left of the elevator. Her sleek red hair was swept up in a ballerina bun, and she wore rust-colored slacks with a forest green silk shirt and a sheer, spotted scarf. A paperback book with a shirtless guy and a woman in a sweeping dress on the cover lay open on her lap.

"Excuse me?" I said. "This isn't the Mmuseumm?" I didn't hold the m's nearly as long as Kerry. It seemed too weird.

The woman snorted. "Oh, no. That's the place, all right." Her raspy, five-packs-a-day voice clashed wildly with her stunning appearance, which I hadn't stopped staring at yet. She jerked a thumb sporting bright green fingernail polish at Kerry. "He's still a liar. He said he didn't bring me anything interesting."

Kerry leaned on the wall beside me and smiled down at the woman. "Lila, this is my friend, Seanan. Seanan, this is Lila Deveroux, and I didn't bring her here for you. I'm just taking her back to her school group."

187

"Through the Halls? Or did you find her there? Because that didn't work out so well last time."

I heard the capital letter at the beginning of the word *Halls*. I also felt Kerry twitch at Seanan's last sentence. Back in "the Halls," Kerry had mentioned he'd saved a shade once, got him out of there, but he hadn't wanted to talk about it more than that.

I guessed something had gone badly wrong with the rescue.

Kerry ignored Seanan's snide comment. "I ran into Jason and his sidekick. Lila followed me in to save me."

"I didn't go in to save you," I protested. "I only wanted to see where to send the security people. I'm not some stupid kid with a hero complex."

Seanan pinned me with a sharp stare. "You made it into the Halls of the Lost by yourself?"

"The door was already open."

"The door shouldn't have been there at all. Not for a normal human."

Wait. What?

She stood, peering with laser focus straight into my eyes. It was strange, and way too personal, and impossible to escape. I tried, but my feet wouldn't move. I couldn't even drag my gaze away from hers. I physically couldn't. My heartrate skyrocketed, and I braced myself for an assault of memory like Thomas had triggered.

The world didn't go away. I had to stand there, frozen, while her eyes seemed to search my very soul, finding out my deepest thoughts and desires. Rifling through my emotions and motivations. Plumbing the depths of my failures. Lots of those.

After what seemed like a very long time, she nodded and released me from her death-stare. "Ah. I see."

"What the actual heck!" I stumbled back to the entrance of the Mmuseumm, ducking behind Kerry. He was weird, yes, but not as weird as this lady. Had the world always been this strange, or was it just New York?

Seanan pointed a green-tipped finger at me. "Listen, kid. The Halls are dangerous for someone like you. Don't know what your issues are, but you've got to deal with them before you attempt to enter the Halls again." She sat back down and picked up the paperback romance from where she'd dropped it. "Of course, once you deal with your issues, the Halls probably won't let you back in. But, hey. That's life for you. Danger or boredom. Those are your only choices."

"O-okay," I said. I had no clue what the lady was talking about.

Kerry took my hand. "Thanks for letting us use your exit, Seanan. I'll bring you something with a really good story next time." He started down the alley, heading for the main street where people hurried past.

Seanan called after us, "Oh, yeah. A little bird told me Ferris wandered out of his territory today. You might want to go check on him."

Kerry groaned. "Why didn't *you* drag him home?"

She raised both eyebrows and settled back on her chair, book in hand. "Had to work today, didn't I?"

I raised my eyebrows. Yeah, I could see how hard she was working.

Kerry sighed. "All right. Where is he?"

"Columbia Park, by Chinatown."

Kerry stopped abruptly. "That's Jason's territory."

Seanan grinned, showing a lot of teeth. "Right."

"I thought Central Park was Jason's territory," I said, totally confused.

"Wait." Seanan's eyes narrowed. "Jason claimed Central Park?"

"At least the Museum of Natural History," Kerry said.

Seanan glared in our general direction. I don't think the burning look was meant for us. Thank goodness, because she appeared to be pretty scary at the moment. "Upstart," she hissed.

"Um," I began hesitantly, "why does Jason hate you so much?"

189

Kerry shoved his hands into his pockets and wouldn't look at me.

"Just tell her, boy." Seanan turned a page so impatiently I heard it tear.

"She'll think I'm crazy!"

"Best to know up front, then, right?" She showed her teeth in a smirk that could not be classified as a smile.

Kerry rubbed his temple like his head was starting to ache, carefully avoiding the bruise on his cheek from Jason's fist and my shot at him with the door stop. "Jason runs a kind of business organization."

Seanan snorted.

"Well, it is!" Kerry said.

Ah. Politics, of a sort. "A business organization like *the mob*?" I asked.

"No, they don't support criminal enterprises." Kerry made a face. "Or, they aren't supposed to. Maybe they do now. I don't know. The point is, they are a secret society. Like the Masons back during the Renaissance."

"Ri-i-i-ght." I said. "A secret society. I get it." I'd fallen in with a bunch of cultists. "You *are* crazy. I've got to go." I turned to book it out of there.

"Wait until you've heard it all, girl," Seanan said. "You love a good story, don't you?"

Darn it. The crazy lady was right. I came back. "Okay. I'll listen. But it better be good."

Seanan cackled. "It's a crap story because the ending sucks. Actually, it doesn't end. It just stops. I hate that kind of story. Why do you think I read romance novels?"

Kerry spoke fast, like he wanted to get this over with quickly, and maybe hoped I'd miss the finer points of his tale. "Leadership of the . . ." He hesitated. ". . . the *group* is generally hereditary, but there was a split, like, a long time ago. One faction followed Jason's family, and one followed mine. There was this big fight, and their side won through strength of arms, but they never managed to get hold of the symbol of leadership, this old sword, so a lot of people never acknowledged Jason's family's supremacy. Especially because they are congenital bullies, and a lot of us don't like them, and some people want my family back in charge. So, yeah. Jason hates me."

I narrowed my eyes and thought that through. "So. A secret society."

"Yeah. Sort of."

"And a magic sword."

"It's not a magic sword . . ."

Seanan snorted again.

"Okay. It's sort of a magic sword."

"And you're the handsome prince." I kept my voice flat, although, dang. He did kind of fit the handsome prince mold. Except he seemed nicer. More crazy, though, unfortunately.

He shook his head. "My brother was supposed to be the handsome prince, not me."

I absorbed the bolt of pain that shot through me at the word *brother*. "Supposed to be? What happened?"

Kerry's face closed down. He turned to Seanan. "Can Ferris wait until after I get Lila back to her group?"

Huh. Touchy subject for him, too. I ignored the stupid hint of insult that he didn't want me to help him rescue Ferris. That he wanted to get rid of me as soon as possible. I didn't want to help him, anyway. Besides, if he wasn't the handsome prince of this story, why would he bother to rescue people in the first place?

"I can find my own way back, thank you very much," I said. "We can't be all that far from the museum. We only travelled the Halls—whatever those are—for half an hour or so. I'm not utterly helpless." And I was done with these people.

I spun, intending to make for the street.

Seanan sucked in a hard breath behind me. "Oh, crap. Hold on a sec, guys." She dropped her paperback, and her eyes fogged over until they were solid white from lid to lid. No iris. No pupil. Just a freaky, swirling, iridescent pearl color. I gasped and fumbled for my phone to take a picture. No one was going to believe this.

I didn't believe this.

My phone wasn't in the pocket I'd expected it to be in. Before I could search more, Seanan's eyes blinked back to normal. "Keep the girl with you, Kerry."

"What did you See, Seanan? Will Lila be safe?" Kerry asked, studying me with a worried expression. Maybe he thought I'd take off down the street, screaming. Maybe he was right.

Seanan buried her nose in her romance novel. "Boredom or danger. Take your pick. But nothing ever changes if you choose boredom."

"You're not going to tell me, are you?" Kerry said.

Seanan ignored us.

Kerry headed for the main street once more. "Come on, Lila. Let's get this over with."

I finished going through every pocket I had. "We've got to go back!"

"Back to the *Halls*?"

"My phone is gone!"

"You want to face the shades again? You were drawing them to you from miles away. Besides, if you dropped something in the Halls of the Lost, it's pretty much gone. Why do you think they're called the Halls of the Lost?"

I threw up my hands and stomped after him. "You guys are crazy, you know that? Crazy!"

Crazy or not, I wasn't going back after my phone. I'd seen Thomas. I remembered what he'd done to me. The thought of meeting up with him and hordes of other shades terrified me more than losing my phone.

"Mom's gonna kill me," I muttered. "How am I going to check in with her? She's such a control freak she might call the police if she doesn't hear from me tonight."

We stepped out of the alley onto a busy street. Yellow cabs clogged a street so narrow I could spit across it, and towering apartment buildings severely restricted any sightlines. I scowled at Kerry, who was pretty much ignoring me almost as well as Seanan had. "Where's the museum?"

Kerry headed for the corner and stepped out into a break in traffic, not waiting for the light to change. "Don't worry about it. We'll stop by Columbus Park really fast and take the subway back to Central Park. Then you can forget all about this."

I jogged at Kerry's elbow across the street, dodging a man and a poodle in an electric wheelchair who also hadn't waited for the light. "Take the subway? We didn't come that far in the Halls, whatever they are."

"Space gets kind of mixed up in there." He stepped onto the sidewalk under a McDonald's sign and pulled me out of the flow of the foot traffic. We stood on cigarette butts. "Look, you know what the Halls are. You've been there. Don't make me say it."

"But—" I began.

Kerry took off walking, jamming his hands into the pockets of his jeans. I considered staying behind and finding my own way back to my group. But I had no phone. No way to find out where I was. No way to find out where to go.

Besides, I couldn't forget that look we'd shared in front of the Old New York exhibit. Kerry came as close as anyone had to someone who could understand the knot of pain I carried buried inside me. Who cared if he was too beautiful to pay any serious attention to me beyond his quest to deliver me back to my tour group?

When I caught up, Kerry glanced over. I didn't meet his eyes. He wasn't going to answer any more of my questions. Guess I'd called him crazy one too many times.

Not that I blamed him. Much. What would he say? Tell me I'd stumbled upon some weird pocket of magic in the middle of New York? Yeah, that was believable. Not. If I hadn't experienced it myself, I'd have laughed in his face.

The Halls of the Lost. That seemed fairly self-explanatory, especially after travelling through them, even briefly. The whole place was a repository of stuff that had slipped out the mainstream of history. Forgotten things, lost items. Lost people.

I frowned at the claustrophobic walls to either side, decorated with fiddly bits of painted plaster that looked like decoration on a grubby wedding cake. A covered construction scaffolding formed a tunnel up ahead, blocking most of the view in front of us. Traffic edged past to one side, and shop windows filled with everything from books to lingerie hemmed us in on the other. I looked away from the lingerie window quickly.

"What should I do if I see Jason?" I asked, mostly to break the tense silence between us.

"Run," Kerry said.

"Not helpful," I muttered as we stepped off the curb in a break in the traffic.

"I mean it, though." His shoulders hunched, and even from the side I could tell the haunted look was back. "Don't wait for me. Just go. Get on the subway. Take the B train to 81st."

"I can't use the subway alone! How do I even find a B train? And if rescuing Ferris is so dangerous, why are you doing this? It's not your job to take care of him, is it?"

"Not really. But if I don't get him out of there, Jason's people will beat him up to remind him to stay where he belongs. Or they'll take all his money for 'protection,' and he doesn't have any to spare."

"So? It's still not your problem. You act like you don't even like Ferris. Why should you bother?"

He studied me, letting his eyes linger an instant too long. "You don't really mean that, do you? You wouldn't let someone get hurt if you could help it. After all, you helped me."

"I didn't! I just—wanted to see what happened."

"Right."

"I'm serious! People do what they're gonna do, and you'll drive yourself crazy if you try to stop them." I crossed my arms, hugging myself, and stared down at the millions of black chewing gum splotches on the sidewalk. Gross.

Kerry was silent for a minute. We passed a little park-type area, not much larger than my backyard back home. A narrow, trash-strewn alley stretched between it and the ornate red brick building next to it, divided from the neat landscaping by a chain-link fence and another porta-potty. The smell suggested the porta-potty wasn't always used correctly.

Kerry said, "Something happened to make you think like this, didn't it?"

"Maybe." I refused to look at him, communicating as hard as I could not to ask me any more questions.

Kerry stopped and looked down at me. People streamed around us, with only a little bit of swearing at us clogging up the sidewalk. "Thanks for following me into the Halls. And coming with me to rescue Ferris."

My cheeks went hot and I knew I was blushing. "No problem. Besides, what else was I going to do? Wander around New York by myself?" I wanted to say more. Tell him I knew how he was feeling. But did I know? How could I tell? Maybe I was projecting my own emotions onto him.

We stood there like fools for an endless minute. I'd have been content to stay there longer, looking at the way his silky hair fell forward, brushing the edge of his perfect eyebrow. The way he had actual stubble shadowing the clean line of his jaw, disguising the bruise from Jason's fist. His eyes locked on mine, and the dark, cold emotions that had haunted me for months retreated before the warmth of his gaze.

His hand came up, as if to touch my cheek.

An older lady with her head wrapped in a pink turban shouldered me into Kerry's chest, trying to get into the boutique we were blocking.

"Sorry!" I yelped to anyone who was listening. The lady was already inside.

Blushing, I pushed away from Kerry. Dang, his chest was wonderfully hard. "So, where is this Ferris guy?"

Kerry's hand slid along my arms in an almost-caress as he let me go. He hesitated, looking down at my bright red face, and started toward the fringe of green visible at the end of the next block. "He plays guitar and sings for people in parks, usually. I expect we'll hear him before we see him. And if we hear him, we'll have no choice but to find him."

"What do you mean, no choice?"

"No choice."

"As in . . . ?"

"No choice."

 chapter four

heard nothing but traffic and distant sirens and conversation and the occasional pigeon call as we neared Columbus Park. The green space stretched a long way left to right, but was narrow from front to back. Oddly deserted tennis courts and a soccer field took up most of the space to our left. An equally abandoned playground lay in front of us. Everyone seemed to be gathered on a concrete-covered plaza in the shade of a bunch of trees. So much concrete. And so many people, all in a tight knot. I smelled Chinese food from a restaurant on the other side of the park.

"You hear him?" Kerry asked as we continued.

The pigeons were getting louder. The delighted screams of little kids got louder, too. Haunting tones of a classical guitar piece filtered through the shrieks and pigeon coos, along with a male tenor singing in some language other than English. The music beckoned, forcing my feet to carry me closer. I had to see the musician, and hear the rest of the song.

"What is that?" I asked, straining to see the man who could make such enchanting music. Kerry was pretty, but not as pretty as the music. I broke into a run.

Kerry swore and took off after me. "Lila! Come back! Don't listen to him!"

Why not? That's what we were here for, right? I ran faster, my pack thumping against my sweaty back with each step. I *needed* to find that musician.

I rounded a low concrete wall into the midst of the crowd, all watching a circle of children dancing around an odd-looking man of indeterminate age perched on a concrete planter. He looked old, but didn't have gray hair or many wrinkles yet. Could be thirty. Could be eighty. It was hard to tell. His woolen trousers, suspenders, collarless shirt, and patterned vest, on the other hand, were easily as old as the park itself, and none too clean.

He played a guitar as battered as his clothes, focusing on his instrument, oblivious to the children and the trees filled with pigeons weighing down every branch and adding avian counterpoints to his melody. Mothers, fathers, and nannies stood around the edges, smiling benignly at the strange spectacle. Was this a flash mob or something?

Would anyone mind if I joined in? My feet started tapping in place as I hesitated. I wasn't a kid any more, but I wanted to join the dance. I forgot about the tour, and the Halls, and why I was here. The darkness inside me, the one that lightened when I looked at Kerry, vanished like a light switch had been flicked on. An unfamiliar but welcome sense of well-being flooded my body. I drew a breath, feeling life and warmth permeate me to my toes. I was content to simply *be*, swaying in the sun, listening to this man play.

Kerry caught up to me and grabbed my arm. "Lila! Fight the spell!"

If this was a spell, I hoped it never ended. I beamed at him. "Kerry! Dance with me!" I peeled his hand from my elbow and kept hold of it, trying to pull him into the circle of dancing children with me.

He came with me into the circle, but wouldn't let me skip like the other kids. He wouldn't even let me clap my hands like the watching adults. A little of the darkness crept back, and I scowled at him.

I shook my hand to get free. Kerry wouldn't let go. He towed me toward the man with the guitar.

My smile returned. I'd go see this guy, no problem.

Kerry dodged a round-faced girl with a million braids in her hair. She was so small she didn't even come to his waist. The girl and I exchanged wide smiles before she danced off with the rest of the kids.

I bounced in place as Kerry crouched in front of the seedy guitar player. "Ferris, what are you doing?" he said.

Ferris startled, as if he hadn't noticed Kerry approaching. With fingers still moving over the guitar, he lifted vacant, bewildered eyes. "What? Kerry? What are you doing here? What's the matter?"

At the loss of the man's smooth tenor, the darkness nibbled at the edges of my consciousness. "Kerry, let him sing." I shoved at Kerry's shoulder with my free hand.

He ignored me. "You're out of bounds, Ferris. This park is Jason's territory, remember? And look." Kerry tipped his head, indicating the gathered crowd, and the pigeons clustered in the trees and planters surrounding us. "Your magic is out of control."

"Oops," Ferris said. He lifted his nimble fingers from the strings, and the music stopped.

My darkest emotions crashed into me, bowing my shoulders under their weight. The sun seemed to dim. I stumbled as my feet quit tapping.

The children stopped dancing, too. A few voices raised in protest, but most of the gathered people shook themselves, glanced around as if wondering how they came to be here, and began to wander off. The pigeons didn't do much, though. But, hey, pigeons. Not the smartest things on wings.

"No," I whispered. I covered my face with shaking hands.

Ferris said, "Sorry, Kerry. It's just that I saw in the paper that a city councilman said they had to do something about all these pigeons. Called them rats on wings. I—I must have had a flashback to the old country. You know, Hamelin Town or something."

A couple grown-ups dropped change into the up-turned hat on the concrete by Ferris's feet before taking their kids by the hands and leaving.

"Don't stop playing," I said, not looking up. I don't think either Kerry or Ferris heard me.

Kerry sighed. "We've talked about this, Ferris."

"Yeah, I know. Stay focused on today. I forget, sometimes." Ferris started to put his guitar in its case.

I grabbed a fistful of his shirt. "Don't stop playing!" I sounded desperate and kind of scary. My cheeks were wet. I hadn't realized I'd begun to cry.

"Kerry?" The old man's voice quavered. He stared at me with wide eyes, holding the guitar out to the side so I couldn't reach it.

Kerry took my wrist and transferred my grip from Ferris' shirt to his. "Shh, Lila. It's all right."

I tightened my fist and yanked him close. "It's not all right!" I yelled in his face, perfect except for the bruise, which just made me feel worse. "While Ferris played I felt all right for the first time in a year! Make him play!"

Ferris jammed his guitar into its battered old case and clutched it to his chest.

Kerry's arms went around me, cradling me much like Ferris was cradling his guitar. "It wasn't real, Lila. Just a trick. Oh, man. Don't cry."

I dropped my forehead to his shoulder, hiding the tears I couldn't stop. I whacked his other shoulder with my fist. "I'm not crying. I'm angry!"

"I—I'm sorry, Kerry," Ferris stuttered. "What should I do?"

"Gather your stuff and get back to our territory." Kerry patted my back helplessly.

My nose was stuck right up against his throat. He smelled like fabric softener and really nice aftershave and something indescribable that was probably just him. I took a deep sniff, and not because my nose was running. Which it was. On his shirt.

Crying was stupid. It never accomplished a thing. I needed to pull myself together. The darkness had been my companion for a long time. Why should I fall apart, simply because it suddenly came back?

Why should I feel so much worse now for having a moment without it?

Ferris bent and picked up the hat full of money. He straightened, and froze. "Uh, oh."

Kerry released me and spun, putting me at his back.

A big guy, all bushy orange hair and splotchy freckles, planted his booted feet on the concrete right in front of us. "Ferris, Ferris, Ferris. What are you doing, man? You busking here without paying up?"

"I . . . I . . . no, I'd never . . ." Ferris stammered.

Fantastic. I'd made such a fool of myself, nobody had noticed this thug approaching. I'd ruined everything yet again.

The guy flung an arm around Ferris' shoulder, squeezing until Ferris was scrunched up against the guy's sweaty armpit. "Where's my money, piper?"

"Leave him alone, Eddy." Kerry stepped up, getting in Eddy's face.

I shook my head. Or maybe I just shook. "Kerry, come on. Let's go." He was going to get hit again.

Eddy wrenched the money hat from Ferris' limp hands and released him. Ferris stumbled a few feet away. The leftover crowd from his busking scattered, unwilling to get involved.

Eddy sneered at Kerry. "Taking care of the trash again, garbage boy?"

Ferris flinched and stared at the ground. He did look homeless, but that didn't make him trash.

"Cut it out," I told Eddy, startling myself. Why was I interfering? Ferris wasn't any of my business. "We just want to leave, okay?"

His narrow eyes swung to me. He could have been good looking, except for the mean expression on his heavy-jawed face. And the freckles. And the orange hair. Okay, he was ugly as sin. "Gonna let your girlfriend protect you, garbage boy?"

Kerry stiffened, and his fists rose a few inches. Shoot, shoot, shoot. I was going to get Kerry punched, again.

"Don't hit him, Eddy!" Ferris moved forward, hands raised placatingly.

"Ferris, get back!" Kerry snapped.

"Why not, Trash?" Eddy glanced at Ferris, but kept most of his attention on Kerry.

Kerry's fists drifted higher.

Ferris tugged at Eddy's sleeve. "I'll come with you, okay? I'll play for Jason. Give him my profits. That's what he wants, right?"

"Shut up, Ferris," Kerry growled. His eyes flicked from Eddy to Ferris and back. His jaw tightened in frustration.

If I were a better person, I'd do something to stop this. To save Ferris. To save Kerry from having to save Ferris. I didn't know what, exactly. But there had to be something I could do.

I couldn't think of anything. The only image in my head was Jason's smug face, feeling the high of Ferris' music, leaving me in misery. "Get Ferris back, Kerry!" I cringed as the cowardly words left my mouth.

Kerry surged forward, as if he were a racehorse and the starting gates had been flung open.

Eddy flung one hand into Kerry's chest. Kerry flew back into me, knocking us both to the ground. The concrete scraped my butt and elbows.

"You don't have enough power to stop me. Not on Jason's land." Eddy laughed, and snagged Ferris in his armpit again. He curled his lip at Kerry. "Hah! The Prince of Trash can't keep the loyalty of even his lowest subjects. Jason will be delighted."

He turned and carted Ferris with him across the park, into the maze of brightly colored signs and storefronts of Chinatown.

 chapter five

Silently, we picked ourselves up and brushed off what dirt we could. I'd received some scrapes and bruises, but nothing major, and I guess Kerry was in about the same shape.

We didn't talk much on the way to Canal Street. We had failed. My feet were beginning to complain by the time we reached the stairs and followed the stream of people going down—and down!—into the subway station.

I'd ridden public transportation back home in Utah, but the trains there were above-ground and the platforms were new and attractive, as if each section of the city they serviced was determined to show everyone whose bit of the metropolis was the coolest.

New York subway stations? Not so much.

Trash lurked in corners, and there was graffiti on the walls, mostly painted over, but not all. It smelled funny, like rotten ice cream and dirty feet and mold. I kept expecting to see enormous rats around the edges of the tiled walls, if I just turned my head fast enough.

The tour company had provided us all with Metro cards, thank goodness. I dug mine out of my backpack as we descended below street level. I fell behind a step so I could watch as Kerry swiped his card and copy how he did it. Maybe I wouldn't look too much like a tourist.

Maps of the subway system lined the white-ish tiled walls, but nobody looked at them. People walked fast in New York, and if I stopped to figure out where I was going, I'd be trampled. Kerry seemed to know exactly what to do, striding confidently to one of the platforms. I followed, trying not to lose him in the crowd. So many people, and this wasn't even rush hour. Some guy with short dreads and a gold button-up vest played a smoky tune on a sax off to the side, nodding as travelers dropped cash into his case. Ferris wasn't the only one busking today.

Brakes squealing, a train came to a stop in front of us. Kerry and I got on and found seats together. New York subways appeared to be configured more for standing passengers than seated ones. The only seats lined the walls, leaving large, clear aisles for standing.

No one was close to us, despite the number of people who'd waited on the platform. It was a big train. And with the noise of the train itself, we could probably talk without anyone overhearing.

"I'm sorry," I said, hugging my backpack on my lap. I glanced over at Kerry. He slouched in his seat with his arms folded. I closed my eyes. I'd really messed stuff up this time. "I mean it. I'm sorry. I don't know why I acted like that. I made you fail to rescue Ferris."

Kerry sighed. He leaned so his arm bumped mine from elbow to shoulder. "Not your fault. I should have realized what would happen when you heard Ferris' magic. *Seanan* should have known."

I shook my head. "Wait. I'm having a hard time with all this talk of 'magic.' What the heck *are* you and Seanan and Ferris, anyway? Because I didn't just imagine getting dumped halfway across the city by a short stretch of hallway. And I didn't imagine Thomas and the rest of the shades, or Seanan's eyes going white all over, or getting sucked into Ferris's weird music so far that the world disappeared. What is going on?"

Kerry shifted uncomfortably. "Look, I know today's been strange for you. It hasn't been normal for me, either. I mean, yeah. I help out

Ferris on occasion, and other people in our . . . secret society . . . but I've never had anyone normal—I mean, someone not in our society— around to see. I've never had to explain all this before." He blew out a breath and scrubbed his hands through his hair, mussing up the tumbled waves even more.

How come guys always had the best hair? Much better than my own not-quite-blond, not-quite-brown, not-quite straight, not-quite-curly hair.

Mine was longer, though. But then, Kerry didn't really need longer hair. His was pretty darn nice just as it—

"You aren't going to believe me."

I jerked my gaze back to his face. "I've had plenty of evidence that weird things are afoot. I'm willing to give any explanation the benefit of a doubt."

"Okay. So." Kerry shot a look over his shoulder, gauging the distance between us and anyone who could be listening.

I looked around, too. On the far side of the train, a tired-looking African-American woman tried to keep her two giggling kids from poking each other. Across from her, a guy in a suit leaned close to read a tablet, manspreading across three seats. A couple guys our age or so wearing yarmulkes and ringlets by their ears hung out by the front doors of the train car, ready to hop out as soon as we screeched to a stop at the next station. No one paid us the slightest attention. The darkness outside the windows created a feeling of intimacy, as if we were enveloped in our own little bubble of privacy.

"Okay," Kerry repeated. He lowered his voice until I could barely hear him. "I'm Irish, right? Or my family was. We came over a long time ago, when everyone was getting out of Ireland. The potato famine, or something. My parents would know more about that, but they never . . . Well." He broke off and looked away.

I recognized the technique. I used it when I thought too much about when my brother went away, and my mom's recriminations

207

afterward. You turned away so no one could see your eyes go red and shiny with tears, and you tried desperately to find something to distract you.

I scooted closer, bumping him with my shoulder. "So your family came from Ireland? Mine are from Wales. And France, of course. Had to be, with a name like Deveroux."

Kerry gave a startled "Huh."

I shrugged. "Genealogy is big in Utah. Wanna hear stories about coming across the plains in a covered wagon? Or about ancestors who were fourth wives of town founders?"

Kerry bumped me back, and, yup, his eyes were a little red as he caught my gaze. "No, that's all right. Sounds like your family is almost as messed up as mine."

My turn to look away, now. My family was messed up for sure. Broken up, smashed up, and gone, gone, gone. Absent emotionally, or just absent for real.

"Hey, are you okay?" Kerry took my hand and began to play with my fingers. Maybe he thought it would be a distraction. If he did, he was right. "Some of the people who came to America with us weren't . . . entirely human. They were fae."

"Fae?"

"Fairies. Magic people."

I stiffened. I knew what the fae were, of course, but . . . "What the actual heck? Are you saying you believe in fairies? Because that's what it sounded like you said, and that's just crazy talk." But what about the Halls of the Lost? And Seanan? And Ferris?

His hand gripped my fingers as if to keep me from running away screaming. "You said you'd keep an open mind. Have you got a better explanation for what happened today?"

"No, but . . . But . . ." I couldn't think of any better arguments except that this stuff wasn't real. Halls, Seanan, Ferris. Maybe it was. "But why doesn't anyone else know about this?"

"Duh. Secret society, remember? Also, New York. Plenty of strange stuff happens here. Everyone just shrugs and goes about their business."

"Right. Whatever. There are fairies in New York. Go on with your story."

Kerry hesitated. "There aren't actually many of the fae left. The world is too full of iron and tech. But there are lots of us halflings around. Lots of the fae-touched."

I studied him with narrowed eyes. "You don't look short, stout, and furry-footed to me."

"Not like the Tolkien halflings!" Kerry snorted. "Loved the books, but that guy played fast and loose with naming conventions."

"You've read Lord of the Rings? All of them?" That got my heart jumping. Even if he didn't look like the cover model from Who's Who, Gorgeous Edition, which he did, his Tolkien love alone would make me give him a second look. Or a twentieth.

He nodded. "Halfling means we've got fae blood somewhere in our background, not too far back. Fae-touched means anyone with any fae blood at all, or anyone who has gotten involved with the fae community." He smiled apologetically. "That means you're fae-touched, now, I guess."

"Okay," I said, drawing the word out as I tried to think what that could mean for me. "Cool, I guess."

"It won't matter once you go home. You're from Utah, right? That's what you said."

"Yeah. No fae there." I frowned. "Not that I know of."

"We're hard to find. It's not like we go around advertising ourselves or anything."

The train stopped and the two guys got out and a couple girls in strategically slashed jeans and designer t-shirts got on. They stayed at the front of the car, away from us.

"So these people want you to be the leader of the society, right? Instead of Jason? And the society is all the fae-touched people in New York." I was trying to put all the pieces together.

"My brother was supposed to be the leader." Kerry's face got that awful look, the one that had drawn me to him the first time I saw him. The one that I knew too well.

"What happened to him?" I whispered. If he didn't want to answer, he could pretend he didn't hear.

"He killed himself."

The abrupt words hit me like bullets. No wonder I recognized something in this boy. I sucked in a breath between my teeth. "I'm sorry. That sucks." Another breath. "My brother's gone, too."

Kerry studied the toes of his battered sneakers. "Why'd he do it?"

I dug in my jeans pocket for a tissue. Dang allergies making my dang nose run. "He's not dead. He just ran . . . He just . . ." I couldn't breathe around the mass of tears in my throat. I glanced over at Kerry's impassive, perfect face. He'd been brave enough to lay it out for me, even after I'd messed up his rescue. Even after I'd slowed him down in the Halls.

I couldn't lie any more. Not to him. I coughed to clear my throat. "Actually, he . . . he *is* dead. He h-hung himself." The words cut like knives, leaving me bleeding inside. I'd never said them out loud before. "He was gay and, well, a lot of people in Utah think that's wrong. And we were way religious. At least Mom is, except she kind of skips the 'love one another' and 'judge not' parts. She told him he was her son and she was forced to take care of him until he was eighteen, but if he didn't 'straighten up' he'd be on the curb that night."

The knives had cut so deep, it seemed like I couldn't stop the bleeding. Everything— blood, poison, and all—was flowing out of my mouth into Kerry's ears. "Dad was so mad at her, but no one sane goes up against Mom when she gets like that. Dad moved to a hotel for a few days to let them both settle down, but it was Abe's birthday, like, the next day. He . . ." I swiped at my eyes and nose. "He didn't wait around for Mom to change her mind."

Kerry didn't say anything. He just waited, staring at me, now, instead of his shoes.

I must have looked awful, tear-streaked, splotchy, and red-nosed. Kerry didn't seem to mind. So I told him the worst part.

"It was my fault," I whispered. "I was the one who told my folks he had a boyfriend. I didn't mean to. Mom kept going on and on about finding a nice girl to date, when everyone knew he'd already found a perfectly nice *boy*. Everyone but Mom, I guess. I lost my temper and shouted at her, which was freakin' stupid. I just wanted to get her off Abe's back, you know?" I shook my head at my own foolishness. "I guess I thought he'd feel freer. He was out with everyone else. I should've kept my stupid mouth shut."

Kerry searched in his pockets and came up with another tissue. He handed it over, as if he handled hysterical girls every day. I was grateful for his tact. And the tissue. And his silence. He knew what I was feeling, what I was going through. He'd been through it himself.

I crumpled the tissue in my fist. "I knew Mom was too angry to make him a birthday cake. I got up early and made one before school. He wasn't in his room, though, when I went to take it to him. I thought he'd gone to his friend's house, maybe was sleeping in his basement or something. I went over to apologize, and to try to get him to come home and talk to Mom again. I thought I could fix it. But he wasn't there. He wasn't anywhere." I shut my eyes, my brother's boyfriend's accusing expression still crystal clear in my memory. I tortured myself with it regularly, just in case I forgot for a moment how useless I was. "Mom and Dad split up not long after that. They each blamed the other for Abe's . . . death. And, sort of, they blamed me."

Kerry hunched over and braced his elbows on his knees. "It wasn't your fault."

I echoed his movement, hugging my backpack on my lap. "That's what my therapist keeps telling me. I guess I believe her. I mean, to have something be your fault, you need to have the power to help, and choose not to. I couldn't help anyone, no matter how hard I tried. I just made things worse."

I straightened my spine and blew my nose. I'd lived with this pain for a long time. I should be used to it by now. Besides, we were getting some weird looks from the little kids on the other side of the train car.

"How'd your parents handle . . . *it*?" I couldn't bring myself to say the word "suicide" out loud. He would know what I meant.

Kerry was silent for a moment. "They're dead, too."

"Wait, what? Not just your brother?"

"No. He took my parents out, too. Stabbed them and then himself. I think he was sick or something. He'd been sick for a while. Video surveillance recorded the whole thing."

"Oh, Kerry," I whispered, shocked and horrified. I reached over and squeezed his hand. Touch sometimes made me feel better. Made me feel as if I were still a part of humanity, and that not everyone hated me. "How long ago?"

"A couple years now." He turned his hand over and clutched my fingers. "He always hated the idea that it was his duty as the oldest son to retrieve that stupid sword and take over the leadership of the fae. He despised politics, and had little patience for those of the fae-touched who had trouble adapting to the modern world."

"Like Ferris?"

"Yeah. Like him. My brother wanted to build things. Design computer boards and things like that. But he was always getting dragged into stuff he didn't want to do. One day he went into the Halls on some errand or other and he didn't come out."

I grimaced, remembering how the darkness had swallowed me whole when Thomas had touched me in the Halls. "The shades got him?"

212

Kerry leaned back until his head thunked on the Plexiglas window behind us. He kept his death grip on my hand. "I went in after him and got him out. My first and only success. If you can call it that. I returned him to the life he hated so much that he went insane and chopped up our parents and killed himself. How is that for the whole thing being my fault?"

The train shuddered to a stop and Kerry lunged for the door. I held on to him, hoping my grip would give him some comfort. He needed it more than I did. I still had my parents, even if I didn't have them both at the same time. And even if I didn't really like Mom much.

A lot of people got off at this stop. Tourists and school kids, mostly, it seemed to me. We blended in and made our way to street level. We passed a food cart, and the spicy smell made my stomach growl.

I headed for the cart. "Let's get food."

"They sell falafel. Does a sheltered Utah girl like you even know what that is?"

"Not really." I shrugged. "But it smells wonderful."

"It's fried bean patties. Still want to try it?"

I hesitated. Beans? What if they made me fart?

What was the matter with me? We'd both just vomited up the worst moments of our lives to each other, and I was worried about a little gas?

Well, yeah. Kind of. But the food still smelled divine. I went up to the man at the cart. "I'll take a number one, please," I told him, and then said yes to everything he said, although his accent was so thick I couldn't understand much. I ended up with three little patties in a paper boat with white sauce and chopped stuff on top and a soda in a plastic bottle. Kerry got some, too, and we cut across the street to Central Park to find a place to sit and eat.

I hurried Kerry past the museum, remembering Jason's threat to beat up Kerry if Jason found him here again.

We wandered on a wide, paved walkway lined with big trees, their branches arching over the edges of the path and shading the iron lattice benches to either side. We chose an unoccupied bench and sat. The falafel was much better than Kerry had made it sound.

I listened to the voices of kids running past and enjoyed the cooling breeze that lifted my hair off my sweating neck. I felt strangely . . . light. As if, by sharing my worst, nastiest secret with someone who really *understood*, I'd left part of the weight of it behind on the subway. I almost didn't recognize the feeling of not hurting.

"I think . . ." I began, licking the yogurt-based sauce from where it had smeared onto my finger. "I think we should make a pact."

"Oh, yeah?" Kerry asked. He looked more peaceful, too. It was nice to find someone who understood you. "What kind of pact?"

I set the now empty paper boat on the bench beside me and turned to face Kerry. "No more helping people."

Kerry frowned, and I hurried to explain. "I mean, little things? Sure! No problem. And maybe if you really want to, and really like the person you're helping, then that would be okay. But we've had nothing but trouble from trying to help people sort out their problems, and it doesn't work. No one ends up happy. Just look at Ferris! You tried to help him, and he got taken by Eddy anyway. We both tried to help our brothers, and that was a complete failure. Can't get much more failure-y than that. And I tried to help save my parents' marriage. I ended up just making Mom hate me more."

"She doesn't hate you."

"You don't know her."

"I know you." He took my hand again. He wasn't grabbing it like he'd fall if I let go this time. No, he held it like he wanted to hug me but this was the best he could do under the circumstances.

I fought to keep a stupid grin off my face. I was trying to be serious, here. "Whatever. Back to the pact. We have a right to our own lives. That's something else my therapist says. We're still kids. It's not our job to fix things. Let the adults handle it for a while." I held up the pinky finger of the hand Kerry wasn't holding. "So. Pinky swear?"

Kerry studied my pinky. "I refuse to make a solemn pact with a pinky swear. What are we, twelve?"

"What do you want to do, then?"

He set our paper falafel boats out of the way and took my hands. "I promise not to try to fix everything, and to learn to live for myself. Your turn."

"I promise not to try to fix stuff for people who should fix their own crap." I looked up into Kerry's teasing blue eyes, and a delicious shiver ran through me. Boy *was* pretty. "What now?"

"This," he said, and he leaned over and kissed me.

chapter six

His lips were warm and soft and perfect, and so sweet I didn't even want dessert. The sounds of cars and buses and joggers padding past and the leaves rustling and someone's dog barking like mad all faded into insignificance. All that mattered was Kerry and me, and this perfect, wonderful moment. This kiss was more than just a meeting of lips. It felt more like a meeting of souls. And maybe it was. A meeting of two people who understood each other. Was every kiss like this?

No. Not possible, or everyone would spend every minute of the day and night kissing, and nothing would ever get done.

My arms rose of their own volition and slid up his arms to his shoulders, skimming his hard muscles. His hand went to my cheek, cradling me like I was something precious and beautiful. No one had ever made me feel like this before. I clung to him, playing with the soft hairs at the back of his neck. No way was I letting him go now.

"Lila Deveroux! What do you think you are doing?" The disapproving voice cut through my distraction, and the world came crashing back.

I jerked away from Kerry, looking up at the strained face of Mrs. W. "Oh! Hello, Mrs. Wilkinson." My face went hot at her disapproving look.

"Don't you 'hello' me, missy. We've been searching for you for an hour! And here you are, making out with a complete stranger . . ." Mrs. Wilkinson pressed a hand to her temple and closed her eyes. "Your mother is going to kill me."

"He's not a stranger." I turned to Kerry, who looked cool and unruffled in his dark jeans and only slightly scuffed-up t-shirt. How had I not noticed the "Got science?" logo? Considering he was half-fae, that was pretty funny. I strangled my nervous giggle.

Kerry stood and stuck out his hand. "I'm Kerry Conner, Mrs. Wilkinson."

She stared at him for a good three seconds of eternity before she shook his proffered hand. I got up, too, and edged between them. "I'm sorry I worried you, Mrs. W. I wanted to explore a bit on my own and I got turned around. Kerry helped me find my way back to the park."

"How very considerate of him." She leaned around me and spoke to Kerry directly. "Thank you for returning Lila. She needs to rejoin her group and you need to leave."

"I can't believe this! He's not going to ravish me in the middle of Central Park, Mrs. Wilkinson." But I knew I wasn't going to win this argument. Mrs. Wilkinson's mouth went tight. I don't think she actually liked teenagers that much. Why did she even volunteer to chaperone us on this trip, anyway?

A large hand clamped down on Kerry's shoulder. "Kerry, my man! What are you doing here?"

I spun. Jason and his bully sidekick stood behind Kerry, pinning him in place. My heart kicked into high gear. "Leave him—"

Kerry cut me off with a swift shake of his head.

Mrs. W missed the rising tension entirely. "Come, Lila. Your little friend has to go now, and so do you."

Jason showed his teeth and let his eyes linger too long on my curves. "Lila? I like it. Why don't you come . . . play . . . with us?"

Not even Mrs. W could miss the innuendo. She crowded close, herding me farther away from Kerry and Jason and his unnamed minion. "The play is about to start, and we need to get to the amphitheater in . . ." She checked her watch. ". . . ten minutes." Her voice shook.

I dodged around her. "I won't leave you, Kerry!"

Kerry winced as Jason deliberately patted—hard!—his bruised cheek. "Go on, Lila. I'll be okay."

He wouldn't. Jason was going to beat him up good, this time. I saw it in Jason's beady little eyes. I shook my head. "No!"

"You promised. Remember?"

No more helping people. I'd promised, but I hadn't meant the promise to include Kerry. "I know, but I didn't mean . . ."

Mrs. W tapped her foot on the gum-stained concrete. "If you don't come with me right this minute, Lila Deveroux, I'm calling your mother."

"Go," Kerry said. He forced a smile. "I'll meet you at the theater entrance before the intermission."

"Oh, no, you won't," Mrs. W muttered.

"But—"

"Go!" he snapped. He turned, jerked his chin at Jason, and began to walk toward the museum.

"See ya, sweetheart." Jason leered at me, and he and his buddy followed Kerry.

I glared after them, vowing all sorts of vengeance I knew I couldn't deliver. My chest hurt, more than I'd thought possible when saying goodbye to someone I'd known for so short a time.

"Lila!" Mrs. Wilkinson was losing what little patience she had left.

I headed in the direction I thought the amphitheater lay. "Come on, Mrs. W."

Mrs. Wilkinson threw up her hands as if disgusted with the whole situation and caught up with me in a few strides. "You could have called, you know, if you were lost."

"I lost my phone."

"You lost your phone?" she screeched. "I am *never* chaperoning teenagers again." She pointed a blunt fingernail at me. "You are to *stay with the group* for the rest of the trip, do you understand, young lady?"

I resisted the urge to turn and see if I could still see Kerry. "Sure, Mrs. Wilkinson." I'd learned how to say all the right things to get adults off your back when they wanted to lecture. It didn't matter what you did, really. Only what you told them. They did whatever they wanted no matter what they said they were going to do, anyway. Like when Mom and Dad said they still loved each other.

A bunch of people were heading the same direction as we were, on a wide sidewalk winding through the trees. We turned a corner, and an enormous open-air theater appeared in front of us, towering overhead. So weird to see trees big enough to hide a structure of this size, right in the middle of a park.

More people streamed from a building kitty-corner to the theater, with signs advertising hotdogs, beer, and bathrooms. We all hit a bottle-neck at the theater entrance.

Mrs. W hurried me past the ticket-taker and led me through the portal and up the stairs to the section where our tour group had a block of seats. "Stay!" she said, as if I were a disobedient dog.

"Yes, Mrs. W," I replied, already tired of this play, and it hadn't even started yet.

I plopped down in the green fold-down seat at the end of the row, waiting for the stage lights to come up.

On stage, a woman dressed like a punk rock fairy welcomed us to the play. The audience grew quiet. There was no curtain, just a backdrop of a forest masking most of the little lake behind the stage. A colorfully-lit castle jutted above the painted branches.

The first act began.

I glanced around. Mrs. W was at the other end of the row, and seemed intent upon the action on the stage. I rose and crept silently down to the portal, like I was heading to the restrooms by the refreshment building. Maybe Kerry had gotten away from Jason. Maybe he'd show up early.

I wandered to the back of the portal and leaned against the wall, listening to the tale of runaway lovers and jealous fairies while I waited, worried about what injuries I'd see on Kerry.

But Kerry never came.

 chapter seven

The first intermission began before I accepted the truth. Either Kerry was in major trouble or he'd stood me up. Should I ditch my tour group—again—and search for him? Or was Kerry trying gently to get rid of me?

Even if I wanted to look for him, where would I begin? We were in freaking *New York City*. And I only had access to places normal people could go, not magical places like the Halls of the Lost.

The actors on the stage struck a final pose, their diaphanous fairy costumes fluttering in the light breeze. The last rays of the setting sun splashed a golden glow across the minimal props and the actors' faces. I hesitated, struck by the other-worldly beauty of the scene.

"That's how fairies should look," I muttered. "Not like Seanan and Ferris." Kerry looked okay, though. I hoped Jason hadn't messed him up too badly.

I pushed away from the wall to go sit back down, throwing one last look over my shoulder in the stupid hope that Kerry would suddenly appear out of thin air. I mean, halflings like him might be able to do that, for all I knew.

One of the extras from the play came around the corner from the back of the amphitheater and noticed me. She stopped in place. She was

223

dressed as one of Titania's fairies in a pale yellow tattered tunic and flowers in her short, curly hair. Her eyes flicked over me, taking in my medium-everything hair, my plaid shirt, my dark jeans, and my Chucks.

She nodded as if I'd passed some sort of test and came over, threading her way between people heading for bathroom breaks and snack runs. "Lila Deveroux?" she said, side-stepping audience members to avoid getting her bare feet trodden upon.

"Yeah . . ." Why would a cast member want to talk to me? My brain whirled, but didn't cough up a single good reason.

She curtsied, a faint touch of sarcasm detectable in the curve of her wrists and the slant of her head. "Seanan must speak with you. Come with me, and I'll take you to her."

She knew Seanan? Weirdness was starting again.

I started forward. "Will Kerry be there? Is he okay?"

She shrugged. "Dunno. I just do as I'm told." Her eyes flicked over me from the top of my messy hair to my scuffed Chucks. "Even if it's escorting some untidy human to meet with someone as important as Seanan."

I winced, and stepped back against the portal's concrete wall. She was rude, but she had a point. I was a mess, physically and emotionally. Why would a boy like Kerry possibly be interested in me?

I should have known he wasn't serious. He couldn't like me for real. He was probably glad to find an excuse to get rid of me. I'd thought we'd connected, but I'd been wrong before. Often. All the time.

Besides. No one went out of their way for someone else. Not usually. Hadn't I already learned that by now? Hadn't I made him actually *promise* that?

I shook my head. "Nuh-uh. No way. Seanan is one creepy lady, and besides, I already got into trouble for wandering off today."

The yellow fairy woman seemed surprised at my refusal. "I think you will want to hear what our 'creepy lady' has to say. It concerns this missing swain of yours."

"Swain? What the heck is a . . . ? Oh." I stopped as the definition of 'suitor' bubbled up in my memory from all the fairy tales I'd read when I was younger. "You mean Kerry? Sorry, I've never heard anyone actually use that word before."

I could have sworn she rolled her eyes, even though I was looking straight at her and her eyeballs never wavered. "Will you come?"

I waivered. I'd promised not to help anyone. And what if Kerry didn't want to see me?

But what if he was in trouble?

"I have to be back before the play is over."

She curtsied again, the sarcasm more evident this time. "I make no guarantees of your ability to move fast enough to return on time."

I was so getting sent home early for breaking the rules. "Okay. Let's go."

The yellow fairy woman moved through the crowd as if they weren't there, and led me onto a path leading into a patch of trees.

Utah parks consisted of patches of land carpeted with grass, with a few slender trees here and there for shade.

Central Park was built on a completely different scale.

It stretched for *miles*, it seemed, with lawns and buildings and lakes and fountains and enormous trees. And big old rocks, too, covered with lichens and moss, scattered among the tree roots like they'd been there since the world began and expected to still be around when it ended.

I don't know how far we went, exactly, me trailing after the fairy woman like another bit of her fluttering skirt. The sun set, throwing the woods into deep shadow before she led me into a little clearing. Seanan sat across from us on a gray boulder, shaggy with dark green moss, shaped vaguely like a throne, romance book in her hand.

Maybe it was Seanan that put the idea of a throne in my head. Instead of a nice blouse and slacks, she wore a long, silver dress that left her arms bare and draped low at the neck. It shimmered in the pale glow of what looked like moonlight, but no moonlight could make it through the dense leaves that roofed the little space. I looked for lanterns, but couldn't see any. I didn't know where the light came from.

The yellow fairy woman curtsied to Seanan—no sarcasm involved—and sank gracefully to a seat at Seanan's feet.

Seanan handed her romance novel to the yellow fairy woman and set her hands gently on the rocks and twisted roots to each side that served as chair arms. Her smooth voice came as more of a shock this time than the gravelly one she'd had the first time we met. "Your boyfriend's in trouble."

My face went hot. "Kerry's not my boyfriend."

Seanan snorted. "He'd better be, girl. You're all the help he's got."

I snorted right back. "If I'm all he's got to count on, we all might as well give up right now. Do you even know what happens when I try to help? Disaster, that's what. I smacked Kerry in the face with a doorstop, I distracted everyone enough to let Ferris get captured, I made my parents break up . . ."

I broke off, remembering Mom's harsh words to Dad—and to me. I swallowed and jammed the memory back into its box. "Besides, Kerry made me promise not to help him. And he stood me up. Why should I care what happens to him?" I hesitated. "What happened to him?"

"Jason and his crew caught him in the park and dragged him into the Halls."

"Kerry has no problem with the Halls." At least when I wasn't with him. "I don't see the problem."

"He hasn't come out," Seanan said, her voice going flat. "This is what I saw when I looked at you today. Kerry going in—and remaining there. Unless you go after him."

Kerry was stuck in the Halls?

Was he a shade?

I stumbled backwards a step. "Me? Make Jason get him. He's the one who left him there."

"Jason is not under my control." She leveled a steady stare on me.

"Will you go?"

"I can't. You told me not to, remember? It's dangerous for me." My hands had gone transparent during my vision of Mom and Dad arguing about me. I'd nearly become a shade. If I met Thomas again, without Kerry there to snap me out of it . . . "No. Besides, I'm not magic. I can't get into the Halls on my own."

Seanan waved away my objection. "The Halls let you in once. No reason to think they won't let you in again. You don't strike me as having found your purpose in life in the short time since we last met. And if you do have problems, I can open the way for you." She rose from her rocky throne, the skirt of her dress flowing over her legs like water. "Come. We have little time to waste."

"No way. You're the one with the magic powers and all. You go rescue him."

The yellow fairy woman hugged her knees, giving me a mocking smirk. "Coward," she whispered.

I ignored her. What could I say? She was right.

Seanan ignored the woman, too. "I can't go after Kerry. I can't directly affect the course of history. I advise. I predict. I cannot interfere. I am bound. No, it has to be you. I saw it."

Interfere in what? I'd think about that later. I shook my head, backing up another step until a sturdy tree trunk hit my backside. Panic fluttered under my breastbone as images of my brother's cold, bluish face rose in ugly memories. "No! You don't understand. I'm just some stupid kid. I can't go around rescuing people. What do you think this is, a fairytale?" I gave a derisive laugh, sounding too much like my mom.

Seanan's eyes pierced me like twin crossbow bolts. "This *is* a fairytale, child. Didn't you know?" Her head tilted as she studied me. "Make your choice. Boredom, or danger? Will you be the hero? Or the villain?"

Her challenge hit home. My vision blurred, and I blinked rapidly to keep the tears from falling. "I'm not hero material." And I'd promised

227

Kerry I wouldn't try to help people any more.

Not unless I really liked the person.

"No one ever is. Heroes work with the material they have. Villains, now? A dime a dozen."

Shivers wracked my body, raising the hair at the base of my neck and making my teeth chatter. I hugged myself hard trying to control them, but the parade of memories wouldn't stop. Kerry's bruised cheek, because I couldn't stop Jason from hitting him. Ferris, under Eddy's not-so-kind control, because I'd freaked out and distracted everyone. My mom's harsh opinion of me. My parents' divorce, my fault as well. And my brother, gone forever because of me.

Thomas's attack, which had dredged all these feelings back up.

I did not want to go back into the Halls. I couldn't live through all that again.

I couldn't leave Kerry there, either. He hadn't stood me up after all. And his nightmares had to be worse than mine.

"H-h-how do I find him?" The hard shivers rolling through me made it hard to speak. "Do you have an amulet or a charm or something to lead me to him?"

Seanan raised a sarcastic eyebrow. "What, you want I should give you a magic kiss on your forehead to keep you safe and guide your feet?"

I gritted my teeth. "You're the one who called this a fairytale."

"Do I look like Glinda the Good?"

I studied her silvery, flowing robe. "Kinda, yeah."

"Well, I'm not," she snapped. Her gaze narrowed and dropped to my lips. "But if I'm not mistaken—and I seldom am—you've already got some kiss action going on. Perfect!"

My face went hot, and I had to force my hands to stay where they were, grabbing opposite elbows, instead of hiding my reddening cheeks. How did she know Kerry had kissed me? Although, considering the sort of kiss we'd shared, maybe it was more surprising that everyone *didn't* see the kiss's effects, shining like opals and sunbeams on my lips.

I sort of felt the opals sparkling there, even now.

The yellow fairy woman snickered.

Seanan circled to the side of her boulder throne and waved me over. "Think of your connection with the boy and follow where it leads. It should take you to him."

"What does that even mean?" Sounded like a bunch of mumbo-jumbo to me.

"You'll find out." She parted a thick curtain of low-hanging branches and jerked her chin at the black opening beyond. "Go on."

"It's dark. And what do I do if I find him?"

"Remind him who he is."

"Well, who *is*—?"

Seanan slapped her hand in the middle of my back and shoved.

I fell headfirst into the dark.

 chapter eight

I landed on hands and knees on a dirt path between thick pillars of tree trunks. Darkness pooled under their canopy like tar. The background sounds of New York—traffic, sirens, car horns, and the constant undertone of human voices—were gone. Silence remained.

"What the heck?" I scrambled to my feet and spun to yell at Seanan. "What was that for . . . ?"

I broke off. Seanan wasn't there. The opening that should have led to her clearing was gone, too, leaving a tangled mass of dense bushes crawling over an outcropping of stone.

"That's just dandy," I snapped. "Another disappearing doorway." I raised my voice, hoping it would carry through whatever barrier had grown between the outside world and me. "Even if I find Kerry, how do you expect me to get him out of here?"

No one answered, but the little rustlings in the branches quieted, and nearby crickets stopped chirping, as if the woods were listening. Creepy.

Okay. No more drawing attention to myself. Avoid notice, find Kerry, and get the heck out of the Halls. That was the plan.

I turned and studied the path. Barely visible in the bad light, it wandered through woods so dense with undergrowth I couldn't imagine trying to force my way through it. If this was a part of the Halls of the Lost, I imagined either the woods or the plants themselves were extinct or had been cut down for development. "Lost" in some form or other. Silvery shafts of moonlight shot through openings in the ceiling of branches stretching over the pathway.

I dusted off my hands and set off cautiously into the dark. With the outcropping at my back and the ranks of trees to the front, I had only two ways to go.

Seanan had said to find my connection to Kerry, and his kiss would help me. I touched my lips, feeling again the warmth of his acceptance. Okay, the kiss had been pretty hot, too, but the part that had felt best was knowing he didn't think I was a freak. He understood.

The woods wavered, as if my eyes were watering. The odor of car exhaust leaked through from somewhere, like I was about to emerge into Central Park. Where Kerry *wasn't*.

This wasn't going to work. These were the Halls of the Lost. When I thought of Kerry, I didn't feel lost at all. Kind of the opposite, in fact. What connection had Seanan been talking about?

Our mutual losses?

Grimly, I closed my eyes and forced my mind back to the day I'd shouted at Mom to quit trying to fix up Abe with girls because, obviously, he wasn't into them. I remembered her cold disbelief and her not-so-cold accusations that I was lying to get attention. I relived my brother's horror and anger that I'd betrayed his secret.

And felt again the panic when I couldn't find him anywhere, and couldn't make Mom try to look for him. I felt the darkness creep over me as I remembered the creak of the rope over the beam in the garage.

My brother was gone, and it was my fault.

The familiar burden of pain settled on my chest like one of the boulders Seanan had been sitting on.

My lips tingled like tiny sparklers going off, far to one side of my mouth.

Was this going to work? Or would I lose myself to misery, like Thomas and the rest of the shades?

Like, perhaps, Kerry was lost?

I opened my eyes and followed the sparkling soda feel of Kerry's kiss, passing through the rows of tree trunks on a rough, dirt path. The top of an old tent peeked over a clump of tangled brush. Its pale canvas picked up what light came through the trees. A few steps farther on, a hiking boot lurked half behind a rock, looking for all the world like some ferret or weasel or something, ready to leap out and bite me. I hurried past, and practically stepped on a shiny silver cell phone. Not mine, unfortunately.

I tossed the phone off the path, straightened, and came face-to face with the filmy, insubstantial form of the shade of an old man.

A strangled shout squeezed out of my suddenly constricted throat. I scrambled back, tripped on a root, and sprawled on the ground at the shade's ghostly feet. He didn't react. His eyes stared past me as if I wasn't there.

I crab-walked a few feet away from him, my eyes fixed on the old dude's gray-on-gray plaid shirt. He still didn't look at me, but he sort of drifted along with me, as if the wind of my very slow movements sucked him down the path in my wake.

"Go away!" I firmed my voice, but honestly, you can't be too intimidating while scooting backwards on your butt.

His eyes swung toward me.

I sucked in a breath. I shouldn't have drawn his attention.

The path curved and I didn't. My hand came down in a pile of detritus under a scratchy bush edging the way. I dug through the dead leaves and broken twigs for something—anything!—to use as a weapon. A smooth wooden handle stuck up from the back of the heap. My fingers curled around the end and pulled. The eighteen-inch-or-so handle ended in the pointed blade of a small shovel, folded up against the smooth wood.

I grabbed the shovel's blade and snapped it open. The shade's gaze drifted past me, as if he couldn't quite focus. I waved the little shovel in his direction. "Back off, buddy."

The blade passed through the shade's trousers at about knee height. His legs deformed, as if I'd waved my hand through dry ice fog, condensing gently back into shape when I stopped flailing. The shade stopped, staring somewhere past my left shoulder.

I stood, holding the shovel out in front of me with both hands. "You stay put, okay? I'll go around."

He didn't move as I skirted him and got back onto the trail. I glanced behind me as I walked. The shade flowed along after me like before, but he kept his distance this time, neither gaining ground nor falling behind.

Okay, I could deal with one lonely shade following me around.

Except the next time I looked back, there were two of them.

And then another shade joined the duo, emerging from behind a particularly thick tree trunk to step onto the path.

I turned and walked backwards, because I didn't dare stop. Pale wisps moved among the trees on both sides, drawn to me like the first time I'd walked the Halls, with Kerry. He'd said the shades weren't usually drawn to living people. What the heck was wrong with me that I just happened to be shade catnip?

The cloud of shades stalking me grew. I counted at least five, although their gray-on-gray translucent coloring made it hard to tell them apart.

No problem, though, right? They moved slowly. As slow as fog. Slower than I could run. And they couldn't hurt me unless they touched me. At least, that was how it had worked with Thomas.

I'd just have to run.

I faced forward, my lips sparkling at their mid-point, where my top lip curved down to touch the center of the fuller bottom lip. Kerry was directly ahead of me. I broke into a fast jog. My pack slapped against my back with every step, and I choked up on the folding shovel until my hand was directly below the blade to keep its weight more balanced.

I made it around one curve before I had to slow to a walk, sucking wind and rubbing at the stitch in my side. My heart pounded, from running and from the thought of all the shades pursuing me through the dark. I seemed to hear Mom's voice in my head, very quietly. *Pathetic*, it said. Not that she'd ever said that to me in real life, but I'd seen it in her eyes. Lots of times.

The path wound through the dense forest, past a pile of discarded jewelry, little things that could fall off without being noticed. Past a rusted-out old car. Past a half-hidden pond with a fishing pole stuck in the muddy bank. Behind me, the shades still came on.

Ahead, another path joined with this one, forming an X. A crossroads.

A clot of pale, transparent shades meandered in loose orbits around the point where the paths met. Not hundreds of them, or even dozens. More than a handful, though. It was hard to keep track of them long enough to get an accurate count, and they kept drifting away or wandering back when I was counting the other side of the crowd. They were so diaphanous they seemed to blend into one another as they moved.

My lips burned, the tingling ramping up to something uncomfortably like pain. I had to be close to Kerry. Maybe he was one of the orbiting shades.

I raised the shovel, hoping the mute threat would warn away the shades long enough to distinguish Kerry from among their number.

I stepped nearer, and the shades began to take notice. Several left their orbits and approached, winding in an indirect path like a cat that wouldn't admit he wanted you to pet him.

"Stay back!" I edged forward, avoiding the middle-aged ghost lady to the right and slipping past the older man beyond her. He reached out and brushed his fingers through mine. A wave of despair swamped me, and I shied away. I had no desire to experience anyone else's nasty emotions. I had plenty of my own, thanks.

I twisted and hopped, waving the shovel to drive back the ghostly forms of men, women, and a few kids. Loneliness, helplessness, and despair rushed through me as each shade drew near. They moved off when I confronted them, as if they'd lost interest.

Or maybe my particular issues didn't line up with theirs.

Where the heck was Kerry? My lips pretty much burned all over. Not much use to show direction. I attracted all these other shades. Why not him?

"Kerry?" My voice squeaked, and I coughed to clear my throat.

I broke through the biggest knot of shades. On the far side of the crossroads, a gray-scale, cloudy Kerry lay under a tree, gazing up into the branches.

Thomas sat beside him.

Crap.

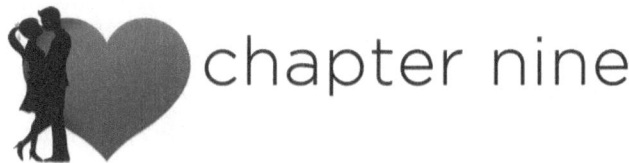 chapter nine

"Kerry!" I called, trying to get him to come to me. No way was I getting close to Thomas. Not unless absolutely necessary.

Kerry didn't seem to notice I was there. Thomas, though. He looked right at me.

He stood and moved toward me, his insubstantial form blurring Kerry's outline. "Have you seen my mom?" His gauzy hand reached out to touch me.

I skittered sideways. No point in going back. Too many shades between me and Seanan's exit. "No, Thomas. I'm sorry."

"My name's not Thomas." He drifted after me.

I had to get around Thomas fast, before he caught me. Thomas's agonies from not fitting in were awful. I had no desire to relive my own, either.

"It's kind of you to sit with Kerry." I stepped to the edge of the path. Thomas followed, slow as a wisp of fog.

"Kerry is nice, not like Evan. Evan calls me names, and he hit me."

I hardened my heart against the pity his words woke in me. I understood all too well the pain of being betrayed by those who should be your friends. Still, I had to find Kerry and get him out of here. I let

Thomas's hand get within six inches, then darted around him on the far side of the path.

Or I tried to. His arms flashed out and grabbed me around the waist faster than I could dodge. The world went black, and I plunged into one of the wretched arguments I'd overheard between Dad and Mom. About my brother, and about me.

Mom was perfectly dressed in a pencil skirt and a trendy blouse. "How can I ever show my face at church again? My son says he's gay, and even Lila knows it. If she picks up on something, the whole world must know it."

I flinched, and closed the door of my bedroom. I didn't want to hear any more. I didn't have a choice, however. Their voices were too loud.

"What's wrong with Lila?" Dad sounded as angry as Mom. "She's a good kid. So's our son."

"He's gay, and Lila's useless!"

Useless. The word echoed in my head. I was useless.

Why was I even *in* this place? I couldn't help Kerry. I couldn't help anyone. "I . . . I'm not useless," I whispered. I didn't sound very convincing, even to myself.

"I'm not gay!" Thomas' words—or were they his thoughts?—broke through my misery. "I'm not a fag!"

I opened my eyes—when had I shut them? Thomas' face hovered inches from mine.

"Who the heck cares?" I snapped. "So what if people call you a fag? Are you gay, or not? Make up your stinking mind, and leave me alone!" I shoved at his arms. My hands slid through his insubstantial form, accomplishing nothing.

I huddled on my bed, listening to Mom's stinging words. "Why do you encourage her to read those silly books? They're useless fairytales! She lacks ambition, and all you give her is pathetic dreams!" Silly. Pathetic. Useless.

The tips of my fingers went transparent and gray. I saw the faint outlines of branches through the bones.

I froze, staring at my hands.

Was this what had happened to Kerry? To Thomas? To the rest of the shades in the Halls? Was this why Seanan had warned me to stay out? Then why had she sent me back in here?

Pathetic. Lazy. Useless.

Yeah, all right. Sure. Maybe I was all those things. Maybe not. Who cared? I needed to rescue Kerry. I didn't have time for this! "Thomas, or whoever you are. Listen to me. I. Don't. Care. Get it? I don't care if you're gay or not. My brother was gay. I loved him because he was awesome, not because he was gay or straight. I *do* care about Kerry. Now either help me save him, or I'll do it on my own, but either way, you've got to let me go!"

I lurched to the side, breaking Thomas' hold on me. Maybe I'd grown so insubstantial he couldn't maintain his grip. I stumbled and landed on my backside in the dirt. Again. Mom's hateful judgments faded into blessed silence.

Thomas stared at me. "Your brother was gay?"

"Yeah. Why does it matter?"

"I'm not gay. I like girls. But I like clothes, too."

"Fantastic." Sarcasm fairly dripped from my words. "You can grow up to be the fashion designer to the shades. Focus, Thomas. *Can you help me save Kerry?*"

He shook his head, but not like he was saying no. More like he was clearing foggy thoughts. Maybe it was more than foggy thoughts, because he grew more *condensed,* and he seemed to look straight at me for the first time. "My name's not . . . Wait. Is Kerry lost?"

I stood and brushed dirt off my jeans. "No, he's right there. He faded." I touched my lips, relieved to see solid fingertips again. My lips still tingled from Kerry's kiss. If he were himself enough for his kiss to guide me, there had to be enough of him left to save, right?

Thomas frowned. "But I don't want him to be . . . You really don't care I like clothes?"

I *didn't have time* for this, but Thomas looked so confused and . . . solid. "Look, Thomas. People will call you all sorts of stuff." *Pathetic. Dreamer. Useless.* I wasn't helping. Not him, and not me. "I don't care, you stupid shade! Be whatever you want to be. Get it? You get to decide, not other people." I brushed past him, heading for Kerry. Heading away from the shades that clustered close to my back. I brandished the shovel to hold them off.

"My name's not—"

"Not Thomas. You keep saying that. What is it, then?"

He stepped forward instead of drifting like a fog bank. "It's . . . It's . . ." He grabbed my hand. I tensed, ready to fall back into the nightmare of parental discord.

Nothing happened. Nothing, except my hand grew warm from Not-Thomas' very real clasp.

"Scott. My name's Scott."

He was totally solid. A normal kid. Well, besides the truly epic 70's bellbottoms and striped shirt.

Huh. Had I yelled him out of being a shade? Who knew that could work?

And what the heck was I going to do with him now that I'd saved him? *Useless. Dreamer.* Maybe Seanan would know what to do. "I'm Lila. I'll help you get out of here, but I've got to de-shade Kerry first."

"I'll help."

"Cool." I rushed to Kerry, dropping to my knees by his chest. "Come over here away from the rest of the shades."

Thomas—no, Scott—planted his little red sneakers on the path between Kerry and me, and the shades. "No. I'm mean. I can scare them off!"

"Scott!" I snapped. "I don't have time to de-shade you again!" I didn't think I had the strength to de-shade *myself*, again.

Scott folded his arms and glared at the shade of a middle-aged woman with her hair in a bun. The shade avoided him, turning back the way she'd come.

Maybe Scott really could scare the shades off. Shows you how good my judgment was. *Useless.*

I turned to Kerry. My hands hovered in the air over his chest. I was afraid to touch him. Afraid I'd be stuck back in my memories. "Kerry?" I whispered. "Look at me."

He sighed, a thin sound in the quiet woods. "I failed."

I let out a breath. At least he was speaking. "Failed at what?" Actually, we'd failed a lot today. Of course, I was used to it.

"I always fail. Why should I even try?"

I went cold. I understood him far too well. *Pathetic. Useless.* My vision blurred, and my mom's voice whispered in my ears, no longer just an echo.

No! I refused to go there. I needed to help Kerry. I had *no time* to wallow in my own crap.

"Kerry!" I snapped. Yelling worked for Scott. Maybe it would work here. "Get up and let's get out of here. Seanan's waiting!"

His eyes didn't move from the canopy of leaves. "I can't save anyone. I promised."

I flinched at hearing my words from his mouth. Did that make it my fault he'd got stuck here? Guilt welled up, and Mom's voice grew louder. *Lazy. Pathetic. Useless.* I ignored her. "You saved *me*, Kerry." I reached for his face, trying to turn him to look at me. My hand passed through his skull, encountering no more resistance than dry ice fog, and his misery threatened to swamp me. "Oh, ick!" I fell back on my butt.

Useless. Useless. Useless.

I gritted my teeth and checked on Scott. The shades were gone. All of them. Weird. Well, at least one thing was going right.

Scott's arms fell to his sides, and he squinted into the darkness down one of the paths I hadn't taken.

I turned back to Kerry. "Kerry! Look at me!"

He blinked, and slowly, so slowly, his eyes turned to me. "Lila?"

"Yes! It's Lila. You helped me, remember?"

241

He shook his head. "I didn't help Ferris."

"That was my fault, not yours. That Eddy guy was too strong. What else could you have done?"

"Nothing. I can do nothing. I have nothing. No family, no girlfriend, no sword."

I flushed. Girlfriend? Did he mean me? I touched my lips, the burning changing to a warm simmer. It took me a minute to pick up on the sword reference. "Kerry, forget about the stupid sword. It's in a freaking museum. You'll never be able to get it."

His eyes lost focus. Great. I was pushing him farther into shade-dom than ever. "Listen to me! You don't need the sword. You're doing a great job taking care of your people without it." I had no evidence to back up this claim, but I knew Kerry. He'd do his best to help people. It was who he was.

Until I made him promise not to.

Useless.

Scott's voice quavered into the silence. "Lila? Someone's coming. I think it's Jason."

I followed Scott's gaze down the left-hand path. Jason, his golden hair swept back and dressed in boots and a white shirt with a sword slung low on his hip, sauntered toward us. He looked kind of like a pirate, and kind of like a thug, and a lot like he was trying too hard to look like the handsome prince. He smiled nastily as our eyes met.

Run away? Or stay and fight?

I couldn't fight. I'd never even hit someone before. Not with the intent to harm. And Jason had a freaking sword.

But if I left now, I'd never get another chance to bring Kerry out of the Halls. He might be trapped here forever. And it was all my fault.

Mom's voice got louder, criticizing my obsession with fairy tales. *What good will those pathetic books ever do her? They're useless!*

Useless.

I had to do something, now, or Kerry was lost.

"Scott, run!" I shouted, dropped the shovel, and slapped both palms on the ground to either side of Kerry's face. "Come back to me, Kerry."

Maybe all I knew about were fairy tales, but Seanan had said this was a fairy tale. And in fairy tales, kisses were magic.

Hoping my lips wouldn't pass through him like my hands did, I bent and pressed a kiss to his cold, ghostly mouth.

The world plunged into darkness.

I juggled the cake box onto one hand so I could pull open the garage door. I'd only had my license for a month and was nervous about driving, especially because it was winter, and the roads were icy and it was still dark at seven in the morning. But Abe wasn't in his room, and I wanted to give him his birthday cake before he left for school. Maybe . . . maybe the cake would make him feel better. Maybe it would let him forgive me.

His bed hadn't been slept in, so I figured he'd spent the night at his friend's house. I pushed the door open . . .

No. I didn't want to see this memory. Not again. Not ever.

The guilt was worse than Mom's disapproval. Names? I could handle being called names. I could shrug off the thoughtless labels.

This memory? This guilt?

It threatened to unravel the fabric of . . . of me.

And this is what Kerry and I both carried at our cores.

I kept my lips on his, and let the vision come.

I pushed the door open. The light switch slipped under my gloved fingers, but it flipped on the second try. I turned to the little hatchback Mom let Abe and me share, and saw the booted feet swaying above the hood. I looked up to open rafters high overhead, where Abe and I had constructed a platform of scrap lumber and cardboard when we were kids. Abe hung from the end of a rope by his neck. His face was purple and gray. His tongue jutted out.

I dropped the cake, and it splattered melty chocolate frosting across the concrete floor.

Tears streamed hot and fast down my cheeks, and I gasped in a breath. "I know you, Kerry," I whispered. His eyes were blue again, not foggy gray. "Abe is gone. Your brother is gone. You're not. Not if you come back."

His eyes focused on mine, seeing me as clearly as he had when our gazes had met for the first time. His pain. My pain. So much alike.

And so much easier to bear together than apart.

"Lila," he whispered. Just that one word, but I heard worlds of meaning inside it. Gratitude. Wonder. Other stuff, maybe.

He brought his hand to the back of my head, bringing my mouth down to his. His lips firmed under mine, going from barely-there mist to warm boy in seconds.

He held me there for a single, glorious moment more. His warmth and the tingling from my lips spread through me until my toes and fingers felt like lightning shot from them to brighten the forest. I almost forgot about Jason and his freaking sword.

Almost.

"Hey, let me go!" Scott yelled.

I tore myself from Kerry's kiss—which nearly killed me, I swear— and sprang up, putting myself between Kerry and Jason. He was only a few yards away, hanging onto Scott by the back of his shirt.

Compared to the memory I'd just escaped, Jason held little power to frighten me. Especially with the warmth of Kerry's kiss to sustain me.

"What is your problem?" I shouted. "Leave us alone, you jerk!"

"Ooooh," Jason said, mocking me. "Whatcha gonna do? Fight me for the little fag?" He shook the boy until I heard Scott's teeth clashing together, and dumped him in a heap in the dirt.

"No," Kerry said from behind me. "You'll fight me."

He stepped around me, flipping the folding shovel in his hand to test its balance, and strode toward Jason. Kerry looked angry, determined, and not at all transparent.

I'd saved him, just in time for him to save me.

 chapter ten

I crouched and scrabbled in the dirt for a rock or a stick or any sort of weapon, watching as Jason kicked Scott aside and began to draw his sword. The blade was long and whippy, and Jason's arm was longer than Kerry's, too. Kerry roared, surged forward and slammed the sturdy shovel head into the center of Jason's blade before it cleared the end of the sheath. Jason's sword splintered, leaving him grasping a complicated basket hilt with maybe six inches of shattered steel jutting from it.

Kerry continued his swing, reversing directions smoothly and bringing the shovel down across Jason's head and neck. Jason staggered, and threw up his empty hand. Ice burst from his palm like broken glass in a leaf blower, pelting Kerry with slivers of cutting projectiles. I gasped, and my hand clenched on a fist-sized rock on the dirt under me. He was bleeding.

He was losing.

Kerry threw up a hand to protect his eyes, leaving only one arm free to swing the shovel at Jason's knees. The shovel connected, and Jason screamed. His leg gave out, dumping him on the ground, but his hand stayed up, and the ice storm cutting Kerry to shreds didn't let up. Kerry raised the shovel, using it to shield his face.

He didn't see Jason draw back the hand still holding the shattered remains of his sword. Didn't see Jason's eyes shift to aim the six-inch spike at Kerry's femoral artery.

Last time I'd tried to save Kerry by throwing something, I'd failed utterly. This time? Well, I couldn't do *nothing*. Even if it ended up being useless.

I chucked my rock, a solid, overhand fastball.

It struck Jason on the elbow of his sword hand. The *elbow*. That's a teeny, tiny target, all things considered.

The broken sword dropped from Jason's nerveless fingers, and the ice storm vanished as he cradled his elbow close to his body.

"Do you concede?" Kerry asked, both hands back on the shovel, ready to swing again.

Jason said a lot of words that would get him grounded for a very long time if my folks heard me say them.

Kerry waited him out, unwavering.

"I . . . concede," Jason ground out through gritted teeth.

Kerry took off his t-shirt and . . . my brain pretty much stopped working. Yup, it was that good a view. I checked to make sure I wasn't drooling.

He grabbed the hem and ripped the shirt into thick strips, using them to tie Jason's hands behind his back.

"Careful!" Jason snapped as Kerry twisted his injured arm into position.

"Good shot, Lila," Kerry said, ignoring Jason's moans.

I shrugged, still kind of out of it because of the no-shirt thing. "I was aiming for his head."

Someone laughed, off to the side.

Scott! How could I have forgotten, shirtless Kerry or no?

I rushed to where Scott sat hunched over, favoring his left side. "Are you hurt?"

He lifted his shirt—to which I had no reaction except pity, thank goodness—and I saw a boot-shaped bruise starting on his ribs. "I think it'll be okay in a few days," he said. He struggled to stand, and I helped him up.

Kerry had Jason on his feet, too. "Now, we get out of here." He grabbed Jason by the collar and me by the hand, hustling us onto the path. The few shades lingering nearby scattered as we approached.

I led us back the way I'd come at a fast jog, past the old car and the pond and the abandoned camp site to the outcropping where I'd come into the Halls.

The outline of a door showed clearly among the tangle of roots that trailed over the rough surface. Kerry hit it with his palm, not slowing.

It swung open, and we tumbled through, into the humid, noisy, warm, smelly, and relatively bright New York nighttime.

"We made it! Kerry!" I gasped, and flung myself at him.

He caught me and swung me around in his arms. My relief was so great I didn't notice the applause, at least at first.

He set me down, and I looked into his long-lashed eyes, smiling down at me. Little cuts peppered his face from the ice, but he didn't seem to notice. "Thank you," he whispered.

He let me go, darn it, and turned to the group of people I only vaguely had noticed gathered under the trees in the little clearing hidden deep in Central Park. He bowed deeply. "Lady Seanan," he said as the applause died.

Seanan lounged on her rock throne in her silver dress, romance novel in hand. Scott slunk over and crouched at her feet, and she lay a hand on his head in welcome. Ferris was there, and the woman who had brought me here from the Shakespeare in the Park amphitheater. Lots of other people were crowded in here, too, perched in the trees or leaning against trunks or clustered near Seanan, including Jason's sidekick and Eddy, who'd bullied Ferris.

And they'd all seen me hanging on Kerry like some silly, love-struck girl.

Which I kind of was. But still.

Seanan rose, setting the book on the arm of her throne. "Prince Kerry, I see you have found the lost sword, and a lost hero. Congratulations. The kingdom is yours."

I sucked in a breath. "Wait. What?"

My words were swallowed in the general uproar. About half of the gathered people cheered and half shouted protests, especially Jason, who had stumbled to his friends and was getting his hands cut loose.

Seanan raised a hand, and silence fell. "Jason," she said, utter calm coloring her voice. "You have something to say?"

Jason stalked into the center of the clearing, rubbing his wrists. I narrowed my eyes at him, ready for him to try something sneaky. He was that kind of guy.

Jason sneered at the folding shovel Kerry had shoved into his belt. "That's not a sword. It's a trenching tool. You use it dig holes to crap in. The Sword of Legend is in the American Museum of Natural History right now."

"No." Seanan shook her head, and her red-gold hair shimmered in the moonlight. "The museum's sword is just a sword. The real Sword of Legend is any weapon that is used by one who is worthy, in the service of others." She held out her hand to Kerry, and he dragged the shovel from his belt and handed it to the Lady.

She held it out into a shaft of moonlight. The shovel shivered, melted, and lengthened. In seconds, a bright-bladed sword balanced across her outstretched palms.

She faced the gathered fae-touched. "Any one of you could have found it. Many of you have royal blood. Many others have courage, or kindness, or wisdom." She turned back to Kerry. "But only one of you has all of these, and the determination necessary to sacrifice their own desires to help others, and, in return, gain the throne."

248

Oh. My. Heck. Even after all I'd seen and done this day, Kerry being the prince of the fairies was too weird to deal with tonight. I shifted my weight, getting ready to slide on out of there.

Kerry caught my hand, keeping me firmly at his side. He didn't say anything, either to confirm or deny this craziness.

Jason scowled. "He's a scrub! He couldn't save his own family from self-destructing. How could he be qualified to be prince?"

"Who should the kingdom belong to, Jason?" I asked. Dang. I was getting involved again. But I didn't care. "A bully like you?"

"Only the weak call the strong 'bully'." Jason's lip curled in disdain. "We need a strong, hard leader for strong, hard times, not a wimp like Kerry, who spends all his time helping fae trash who can't be bothered to show proper gratitude."

My eyes flicked to Ferris, who flushed and looked down.

"He was strong enough to defeat you!" I took Kerry's hand, only flinching a little at the blood smears on his fingers.

Seanan's gaze sharpened on Jason's face. "Is this true, Jason?"

Jason's face went dark red with rage. "Only because he cheated. That girl threw a rock at me, in the middle of a duel!" He pointed straight at my face, and Seanan's eyes flicked to me.

One corner of her mouth twitched up, and she looked like a cat with an open quart of ice cream. "She did? And this weak little girl, who has not the slightest bit of magic beyond what most mortals have, was able to swing the balance of the fight with one thrown pebble?" She shook her head, faking sadness. "Who is the weak one now, Jason?"

Jason's fae-touched faction muttered, and some of them laughed. Jason scowled, and slunk away from the clearing, and not many of the fae-touched people went with him.

"He's still gonna be trouble," I whispered.

Kerry squeezed my hand. "I can handle him," he said.

"Indeed, you can, young prince. And not alone, I suspect." Somberly, Seanan dipped her chin in my direction. "Thank you, Lila

249

Deveroux, for your assistance this night." She raised her gaze to take in the rest of the people in the clearing. "Look well on this one, all of you. She has done us a great service. You are charged with her safety for as long as she is in our territory."

The gathered fae stared at me and, one by one, bowed or curtsied, even the ones in the trees. Even the yellow fairy woman, and it hardly looked sarcastic at all.

Should I curtsy back? Difficult to do, with Kerry hanging on to me so tightly.

Not that I minded.

Seanan placed a hand on Scott's shoulder and urged him forward. He came to me holding something small, dark, and rectangular in his hand.

"Seanan found this in her Mmuseumm. It's yours, right?" he said.

It was my phone. Yes! I snatched it up and checked to see how many texts I'd missed. "Thank you, Scott." I bit my lip and leaned in close. "Are you okay, kid? Do you have a place to stay?"

He smiled. "Seanan says she's going to take care of me."

I guess that was okay. His mom had probably given up on him decades ago. It would have been hard to explain how he hadn't aged in all that time, anyway.

Scott ran back to Seanan, who bent and kissed his forehead, which she'd refused to do for me. I guess the kid rated higher than I did.

"Is there anything else you would ask of us?" she said, turning back to me. "We owe you a debt."

What should I ask for?

I wanted my mom to accept me as I was. I wanted my dad full time. I wanted my brother back. I wanted Kerry. The first three things, no one could give me. And Kerry? I only wanted him if he wanted me back.

"Um," I said, not so eloquently. "That's okay. I don't need anything."

Her eyebrows rose. "You would leave the weight of obligation so unbalanced? Surely we can help you in some way."

"Get me back to my tour group unnoticed?"

"Granted!" Seanan gestured to the yellow fairy lady, who rolled her eyes and walked to stand at the entrance to the path back to the theater. She tapped her foot impatiently when I didn't follow her.

Seanan waved a hand at her rock-seat. "Come, Kerry. Take your place on the throne."

His grip on my hand didn't loosen. "No."

Seanan's eyebrows went up. "Why not?"

Kerry began to shake. I'm not sure anyone else could tell, but I was so close to him it was unmistakable. "I have given you everything I have. My dreams. My ambitions. My family. All of that I sacrificed for the good of our kingdom. But this is one thing I won't give up."

What now?

Seanan looked from Kerry to me, and back. She laughed. "Score another one for me!"

I frowned, utterly confused.

"What are your terms, Highness?" Seanan rasped, her voice falling back into the harshness it had held when I'd first met her.

Kerry's chin lifted. "I hold the throne in absentia while I go to college, which the kingdom will pay for."

My shoulders drooped. For one second there, I'd thought he'd meant he wouldn't give me up, not his dream of going to college. And it wasn't really *his* dream at all, but his brother's.

Seanan nodded, watching us both with a sly smile. "Tell the girl where you want to go to school."

Kerry studied me. I wondered what my face told him. If he figured it out, maybe he could tell me, because I wasn't at all sure what I felt.

"How about if I go to school in Utah?" he asked. "That's where you live, right?"

Now I knew what I felt. A huge grin burst from my core, right where my heart danced merrily inside me. "Right. That'll work."

Seanan said, "Done."

I glanced over, breathless, just in time for her to settle into her throne and lift her book into her lap.

I could have sworn the couple in a clinch on the cover bore an uncanny resemblance to Kerry and me.

"Kiss your hero, Kerry," Seanan said, "and get her back to her tour group before she's missed."

I blushed. Was he going to kiss me in front of everyone?

Apparently, the answer was yes.

"Aaaw," Seanan cooed. "I just love a happy ending."

about the author

MAUREEN MILLS lives in Draper, Utah, and is the happily married mother of five grown children, all of whom are proud geeks like their mom and dad. Her debut release, *Fires of Hell*, is an adventurous steampunk with a mysterious flare. When she's not playing with her imaginary friends, she enjoys knitting, reading, and sewing cosplay outfits for her kids—who look a lot better in them than she does. She and her husband are in the process of creating a steampunk truck camper from scratch. She also enjoys teaching beginning fiction writing for Canyon District's continuing education program. Reach out to her on Facebook at Maureen L. Mills or at www.maureenlmills.com.

About *Fires of Hell*

Murder, sabotage, and dashing airship captains—Airship Engineer Amelia Everley can handle them all. She hopes.

TERESA RICHARDS

you,
me, and
comic con

Teenacity
BOOKS

chapter one
SHOCK

The news came in a text, wicked early on the Saturday morning of our three monthiversary.

I stared at Jake's message:

we're nor working out. L8r.

The present I'd gotten him sat on my bedside table, still in the overnight packaging. Jake had been trying to get this special edition Pink Floyd grip tape for his skateboard for weeks, but it'd been out of stock at all the local stores and backordered online. I'd found it on eBay, paid way too much for it, and had it rush shipped to get it on time. Before today.

Was he seriously breaking up with me in a text? One that he hadn't even bothered to spell-check?

I typed in a response:

We're competing today, stop being an idiot.

I sat on the edge of my bed. My hands clenched and unclenched the fabric of my flannel pajamas.

I would not dissolve over this.

Jake was the first and last good thing to happen to me since my cousin Griffin left. Jake had kept me from falling to pieces. He'd watched me skate, then said I could do better. He'd pushed me, convinced me my skating was good enough to take to the next level. I was better and more confident because of him.

That was why I'd signed up for my first competition. Which was today.

Jake didn't respond to my text, so I called him while I worked the Fed Ed box open and took out his gift.

With my cell to my ear, I waited for him to pick up, practicing what I was going to say under my breath. "Will you please tell me why you're breaking up with me today, of all days, with no explanation? Because 'we're not working out' is not an explanation and, anyway, you know that's not true."

His phone rang again.

My words came tumbling out faster, louder, more insistent.

"We're good together. We have Green Day, black coffee, Zumiez skateboards, and twenty-three hours of accrued detention between us." My fingers tightened around my phone. "We are the very definition of good together."

Third ring. Why wasn't he picking up?

My blood turned hot in my veins.

"What more do you want, Jake? Are you expecting Katy Perry to jump out of a cake for you?"

Wait. Maybe I should dress up as Katy Perry and jump out of a cake.

No. Too much.

I took a deep breath. "I don't want to lose y—"

"This is Jake. Catch you later."

It was his voicemail. I felt myself deflate.

"Hey Jake, it's me. Can we talk?" I stopped, suddenly at a loss for words after hearing his voice. The fire inside me had gone out and, just like that, smoke was the only thing I had left. "Call me, okay?" I pressed end.

Jake's gift was still clutched in my fist. Standing, I found an old shoebox, rolled up the grip tape so it would fit inside, and scrounged in the hall closet for some wrapping paper. I scowled when I pulled out my only two choices—Christmas paper featuring soccer-playing snowmen, or a pink monstrosity with polka dots and yellow ducks.

Ugh. I did not have time to be creative. But Jake's gift had to be perfect. I pulled out a pile of skater magazines and flipped pages until I found a few that would complement each other. I cut them into strips and glued them around the box to make a pattern. As a joke, I cut out a tiny Superman shield and glued it to the front, right in the center.

Jake hated people who dressed up as superheroes. We'd spent Valentine's Day in the city, and there'd been this couple dressed up as Superman and Lois Lane mooning at each other on the subway. We'd spent the rest of the night laughing over how lame they looked. The next day, Jake drew a Superman shield in my notebook when I wasn't looking and when I saw it later in class I laughed so hard the teacher almost added another hour to my detention. The Superman thing had been a running joke between us ever since.

A lump formed in my throat and I summoned my anger to squash it.

Jake couldn't have meant to break up with me. He wasn't thinking straight. Or hadn't had enough sleep. Or was pissed about something else and was lashing out at me.

I had to make him remember why he'd asked me out in the first place and why we'd stayed together for so long.

So. My plan.

I'd go to the competition, where Jake was skating in three separate events, and skate my best set ever in my own event. My moves would win him back. That's how I'd caught his eye in the first place, and I could do it again.

When I was little, my cousin Griffin babysat me every day after school while my mom was at work. Instead of taking me to the regular park, like he was supposed to, Griffin took me to the skate park so he could practice his ollies and kickflips. Watching the skaters fly through the air, spinning and twisting with nothing but a board between them and the concrete, was life-changing. It went against every rule I'd ever known. I asked Griffin to teach me how to do it. He got me my own child sized board and the next day, my lessons began.

The first time I fell, it hurt. A lot. I sat there with tears in my eyes until this boy skated by and asked Griffin, "Is she just going to sit there crying all day?" Another boy said, "Yeah, get the girl off the ramp." They said it like I wasn't even there. Like I didn't even count as a person.

I'd hopped up, anger simmering inside me, and kept skating. The next time I fell, I only cried on the inside.

And the time after that, I didn't cry at all.

I had my ollie within a week, and pretty soon, I was showing those boys what was what.

My cousin had been the closest thing to a dad I'd ever had—just younger and more fun, I imagined, than a real dad would be. When Griffin left for his first tour of duty, I didn't cry, even though I wanted to. Instead, I went to the skate park and raged on the pavement, daring the concrete to try and take me down.

It hadn't. Nothing had.

"Avery, what are you doing up so early?" Mom asked when I entered the kitchen already showered and dressed for the day. "Are you going to the skate park in that?"

I followed her gaze to my outfit: black leggings under a stretchy purple miniskirt (the purple matched the streaks of color running through my dark hair), a loose-fitting tee layered over a black tank top, and my magazine-print, DC shoes. Okay, so the skirt wasn't practical for skating. Obviously. And neither was the tee that tended to slip off one shoulder when I moved. But this outfit was better than my standard tee-shirt and jeans combo for reminding Jake that he didn't want to break up with me.

Mom was dressed for work—today it was sky-blue scrubs with little rainbows. Sick kids liked little rainbows.

"I'm going to the city. The competition's today, remember?" I tucked back a piece of hair that had slipped out of my messy-on-purpose up-do.

She squinted at me. "So, you're *competing* in that outfit?"

I fidgeted. "Of course not. Duh." I turned so she could see the sling-bag on my back, which held Jake's awesomely-wrapped present, my knee pads, my helmet, and zero extra outfits. But she didn't know that.

"Okay," she said, her gaze slipping off me and back to her phone. She continued scrolling through her emails. "Don't forget your Metro Card."

"Got it," I said, patting the side-pocket on my bag.

She clicked off her phone and looked at me. "Good luck today. You and Jake are going to kill it."

"Yeah," I said, grabbing a bag of Cherry pop-tarts from a box in the sparsely stocked pantry. I ripped it open and took a giant bite, then headed for the front door.

"Did you see the email from Griffin?"

I froze. My cousin had sent an email? It'd been two weeks since we'd last heard from him and I'd been worried. "When did he send it? Is everything okay?"

"It came late last night. He's okay, but . . . well you should just read it."

Already I had my phone out and was searching for the email. "Why, did something happen to him?"

"No. It's just rough over there."

There it was. An email from Corporal Griffin Beckley.

"Why haven't you written him?" Mom said.

My head whipped up. She was staring at me, pinning me with one of her *I'm supremely disappointed in you* looks.

"I, um, just haven't."

Wait, *Corporal* Griffin Beckley? I glanced again at the email. He wasn't up for a promotion to Corporal yet. He needed another few months under his belt.

Unless . . .

My mouth went dry.

Unless a spot had suddenly gone vacant.

"Avery, he needs to hear from you."

I stuffed my phone in my pocket. "I know." My voice sounded scratchy. Hollow. I hesitated, then walked over to her and kissed her cheek. "Bye, Mom."

Her eyebrows lifted in surprise. I retreated.

My skateboard was leaning by the front door. I grabbed it, holding it in front of me like a shield as I left the house.

"Bye, honey." Mom's voice was cut short by the door banging shut.

When you see the jagged New York City skyline every day from across the river, with its bursts of high-rises and valleys in between, it kind of loses its magic. The train ride in from Jersey was a good warm-up in pointedly not looking at anyone—an essential life-skill for the streets of New York.

I read Griffin's email. A bomb had gone off during what was supposed to have been a routine drill. It killed one of his friends, leaving a vacancy that Griffin had been promoted to fill.

I couldn't read the rest. And I couldn't write a response. I tried, but the only word I could come up with was *why?*

Why had he chosen such a dangerous job? Why had he left me when I needed him so much? Why was he okay with the fact that we might never see each other again?

And I couldn't write any of that. He needed to focus on staying alive, not the fact that I sucked at life. So I sat back and closed my eyes, tightening my hands into fists and turning my thoughts to Jake.

By the time I got to Penn Station, my body was jittery with a tangle of nerves, anger, and hurt. I stuffed the feelings down and stared at a dot on the Find My Friends app. Time to focus.

Another sign Jake hadn't actually meant to break up with me: he hadn't blocked me from finding his phone.

The City was warm but not too warm, with a light breeze kicking off the buildings. It was crowded just to the point of feeling like you were in *the* place to be. I joined the throng of pedestrians ignoring each other on the sidewalk, heading away from Penn Station. A cloud of steam rose from the subway tunnels through a patch of metal grating on the ground. Hot dog stands dotted the way, selling overpriced and under-heated mystery meat.

And the cabbies honked. Always the cabbies honked.

I maneuvered around a group of tourists taking pictures with someone dressed up as Spiderman. A few feet away, Batman vied for the tourists' attention. Beyond him, Hello Kitty, Dora the Explorer, and Elmo all smiled and waved at passersby, trying to coerce them into posing for a photo. Once the tourists posed for the photo, they'd be guilted into tipping the actor sweltering inside a polyester suit.

I scowled. These actors were turning Times Square into a circus— I'd been noticing them more and more recently. And I wasn't even in

Times Square; I was several blocks south of it. The madness seemed to be spreading.

Just ahead, the third Hello Kitty I'd seen in the past five minutes retreated to an alcove and pulled off her plush head, revealing the person beneath the costume: an elderly woman who looked like she belonged at a Bingo match. Her silvery hair was streaked with dyed-blue sections. The woman took a drink of water, counted some bills, and stuffed them somewhere in her costume.

A laugh bubbled up inside me and I wished Jake were here to share the moment. Because, really, this was priceless. Hello Kitty could become our new Superman. I snapped a picture of the woman, skirted around a mom pushing a stroller, and continued following my phone toward Jake.

But . . .

I stopped walking, squinting at the dot on my screen. I turned in a slow circle, glancing at the nearest street sign to make sure I was where I thought I was.

Umm.

The dot on my screen was definitely not at Pier 62 Skate Park, where the competition was being held. That was further south. Right now I was heading straight west, toward the Hudson River.

What the heck, Jake?

I had an hour until check-in closed—enough time for a quick detour—but if I followed the dot, it would cut my warm-up way short.

I tried calling Jake again. This time, the call went directly to voicemail. I didn't bother leaving a message.

I called his sister next.

She picked up on the first ring. "It's Cassie," she said, a little too brightly.

"Hey, Cass, I'm looking for Jake. Do you know where he is?"

"Don't you guys have that skate thing today?"

"Yeah, but I can't get ahold of him and I don't think he's at the park."

"He left the house ages ago. Said something about wanting to be early to get a good warm-up spot. He should be there by now."

"Do you think he's hurt?"

"Umm, we haven't gotten a call or anything. Hang on a sec." In the background I heard her yell "Mom, have you heard from Jake at all?"

Pause.

Then she said into the phone, "We haven't heard anything. I'm sure he's fine."

Huh. "Okay, thanks."

I tapped a finger against my phone, thinking. The only social media account Jake kept active was his YouTube channel, and he only posted after he'd made a new skating video.

Still, I checked it.

Nothing new since yesterday.

He wasn't one to post status updates or pictures or inane social commentary, so I couldn't track him that way.

I called Ben, a friend of Jake's whose number I only had because they'd included me in a group text once. When he answered, he sounded out of breath. "Yeah?"

"Hey Ben, it's Avery."

Silence.

"Jake's girlfriend," I added.

"Oh." Heavy breathing. "Hey, Avery."

"You're competing today, right? Are you at the skate park?"

"Yeah, I'm here."

"Is Jake there? I need to talk to him."

More heavy breathing. Was he skating right now?

"I haven't seen him," he said.

"If you do, could you text me or something?"

"Sure." Ben's voice got softer, like he'd pulled the phone away from his mouth. "Yeah man, I'm coming." Then, back to me. "I gotta go."

"No problem," I said.

He'd already hung up.

Okay, so Jake had left his house ages ago, and he wasn't hurt. Which meant he should have already been at the skate park. But he wasn't.

So . . . where was he?

I checked the time again. Fifty-two minutes left. Argh, if I was going to go after him, I had to do it fast. I hopped on my board and sped away.

The closer I got to Jake, the thicker the tourists got. And the thicker the Spiderman look-alikes got. I started to see Avengers, anime characters, aliens, and those white soldier guys from Star Wars. I had to get off my board and walk, the characters got so thick.

I gazed around, my mouth dropping open. My pace slowed. My mind slowed.

I'd stepped into an alternate reality.

I bumped into a guy dressed as Captain America. He turned around.

Oh, wow, this one actually looked like the character he was dressed up as. Like, in a really good way. I'd found the teenage version of that guy in the movies!

"What is this place?" I breathed.

Captain America smiled. "It's Comic Con."

chapter two
OGLE

My gaze travelled beyond Captain America, beyond the crowds, and up. I was standing in front of a convention center. Beyond it was the Hudson River. A long line of people, many of them dressed up as characters from comic books, movies, and TV shows, snaked away from the entrance.

I took it all in. Was I still in Manhattan? The square at the base of the building was packed. Loud music blasted.

How had I not noticed the music until now?

Vendor stands were crammed into every available space. Artists offered prints at ten dollars a pop. A steampunk society handed out cards. Writers offered sample sheets of their comics. And people sold Comic Con merchandise, from light-up swords and foam Thor hammers, to Christmas ornaments and Pokeball bath bombs.

"Crazy, right?" Captain America said, nodding toward the vendors. "The good stuff is inside." He paused, giving me a once over. "Is this your first time? They'll be opening the doors in an hour—you made it just in time. Although, if you come again next year, you should get here earlier. I would have, only my dad had car trouble this morning. I had to get a cab to the train station, but the cabbie drove so slow that I missed the train."

I gawked at him.

"I came in from New Jersey," he continued. "I didn't want to wait for the next train so I took a ferry in and hopped a bus. It took forever." He glanced down at the skateboard dangling from my fingers. "Is that part of your costume?"

"Umm."

"Yeah, it's a little overwhelming your first time. But the line moves fast once the doors open. We'll be in soon."

Wait, what? I looked around, realizing I was in a line. *The* line. For Comic Con.

Seriously? I looked at my phone again. I was right on top of the dot. Jake was here. Somewhere in this madness. He could be anyone; half the people here had masks. Or other—bigger—head coverings.

I turned a circle and eyed a guy—or it could've been a girl, I guess—who was dressed like some sort of alien octopus with huge tentacles snaking several feet above its head. Its face was covered by a mask with bulging eyes and a mucous-y looking film. Another person was dressed like a giant tarantula, complete with a black head covering and six giant eyes arranged around his own. He crouched low to the ground and walked on all fours so he was creeping along, like the spider he was dressed as. He also seemed to be getting a kick out of terrorizing the people in line. I shuddered.

This was an official crazy-fest.

Could Jake have gotten up early this morning and dashed off a hasty break-up text, just so he could pursue some secret, creepy passion and be the first in line at Comic Con?

No. It was impossible.

Jake and costumes. No.

Jake and comic books. No.

Jake and superheroes. So much no.

So . . . why was he—

A guy in a yellow shirt stumbled backward, stepping on my toes and splashing something—beer, it smelled like—all over me. "Dude, watch it!" he yelled at the guy dressed as a tarantula, who was trying to edge him out of line.

Yellow Shirt Guy grabbed my arms, pinned them at my sides, and put me between him and the giant spider. He was breathing hard and trembling, like he had some major spider issues.

"Hey, let go of me," I said, trying to free my arms so I could pelt him with my skateboard.

Tarantula Guy got closer, like he could sense this dude's fear and was getting high on it.

Yellow Shirt Guy cowered behind me, trembling.

I tried to wriggle free, but his grip was solid. His fingernails dug into my skin.

"Ugh, you smell like year-old gym socks," I said.

"Using a lady as your shield? Not cool," said a voice from behind me. A Captain America-y voice.

Then a thud. A grunt. A shift in body weight.

My captor's arms fell away from me and I stumbled over, my skateboard flying out of my hand.

My reflexes took over. I tucked my elbows into my sides and twisted so my shoulder would hit the ground first. Tucked into a ball, I landed and rolled once.

I wasn't hurt. But I also wasn't done. Staying safely on the ground was beginner stuff.

I slapped my hand to the ground and used my momentum to push myself up, swinging my feet around so they were under me.

I stood up. Ta-dah! A perfect safety roll. Griffin would be so proud.

There was a smattering of applause. A circle had formed around me and everyone was gaping, wide-eyed, at me. Including Tarantula Guy with all eight of his eyes, though, of course, six were plastic.

269

"What?" I asked. "I used to fall off my board a lot."

Captain America stepped forward, holding his shield in one hand and my skateboard in the other. He handed me the board. "Are you okay?"

I shrugged, using the movement to check my body for damage without being too obvious about it. "Yeah, I'm fine."

The tension in the circle evaporated. Yellow Shirt Guy seemed to evaporate, too, slinking into the crowd. Tarantula Guy moved on.

"Your shirt's wet," Captain America said.

"It'll dry. I'll just smell like beer for the rest of the day." I wrinkled my nose. I'd have to buy a new shirt before I went home or my mom would kill me.

"I'm Cameron," Captain America said, shifting his shield and holding out a hand. He smiled again. He had very straight teeth.

I let him shake my hand. "I'm Avery."

"Nice to meet you, Avery. You're going to have a blast today, I promise. Did you come alone?"

"Uhh." I met his gaze. His eyes were very blue. I really just wanted to look into them and forget everything else.

"I'm meeting some friends here," he said. "They're further up in line. We'll show you around, if you want."

"Oh. Okay." I shook my head, clearing it from his blue eyes and straight teeth and Captain America-y good looks. "Actually, I'm looking for my boyfriend."

He raised an eyebrow.

"I mean, um, he's already here, I just don't know where. Maybe further up in line?"

"Oh," Cameron said. "He's not answering his phone?"

"Nope." I left it at that. I was not about to admit that Jake had maybe broken up with me and was now avoiding my calls so he could come to some geeky comic book conference instead of skating with me. Because that was apparently what he was doing.

Unless . . .

My stomach dropped.

What if his phone was here, but *he* wasn't? What if he'd lost it on the train or loaned it to someone and I was following a total stranger?

Why hadn't I thought of that earlier?

I texted Ben:

Any sign of Jake?

Ben responded quickly:

nope but he needs to get here quick. wrmups almost over

Which meant I needed to get back quick, too.

If Jake wasn't at the skate park, and his phone wasn't at the skate park, then the logical conclusion was that they were both here. Which was insane, but still made the most sense.

"I'll help you look for him," Cameron said. "He's got to be in this crowd somewhere."

I squinted at him. Why was he being so nice? Must be desperate for friends or something.

Cameron turned to the group behind us—these ones sporting elaborate costumes à la Game of Thrones. Fur and armor and . . . was that a wolf head?

"Hey, will you save our spot in line?" Cameron said. "I have to help Avery find her friend."

"My boyfriend," I clarified, trying not to focus on Cameron's perfectly square jawline, and looking instead at his hair. Which was the color of sand. I wondered, if you dribbled a handful of sand on top of his head, would you be able to see the grains or would it blend in perfectly with his hair?

I shook my head. *Stop it, Avery. You're here to find Jake, not ogle some nerdy Captain America look-alike.*

Cameron nodded. "Your boyfriend. Got it." He eyed my skateboard. "It'll get pretty crowded farther up in the line—keep that thing close so you don't whack anyone. Why'd you bring it anyway?"

I clutched the board to my chest, bristling. "This *thing* happens to be the coolest thing I own. And my favorite thing I own. I'm skating in a competition later today. Assuming I make it back in time." I checked my phone. Thirty-seven minutes left.

The smile died on Cameron's face. "Wait, you're not going in?" He gestured to the convention center.

Oops. "Well, not exactly."

"Do you have a ticket?" he pressed.

"No."

His shoulders seemed to deflate.

I spoke before thinking. "But, maybe I could come back after I compete—you can show me around then." Okay, Jake really *would* blow me off if he knew I was offering to go inside with this nerdy, though admittedly easy-on-the-eyes, comic con guy. What was wrong with me?

I snapped my mouth shut to keep it in freaking check.

"It's sold out," Cameron said.

One of the Game of Thrones guys piped up from behind us. He had a sword slung across his back and very hairy arms. "I saw a scalper back there—you could probably still get a ticket."

"But what about the verification?" said a girl wearing a long, velvety red dress that accentuated her excessive boobage. "How's she supposed to get around that?"

"What verification?" another guy said, this one wearing a green cape and holding a severed wolf head—fake, I hoped, even though it totally looked real.

"It's new this year," the girl said. "You had to register before you bought your tickets, remember? They're trying to cut down on people buying the place out and reselling—"

"It doesn't matter, I'm not going in," I interrupted. "I just came to find my boyfriend."

Silence. Chirping crickets and all that.

The Game of Thrones crew looked at me with varying expressions of sympathy. Like one might look at a mouse that wanted to be a lion.

I turned to Cameron. "You don't have to come with me, I don't want you to lose your spot in line. I'll find Jake on my own."

He sniffed. "I said I'd help and I'll help."

I scrutinized him. "Why? Why do you want to help me?"

He shrugged. "I like helping people. I *am* a superhero, after all."

I raised an eyebrow.

"Okay, that was lame. Sorry. I just . . . get so excited by this stuff. You've obviously never been here before and I think it'd be fun to show you around, even if it's only outside the convention center. That's all. I promise."

Ugh. If I let Cameron tag along, he might figure out the truth about Jake impulse-breaking up with me. And how lame would I look? I was clearly a horrible girlfriend for not knowing my own boyfriend harbored a secret passion for nerdism. Had the whole Superman joke been no more than an act to make him look tough?

Cameron interrupted my thoughts. "Do you know the difference between Spiderman and Deadpool?"

"Dead-what?"

"What about Marvel verses DC?"

I opened my mouth, but had no answer. Weren't they both comics?

Cameron grinned, like tripping me up was better than winning the lottery, and added, "And why is everyone okay with the fact that they keep changing the actor who plays Doctor Who?"

"Umm."

"Exactly! You need a guide, even if it's just while we're waiting around outside. The costumes are so much better if you know the context behind them. Like," he paused, scanning the crowd. He pointed at a guy holding the end of a leash. "Take the guy with the turtle, for example."

Wait, what?

I looked at the guy again. Followed the leash with my eyes. On the end of the leash was, in fact, an actual, real-life turtle. On the turtle's back sat . . .

I squinted. "Is that a severed head?"

"Yep."

"Geez, the special effects around here are amazing."

"Yep."

I waited for him to explain the turtle-with-severed-head.

He didn't.

"Fine, I'll ask. Why does that turtle have a severed head on its back?"

Cameron grinned. "What an excellent question. I'm glad you asked. It's from Breaking Bad. Season two. These bad guys killed this other bad guy and then sent his head into the desert on the back of a turtle for the police to find. Because the bad guy's nickname was Tortuga. Get it? Turtle in Spanish? Anyway, the turtle comes hobbling through the desert, the police guys close in, and then—Bam!—the turtle explodes, taking the police down with him.

"The funny thing is, that scene was such a big hit, but it actually started out as a joke. Like, the writers were brainstorming and someone threw it out there and they all laughed at the thought of an exploding turtle and it became this running joke and then someone thought, *Hey, that might actually work. We totally should do that.* So they did. And it was epic."

"So . . . if the turtle is going to explode, maybe we should get moving?" I said.

"Exactly! You never know what these crazy nerds will do next. The turtle might be wired to pop confetti out of its butt. It could explode at any minute."

I laughed. "Because confetti is the worst thing that could pop out of something's butt."

"Right? Okay, I think I've proven my worth." He put a finger on my elbow—just the whisper of a touch—to guide me away from Turtle Guy.

After the briefest hesitation, I let him. He was so easy to be with. So lighthearted. None of the brooding, angry, rage-against-the-world energy I created just by breathing. "Fine, you can help me. But just until we find Jake, then I have to leave. I'm already cutting it close."

His whisper-light touch became more firm.

I tucked a loose strand of hair behind my ear. "And, um . . . thanks."

Cameron led me toward the convention center and the ever-thickening crowd of fans. The music got louder as we neared the entrance.

"So, what does your friend look like?" Cameron said.

My boyfriend. Even though I said it in my head, I refrained from correcting him yet again.

"He's got dark hair—almost black—about shoulder length, and he's just a bit taller than me. Olive skin. Usually dresses like a skater." I scanned the crowd for his signature baggy jeans and t-shirt.

"He could be wearing anything here," Cameron pointed out. "Who are his favorite superheroes?"

I snorted. "Jake doesn't have favorite superheroes."

"Favorite comic books?"

"Nope."

"Favorite TV shows, then. Or a favorite movie? There has to be something."

"There really isn't. At least, not that he's ever told me. Honestly, the fact that he's here is a total shock. I've never heard him talk about comic books or superheroes or anything, except to make fun of them. He doesn't even really like movies. He spends all his time boarding and making boarding videos for his YouTube channel. He's trying to get a sponsor, and having a following helps."

Cameron snapped his fingers. "YouTube has an exhibit this year. And a panel or something—it might even be on the main stage."

Hope whooshed into my chest like a breath of fresh air after a stuffy subway ride. For the first time this morning, something finally made sense. Jake hadn't sold out and he hadn't been lying about hating Superman. He was just trying to get his channel on the radar. That would be the only thing more important to him than competing. "Yes! He must have come for that."

I felt my spirits lift. I might be able to find him and convince him to come watch me skate, even if he'd decided to drop out himself. This was not over. I could still wow him with my set and win him back.

"So he probably wouldn't be dressed up?" Cameron asked.

"Honestly, I think Jake would rather die than dress up in a superhero costume." Pause. "No offense."

Cameron smiled. "Hey, I get that cosplay isn't everyone's thing. That's okay."

I quirked an eyebrow at him. "Cosplay?"

"Nerd-speak for *dressing up*."

"Oh. So . . . what makes it *your* thing?"

Something sat on the tip of his tongue. I could almost see the struggle as he debated letting it out. But, after a moment, he just shrugged. "Check your phone again—is Jake close?"

Cameron's expression betrayed nothing. What was he holding back?

I tore my gaze away from his and examined my phone. "Find My Friends says we're right on top of him, but in this crowd, we're right on top of everybody. All this tells me is he's here, somewhere."

I zoomed into the map on my phone, studying it to see if my dot would separate from his at all so I could tell which way to go. It did, a tiny bit, and I turned left, angling toward the convention center entrance, and a large open space packed with people. We walked toward it.

A booth came into view, with a canvas banner stretched across the top that read: '*Z105.1—NOT your mother's radio station*' in graffiti-style writing. This was where the music was coming from.

Cameron nudged me. "What's Jake's last name?"

"Powers," I said.

Cameron sucked in a breath and bellowed, "Jake Powers! Jake Powers! Does anybody know Jake Powers?"

Heat rushed to my face. Kill. Me. Now. In addition to explaining to Jake—once we found him, of course—why I was looking for him even though he clearly didn't want to be found, now I'd also have to explain why I had an over-exuberant new sidekick.

I resisted the urge to shush Cameron. I'd agreed to let him help and, apparently, this was him helping.

"Has anybody seen Jake Powers?" he yelled.

A handful of people turned their heads. Well, a few people, a few superheroes, and a few Wookies.

One of the Wookies reached up to take off the headpiece of his costume.

A cascade of auburn hair tumbled down as the headpiece came off. I blinked.

Oh. This Wookie was a her. A Chewbacca-*lina*. And she looked old enough to be my mom.

"Did you lose your child?" she said to Cameron, concern wrinkling her brow.

"No, she lost her boyfriend," Cameron said, winking at me.

Oh, of course *now* he would get it right. Saying I lost my boyfriend sounded utterly immature and stupid, especially when this poor woman thought we'd lost a kid.

"Oh." Her features relaxed. She cradled the Wookie head in the crook of her elbow, as if she held a baby. "I'm Annalise. I'll help you look."

She turned to the rest of the Chewbaccas. "Hey, ya'll we have a missing boyfriend. Spread out and look for Jake Powers. Ten points to the first Chewy to find him!"

Ya'll? This woman was a long way from home.

But the Chewbaccas listened to her. They were a mix of people wearing full-on Chewbacca suits, fur and all, and others who just wore the masks or headpieces with brown clothing. A few of them took off their masks, but most left them in place. They fanned out and started asking around for Jake Powers.

"Don't worry, we'll find him," Annalise said.

Cameron had wandered away while Annalise was rallying the Wookies. I spotted him with a group of Avengers. He punched one of them in the arm and they both laughed at something.

I walked over. "So, you found your friends?"

"Yeah." He held out an arm and invited me into the group. "Guys, this is Avery. I'm helping her find her boyfriend."

"Ooh, you need help finding a boyfriend?" A girl dressed as . . . Supergirl maybe . . . sidled up to me. "What's your type?"

I eyed her, my body tensing up. I'd never gotten along well with other girls. They didn't understand me and I didn't understand them. I pointed to her outfit. "Isn't Supergirl from a different show?"

Cameron focused on the girl. "No, no, no, she already has a boyfriend, she's just looking for him. He's here somewhere but she doesn't know where."

"Oh," Supergirl said, her mood deflating like she'd really been looking forward to hooking me up with one of her geeky friends. The rest of the group included an Iron Man, a skinny Hulk, and a guy dressed in black with a bow slung over one shoulder. Cameron was definitely the best-looking of the bunch.

278

"I'm not Supergirl," the girl said. "I'm Scarlet Witch."

"Scarlet who?" I said.

"Her name is Brynn," Cameron said.

The girl shook her head. "Don't listen to him. I'm Scarlet Witch. You know, the girl with the twin brother who dies saving everybody?"

"Oh . . . right," I said, even though I had no idea what she was talking about.

I risked a glance at Cameron. One look at his face said he totally knew I had no idea what she was talking about. But he didn't call me out on it.

"I thought you were in line already." Cameron said to the group.

"Carly's holding our spot," Iron Man said. "We wanted to see the Chewbacca dance-off."

I laughed, thinking he was joking.

Oh, wait, he was serious. "Really? The Chewbaccas had a dance-off?"

"Yep," said Brynn. Or Scarlet Witch. Or whatever. "The DJ called all the Chewbaccas over to compete for an early-bird wristband to the George Lucas legacy exhibit. The dance-off ended a few minutes ago, and it was totally awesome."

I was having a hard time keeping a straight face. Had Jake seen the dance-off? I could only imagine how much fun he'd have making fun of it.

"Wow, the things you miss when you're stuck in the back of the line," Cameron said. "Stupid train. But, hey, if I'd gotten here on time I never would have met Avery." He winked at me.

Heat crawled up my neck and my insides went gooey.

Stop it! I gave myself a mental slap.

Annalise, the leader of the Wookies, came up behind me and clapped her hands together like she was calling order to an unruly classroom. "Come on, people, let's find Jake!"

The Avengers joined in the hunt for my boyfriend.

And I tried not to die of embarrassment. Well, embarrassment and amazement, really. It was a little overwhelming—all these people jumping to help a total stranger. Where were the brash New Yorkers I knew and loved who ignored each other unless the sky was literally falling?

"Your friends are so nice," I said to Cameron.

"Yeah, we take care of each other."

Brynn-slash-Scarlet-Witch was still standing beside us, even though the rest of the Avengers had split off to look for Jake. She was staring at something on her phone, her eyes tight. She grabbed Cameron by the elbow. "We have a problem."

 chapter three
SCRAMBLE

"Uh, oh. What problem?" Cameron said.

"You know that project my boss put me in charge of?"

"The Star Wars finale thing?"

While Brynn and Cameron talked, I scanned the crowd for Jake, spotting several Wookies still on the hunt.

"Yes, the Star Wars finale. Well, apparently the acting company we hired has been hit with the stomach bug and all their actors are puking their eyeballs out right now. They've completely bailed—the manager just sent me an email—and now I have zero actors. And I can't get ahold of my boss." Her voice was rising in pitch by the second. "I knew we should have hired a bigger company—one with more actors or a guarantee or *something*, but no, my boss had to save a buck, and now I'm the one who's gonna get fired."

"Wait, you work for Comic Con?" I said, still picking through the crowd with my eyes. "Aren't you a little young?"

"She's an intern," Cameron said. "Her dad knows someone."

He gripped Brynn by the shoulders. "We'll figure this out. Hire different actors."

Brynn's lower lip trembled. "The other big companies are already booked up. But this is the *Grand Finale*, Cameron. It has to be huge."

She sniffed and wiped at her nose. "And what about the fundraiser? We can't expect people to donate to the troops if there's no show!"

My head whipped around. "Donate what to the troops?"

Cameron explained. "Her boss is the marketing director for Comic Con and he had this idea to have convention goers donate to a worthy cause, in order to . . . how did he put it?"

"To demonstrate that the Comic Con franchise is globally aware and socially responsible." Brynn said, like she was reciting a line she'd heard a thousand times. "This year, they're collecting donations for a group that helps injured soldiers transition back to real life when they return from active duty."

I felt my mouth drop open.

Griffin.

Maybe something like this would help his friends, and . . . him, if he ever needed it. "That's really great," I said.

"I know, right?" Brynn was full-on crying now, her voice going all high and squeaky. "Collecting for the troops was my idea." She hiccupped. "And now we're not going to have anything to send them."

I hesitated. I couldn't bring myself to write Griffin a measly little letter, but maybe I could support him in a different way.

"So, what exactly do you need to get this show back on track?" I asked. "Just actors? Anything else?"

"No, just the actors. We rented the costumes; they're already here."

"What about the script?" I pressed. "How long is it?"

"Aren't the parts pre-recorded?" Cameron asked Brynn. "You really just need stand-ins, right?"

Brynn cocked her head. "Yeah, I guess so."

"So, you just need people to wear the costumes and stand onstage?" I said.

"Well, they can't just stand there doing nothing. There's a fight scene at the end. And they'll have to pretend they're talking to each other before that."

"Right, but if they don't have to learn lines, how hard could it be?"

Brynn shrugged. "Not hard, I guess."

Okay, I was getting excited. Here was something I could *do* for Griffin. Finally. Something other than just sitting around worrying.

I checked the time—twenty-four minutes to check-in. How long could it take to recruit some actors from this bunch of people who clearly loved attention? I'd be fine without a warm-up if it came to that. Griffin was more important. "I'll help you find actors. Let's save your show."

Cameron was staring at me, one eyebrow raised. The look on his face was one I'd seen before—on other guys' faces when my ollie went higher than theirs. A mixture of awe and respect.

Brynn made a quick list of all the parts that needed to be filled for the production and texted it to me. Cameron and I went around looking for recruits, while Brynn worked on an incentive to offer them. She thought she could get them wristbands for one of the next-day events but had to make some calls.

"So, how should we vet these actors?" Cameron asked. "We don't want to recruit any crazies."

"Good point. What if Tarantula Guy took off his costume to go to the bathroom and we accidentally hired him?" I tapped my phone against my thigh, thinking. "Okay, what if we played a little trivia game? See how they answer some simple questions?"

"Yeah, that could work," Cameron said. "They can't be yes or no questions, though. We need something that'll show us their personalities. Or at least how easy they'll be to work with."

"Okay, how about *Which Star Wars character do you identify most with and why?*"

Cameron glanced at me sideways. "What would your answer to that be?"

I hesitated. Crap. I couldn't think of a single Star Wars character's name.

He laughed. "I knew it. Have you ever even seen Star Wars?"

I lifted my chin. "Of course I've seen Star Wars."

"Which one?"

"Umm."

"An original or a new one?"

I shook my head. "I don't know. I watched it with my mom. There was this big, giant space ship. Does that help?"

Cameron laughed. "Nope. Sorry, you wouldn't be allowed to join our stage production based on your answer to that question."

"Hey!" I punched him in the arm.

"That means it's a good question. Its weed-out success rate is now tried and true."

"But I'm not crazy; just uninformed," I pointed out. "Ignorance wouldn't ruin the show."

"Maybe."

"Okay, how about this question?" I said. "*When the zombies rise up to take over the world, what's your plan of action?*"

Cameron hesitated. "Run?"

"Lame! That is such a cop-out answer."

"All right, smarty pants. What's your answer?"

"Easy," I said, thinking fast. "I would write a best-selling book about the benefits of a brain-based diet and call it The Seven-Day Zombified Fix. It would be the latest and greatest diet fad, guaranteed to melt away those extra inches and pounds. The slogan could be 'Brains for breakfast, lunch and dinner.' Zombies are people too, and everyone wants to be told their cravings are good for them. They'll buy up my books by the dozen. Then when I become filthy rich, I will fly my private jet to my own personal island and live there in peace and tranquility for the rest of my life."

Cameron looked at me, like he was deciding if I was crazy-weird or crazy-brilliant. "Wow," he finally said. "That is a very detailed plan. So, will you be a zombie living on your personal island or is the plan for you to keep your humanity long enough to escape?"

"Oh, I'll be the last human left. Obviously. They won't kill the one person telling them it's okay to eat brains. I'll be, like, their favorite celebrity." I paused, cocking my head. "The other option is to challenge them to a skate-off and laugh when their limbs start popping off. But I'd go with the diet plan first."

"Okay, I have to admit, that was a cool answer. You're hired again."

"Aw, thanks."

We went around asking people the zombie question, and getting reactions that ranged between *That's the dumbest question I've ever heard* to *I've been waiting my whole life for someone to take me seriously on this and I have the perfect answer and here's why*. There was a sweet spot in the middle, somewhere between indifference and psycho conspiracy theories, and those were the ones we invited to be part of the show. Most of them jumped at the chance to be on the main stage for the final number. The fact they'd get a wristband to one of tomorrow's events, and free lunch during the dress rehearsal at noon, sweetened the deal.

Soon, we had all the parts covered but one: Jabba the Hutt. Brynn had told us that whoever played Jabba had to be tiny in order to fit into the Jabba suit—which was lined with layers of rubber flab—its own built-in fat suit. We found a few teenage girls that could have done it, but they all flat-out refused as soon as we mentioned the fat suit.

"Maybe one of the interns could do it," Cameron said, after we'd been rejected by the fourth super-skinny girl we saw. "Let's go find Brynn."

"Hey, why are you helping with this?" I asked as we walked. "You don't work for Comic Con, too, do you?"

"Nah. But Brynn's my friend and I hate to see her so stressed. Plus, my brother Joey served in the army for a few years. I want to support the fundraiser."

"Really? Where's he stationed? My cous—" My voice hitched. I swallowed and tried again. "I know someone in the army. Maybe they're serving together."

A shadow crossed Cameron's face. "Joey's not in the army anymore."

For the first time since we'd met, silence stretched between us. It was a searching kind of silence, like a spotlight trying to find the actor on a dark stage.

The silence felt too raw, too real. I had to break it before it exposed me.

I said, "Well, hopefully we saved the show. Brynn will be able to find someone to play Jabba, right?"

"Sure," Cameron said. But he still seemed lost in the silence.

We spotted Brynn and I sped up, weaving through the crowd. I handed her the list we'd made of our volunteers and their cell numbers. "Ta-da! They're all planning on a dress rehearsal at lunch. Your show has officially been saved!"

Brynn scanned through the list, her eyes lighting up. "Oh, this is perfect! Thank you so much!"

Cameron caught up to us. "We can't find a Jabba—that's the only part missing. Are there any interns that would fit into the suit?"

Brynn shook her head. "Nope. I already thought of that. I'd wear it myself, but I'm too tall." She paused, her eyes landing on me. "But Avery would fit."

chapter four
RUN

O h, no.
    I stepped back, squirming under Brynn's gaze.

Cameron looked at me too, as if with new eyes.

My face went hot. I was not going onstage, in a fat suit, in front of thousands of people. Even for Griffin. Recruiting other people to wear the costumes was one thing. Wearing one myself was another thing entirely. Especially a costume as embarrassing as an ugly, blubbery alien. What if Jake saw? I would never live it down.

I scrambled for words. "Um, hello? I'm not going in, remember? I don't have a ticket."

"The actors don't need tickets," Brynn said.

"But the competition. I have to go, like, right now. I'm already going to miss my warm-up." Crap, what time was it? I pulled out my phone. Thirteen minutes left. Oh, crap, crap, crap. I was going to have to ride hard to make it.

"Jabba's part is really easy—you can miss the dress rehearsal. Just come back when you're done skating."

I took a step back, trying to think of another excuse. My phone buzzed with an incoming text. I scrambled for it, thankful for the distraction. The text was from Ben:

287

Jake is here. Don't no where he came from, he's been MIA all morning. Where are u?

My pulse ticked up. *What?!* Jake was at the skate park? When did he leave, how did I not notice, why would he stay here all morning and leave right before they opened the doors? My fingers curled around the bottom hem of my shirt and I squeezed, trying to ground myself. "I have to go."

Cameron caught my elbow. "Are you okay?"

"Yeah, I'm just really late. I've got to go."

"So, will you come back later?" he said. "Will you be Jabba tonight?"

I hesitated. Brynn was staring at me, her hands locked together in front of her in a pleading gesture.

Cameron stepped closer to me. Way closer, like he wanted to tell me a secret. His breath was hot against my ear. His fingers curled gently around my arm.

I shivered.

"Hey Avery?" he said, quiet enough so it was just for me. "It's okay to let go and have fun—even nerdy fun. You don't have to hide all the time."

I turned so I was looking straight in his eyes. Those deep, blue, piercing eyes. How had he seen me? How had he known?

My skin was on fire. His face was inches from mine.

"Yes, I do," I whispered. Then I turned and ran.

I ran right into Annalise, who was still cradling her Chewbacca mask in one arm. "Hey, honey, the Wookies have searched the crowd. There's no sign of a Jake Powers anywhere."

"Thank you," I said, unable to look her in the eyes. She'd helped me—a messed-up skater girl from New Jersey—without knowing me at all. Brynn and Cameron were helping the veterans. And here I was, ditching out on them.

288

But I had to. I didn't know what else to do.

I left Comic Con.

And Cameron let me.

I wanted him to stop me—at least, part of me did. Part of me wanted to stay here all day. To show Cameron—everyone—the real me without fear of what they might think. Part of me wanted Jake to have come here in some wacky costume—to have been hiding this part of himself—so I could have admitted I'd been hiding, too. That I was still that little girl at the skate park who refused to cry, even when I really wanted to.

But he didn't. He hadn't. And the real me was buried so deep that sometimes I felt I didn't know her at all.

I shook my head, trying to clear out the crazy. I didn't belong at Comic Con. It was time to get back to something I knew. The aggression, the passion, the anger—that was my world. That was where I felt safe. Not here with these costumes and dancing Wookies and tenderhearted superheroes.

A line of sweat dribbled down my back, right between my shoulder blades, as I hurried away from the convention center. My fingers ached from being curled around the wheels of my board all morning. The straps of my bag cut into my skin and my helmet thumped against my back as I ran. Once I got far enough away for the crowd to thin out, I dropped my board and hopped on.

My legs pumped, in sync with my racing heart. Why had I let myself lose track of the time like that? Why had I let myself get sucked into the atmosphere? How had Jake gotten back so fast?

Why had those people been so nice?

I refocused, pumping harder. I did not want to be disqualified from my first competition because I'd missed check-in.

A traffic light ahead turned red.

I sped up, shooting into the street out of turn and cutting off a cabbie, who leaned on his horn and flipped me off.

Six blocks down, only eight more to go.

A stitch started in my side.

I pumped harder, wishing my board could somehow grow wings. Too many people lived in this blasted city.

At ten blocks down with only four more to go, I was forced to stop at a busy intersection. I pulled out my phone to check the time.

An invisible, thousand-pound weight slammed me in the gut like a sucker-punch.

I had four minutes till registration closed.

When the street cleared, I launched myself into it and worked my board harder than ever.

I rode as fast as I could. Even though my feet ached and the stich in my side now had a death grip on my lungs. I'd been training for this competition—looking forward to it for months—working out the best way to introduce myself to any brand reps that might be there. I couldn't just give up now.

Three blocks to go.

I kept skating. Dodging around people and strollers and street vendors. Dashing into the streets before the signals turned, narrowly missing some up-close-and-personal contact with a few choice vehicles.

Two blocks. I hissed at the cramp in my side.

My time had to be up.

One block.

But maybe they'd still be open. Just a smidge longer than they were supposed to.

I redoubled my pace and sped down the last block. I scanned the crowd ahead, trying to spot the registration table . . . there it was . . . I adjusted my course. Arrived at the booth. Skidded to a stop and smacked a hand down on the table.

The girl behind the table jumped. A guy seated next to her stopped what he was doing—cleaning up, it looked like—to gawk at me.

My pulse thrummed in my skull. Pain stabbed at my side. "Am I too late?"

They exchanged a glance and the girl said, "What's your name?"

"Avery Rollins."

The guy shuffled through a box and pulled out a card. "Got it. Here ya go." He handed me a number and a foil sticker with the competition's logo on it.

I clutched my chest, trying to work out the stich. "Wow, so I made it? I'm in?"

"Sure, why not? We're still here," the girl said. She consulted a paper attached to a clipboard. "You skate at 2:15. General warm-ups are over, but Area One on the far side of the park will be open all day." She pointed it out on a map.

I laughed. It came out sounding giddy and maniacal. I swallowed, trying to slow my breathing. "2:15. Got it." I stuffed the number and sticker into my bag. "Thanks!"

I pressed a hand into my side.

Wow, I'd made it. I had to tell Cameron.

I pulled out my phone to send him a text, then stopped, my fingers hovering over the screen.

I couldn't text Cameron. I didn't have his number.

My happy-bubble popped. It hurt worse than my cramp.

Whatever, he wouldn't have cared anyway, said a voice inside my head.

But I squashed the thought. Because, actually, Cameron would have cared. He cared about a lot of stuff he had no business caring about. Was he just unique like that or was it a Comic Con thing?

My stomach churned as I realized I'd never see him again. Why hadn't I thought to get his number? At least so I could have thanked him again for trying to help me. I'd spent the morning thinking only about myself.

And I couldn't ask Brynn for his number—not after I'd left like that.

I found a spot to sit and catch my breath.

So many of the girls I watched were tiny enough to play Jabba at Comic Con. Brynn might have to sweeten the deal, but one of them would go for it, surely. Or maybe their skinny Hulk friend could help them out if he slouched down a bit. Either way, they'd find someone for sure. It'd just take some time. And, anyway, it wasn't my problem.

I got on Twitter and typed #NYCC, the official hashtag that had been plastered all over outside the convention center. There were pictures of people posing with their favorite superheroes. Pictures of the wildest, wackiest costumes imaginable, and some that were beyond imagination. Also, a video of some Wookies dancing.

I peered closer. The video was tagged, #epicwookiedanceoff

Two or three of the Wookies were clearly better than the others. Was one of them Annalise?

I watched the video three times and scrolled through some more pictures and tweets:

so excited for #NYCC. waiting in line to score some wristbands.

Who's going to win the costume contest today? This guy!

first time ever at nycc im so nervous!!

One tweet stood out from all the others. Posted a few minutes ago by @CammerMan_52:

The tradition lives on. This one's for you, Joey. #ComicCon #brothersforever

Included was a picture of Cameron inside the convention center, posing next to a giant spaceship that looked like it came straight out of a movie; I just had no idea which one.

I squinted at the picture—his sandy blonde hair and perfect smile—while warmth trickled through my body and erased the pain in my side. What was Cameron doing right now? Had the first panel started yet? Where was his brother, if he was no longer on active duty, and why weren't they at Comic Con together?

I clicked on Cameron's profile. My finger hovered over the Follow button. I almost pressed it.

Almost.

But what about Jake? I could still find him—try to get him back. Nothing in my life had to change.

If I wanted to know Cameron's secrets, he'd want to know mine. He wasn't like Jake, who'd never even considered that I might have emotional baggage and that's why I skated so hard.

A whoop from the crowd made my head jerk up. I put my phone away and wandered over to Area One, where the noise was coming from.

This was the only space still open for warm-ups. Skaters competed for space on the ramps like ants on a slice of cake. But the half-pipe had cleared and everyone in that area was watching a single boarder. He was tricking out, and he was on fire. His skating was effortless. He moved like the board was a part of him, and when he flew through the air, it was almost like he had wings.

My gaze travelled down the skater's body. The black tee-shirt that fluttered to reveal muscled abs at the apex of each move. The way his body curved when he gripped the board at the height of each trick.

Then I noticed his helmet. And the familiar Pink Floyd sticker. My breath hitched in my throat.

It was Jake.

chapter five
SKATE

Jake was the boarder holding everyone captivated.

He wore no costume and he had nothing to hide. He was not out of breath like I was—like he should have been if he'd really been at Comic Con all morning. Jake was confident, and strong, and sure. Just the same as he'd always been.

My lungs threatened to collapse. I couldn't breathe.

I wasn't confident and strong and sure. I was a lonely girl with no dad, a worn-out mom, and a best friend halfway around the world getting shot at every day. I was terrified for Griffin, and it was eating me up inside. How was I supposed to be strong all the time? I was not as strong as Jake, even though I'd been telling myself I was.

Someone grabbed my arm.

I jumped.

"Avery, you made it." It was Ben.

I rounded on him. "Where was Jake this morning? Was he here the whole time? Were you just covering for him? Did you both laugh at how stupid I was to believe he wouldn't be here as early as humanly possible?"

Ben's eyebrows shot up. "No. What are you talking about? I texted you as soon as I saw him, I swear." He peered at me. "Are you okay?"

I was not okay. Jake had sent me a cryptic break-up text, and then he'd turned into a ghost. Where had he been all morning?

"I'm fine." My feet were frozen for a fraction of a second. Then the ice melted and I stormed forward, pushing my way through the crowd.

I got as close as I could and waited. Waited for Jake's little show to end. Waited for my blood to cool. Waited for the knot around my lungs to loosen its death grip so I could breathe.

I clenched and unclenched my fists. Wiped my palms on my skirt. Practiced what I was going to say to him.

What was I going to say to him?

When Jake got off the half-pipe, people swarmed around him, clapping him on the back and asking him questions in rapid-fire succession.

"Great warm-up, man."

"Dude, you've got moves."

"Where do you practice?"

"How long did it take to get your kickflip?"

A girl wearing a skimpy outfit clearly not meant for skating sidled up to Jake, grabbed his face, and full-on kissed him. With no warning.

The crowed whooped and cheered.

The girl pulled away, but stayed glued to Jake's side, looping her arm through his. He made no effort to shake her off.

So. He *had* dumped me.

My blood caught fire, but I had to be tough about this. Show him he couldn't hurt me and that dumping me was a big mistake.

I stepped into his way. "Where were you all morning?"

Jake froze. His jaw tensed, but his eyes darted to the side, like maybe he'd been expecting a fight from me but not a scene.

The air around us went still.

The girl on his arm narrowed her eyes at me in a death glare.

Jake pulled his helmet off. "Avery. Didn't you get my text?"

Oh, his voice. It was so rugged and sexy.

I squared my shoulders, determined not to let him see what he did to me. "Yeah, I got your text. Nice timing, by the way, the *day* of the competition. Real classy, Jake."

"I wasn't trying to be classy, I was just trying to break up with you." His tone was matter-of-fact, but his words stung.

"Burn!" someone said.

My cheeks went hot, like I'd been slapped. I fired back with the only thing I could think of. Even if it wasn't true, it would embarrass him. "I followed you this morning. I know you went to Comic Con."

Jake laughed. "Why would I go to that geek-fest? I've been here since dawn."

"No you haven't; I followed your phone signal." I bit my lip, realizing I'd said too much. But I couldn't take it back now.

He shook his head. "You're insane. You must have been following the loser who stole my phone on the train this morning. Yeah, that's right," he said, seeing the wave of panic that must have crossed my face. "The creep got my wallet, too. So maybe you could run on back to that slime pit and get it for me."

Shame crawled up my neck. "But Ben said you were gone all morning."

The girl hanging on Jake smiled, all saccharine sweet. "He wasn't on the ramps 'cause he was with me. My apartment's right over there." She pointed across the street. "He's been with me for weeks, he just didn't have the guts to tell you."

All the air whooshed out of my lungs like I'd been sucker-punched in the gut.

Jake blinked, like her words surprised him just as much as they had me. But he didn't deny it. "Avery, I'm sorry," he finally said. "It just happened."

I couldn't look at him. My stomach twisted, threatening to expel everything inside it onto the ground. My whole morning had been a waste. "Whatever, Jake."

My hands clenched into fists. Why hadn't I just stuck to the plan? Show off on the ramps. Be hardcore. Win him back. That little tramp hanging on him looked like she'd rather die than step on a skateboard—Jake couldn't want someone like that.

But . . . did I really want someone like Jake? Someone who would cheat on me?

A man approached Jake and shook his hand. "I'd like to talk to you about representation, son. I hear you can land an ollie 540."

Jake grinned. "You heard right."

"He's the best there is," the girl said.

I spoke before the man could continue. "You know what, Jake? I'm gonna save my moves for someone who deserves them."

The crowd laughed.

I hopped on my board and skated away, my face burning with a mixture of shame and vindication. I fumed through a horrible warm-up—there was no room to do anything with all the other skaters fighting for space.

I waited for my turn to skate. I watched some amazing skaters. And, also, some not-so-amazing ones. I sort-of made some friends. I fell in with this group of skater girls who all seemed to know each other, and one of them asked where I lived and how long I'd been skating while we were eating lunch. They lived in Jersey, too, it turned out, and said we should skate together sometime.

I told myself Jake was a jerk and I shouldn't be sad he was gone. Still, his betrayal hurt.

I stalked twitter to distract myself—the Comic Con feed in general and @CammerMan_52 in particular. I found a tweet from @FanGirlBrynner—that must be Brynn—that Cameron was tagged in:

Never been so stressed in my life. Skinny short people suck. #NYCC finale @CammerMan_52

My chest tightened. So she hadn't found a Jabba yet.

298

True, it wasn't my problem. But I still felt bad, knowing I could have solved it and chose not to. What kind of a person did that make me?

Cameron had posted again, this time without a picture:

George Lucas exhibit was jaw-dropping. Joey would have loved it. #NYCC

My brain caught on the words *would have*.

I chewed my food slowly, musing over all the things I didn't know. Where was Cameron's brother and why wasn't he at Comic Con? Would Brynn be able to find someone to wear the Jabba suit in time? Why had Jake cheated on me and why did it hurt so bad?

Also, what was Griffin doing right now and why couldn't I bring myself to write him a freaking letter?

I wrote Brynn a text, asking if she'd found a Jabba yet. Then I deleted it. Then I re-wrote it. And deleted it again.

When it was my turn to skate, I put it all out there. Channeled my anger and hurt and fear into my skating. My turns were sharp, my landings clean, my skating bigger and more aggressive than ever. I tore through my routine and placed second overall in the women's round.

But it didn't make me hurt any less.

I managed to avoid Jake and his friends the entire day, but after it was all over, Ben found me. He held his board in one hand and an energy drink in the other. "Hey, great run. Congrats on your medal." He pointed at the paper certificate they'd given me, with a picture of a medal in the center.

"Thanks. Good for fifteen percent off skate accessories at the West Side Skate Shop." I held it up so he could see that the award doubled as a coupon.

He hesitated, like he wasn't sure if he should say whatever he was thinking.

I saved him. "I'm sorry I yelled at you this morning."

His eyes went wide. "No, don't be! I'm sorry about Jake. He's an idiot."

"Yeah."

"You're better off without him."

"I know." I looked away. My phone buzzed with a text but I left it in my pocket.

"Hey." Pause. He waited for me to look at him. When I did, he said, "If you ever want to hang out, give me a call, okay? I think you're a really cool girl."

"Oh." My cheeks went hot. "Okay."

He finished the last of his drink and tossed the container into a bin. "I guess I'll see ya around."

The way he said it, I wasn't sure if it was a question or a statement. "Sure."

I watched him walk away. Pulling my phone out , I gathered up my stuff. The text was from Brynn:

The girl who finally agreed to play Jabba quit after the dress rehearsal and I'm having zero luck finding anyone else. Any chance you'd reconsider? Please, oh please, reconsider.

Before I could respond, or even begin to reconsider, Amy came over to congratulate me. She was one of my new friends from lunch and she'd taken fourth. "Tight set, lady. We should skate together soon."

I was trying to stuff my helmet and pads back into my bag. "Yeah, that'd be cool."

"Are you doing the Summer Classic next month?" she asked.

I squinted at her. "I haven't heard of that one."

"Registration's still open, I think. You should sign up—we can go together."

"Sounds fun. Maybe I will."

I gave my helmet another shove before realizing why it wasn't fitting into my bag—Jake's present was in the way. I pulled out the carefully wrapped box. Stared at it. What was I going to do with it now?

"Amy, let's go!" a girl said. Danielle, maybe? She'd fallen on her initial drop-in and been disqualified, but everyone said she was really good.

"I'm coming." Amy turned back to me. "Want to get some food with us?"

"Sure," I said, rearranging my bag so everything would fit and stuffing the present back in. "Where are we going?"

"Hard Rock Café."

"You know that's right in the middle of Times Square, right? You really want to fight the tourists for The Hard Rock on a Saturday night?"

The other girls joined us. "It's tradition," Amy said. "We always go there after skating. Emily's in love with their sweet potato fries."

"And one of the bartenders," Danielle added, nudging Emily in the shoulder.

Emily made a pouty face. "Rico doesn't work there anymore."

"The Hard Rock has plenty of hot bartenders," Amy said. "We'll find you a new one." She hopped on her board and skated out of the park. "Unless I find him first!" She dodged to the side for a quick trick on the curb while the others scrambled to catch up with her.

I needed to respond to Brynn, but I didn't want to get left behind. What would I say to her anyway? I still couldn't bear the thought of going on stage in a fat suit in front of thousands of people. But maybe that wasn't a good enough reason not to help.

We boarded until the sidewalks got too crowded—a few blocks away from Times Square—then continued on foot.

That's when I saw it—the red, white and blue shield.

My breath hitched in my throat and I stopped walking.

Danielle bumped into me from behind. "Ugh, what's with all the losers?"

Captain America turned. It wasn't Cameron.

Of course it wasn't Cameron. Why would he leave Comic Con to try and mooch tips off of the tourists in Times Square? Still, I was disappointed. It was like seeing a great half-pipe only to get closer and realize it was full of potholes.

Beyond the imposter Captain America stood another one. And beyond him, a cluster of Spider Men were trying to photo bomb the tourists.

Amy turned around. "I know, right? I hate Comic Con. They're turning Times Square into a circus."

I felt my defenses go up. "It's not Comic Con's fault. These people are just independents."

"How do you know?" Emily said.

"Well. Uh, I met some of them this morning and they were really nice. The ones at Comic Con, I mean. And they're all at the Javits Center right now, not out on the streets."

"Hey," Danielle yelled to a group of them. "Standing around looking stupid and bullying tourists is not a job, or a legit hobby. You all need to get a life."

My grip tightened on my board and my face flushed with heat.

We got in line for a table, but my mind was suddenly somewhere else. On someone else.

Someone who carried a shield, just not the same kind I did.

Man, what was wrong with me? Scoping out hot bartenders at the Hard Rock was a great way to end the day.

It just wasn't—I realized—how *I* wanted to end my day.

I checked twitter to see if Brynn had written anything else. She had. Thirty-seven seconds ago:

I'm done #PeopleSuck

My face burned with shame. People did suck. *I* sucked.

Okay, maybe I could help her without embarrassing myself. Sure, I would know it was me beneath the suit, but no-one else would. My face would be completely covered, right? All I had to do was wear a costume and go onstage. If I did, I'd be helping Brynn and doing something brave for Griffin, hopefully without exposing myself in some embarrassingly public display. Then, when it was over, I could go find Cameron and . . . well, I didn't know what I'd do. But at least I'd get to see him again.

I said, "Hey, guys, I have to go."

"Aw, why?" Amy pulled a pouty face.

"I'm not feeling well. The thought of sweet potato fries is making me sick." I clutched my stomach for show. Actually, sweet potato fries sounded pretty darn good. Or, at least they had. Until . . . they hadn't.

"Boo," said Amy.

"I'll text you about skating together next week," I said.

"Fine," she grumbled.

Danielle waved, "Bye, Avery. We'll send you pics of all the hot bartenders!"

I worked my way through The Hard Rock crowd, glancing at my phone. It was almost five o'clock. What time did Comic Con end? I texted Brynn:

I'll do it

As soon as I had a clear stretch of sidewalk outside, I dropped my board, grappling with the fact that I was now officially crazy.

I, Avery Rollins, was going to Comic Con. On purpose this time.

chapter six
BEG

Fifteen minutes later, out of breath and crazy nervous for what I was about to do, I stood outside Comic Con. I was ready to save the day.

Also, I was stuck outside.

Brynn wasn't answering her phone or responding to texts. Maybe she'd had a nervous breakdown and flushed her phone down the toilet.

I commented on her latest tweet, and also on one of Cameron's from earlier in the day, that I was waiting outside to help. But neither of them wrote back.

I went to the entrance, where an attendant sat in a booth popping Cheetos into his mouth three at a time. "Cutting it a little close, are we?" the attendant said around his mouthful. "You know it's over in two hours?"

Oh, good, I still had two hours. "Well, I'm just here for the final show. I'm in it—is there a back entrance or something?"

The guy looked at me, his mouth hanging open slightly. Orange Cheeto bits clung to his teeth. "You're in the show?" He repeated, like he wasn't sure he'd heard me right.

"Yes. I'm Jabba the Hutt. But I don't know where to go."

He gave me a once over. "Do you have a ticket?"

"No, but the girl in charge said the actors didn't need tickets."

"So, you're an actor?"

"Well, not really, exactly. That is, normally I'm not. But they needed someone to wear the Jabba suit that was skinny and short and, well, I guess I fit the bill. So, where do I go? It's starting soon, right? I'm sure they're wondering where I am."

The guy stared at me. Narrowed his eyes a bit. "Nice try, sweetheart."

My mouth dropped open. "Seriously? You're not going to let me in?"

"Nope."

I stood there, staring at him, while he went back to his Cheetos.

Okay, new plan. I whirled around and went in search of a scalper.

The forty bucks in my wallet turned out to be just enough to buy a ticket from the one and only scalper that was still hanging outside the building.

"You're gettin' a deal, sweetheart," he said in a thick Bronx accent. "This same ticket was selling for two-fifty this morning. You're lucky I'm in a good mood."

"Thanks," I said, pocketing the ticket and speeding back to the entrance.

The attendant had moved on to a hoagie, and had just taken a giant bite when I slapped the ticket down on the counter. "Here's my ticket."

A few bits of lettuce fell from the sandwich. He left them and reached for my ticket.

He scanned it while I fidgeted with the wheels on my board.

His brow furrowed. "ID please?" He set down his sandwich, peering at something on his computer screen. "Mister . . . Izaq Abdul?"

"Oh, my ID." I pawed through my bag. Then . . . "Wait, what?'

"Your ticket says your name is Izaq Abdul." He raised an eyebrow at me. "Miss, did you buy this ticket from a scalper?"

I swallowed. Was buying tickets from scalpers illegal or just generally frowned upon?

"Before you answer, you should know that it's illegal to buy or sell tickets that were not registered to you. New policy this year." He studied me.

"Umm."

"You know what? I'm in a good mood. So I'll pretend I never saw this."

I relaxed. "So, you'll let me in anyway?"

His face hardened. "No. But I won't detain you and I won't call the cops. It's late and I'd like to be home in time for dinner."

I eyed the hoagie, which looked an awful lot like dinner to me. "But how am I going to get in?"

"You're not." He picked up his sandwich and took a giant bite.

My leg bounced up and down, bumping into my board every few bounces. I sat on a concrete block, a hundred or so yards away from the back of the convention center, staring out at the Hudson.

I'd skated around the entire center, but the creep who'd sold me the ticket was long gone. The only doors I'd found were locked. I'd looked up the main number for the convention center and called it—I got a recording. I'd looked up the number for the marketing director of Comic Con—another recording. It was after business hours and, apparently, no one wanted to be bothered on their cell phones, so only office numbers were listed online. And Brynn still wasn't answering her phone.

So much for saving the day. So much for seeing Cameron again.

A boat chugged its way upriver, breaking through whitecaps kicked up by the wind. A man stood nearby, a cigarette hanging out of his mouth as he argued with someone on the phone. I opened twitter and went to the Comic Con feed. It was becoming my default—like a bad habit I didn't want to kick. I scrolled through the tweets, almost on autopilot.

My eyes caught on something. A picture posted by someone else:

Cameron stood between two men wearing army fatigues. He was smiling, but only barely. The caption read: *#InMemoryOfTheFallen*

I gasped, my hand flying to my mouth. I stared at the hashtag, my brain struggling to process what I must have known all along.

Cameron's brother was dead. One of the fallen.

My lungs started to burn. I'd been holding my breath.

I exhaled, shakily.

The thought of Griffin dying had always sent me running to a dark hole in my mind. I'd been hiding there ever since he enlisted, building up walls to keep myself safe. Losing him was the thing I feared most.

But Cameron had lost his brother, and he'd managed to go on living. He even seemed happy.

How was that possible?

The impossibility of it sent my brain into a tailspin. It was too much to handle—too much to process. The idea that your worst nightmare could happen and that you'd be okay.

My stomach twisted into a knot—tight and impenetrable. But one thing became clear: I had to write Griffin a letter. If he died tomorrow not having heard from me once, I would never forgive myself.

I pulled out my phone and started an email.

Dear Griffin.

I tried to do something brave today. Tried to help someone like you do every day. But it didn't work out.

I'm sorry I haven't written. I guess I just didn't know what to say other than I'm a mess. And I know you probably don't want to hear it, but there it is. I'm scared and I'm sad and I'm afraid to let anyone in. Keep being safe. I miss you.

Avery

I re-read it. It wasn't perfect, but I made myself press send.

I opened my backpack and rifled through it until I found Jake's gift. It was still carefully wrapped in layers and layers of disguise—just like I'd been when I was with him.

I peeled off the Superman logo first. Then I peeled off a strip of paper. Then another one. And another one after that.

They came off one by one, layer by painstaking layer, until my masterpiece lay in a shredded heap by my side. I gathered it all up and threw it into the nearest trash bin, grip tape and all. Goodbye, Jake.

And then I had a thought. A little bit like a lightning bolt.

What if it hadn't been Jake who'd kept me from falling to pieces after Griffin left? What if it had been me and Jake was just a bystander?

I hopped on my board, considering this new possibility. Skating up and down the walking path by the river, I suddenly felt lighter. The curb wasn't great for tricks, since chunks of cement were missing in random places, but I did a few slides anyway.

The more I skated, the more I knew it was true.

I could be strong all by myself.

The man that had been arguing on his phone earlier was now pacing. I narrowly avoided running into him as I came out of my last slide. He barely noticed. His face was flushed and his eyebrows angled sharply together, almost meeting in the center to form a severe V.

"... don't care if she's puking her intestines out. We had a contract. I want that girl here, right now, with a barf bag sewn to her face if necessary, or we are never working with you again. I've got thousands of people in there waiting to see this show, and they don't want it without Jabba."

I did a tailstop.

"Get me someone now or you can kiss your job goodbye." He stuffed his phone in his pocket and pushed a stray hair out of his face. He saw me for the first time. "What are you looking at?"

"Um, sorry," I stood frozen on the pavement, my board propped up at an angle. "I couldn't help overhearing—are you looking for someone to wear the Jabba costume for the final event at Comic Con?"

His gaze went from venomous to appraising faster than a Times Square spider man could jump into your shot. He looked me once up and down. "You want a job?"

"Well, I kind of already have it. I mean, Brynn was begging me to do it earlier, and I texted to tell her I was coming, but when I got here, they wouldn't let me in the building. And Brynn's not answering her phone so I couldn't tell—"

The man cut me off. "She's not answering because I've got her taking the cast through a last minute run-through. The dress rehearsal was terrible. You're hired."

I laughed, relief bubbling up inside me. "Really?"

"Of course, really. Do I look like an idiot? This will solve everything." He whirled and led me to one of the doors I'd passed earlier, unlocked it, and yanked it open.

I took a deep breath. Embarrassingly public display, here I come.

chapter seven
COSPLAY

Vinegar. Tar. My grandmother's potpourri. All rolled into one. That's what the inside of the Jabba suit smelled like.

Yep, I was now dressed as that gross blubbery alien guy with the slitty eyes and snake-like tongue, for the Star Wars finale at Comic Con. I was crazy. I had to be.

"Did I hear you say something about toxic fumes?" I asked Mr. Crombie—the guy I'd met outside. He turned out to be Brynn's boss.

He fit a giant, rubbery head on me. "They're not toxic," he said . . . grunted, really, as he gave the head an extra shove

He yanked up the zipper at the back of the suit. I was so huge I could barely move. My hands were hidden inside Jabba's, which were like a pair of waxy rubber gloves connected to the body of the suit. I was surprised that Jabba had fingers. I thought he just had, like, tentacles or something. The head limited my vision, but—bonus—it would definitely hide my identity. I could go out there and save the day without anyone knowing it was me.

A trickle of sweat made its way down my back. I moved to wipe it away but found I could no longer reach my back or my neck. I fidgeted.

"All right, let's get you onstage. They'll be starting any minute."

"So, what exactly do I have to do? Throw someone in a dungeon? Laugh like a psychopath?"

"You'll be dying. All you have to do is fall down."

"Oh, okay." Sweet, all I had to do was let someone kill me and I could go find Cameron.

He pressed something squishy into my hand. "Make sure you fall on this. If it doesn't burst, give it a squeeze. It'll slowly pool around you as you lie onstage."

I held my hand up in front of my face so I could see what he'd given me. It was a bag of red goo, like the size of an orange. "Stage blood? Shouldn't it be green or purple or something? Jabba's an alien, right?"

A vein in Mr. Crombie's forehead bulged.

"Never mind," I said.

He ushered me around a pole and behind a curtain. Past lots of black drapery and costume racks and people. "Up the stairs, please."

My right foot knocked into the bottom step before his words could register. He grabbed my elbow to keep me from falling. I felt sort-of dizzy. It smelled like they'd dunked the Jabba head into a vat of industrial chemicals before putting it on me.

"There are four stairs and then the stage." He let go of me. "Brynn, could you take Jabba to his spot?"

Wait, Brynn was here? I jerked my head around, but had zero side vision. I heard her before I saw her.

Her voice was crazy with relief. "You found someone?"

"No. She said you hired her. I found her outside."

Brynn stepped into view, squinting at my eyes, which were the only part of me visible. "Avery? Is that you?"

"Yeah, it is." I paused. "But don't tell anyone it's me, okay? This is super embarrassing. I feel like a sumo wrestler on drugs."

She laughed. "It's our secret. Thank you so much! My backup plan sucked—we were going to lay the Jabba suit onstage before the curtain

312

came up and pretend he was either sleeping or just too lazy to move. But the fans would've known no one was in the suit and they would've been pissed. The die-hards are a feisty bunch."

She grabbed onto my arm and guided me across the stage. "You are a real life saver—I'll owe you forever for this."

Through my eye-slits, I could see a bunch of other people—the ones we'd recruited earlier—finding their places. Some were decked out as aliens. Some held light sabers and some held giant guns. Some looked like civilians. I couldn't tell which ones were supposed to be the bad guys and which ones were the good guys.

Brynn brought me to a spot. "Stand here and move forward when the curtain goes up. Your lines are prerecorded and will come over the loudspeaker. Just jostle around a bit when you hear Jabba cackling. The rebels will kill you pretty quickly once the fight breaks out. Maybe writhe around on the ground for a bit before you go comatose. Then you just have to lay there until the end. Got it?"

An army of guys in white plastic uniforms arranged themselves onstage. Okay, now *those* were bad guys.

Wait, I had to stay onstage until the show ended? But then I wouldn't have time to find Cameron.

"Um, could I maybe stagger off the stage as I'm dying so I have time to get out of the costume before everyone leaves?"

"Well . . . not really, no. Jabba has to stay onstage bleeding while the fight goes on around him. It's a powerful statement. You can't leave until it's over."

Oh, man, how was I going to save the show *and* find Cameron? Maybe this wasn't such a good idea.

"You okay?" Brynn waved a hand in front of my face. "You understand what to do?"

I was starting to feel light-headed. The chemical-y scent of the Jabba head was horrible. No wonder the earlier girl had quit after the dress rehearsal. "Yeah. I got it."

"Okay, people, we're on," said a guy carrying a clipboard.

The Star Wars theme song came on over the loudspeakers and a roar went up from the audience.

A very big, very loud roar. From a massive crowd.

I hadn't expected a *massive* crowd. I mean, big, yes. I'd seen the crowds out front earlier. But not *massive*. The sound coming from the other side of the curtain was deafening. Either they were really, *really* excited to see this, or a lot more people were out there than I'd thought.

I tried to clasp my hands together, but my costume got in the way. Instead, I gripped the bag of stage blood in my rubber-encased hand and squeezed ever-so-slightly. I loosened my grip. I squeezed again and loosened again. The action was calming. Well, a little bit.

I felt about as calm as a skater girl wearing a Jabba suit preparing to make a public display of affection to a near-total stranger could possibly feel.

I still wasn't sure what I'd do when I saw Cameron.

Or worse, what I'd do if I didn't. He'd be in the audience, right? He wouldn't miss Brynn's big show.

Right?

The curtain came up. Actors surged forward. A hissing to my left made me turn my head. It was a fog machine.

An actor beside me said, "Time to move, Jabba. Stage left."

Umm. Which way was stage left?

"That way," he hissed at me, shoving me to the left.

Man, why hadn't he just said, 'Go left?'

I found my spot. A scene played out over the loudspeaker, the parts all pre-recorded with the actors carrying out their roles silently onstage.

The rebels were moving in. They'd stolen some top-secret plans. They were on a mission to save the galaxy.

My head pounded. The Jabba suit was really smelly.

Then the actors were in my face. Threatening me. Someone had asked me a question. A creepy laughter sounded over the intercom.

Oh, was that my cue?

I wiggled in my costume, trying to make it look like Jabba was laughing.

So, when were they going to kill me? My gaze shifted between the actors in front of me, trying to figure out which one would deliver the death blow and which way I should fall when it came. I tried not to breathe too much—the plastic-y fumes from my costume were overwhelming.

From the corner of my eye-slit, I saw it: Captain America's shield. And a boy with sandy-colored hair, deep blue eyes, and a melt-in-your-mouth smile.

Fireworks exploded in my chest and my stomach turned all hot-caramel-y deliciousness.

Cameron was sitting in the third row along with his entire Avenger crew, minus Brynn.

And, oh gosh, I was crushing on him hard. Even though he was into cosplay, comics, and all things nerdy, we had more in common than I'd realized. And I couldn't get over the fact that he'd treated me better than Jake ever had.

In fact, no boy had ever treated me like Cameron had—like I mattered for no particular reason at all. Not because of what I could give him or what I could do on a skateboard or even because I was wearing a miniskirt. Cameron had treated me like I mattered just because.

I wanted to spend more time with him. Lots of time. All the time.

I needed to find out why he was nicer than any guy I'd ever met. What had made him treat me, a perfect stranger, better than my actual friends treated me.

I had to tell him I was sorry about his brother. I wanted to tell him about Griffin. I needed to know what else he liked, besides dressing up as Captain America. What made him happy, angry, sad, excited.

I wanted him to know me. The real me.

My emotions felt too big to keep inside. I couldn't even try. Surely, a flashing, neon light display must have been somewhere above my head.

I looked at Cameron again and felt my cheeks flush.

He was perfect, beautiful man-candy, and I was standing in front of him dressed as a giant, alien slug.

My head swirled.

Man, this suit smelled bad.

I needed air. If I could crack the suit open, just a tiny bit, maybe I wouldn't suffocate.

Over the loudspeaker, I heard the creepy Jabba laugh again. I jiggled myself appropriately. The actors were getting worked up. It had to be about time for me to die.

But if I didn't get some air fast, I'd die for real.

I worked one of my hands—the one that wasn't holding the packet of fake blood—out of the arm of the costume, pulling it in toward my chest. From the outside, Jabba's arms wouldn't look much different whether there were actual arms inside them or not.

Once my arm was free, I tugged at the Velcroed spot where the head connected to the rest of the suit. I worked my fingers into the Velcro near my neck, making a space a few fingers wide.

Fresh air dribbled in and I sucked it up, like some heavenly elixir. But I couldn't get nearly enough.

I worked the hole open farther.

A fight broke out before me. The two guys who had been in my face were now fighting each other, light sabers whirring through the air.

Wow, the special effects on those things were great. They looked nothing like the plastic toy ones my mom's hospital had for the kids.

Suddenly, one of the guys turned toward me. He slashed at my belly with his light saber, then shoved me. I teetered.

Crap. My fingers were still poking through the Velcro hole I'd made in the neck of the Jabba suit. I'd need that arm to catch myself when I fell. I yanked my arm out of the neck hole—tried to work it back into the arm hole—but only managed to rip the hole in my neck open further.

The fresh air felt great, though; I drank it in, feeling my senses clear. But now the Jabba head was in danger of coming off altogether. And it had shifted so that the eye slits no longer aligned with my actual eyes. I was totally blind to what was going on on-stage.

Another shove from one of the actors. I shuffled my feet, trying to keep my balance.

Where was that stupid armhole?

Oh, wait, I was supposed to fall on the arm with the fake blood. But the actor was pushing me the opposite way. How was I going to smash the blood bag underneath me if I fell on the opposite side?

Ugh, I should have insisted on a more detailed job description.

One last shove and I was on the ground, with no plan in place. The hand holding the blood was up—if I squished it now, it would just dribble on top of me, not pool out from beneath me like it was supposed to. My other arm was smashed somewhere between my body and the layers of fat suit, no closer to finding the armhole than it'd been a moment ago.

And, I realized, the Jabba head was coming off.

I gasped, reaching up with the only free arm I had to jam the head back into place. The blood bag flew out of my grip, rolled off the stage, and landed on the ground. It burst open, splattering the people in the front row with fake blood. I saw it all through my eye-slits, which were now back where they should be.

A collective gasp-slash-giggle went through the first few rows of spectators as people scrambled out of the way. Cameron's group was barely out of the splash zone, but they had a front-row seat to the spectacle. Those caught in the crossfire gasped as the liquid hit their costumes or clothes. Some were laughing. But others shot death-glares at me as they wiped at their clothes.

Oh, no! Had I just ruined the show? Should I say something?

The fight continued onstage; most of the spectators hadn't seen my mistake.

But still. Brynn had said the die-hards were feisty, and who else would be sitting in the front row but die-hards? I had to say something to them.

I made my voice as deep and creepy as I could and bellowed, "When Jabba goes down he takes everyone down with him." I shifted my weight, finally freeing my pinned arm, and lifted myself up like I was struggling for life. I shimmied forward on the stage, pretending to be in the throes of death.

"Let this be a warning," I wheezed. "Never . . . underestimate . . . a Hutt." I gasped and dropped to the stage, like the life had finally gone out of me.

I risked a glance at the front row. Only those closest to me would have been able to hear what I'd said—the background noise of light sabers and laser guns from the fight onstage would have drowned it out since I didn't have a mic. But the people in front were the ones I'd splashed blood at so they were the only ones who mattered.

For a moment, their faces were stone. But then, one by one, they started laughing. The girl who'd been hit the hardest said, "It's just stage blood—it'll wash off."

A guy next to her clapped at me. "Good save, Jabba. Well done!"

Cameron and his friends were in hysterics, too.

Things were wrapping up onstage, actors falling in fake death everywhere. But I couldn't take my eyes off Cameron. When I'd met him this morning, I'd been all full of anger and fear and aggression. But Cameron had added humor and friendship and heart.

And I realized something: the fear, the anger, the aggression—everything I felt when I skated—that was all a part of me and made me good. I didn't have to chase those feelings away. But maybe there was room for more—pieces of myself still missing that I hadn't discovered yet. Maybe a mixture of passion and aggression and heart and humor could make me happy. Maybe that's what would make me strong.

My heart swelled, processing this new revelation, as I gazed at Cameron and pretended to be dead.

Soon the good guys had killed all the bad guys onstage. The Star Wars theme song came on, accompanied by thunderous applause. The audience stood.

Cameron stood.

Wait, was he leaving? I panicked. There was no way I'd be able to get backstage, get the costume off, and get back here fast enough. I didn't even know if I could get myself up off the floor.

But I wanted Cameron to see me—the real me—even if it meant sharing all my secrets. Even if it meant that all these people would see me wearing a fat, blubbery, alien suit. I didn't want him to leave thinking I was the same girl I'd been this morning. He needed to know he'd changed me.

So I did something stupid. Or maybe it was something brave.

Either way, I was done hiding.

I took my Jabba head off.

"Cameron!" I called out. "Hey, Cameron!"

He turned and, after a moment of searching, his gaze landed on me. His eyes widened. Then his mouth quirked up in a half-grin, like he was in on some hilarious joke nobody else knew.

He pushed his way to the edge of his row and approached the stage. The audience was on their feet, still clapping. The ones who'd heard me yelling Cameron's name were now gawking at me.

I scooted myself to the edge of the stage, maneuvering my fat-suit-encased body into a sitting position. Actors scurried about onstage, getting themselves in a line for the final bow. The audience roared in appreciation.

The curtain came down behind me, leaving me all alone onstage—the center of attention. But I didn't care. For me, time stood in place as Cameron came forward, still carrying his Captain America shield.

He said, "So, you're a closet Star Wars geek who impersonates Jabba in her spare time? Really, Avery, you should have told me. I would have understood."

"I'm not a closet Star Wars geek! I just wanted to help Brynn and support the troops and . . ." I trailed off, seeing the teasing grin on his face.

"So this isn't your Jabba head?" he asked, patting the grotesque rubber head sitting next to me. "How very disappointing."

"Just my ticket to Comic Con," I said.

"Why'd you want to get in so badly?"

I felt my cheeks flush. Hopefully he'd think it was just from being stuffed inside a giant incubator and not because of the full-on rocket launch happening inside me. "Um, well, I wanted to thank you for helping me this morning."

"You're welcome. I guess now we're even, since you just saved the show."

Oh, how could I tell him everything I was feeling without sounding totally lame and forward? I'd only known this guy a day.

"Hey, how'd the competition go?" he said.

I smiled. "It went well. I killed it."

He held out a hand for a fist bump, then looked at my Jabba hands and laughed. "Good job. I don't think your boyfriend is here. I've been asking around for him all day."

My insides melted. Did that mean he'd been thinking about me all day?

"You're right, he's not here," I said. "He never was, it turns out. His phone got stolen on the train this morning."

I waited for understanding to dawn in Cameron's eyes. It did. "So we were tracking a thief all morning, not your boyfriend."

"Yep. Jake was at the skate park the whole time." I kept my eyes locked on Cameron's. "But he's not my boyfriend any more."

Cameron's lips quirked up into a grin. "Oh, really?"

He was totally flirting with me. I so did not want to spoil the moment.

But I had to tell him he'd changed me—that he was right—I had been hiding and I didn't need to any more. I wanted to tell him about my cousin. I needed to tell him the truth about Jake breaking up with me this morning. "Stop looking at me like that."

Cameron's grin widened. "Like what?"

"Like that." I took a shaky breath. "Jake broke up with me early this morning. Before I even met you. I was lying to you all—"

"Want to hang out tomorrow?" he said, interrupting me.

My brain stuttered to a halt. "I just said I lied to you."

"I know. And I said, want to hang out tomorrow?"

I hesitated. "Aren't you coming back to Comic Con?"

He shrugged. "I'd rather hang out with you, if that's an option. We could sit outside coordinating dance-offs. Or you could get another acting gig and join me inside. Or you could teach me how to skate. Whatever."

The caramel-y deliciousness came back. My insides twisted into a delightful knot. There would be time to tell him everything later. For now, I just smiled. "That sounds perfect."

"Which part?" he said.

"All of it."

He grinned and nodded at something behind me. The cast is coming out for another bow. "You should really take some credit for saving the show."

"The show which I then ruined."

"You didn't ruin it, that blood bag mishap was hilarious. I only wish I'd known it was you in there—it would have been even better!"

He held out the Jabba head. "Want some help putting your head back on?"

Oh, if he only knew. My head would never be on right again, he'd scrambled it up so good. But I said, "Yes, please."

He stepped forward. Held up the monstrous head piece. Just before placing it on my head, his smile went a touch mischievous.

Then he leaned in and kissed me.

It was just a peck, really. The whispery-est whisper of a kiss. But my insides exploded, heat melting me into a gooey puddle.

He pulled away. Held my gaze for the tiniest moment.

Then he eased my Jabba head back into place. Through my eye-slits, I watched him step back, examine me to make sure it was on right. He helped me stand up.

I did what I was supposed to do. I joined the cast and took a bow, my body still tingling from the feel of his lips on mine. But I kept my eyes on Cameron. I had a feeling he'd be in my sights for a very, very long time.

 about the
author

TERESA RICHARDS writes speculative and contemporary Young Adult, and loves anything that can be given a unique twist. Her debut, *Emerald Bound*, released with Evernight Teen in 2015. When Teresa's not writing, she can be found chasing after one of her little kids, driving one of her teens around, or hiding in the house with a treat she doesn't plan to share. She is represented by Mallory Brown of Triada Literary Agency. Connect with Teresa on twitter @BYUtm33, Facebook @AuthorTeresaRichards or Instagram @authorteresarichards, or at www.authorteresarichards.com.

.

About *Emerald Bound*

A dark retelling of The Princess and the Pea, *in which the pea is an enchanted, life-stealing emerald.*

Thank you for taking a chance on Teenacity Books!

"I never said dance wasn't a workout," he says. "I said dance wasn't a sport."

"Have you ever thought maybe ballet is harder than flipping tires? You've got to hit the poses in step. There's no time to scratch yourself and burp."

To get the scoop on all new releases, visit www.nikkitrionfo.com/teenacitybooks.

While you're there, consider joining the Teencity Books Reader Crew! Teenacity Books Reader Crew is for test readers who love hip, sweet romances. We are a new publishing company and eager to get our work out there. We'll give you free short stories, the best sale prices on books and access to projects before launch date.

We also love to share character memes and discuss stories with our fans. Simply follow Nikki Trionfo on Facebook or Instagram.

Also, did you know? The reading community relies on honest reviews to find books that are a good fit. Now that you're ready to rate *Under a New York Skyline* on Amazon or Goodreads, take screenshot of your review and send it to TeenacityBooks@gmail.com. You'll get Nikki Trionfo's free short story *Darkly Bound*, a fairy-godmother-filled tale about a dark enchantress and the innocent sixteen-year-old fairy she magically controls. Little does the enchantress know how crafty innocence can be.

We love our readers! Thank you!

www.ingramcontent.com/pod-product-compliance
Lightning Source LLC
Chambersburg PA
CBHW020334180626
46812CB00001B/197